MW01286302

Books by J. D. Evans

Mages of the Wheel Series

Wind & Wildfire (Prequel)
Reign & Ruin
Storm & Shield
Siren & Scion
Ice & Ivy (2022)
Mountain & Memory (2022)
Fire & Fate (2023)

MAGES OF THE WHEEL BOOK ONE

Reign & Ruin

J. D. EVANS

To my family, whose patience, generous sacrifice of time, and loving encouragement were the balance paid for this book.

Tero
Corsan Republic
Corsyra
Marceo
Aklion
Eannea
Isla Sora
Rieta
Haenna
Tyrus
Sun Sea
Nasiye
Menei

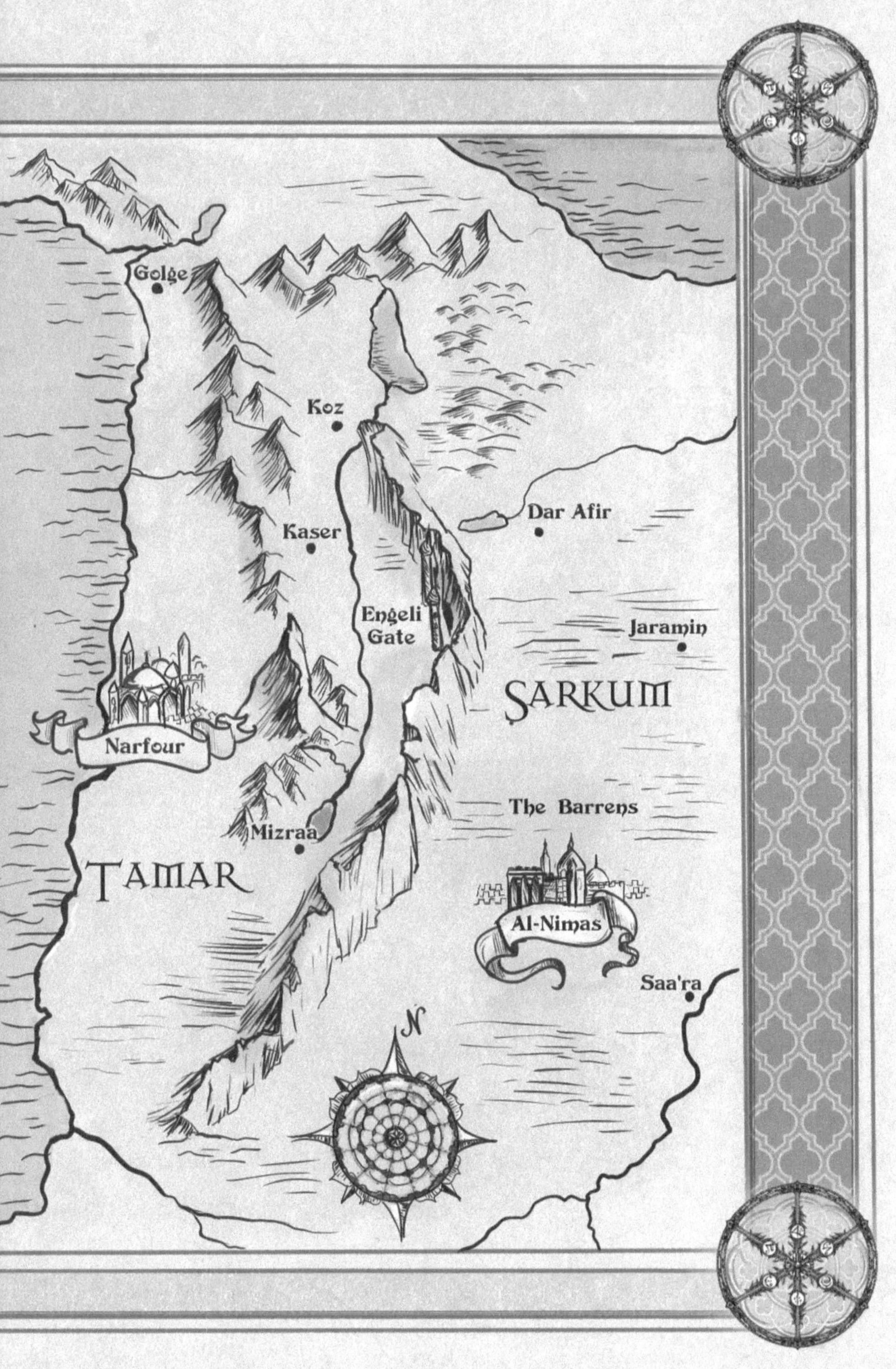

Golge
Koz
Kaser
Dar Afir
Engeli
Gate
Jaramin
Sarkum
Narfour
The Barrens
Mizraa
Tamar
Al-Nimas
Saa'ra
N

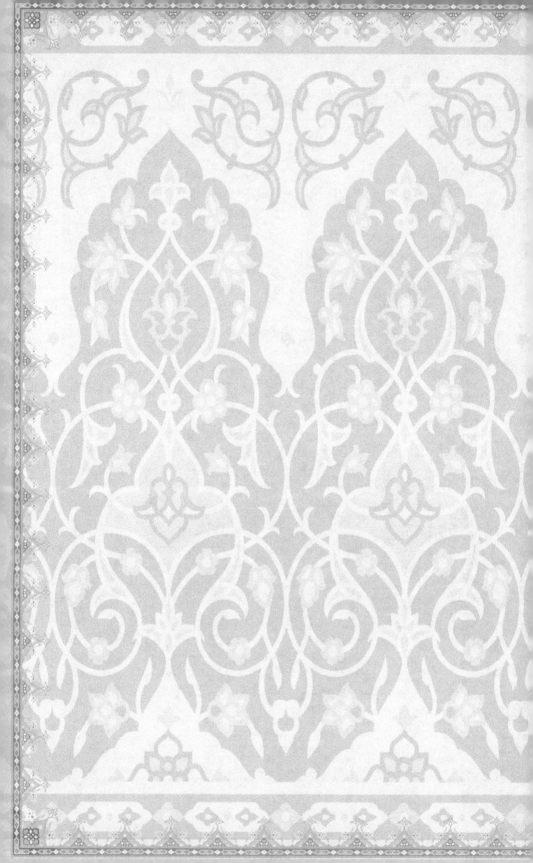

Poem of the Wheel

I am balanced for I am broken
Parts that make a whole
Each joy and sorrow token
Paid to mold my soul
For we are nothing
And we are all
The darkness that is rising
And the light that cannot fall.

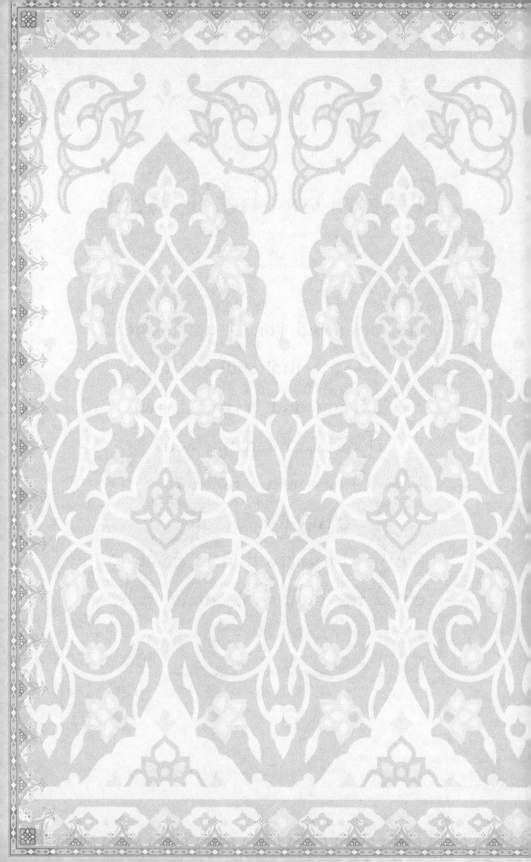

One

THE GALLERY THAT LED from the main palace to the Council Hall had never stretched so long. Perhaps, if the Wheel favored her, this was as close as Naime would ever come to understanding what it felt like to walk to the gallows. Her father strode some distance in front of her, his steward and his favorite Lightbringers flanking him, as three more attendants walked between her and him in an arc. The Lightbringers' mage orbs lit their progress through the hall, which remained untouched by dawn's wan light. Her father walked as though he were strolling through the park at leisure, and not heading for one of the most momentous encounters of Naime's life. He seemed himself today. Though what she considered normal for him now was not what it had once been.

He'd been a man of confidence and strategy. His plans and schemes were so well laid the High Council rarely knew what was happening until it was far too late to change things. Then he would simply weather the storm as the Council erupted into chaos. That was how he had handled their bickering, their currying for favor, their divisions. He ignored them and did as he wished. Now, when his emotions were stoked, he became confused. Sullen. Temperamental. Words Naime never would have used to describe him before her mother had died and taken something of him with her. Before a lifetime of breaking open minds finally began to break his own.

It should have been many more Turns before she had to consider taking over the rule of Tamar in earnest, more time to shape the Council in her favor. But the Wheel did not turn for comfort, it turned for balance in all things. With balance came hardship in equal measure to joy, and Naime had enjoyed more than her fair share of ease.

She sensed the coming of balance in her life as she might have sensed a storm on the horizon, the same edginess shaped her moods and thoughts, the same feeling of excitement and fear.

Behind her, someone's muffled steps scuffed the carpet and she sighed as her cousin, Ihsan, reached her side and slowed his pace to match hers. She took his offered arm and lifted her eyes only to glance at him.

"Running is unseemly."

"I know," he said. "Forgive me." His skin was pallid, his eyes red rimmed, and his brow set with lines of tension. The nightmares had returned. Naime swallowed any further admonition and focused on her father's broad back.

Ihsan avoided all palace functions and duties as much as he could. Not out of inherent laziness or selfishness, as so many assumed. Ihsan's misery balanced her contentment, and he was long overdue for his own equal measure of joy. Before he had moved from the palace to the city, she had been present for some of the nights the nightmares plagued him. They were beastly things that gripped him in a world of memory, pain, and fear like nothing she had ever personally experienced. They came most often when he was forced to face the Council. To face the Grand Vizier, as he would today.

"Thank you for coming, San," Naime said. He nodded once, though he remained stone-faced and silent as they walked. The expression was almost comforting, as it had dominated his countenance for nearly a decade. Despite his seriousness, she felt less isolated with him—he understood what she wanted in a way she was not certain her father did. Not anymore.

Their procession reached the Council Hall doors, as tall as two men and made of gold leaf latticed wood. The Lightbringers, first-level fire mages, moved away from her father to open the doors. The long, rectangular room was tiled with the swirls and colors of the Wheel. The ceiling soared, domed above them and painted with geometric formations of the sigils for each magic House, each of the six spokes of the Wheel. It was meant to be a room where equity reigned, a place where everyone was represented.

Generations ago, that had been true. But power and fear had brought war, had broken the Wheel, and now the Council was made up of men whose power lie in wealth, in oppression by avarice, in customs and old ways that were comfortable.

Naime squeezed Ihsan's arm, and he reciprocated. Her whole body was her heartbeat, a cage that barely held her together.

This Council meeting held promise, for all the things she hoped for Tamar, and dread, for the threat of seeing all those hopes pulled out of her grasp.

The Sabri family line had ruled Tamar, and before the Sundering War, the Old Sultanate, for generations uncountable. Their blood was spun of the First House, a birthright of air and beginnings, dawn and change. Her mother had called Naime her little light, had told her from her earliest days that she would be the first woman to rule Tamar in her own right. That she would be the change and the balance the Wheel demanded to correct the wrongs of her ancestors.

But now she was gone, and Naime feared her father's mental decline would take him too. Alone, Naime would rule a Council that saw her as nothing more than a steppingstone for their sons to the Sultan's seat. She must not fail. She would not, and today brought the first test.

Naime paused in the doorway to the hall. Already nervous, skin alight with the cold fire of anxiety, Ihsan's tension only worsened hers. Her father continued down the aisle toward the padded bench in an ornate alcove at the far end. The Viziers bowed as he walked, followed only by his steward, between the rows of seats to either side. They lowered their heads and spread their hands palm up before them, offering and receiving balance. Naime surveyed the Viziers surreptitiously as she waited for her announcement. They could not all be present today, which was not unusual, they had estates, land, and people to manage.

Of the thirty-six Viziers, only twenty-four were present. And at first tally their number was comprised of a suspicious majority of the Grand Vizier's supporters. That did not surprise her. The Grand Vizier was a man who planned as carefully as her father once had.

Beside her, Ihsan exhaled audibly, and when she glanced at him, she just caught his gaze slipping away from the Grand Vizier, who stood nearest to her father's seat. The steward announced Naime and Ihsan, and the men of the Council remained bowed as they walked toward her father. Ihsan's skin grew cold beneath her hand as they approached the end of the hall and the Grand Vizier. Naime gripped his wrist, reminding him to constrain his magic, and the ice of his power sank away.

They sat, she on the end of a long bench set at a right angle to her father's place, within reach of him. Ihsan slid beside her. Each person in the room sat closer or farther from the Sultan as dictated by their rank. She would always be closest, then Ihsan, second in line for the Sultan's seat. In the center of the bench opposite them, the Grand Vizier sat one seat closer to the door than Ihsan. He would not be happy until he sat in front of them all, and there wasn't a person in the room who didn't know it. Many even supported it.

Behram Kadir, Grand Vizier of the High Council, was a Sival of the Fifth House and master of its charisma and gift for lies. He had once been her father's best friend, but now sat as his most powerful rival. He wore the guise of trusted adviser so comfortably that even her father was sometimes fooled. Especially now, when the Sultan's confusion more frequently surpassed his sense, and he reached for the familiar to feel settled, to push back the remnants of other minds that overshadowed his own.

"The Sultan, Princess Sultana, and Sehzade have arrived. I call this Council to session." Kadir executed a formal bow, with hands spread, then took his seat, beside Yavuz Pasha, the palace secretary, and beyond him the Vizier of Finance, Esber Pasha.

When Ihsan had come to live at the palace, they had decided they would never call Behram Kadir by his first name, which would suggest respect, humanization they did not think he deserved. He had been Kadir to them both ever since. Once he had arranged his crimson robes to his liking, he smiled at Naime. She acknowledged him only with a tilt of her head.

Though she shared her father's gift, and affinity, for plans and schemes, she could not treat the Council as he had. She was not a man, not a prince, whose temper would be seen as strength or whose unusual methods might be seen as visionary instead of disruptive. Neither was she a princess the way they believed she should be. They believed her indulged, spoiled, given too much freedom. Because she was also her mother's daughter, a lowborn woman who had made her way to the top tiers of the University on her wits and tenacity alone. In so doing, Naime's mother had attracted the notice of the most powerful man in Tamar. Two of them, actually.

Naime shifted her gaze from Kadir to her father. He had married her mother against the wishes of the Council at the time, and she had turned many traditions on their head. A legacy Naime intended to continue, when the time was right.

"Today is a momentous day," her father said, and a familiar spark of mischief lit his eyes, one that hinted he was about to announce something he knew would displease the Council. It was the same look he had worn when he watched her and her mother plot Naime's rise to the Sultan's seat. "My daughter has completed her fourth full Cycle of the Wheel."

Then came an eruption of polite, unenthusiastic applause. Twenty-four Great Turns of the Wheel had passed since her birth—she was of age. No longer to be a semi-silent bystander in the High Council meetings. She was permitted to speak, to address them as a superior. It also meant she could marry. This day heralded the beginning of the race for her to take control of the Council before they managed to marry her to one of their sons.

Naime's body was still and charged all at once, as though something shivered beneath her skin and would burst forth at any moment. She had to remember to breathe deeply to keep herself calm and focused.

"It is my wish that the Princess Sultana begin addressing the Council in my stead, to prepare her for ruling."

A discontent quiet lingered, and Naime was aware of each meaningful glance, shifted seat, or quiet cough of surprise. She stood, hands folded to hide her desire to fidget under their scrutiny. Kadir's dark eyes fixed on her, a tiny smile on his mouth. He was as capable of hiding himself from those around them as she was, though in a different manner. Air gave the gift of composure. Fire gave the gift of deception.

"It is my honor to stand before the High Council and its wise Viziers. I hope our future work together provides only prosperity to Tamar and its people, who look to us for balance and temperance." She bowed, spreading her hands. It would be the last time she bowed to any of them. She wondered if they realized that. If they knew what she intended.

More quiet applause trailed her declaration.

"Of course, I have also reached the age to marry." She used the tiniest thread of her power to lift the sound of her voice. She wanted what no Sultana before her had managed. Not to be the stepping block for a new Sultan, but to be ruler herself. Her father, in his moments of lucidity, approved. They had spoken of her plans for the future, for holding back the Republic and uniting the Old Sultanate again to reenergize the Houses. This was the first step toward those goals—controlling the Council. Yet she took it without her most powerful ally, because her father's age had been a more insidious enemy than any she faced in the Council now.

She let her words hang in the air. The night before, she had rehearsed every word, every subtle movement, every glance. It was best to let them rejoice, to approve, to hand her their weaknesses, before she revealed her true move.

Kadir stood. He held his staff of office in one hand and leaned on it slightly to support his weight off his left leg. He'd been injured in an accident a decade ago. It had left him with a severe limp he tried to hide and a crescent scar marring what many still considered a very handsome face.

"May your next four Cycles be as well as the first, Princess Sultana. The High Council has considered it an honor watching you grow to womanhood and are confident you will make a fine Sultana for whoever succeeds your father. The Council will submit a list of appropriate candidates to you," he addressed the Sultan, "as soon as possible."

Naime did not miss the calculating look in his brown eyes. She knew his son would be at the top of the list. The thought turned her stomach.

"Please do, Grand Vizier." Naime cloaked herself in her power, warding her tone and her body against the imminent backlash. "But also, please be aware that my betrothal may be delayed in the near term by our alliance negotiations with Sarkum, which the Sultan has appointed me to oversee." It was not what she wanted, to flaunt her father as a kind of shield. But it was not time to stand under her own power, there was not enough of it yet. They still thought of her as a girl, a pretty ornament in the palace that would be handed off as a kind of goodwill token to whoever was chosen to succeed her father.

Admirably, Kadir managed to contain his surprise. Only one peppered brow rose, and his fingers tightened against the scepter. The corner of Naime's mouth curved up in response. He saw, and his brow lowered and fingers loosened.

The other Council members began to stir. A few of those she knew to be moderate leaned in to whisper to each other. The Council had refused to look at the alliance terms she had drafted, because the Grand Vizier convinced them there was little point, that an alliance with Sarkum, their eastern neighbor, was foolhardy.

Only a very few of those closest to her knew she had already sent a letter to Sarkum, suggesting the alliance, requesting the presence of a delegate. She had stamped it with her father's seal and sent it with his approval turns ago. Sarkum and Tamar had once been united under the Old Sultanate, before the Sundering War. It was time to heal old wounds and bring them together again.

The Sundering War had come at the behest of Naime's forefathers, after court-sanctioned atrocities committed by the destruction magic of Sixth House mages. Destruction mages were murdered or driven from Tamar, and were still regarded with fear and superstition, even so many generations later.

Uniting with Sarkum meant bringing back Sixth House power. Despite that it would once again balance the Wheel and mend what was broken, Kadir would never agree, and he controlled the Council majority. He was as tied to history and tradition as the most crumpled of old greybeards, unflinching in his adherence to the earliest edicts of the Tamar Sultanate. So, she had set the Wheel in motion before they could stop its turn. Now she must maneuver obstacles into their path to give herself time to complete her plan, to complete an alliance and take her father's place on her own.

There was a pause as the Council chattered amongst themselves, Kadir waiting for Naime to elaborate, Naime smiling serenely at him. He was no fool. He would not underestimate anyone until he knew it was a safe.

For more than a decade, Naime had watched Kadir bully and manipulate his way to the position of Grand Vizier. Watched him slither his way out of crimes, manage unfailingly to hide the literal and figurative blood on his hands. Forced to stand idly by while Kadir used every opportunity to garner power for himself in the Council, appointing governors more loyal to him than to their country and their Sultan. Finally, after so long, it was time for her to break him over the Wheel as her father had never had the heart to do. Watching him now, stiff and chaffing under the fact she was momentarily in control of the room, was her first real taste of revenge. It banished her nervousness and replaced it with determination that settled her.

"I apologize, Sultana Efendim, but I seem to recall that the Council did not support alliance negotiations," Kadir said, and the Council quieted in anticipation. He smiled. She smiled back, tilting her head in a slight approximation of deference.

"If the Sultan had required the Council to support negotiations, I am certain he would have sought their approval. But he is quite sure of his decision." She smiled to her father, and he nodded. Sarkum had not responded yet. If she had an actual delegate to present, things would have gone much more smoothly. To maintain her command of herself and the room, she had to bury the skittering unease Sarkum's silence caused her.

"We had hoped to present the matter again to the Council today, but I am afraid the Sarkum delegate has been delayed in coming." It was a small lie, one she hoped would prove in the end to not be a lie at all, or everything she planned would be for naught.

Naime had never experienced the depth of silence that fell over the Council Hall in the moment that followed her declaration. It was as if she could feel each word sinking slowly into their understanding, like small stones in vast water, until they hit the bottom and stayed, kicking up clouds of sediment and disapproval. Then at once, the men leapt to their feet in outrage and disbelief, all shouting over each other, and Naime's breath left her in a rush. Her father moved as if to rise, expression tight with alarm. Naime stepped to his side, but not onto the dais, and touched his hand as she smiled. "It's all right, Father. Be at ease. I am here."

He smiled back, relaxing into his seat. Ihsan turned to her, concern and bitter amusement in his pale hazel eyes. "And now?"

"Let the typhoon blow itself out, Cousin," she said, and remained as she was, her fingers against her father's hand, waiting. Kadir managed to bring the Council under control, shouting and even going so far as to release his hold on his magic enough that the temperature of the room raised a few degrees. Ihsan shuddered, his hands tightening around his knees, but he rode it out in silence. She was proud of him for his effort and felt shame for needing him with her on this day, when it caused him obvious discomfort.

Naime frowned at Kadir when he finally turned. The Council sat, one by one, but war still raged in their expressions, even those few she had hoped might be willing to listen. But outrage was infectious, and it had spread before her reason could. Always, fire faster than wind. Kadir's special talent.

"Sultana Efendim. I am certain I misheard you—"

"You did not. The Sultan and I intend an alliance with Sarkum. The letters have already been sent. I will not aggrandize myself by lecturing into the vast wisdom of the Council, as I am certain they are aware the Republic is on the move. Already the Eannean Islands have been swallowed whole, and the Republic has outposts against the northern border of Sarkum. They mean to wipe out mages."

She paused to allow the dire proclamation to quiet tempers. "We are not strong enough to stand against them. An alliance with Sarkum is not only long overdue, but vital to our survival."

"Sultana Efendim. The Republic has given no indication that it means to go to war with us." Kadir spoke as if to a silly child, thinking he might provoke her into losing her temper, no doubt. A show of temper or pique would ruin her credibility.

Though his tone and placating smile made her furious inside, she swallowed the desire to correct him or insult him back. When she replied she did so in a cool tone helped into existence by a thread of her magic.

"Yet I will not wait until their armies and machines have descended into Narfour and taken the palace before I enact countermeasures. I know the Grand Vizier sees the wisdom in being proactive." She stood tall, though she was still shorter than many of the Viziers, keeping her face calm and neutral to match her voice and veil her exasperation. She could not be the only person in the room who understood the imminent, if not direct, threat?

"And what will you do when Sixth House mages unleash death and disease in the streets? Will that help us against an enemy?" one of the other Viziers shouted. He did not have courage enough to stand and make himself known, but she focused in the direction his voice originated.

"Superstition and old wives' tales are not solid foundations to make decisions upon," Naime said. "Especially decisions regarding an entire nation."

"Destruction mages?" Her father shifted, growing more agitated at the mood in the room. When she looked at him his brows were drawn together as he peered at the faces around him. He no longer always understood where to take his cues from, and his uncertainty now led to temper or fear. Rumors in the palace spoke of him getting confused easily, but as far as she knew, no one understood how far gone his mind was to his illness. Not yet. She had to keep it a secret as long as possible.

Naime cut her gaze to Ihsan, who went to the Sultan's other side, leaning down to speak in low tones, trying to calm him before he gave any more sign he was disturbed.

"These are not old wives' tales, Sultana Efendim." Kadir turned and directed his speech at the Council, fanning the flames of their discontent. "You dishonor the history of your own family and the decision they made to end the Old Sultanate. Thousands died to free us from the dangers of the Sixth House. You would undo that now for protection against an imagined threat?" He tapped his staff against the marble floor and waved his other hand in dismissal. "Even if the Council agreed with this, we are far too vulnerable. There are no Third House mages alive. Rumors say even in Sarkum none exist. There is nothing to counter the vile magic of the Sixth House. I cannot accept this, Sultana Efendim." Kadir's voice grew in volume until the last words. The Council cheered him on.

Naime exhaled the building frustration that ate a windswept hole in her temper. Her fingers curled into the white and blue fabric of her entari as she imagined wrapping her hands around his throat. Kadir turned from her to her father, and smiling, said, "You would never agree to allowing Sixth House mages in the palace, would you, Sultan Efendim?"

"What?" Her father launched from his seat, and only Ihsan's nearness allowed him to grasp the Sultan's arm before he went over the edge of the dais. "Of course not!" His brown eyes were wide with fear and confusion when he looked at Naime. The expression made him seem more child than man, and defeat prickled through her, until she felt small, and hopeless. "What is he saying? What are you doing?"

"Father." She kept the desperation out of her voice, trying to soothe him. She needed to get him out of here, away from them, immediately. "You agreed. You sealed the letter I sent to Sarkum. It is necessary to balance the Wheel. You know that. Do you remember, we talked about this—"

"No!" he said, sharply. Naime grit her teeth. She had spoken to him, said the same exact thing, for three small turns, every night. But her hope that it would make him remember when she needed him to had been in vain. Ihsan tried to murmur encouragement to the Sultan but he twisted out of her cousin's grasp. "No, absolutely not. Behram, what is going on?" he said to Kadir, whose face shone with serene triumph. Naime squeezed her hands into fists.

"Sultan. Be at ease. The Council will handle this." Kadir bowed deeply, a gesture of profound humility, yet it oozed only arrogance from Kadir.

"Yes," the Sultan said, visibly calming as Kadir straightened. "Yes, that will do."

Ihsan helped him as he fumbled to find his seat again, his gaze flashing to Naime's then to the doors. She put her hand on her father's shoulder. He patted her hand with his and smiled at her as if nothing at all had happened. As if he had not just destroyed her best hope to secure the future of Tamar. And her own.

Two

NAIME STOOD IN THE garden just outside her rooms. They had been her mother's before her, and Naime had taken them over as consolation when her mother died. This section of the garden had been carefully cultivated under her mother's direction, a place where she could find silence and peace away from the scheming.

That silence was poisoned by Kadir's burning presence. They faced each other, both with feigned expressions of politeness. Kadir's steward, Mahir, stood beside him, holding a golden tray in both hands, the interior of it cushioned with gold-embroidered white brocade. Naime stared at the stack of small papers on it, each carefully tucked into a folded envelope. There were four of them. There should have been six, a candidate representing each of the Houses of the Wheel, but that was impossible, because of the absence in Tamar of mages from the Third and Sixth Houses. Every direction she turned, the Wheel demanded balance. Why was she the only one who noticed? Or cared?

"Samira," Naime said. Samira Azmeh Sabri-ih, her highest-ranked attendant, stood beside her, and at her command, reached to take the tray from Mahir. She was the only Fifth House mage Naime kept in her entourage. Her family one of the few that did not align with Kadir in politics.

Naime did not look at Kadir as she took the envelopes from the tray.

"I think you will be most pleased," Kadir said, the smug pleasure in his tone more grating and offensive than anything else he could have done.

"Do you?" Naime sighed, opening the first envelope with a flick of her thumb. *Cemil Kadir.* His name was written in perfect calligraphy. Samira could see it from where she stood, and Naime did not think she imagined the soft, restrained exhale from her friend. Her heart squeezed, but she did not look at Samira to offer comfort or silent promises. She could not promise anything, or indicate to Kadir weakness from either of them.

Below Cemil's name was a detailed list of the bride gifts he would provide. Naime scanned the list only as a pretense. She did not care what any of them had to offer. She didn't care for their wealth or proof of their nobility.

None of them could give her what she needed, a way to protect her people from extinction at the hands of the Republic.

She tucked the card back into its envelope and returned it to the tray.

The next name was the son of Yavuz Pasha, Vizier of the northern province, her father's secretary, and the most well-respected and moneyed minister besides Kadir. Yavuz supported the Grand Vizier in most things, but he was also a steady man of logic and thought, and if all her plans were ruined, he was her best choice for an ally. His son was another matter. Where Cemil Kadir was intelligent but a useless, bitter drunk, Sadiq Yavuz was vain and silly. Naime slid a cursory glance at his proposal, then placed the envelope with Cemil's.

"These bride prices are far too lavish," she commented dryly. "I am honored by the generosity of my father's governors." The words were customary, but they tasted like ash in her mouth. She read the next two and was surprised by neither. All sons of the wealthiest and most influential Viziers on the Council, all men who offered her nothing but useless items and land as coercion to push her out of her rightful place as ruler of Tamar.

"They are not generous enough, Sultana Efendim," Kadir said with all the passion available to a fire mage of his ability. "You are the jewel in your father's palace, and there is not a man alive who would not lay down all he has to have you at his side."

Naime lifted her eyes to his and raised one brow as she handed the rest of the envelopes back to Samira. Mages of the Fifth House were the best liars on the Wheel. In balance, water mages like Ihsan were almost impervious to lies. But Naime did not need to be a Second House mage like her cousin to feel Kadir's lie as if it were oil poured over her skin.

"I will speak with my father, and you will be notified." She had to stall for a time. She had to believe Sarkum would want an alliance and send a delegate.

"I have already spoken with your father, Sultana Efendim. We agreed the end of this small turn would be an auspicious day for such a joyous decision."

Of course he had approached her father first, the conniving bastard. That was only three days away. Naime subdued her panic with a smile and a laugh.

"I cannot possibly be expected to prepare for such a thing in only three days." A messenger could deliver another missive to Sarkum in as little as three days, if the winter pass cooperated. If a delegate left immediately from Sarkum upon receiving a letter that suggested haste, it might take twice as long for them, traveling more slowly. That was at least a small turn and a half. If she stalled too long, Kadir would convince the Council she was defying them and demand an immediate decision.

She folded her hands in front of her and ducked her chin to appear deferent. "I wish to treat the offers with the respect they deserve. A day to consider each in detail, a day to discuss them with my father, then the traditional three days of cleansing, meditation, and fasting."

They were antiquated traditions from the Old Sultanate, rarely observed anymore. But it was her right to request them, and Kadir did not have authority to deny her.

His mask slipped a fraction and he proffered a calculating smile. "I always told your father I thought your mother's insistence that you study law would be a great boon to whoever you marry." He'd loved her mother's intelligence and knowledge, until she'd turned it against him.

"I live to serve." Naime smiled demurely. She suspected he'd told her father exactly the opposite. He would never encourage another player in his game.

"Be careful the way you shift the Wheel, Sultana Efendim, without knowing who will be there to stand in balance." Fire flashed in his eyes.

"Your concern for my welfare has always warmed my heart, Kadir Pasha," Naime said. "And yet I, like my mother, recognize a serpent disguised as a rope."

His cool facade evaporated, the force of his anger pushing his magic against hers, so heat met cool in the air between them. Naime remained calm, smiling, as if she didn't notice his slip at all. Using her mother against him was not a trick she would normally employ, but if she did not distract him, she would lose to him again. Besides, his love for her mother had been the only virtuous thing about him, and she did not wish to sully it.

"I will inform the Council of your wishes, Efendim." Kadir bowed and his steward did the same. Naime did not return it but watched him as he straightened and shambled away.

When he was out of sight, she spun toward her rooms and Samira followed.

"What do you intend?" Samira set the tray on a small table inside the sitting room so she could close the arched glass doors behind them.

"I must make my next move on the board before Kadir captures all my pieces." If she was forced into a betrothal by the Council before a Sarkum delegate arrived and allowed her to stall the ceremony, there would be no hope for alliance. She knew there were Viziers on the Council who could be convinced that alliance was necessary, that the power a balanced Wheel would bring back to Tamar and Sarkum was needed to stave off the Republic. But they would not do so with Kadir at their helm, whispering his lies and coercions and nurturing the seeds of his bigotry against the Sixth House.

None of the candidates offered in marriage would be amenable to her plans. They would take their newfound power and wreak havoc. Or perhaps worse, do nothing.

Naime sat on the floor cushion in front of her low-slung desk and withdrew a fresh sheet of paper and a pen. Samira pulled the stopper from the ink bottle and set it by Naime's hand, then knelt beside her as Naime began to write. She would not risk speaking her plans aloud, not without an earth mage who could cast a dampening and silence her words to those beyond the spell. But Samira could read over her shoulder and come to them herself.

"This seems risky," Samira suggested.

Naime held her hand above the sheet and a thin breeze of her power dried the ink. She did not normally expend her power for trivial things, but every moment counted now. Samira was right, it was a risk. By sending a missive indicating time was short for an alliance, she also suggested Tamar was desperate, and gave Sarkum an upper hand in their dealings. In this case, she had to tip her hand a little, or risk losing her chance at all.

If the Wheel demanded balance, this was the only way she saw to achieve it, and in that, she hoped it would turn in her favor.

"Kadir will try to convince my father to go against my wishes. He will push to sign the betrothal as soon as possible, so that even if Sarkum does send a delegate, I will no longer have authority to deal in negotiations. I would have to break a betrothal promise to do so." A dire affront to tradition and the Wheel itself.

"Which would make the Viziers' heads explode," Samira said dryly.

"It would be troublesome to appoint a new Council," Naime replied in a similar tone. "And someone would have to clean up the mess." She sighed theatrically.

Samira made a sound of agreement, fighting her smile. Humor helped, but was not a solution. Naime could not go against the Council so overtly again, or she would lose the faith of those who chose to support her, and the chance to persuade the rest by careful maneuvering. Though in truth the Council was only in place to advise the Sultan, and not command him, they held all the power of the noble families. They could not be ignored or insulted, lest she begin a civil war. It had always been a game, steering the Tamar Sultanate. Naime was a mediocre player for the time being, gifted what power she had over them by her mother's reputation and her father's blood. But until she proved her own validity to them, she would continue to balance precariously on the edge of ruin because she was a woman trying to attain a man's position. Thankfully, she had always been a quick study.

Naime signed the letter with her father's name and title, in his hand, something she had learned at an early age. This time she blew on the ink, staring at the script, missing him intensely. He could not be trusted anymore, and each time she made a decision without him another fine crack fissured her heart.

"I worry this puts you at too much of a disadvantage," Samira said.

"Is there not a time during swordplay when one must step into a blow to achieve a victory? I shall think of it like that." Naime selected a stick of sealing wax.

"One only does such a thing when they are willing to sacrifice themselves for the sake of that victory." Samira touched her finger to the wax, and it melted. Naime pressed it to the paper.

"In the end, you know what I care about most is protecting us from the Republic." Naime picked up her father's seal and pushed it against the wax. When she pulled it away, it left the impression of her father's *tughra*, the seal designed for him by the court calligrapher. She rolled the parchment and sealed it with more wax, and the seal bearing the Sabri family crest, an air sigil pierced by a yataghan and crowned with a radiant sphere.

"You mean becoming Queen Sultana, and then protecting us from the Republic," Samira said, her teasing smile buried in a stern look.

"I only want that because I know, as do you, that there is no one the Council will offer as a potential husband who would care for Tamar as I do. They do not see what I see." She handed the letter to Samira. "We need Sarkum. We need a balanced and powerful Wheel and a full Circle of Chara'a. Besides, what would I do if I did not rule? I could never spend my days sitting in contemplation." She touched a finger to the letter. "Send this now. Do not use a palace messenger or horse. I do not want the esteemed Grand Vizier to know what I have done." Naime raised an eyebrow and Samira responded with a conspiratorial smile. "Not until it is far too late for him to counterattack."

THREE

THE DAY WAS COLD, the sunlight insipid in the way it was as the end of autumn met the beginning of winter. This was Makram's season, when his power waxed most powerful. Yet he felt stifled and pent up, watching his brother peruse the Tamar Sultan's letter yet again.

Kinus sat on the gold-embroidered, tan divan that served as his throne in this section of the palace, hunched over the letter he held in one hand, his other arm propped on his knee, his brow furrowed. Makram had been staring at him off and on as he sat, and the sight grew more tiresome with each moment that passed. The light that shone through the western wall of windows had changed from the pale wash of morning to the unnuanced light of midday, and soon it would dim to silver evening. Kinus had neither moved nor uttered a sound more enlightened than a grunt since he had read it. Makram had dismissed the secretary, and hoped he, at least, was managing something more productive than standing around in chafing silence.

"Clearly"—Kinus lowered the letter and the paper crackled as he shifted, straightening his back—"they are in desperate need of something." He lifted his arm from where it rested over his knee and stroked his fingers over his black, thick mustache, frowning as he did.

"An interesting observation," Makram said, careful to keep his voice even. "That was not the tone I took from it." Because his brother had been lost in thought the better part of the day, Makram could not read with certainty his mood, and was therefore hesitant to speak his mind lest he turn Kinus off to his opinions completely. He'd had plenty of time to read and reread the letter over the turn since it had arrived, since Kinus refused to even look at it until today.

The letter was written by someone who believed they were utterly in control, everything from the measured script to the terse, conservative wording told Makram all he needed to know, despite never having met the Sultan of Tamar.

Kinus regarded him from beneath lowered brow, in his eyes a command for silence. Makram quelled the rest of his assessment behind clenched jaw and a perfunctory duck of his head.

"This gives us the upper hand in negotiation." Kinus stood and stepped away from the dais and divan, toward the windows. "He says he wishes for an alliance, but the advisers agree we should not trust that to be his true intent. Do they wish to bog us down in negotiations while they assess the strength of my military? Or spy out how many Sixth House mages reside in Sarkum?" All the things he said, Makram had already heard whispered by the Elders behind their hands and as he passed them in the halls.

But Kinus wasn't speaking to Makram now. He paced beside the narrow, arched windows that overlooked the winter-cloaked courtyard. The mirrors that lined the wall behind the dais reflected back the wan light, casting columns of shadow and daylight across the floor. Fire and water, darkness and light. Second and Fifth House attributes, though many wrongly associated darkness and shadow with destruction and the Sixth House. It was significant, if one bothered to pay mind to portents, that the crown prince walked through the manifestations of opposite Houses on the Wheel. These were the scales that must be balanced in any decision.

Makram scoffed. Only the superstitious ninnies in the council believed such nonsense. Common sense was all one needed. But there were too many voices for Kinus to listen to, too many opinions. Navigating the intensifying dealings with the Republic and now adding negotiations with a generations-old enemy might cause even the most resolute to start looking to signs and omens for assistance. Makram would much prefer Kinus look to him for that help as he had done in their youth. Now he could only do his best to push his brother in the right direction when Kinus allowed it.

"I fear we are complicating things before they have even begun," he suggested, as Kinus stepped through a shaft of light and it glinted on his gold caftan. An alliance with Tamar would benefit them greatly. While Tamar had put a permanent moratorium on Sixth House mages after the Sundering, more mages were still born in Tamar than Sarkum. In addition, those mages born in Tamar were much likely to be of a high order than those born in Sarkum. If there was any hope of fending off the Republic, it lay in an alliance with their neighbor despite animosity. Even putting aside the thought of war, the Blight continued to spread, even in the root crops, and Tamar and its mages might be their only salvation from it. If the Sultan was reasonable, as his letter indicated he might be, then there was no better time to put the past behind their countries and unite again.

"And yet as a ruler I must be aware of these complications you dismiss so easily." Kinus bestowed a mixed look of hauteur and disapproval on Makram.

"Save your sanctimony for your subjects foolish enough to be led around by it, Brother. If anyone is in need of something, it is us. We need power, we need help with the damned Blight or the only upper hand you'll have is a mountain of starved citizens to stand upon." Makram kept his voice deferential, even if his words were not. "If Tamar can offer that and is willing, why would you not hear them out in a negotiation?"

"This is a chance to put them back in their place." Kinus stopped at the windows, his voice taking on the dark, bitter tones that accompanied his lapses into righteous fury at the wrongdoings of the past. Makram rest a hand against the hilt of his yataghan, channeling his tension into the grip. "They ruined us when they began the war and broke the Wheel, and I will not go crawling on hands and knees to them. They are half the size of Sarkum and their military is all but non-existent. This is the time to bring them to heel. And you, of all people, should be against an alliance." Kinus clasped his hands behind his back. "You think they will allow you to keep your place as Agassi? Will they allow you to be anything at all?"

Instead of putting you down like a cur. Kinus would never say such a thing to Makram, but others had. Behind his back, whispered as he passed. None of those who feared his magic would look him in the eye and say *better you were never born.* Kinus' truths were harsh, but they came from caring, at the very least, and were honest. Besides, he was only harsh when he felt tested. Makram ignored the ache of old emotional wounds. What mattered was helping Kinus see the bigger issue.

"Yet I am willing to risk this, and I have the most to lose. The Republic is breathing down our neck—what do you think they would do if we entangled ourselves in a conflict with Tamar? Sneak in and hamstring us while we are preoccupied." That's what he would do, were he in command of the Republic's army. "Please. Let us send delegates to Tamar if you do not wish to go. The Sultan has offered negotiations. At least hear their terms. We could breathe power into the bloodlines—"

"*Enough*. Do not bring power into this." Kinus' voice cracked. The sunlight framed him in pale glory, his robes glinting, his black hair oiled and pulled into a knot at the crown of his head. At thirty-six he was a decade older than Makram and young to rule, when measured against tradition. Yet, he was the picture of a ruler, an exact replica of their father. Almost. He lacked their father's confidence, a fact the Elders took wholesale advantage of and the reason for him setting his feet at inappropriate times. Such as now. Makram only needed to convince his brother he wasn't trying to overstep, and he would be more reasonable.

"The Republic would be a far better ally than Tamar. They are a military force. They have technology we cannot conceive of. What does Tamar have?" Kinus gave a little laugh of derision. "A broken Wheel and powerful mages. They will fall to the Republic just as easily as us."

He couldn't be serious. The Republic would demand the lives or imprisonment of all mages, to include both of them. "And the Blight?"

"I said enough, Makram. I've made my decision. If Tamar wants something from us, they can wait until I have time to respond. They have no other choice. We lie between them and any allies besides Menei, who isn't united enough to align with anyone. Let them understand I will be maneuvered by no one."

Kinus crumpled the letter and tossed it on the mosaic tiles at Makram's feet. "You may go."

Makram stood a moment longer, allowing his desire to argue further to fade. To rant at him would do nothing but root him more firmly in place. He would have to concede for now and try again later, once his brother had a chance to cool from his flux of pride.

"As you wish." Makram retrieved the crumpled letter from the floor and strode out of the cavernous room.

Four

SEVERAL DAYS AFTER KINUS had initially read the Sultan's letter, Makram sat on the veranda that linked his rooms to the central atrium garden of the palace living quarters, waiting. All the rooms opened to this area and were reserved for family and servants to the royal family. The trees in the garden had given up their fruit already, and many of the flowering plants had lost their blooms, everything transitioning from autumn to winter.

The palace had been built after the Sundering War, a smaller replica of the palace in Narfour, where the Old Sultanate had ruled. Ediz Rahal the First, who built it, intended it to be occupied with people enough to rival the Old Sultanate, and so built it with room to expand. But Sarkum had languished. The palace stayed too large and quiet. They had dwindled with each generation, magic dimming in the bloodlines. The rulers in Sarkum had never been prosperous enough after the Sundering to build their dreamed-of empire, only maintain it from diminishing to nothingness.

Makram lowered his gaze from the garden to the smoking pipe that sat beside the table. The nargile was cleaned and set up between the bench he sat on and the two chairs that faced it. Tareck Habaal, his steward and friend, claimed it helped him center his thoughts and calm his mind when he smoked. They spent most evenings here, talking, even now, as the evenings grew colder. Makram rarely minded the cold, and Tareck was far too stoic to complain, despite his magical affinity to Fourth House's earth and summer's warmth.

Being outside helped to slow the thoughts that came too fast and jumbled to make sense of. Tareck had been summoned to attend Kinus, and Makram was too on edge wondering why to do anything but wait. He hated waiting, had since he was a boy. When he'd return home on a break from training, and be forced to wait for his parents to make time to see him. He'd had Kinus to wait with him then, to distract him with games. And those times when Makram's parents never made the time to see him, it was Kinus who found ways to make him forget, to keep him occupied.

The door from the hall to his rooms, a modest combination of bedroom and sitting room, opened. Makram stood as Tareck entered the sitting room and crossed it to emerge on the veranda.

Tareck moved as all the other attendants and servants of the palace did, with grace and subservience, but his silence had an edge. He was first a soldier, a fighter, and though he had not been trained to the position of steward, Makram enjoyed his unadorned, outsider's opinions. Too many attendants in the palace were concerned with garnering favor and moving upward. Tareck would be most happy to return to the barracks and spend his days wielding sword and rein. Until that changed, Makram would keep him exactly where he was because it was his longing for his former life that kept him keenly observant of his new one.

"What did he want?"

Tareck held out a piece of paper and shook his head as Makram took it to examine. Makram scanned the words, disbelief sinking cold through his body then igniting with impotent frustration. He brushed past Tareck and into the sitting room, then the hall that led to the palace proper. Tareck followed, keeping some distance. It took everything of Makram's will not to crumple his brother's reply missive into the smallest ball he could. It would be too tempting to throw it in Kinus' face when he found him.

At this time of day, he suspected his brother would be in the sword hall, practicing in the interest of exercise rather than skill.

Something Makram found doubly offensive for the fact his life had been nothing but the sword. Though the sword and battle suited him fine, he'd had little choice in the matter when he'd been shipped off to training as a child.

"Perhaps a moment to curb your temper," Tareck suggested blandly from behind him. Makram waved the letter without looking back at him.

"I'll curb my temper against his teeth if he won't see reason."

"As you wish."

The doors to the sword hall, an addition to the palace armory, were thin wood carved in quatrefoil repeats. Makram did take a moment to relax before he pushed through them. No sense going at Kinus like a charging ox. It would not serve his purpose to irritate his brother from the outset.

Kinus stood at the far corner of the room, setting a yataghan on the long table that ran the length of the western wall, beneath a row of arched, mullioned windows. His opponent, the same aging martial instructor who had taught their father, bowed low as Makram crossed the room. Kefah Behnassi was in his sixtieth turn of the Wheel, and though Makram had devastating magic to call upon and Kefah did not, he far outmatched Makram in skill at the blade.

"Have you come to practice as well, Efendim?"

The politeness of the question was warning. Makram halted, took a deep breath to gather himself, and ducked his head in the man's direction. "Another time, Behnassi Bey. I have an urgent matter to discuss with the Mirza."

Kinus ignored Makram, examining the blades laid out before him, his back to the room. That did not bode well for Makram's chances at changing his mind.

Kefah retrieved his charcoal-grey ferace and pulled the coat over his caftan, glancing between Makram and Kinus as he buttoned and belted it. "I am certain your steward is not presenting you enough challenge and I am afraid your skills will molder. I am at your disposal, as always." He bowed. When he rose he cast a bright-eyed, taunting smile at Tareck, who gave a mocking bow in return. They were master and pupil as well as longtime friends.

"I will remember your generosity, Master. I do not mean to neglect my skills." Perhaps being thoroughly beaten in a sword match was exactly what he needed to remind himself why he preferred soldiering to politics.

"Of course, Agassi. Your position is a busy one, and these are troubling times." Kefah glanced at Kinus' back. "I will take my leave. Captain Habaal, perhaps you will join me?"

Tareck looked to Makram, who nodded, and the two soldiers left together. When Tareck had once again closed the carved doors, Makram held the papers out to Kinus' back.

"This is madness," Makram said. "You know I would do anything you ask of me. But this…I cannot sit idly and allow you to make this mistake."

"Allow me?" Kinus laughed, slamming down his blade as he spun toward Makram. "You, the second born? You are not Mirza. You are not the ruler. You are nothing."

Makram's frustration chilled and sank, becoming a bitter, acid feeling in his chest.

"Elder Attiyeh and that war dog you call a steward have been whispering in your ear again. Their opinions and your power do not give you the right to dictate to me, Makram. Everyone else might be awed by it, but I am not. There are other considerations in this world than magic."

"I am not trying to dictate to you. This is about protecting Sarkum from annihilation." Makram leveled his voice, pushing past the pain his brother's words had caused. What had happened to make him write such a scathing refusal to Tamar, to use such harsh language now? The Elders must have done something to raise his ire and Makram was the only one he could safely unleash it on. While he might understand that, he still could not allow a fit of temper to be the reason they lost their chance at gaining a powerful ally and a cure for the Blight.

"The Elders have kept you in council too long lately. You are not yourself. I will forgive the words, but *this* is not a solution." He tapped his fingers against the missive. Kinus glanced at it then away.

"No? What solution do you have? Shall we help to destroy the Engeli? Let Tamar sweep in and eradicate what's left of the Sixth House, along with you?" Kinus' words echoed off the tiled walls. He sighed, putting his back to Makram again and pressing his fists to the top of the long table beside the row of practice blades.

"Brother." Makram crossed the room and gripped Kinus' shoulder. "Listen to *me*. The Elders scheme and posture and maneuver their families about like chess pieces. They will do the same to you if you allow it. But you have always watched out for me, and now I am only attempting to return the favor, for you, and for Sarkum."

"Even if the Elders were not opposed to it, I would be. Trading assets and shaking hands does not make allies of enemies." He shifted from where he leaned over the desk and grasped Makram's shoulders. "The way forward is not through the past."

"That is ridiculous."

"How do you know the letter isn't a prop to lure me to Narfour so they can have me murdered?" Kinus dropped his hands. Makram pressed his fingers to the space between his brows and closed his eyes as Kinus moved away. Kinus did not wear paranoia well. It was a mantle bestowed by the Elders and their scheming, one he felt obligated to wear.

"If you are concerned, then send me in your place. Do not put the musings of the Elders above your own good sense. Only some of them are trustworthy."

"Which is for me to decide, not you. In fact, I forbid you to engage with them without me present, especially Attiyeh." Kinus gripped the ivory hilt of a yataghan, lifted it to examine it one way, then the other, looking at Makram over his shoulder as he set down the ornamental blade.

Makram had lost the fight, but what could he do? Arguing further was pointless, yet he did so anyway. Kinus could change moods as quickly as fire changed direction, and Makram never knew when he might say exactly the right thing to remind Kinus he was an ally. Or exactly the wrong thing.

"I am a palace official, Commander of your armies. Such restrictions will prevent me doing my work. I have been nothing but loyal to you, and will always be."

"It was I who brought you out of the janissaries, where our parents cast you, and into the palace. Prove to me your work is still of benefit to me, and I may consider lifting the restriction. You are dismissed."

"Kinus." Makram closed his eyes, ignoring the sting of old hurts. Kinus did not mean to wound him.

"Address me formally or not at all." Kinus walked away, so all that was left for Makram to do was stare at his back or leave. He carefully rolled the letter he held into a cylinder and tucked it into the breast of his ferace. Then he bowed to Kinus' back and left. Tareck and Kefah were not in the hallway, so Makram strode for his office.

The offices for all palace officials were housed in one hall, and though they were some distance from the main palace, the walk was not long enough to clear Makram's head. The office of the Agassi, Makram's office, was at the very end.

It was the closest thing to sanctuary he had in the palace, and he walked to the back of the room, where a narrow bench spanned the base of the only window. His low desk stood in front of it for the light the window gave to his work. He pulled the rolled letter from his coat and flattened it on the table, smoothing its edges as he sat to read.

Kinus had refused everything. He wouldn't even entertain talks of negotiation. He didn't threaten them—thank the Wheel for small favors—but the wording was arrogant at best.

Makram propped his elbows on either side of the letter, pressing his palms against his eyes. He could reword it, so it was at least polite. It might leave the slimmest possibility of future negotiation open. No, that was wishful thinking.

Early winter's damp cold seeped in through the thin glass behind him, and Makram lifted his head, glad for the chill that energized his magic and his body. There was clarity in cold. It had not been so long ago that he and Kinus had been inseparable. In the Turns since their father's death the Elders had succeeded in driving a wedge between them that Makram had been too physically distant to prevent. If someone had asked him, back then, if he thought that might ever happen, he would have laughed. Kinus had been so protective. It had always been Kinus who soothed the wounds caused by parents that viewed their second son with no more love than they would have viewed a trained hound. What had happened? How could a gaggle of alarmist old men have damaged the bond between brothers?

A knock on the door broke him out of the sinkhole of melancholy. He knew the rhythm to be Tareck's.

"Come," he said, folding his arms over the letter. The door opened and just before Tareck stepped over the threshold someone in the hall called for him. Makram watched as a messenger handed a leather-carrying tube to Tareck, the white wax sealing the buckle on it still intact.

Once Tareck closed the door, Makram announced, "I think it might be best if I leave the palace for a time."

Tareck grunted, producing a dagger from the cloth belt that wound beneath his ferace and around his waist, and slicing open the wax seal on the leather tube. He could go back to Jaramin, where the janissaries trained, and spend his frustration in training, as Kefah had suggested. Nothing vented an excess of emotion better than sparring or battle, and besides Tareck and Kefah, there was no one in the palace skilled enough to challenge him.

"Angered the Mirza with your infernal devotion to logic, have you?" Tareck pulled the rolled missive from inside the tube and set the case aside.

"Don't start," Makram said. "How is he to know which voice to listen to when so many are chattering in his ear?"

"*You* have never suffered from an inability to tell an eagle from an ass. Perhaps another deficiency allowed the second son." Tareck shrugged one shoulder. "How far will you run to ensure he forgets you've angered him?" Tareck unrolled and scanned the letter, partly as a way to hide himself from Makram's glare. He could not keep Tareck around for his honesty and then rant at him for the same. This was an old battle between them, about Kinus' fitness to rule. It was not an argument Makram ever participated in, but still Tareck needled him. Still occasionally broke into lectures.

He didn't want to return to Jaramin and be so far from the palace, in case Kinus changed his mind. There was only one place closer that would not make him appear to be hiding out to scheme.

"The estate in Saa'ra. I'll see to the stables and the eagles. I haven't been in some time." Makram straightened, watching as Tareck's brows drew together, and the muscles in his jaw jumped as he clenched his teeth. "Something of interest?"

"From Tamar," Tareck said, crossing the room and pressing the letter over the top of Kinus' where it lay on Makram's desk. He took in Tareck's troubled expression before he considered the letter. Another from the Sultan, in the same thoughtful script. Yet this one was worded strangely, or rather, even more precisely than the last.

Makram read it once, then again.

"...a faction of my Council is not eager for alliance with Sarkum. I fear if no word or delegate is sent by the end of the small turn negotiations will become impossible."

It was signed by the Sultan and bore the seal of his *tughra* in white wax. Makram's hands spasmed against the paper, everything inside him screaming to tear it to shreds and bellow his frustration. They were going to lose their chance before they'd ever even had it.

"The Council in Tamar sounds as though it might be kin of our own," Tareck said dryly.

Makram shook his head. Everything felt suddenly constricting, his clothes, the etched metal closure that held his hair up, the room. He needed to be away from this place, from those who wanted to harness Kinus and him to the same slow, rickety political system that had been in place since the Sundering. A pair of matched fools to continue on the same rutted path.

"I am more concerned with what he didn't say. If his Council is against an alliance, then we have very few supporters at all. Kinus will never agree to send someone. He will send this instead." Makram tapped the refusal missive from his brother.

"Have you considered consulting with Elder Attiyeh?"

"No. The last thing I need is to give him cause to stir the Council yet again with talk of me succeeding instead of Kinus." Makram closed his eyes. There was one solution he could think of, but it was an incredible gamble. It would test his brother's trust in him, possibly to its breaking point. But it had always been better to ask forgiveness from Kinus than permission. He was far more likely to grant the former.

Makram could not sit back and do nothing. He could not let the Blight continue, threatening the lives of every person in Sarkum, could not wait in silence while the Republic plotted their end.

He stood. "We're leaving in the morning. Prepare horses and an escort. Keep it small, six men at most."

Tareck let out a breath that puffed his cheeks. "But not to Saa'ra."

Makram ignored Tareck's triumphant expression, rolling up the new letter from Sultan Sabri together with Kinus' letter. Tareck handed him the messenger tube and Makram stuffed them inside. "Seal this and keep it with you."

"Shall I inform the Mirza you will hand-deliver his missive?" Tareck asked, with all the might of his sarcasm in his face and his tone.

"Best keep it between us for now. I'll leave a written explanation with Elder Attiyeh to be delivered in a few days." Makram considered. There were several routes they could take, some safer than others. "We'll take the northern route to the Engeli Gate. It is fastest."

"And more dangerous," Tareck said. "No need for Kefah to be concerned about your skills rusting. You'll be needing them soon enough."

Five

Numbness permeated the spaces inside Naime, the stillness of disbelief. The days had come and gone with no news from Sarkum. There were no more ways to stall, no more pieces to move into position. She had lost. The very best she could hope for was to convince her father to marry her to the most easily manipulated of the lot. Even then there would be no alliance, no way to work toward balance and magic strong enough to repel the Republic. This would be the end of them.

Yet she sat in her lavishly appointed rooms, on her velvet-cushioned stool, in front of a jewel-encrusted mirror while Samira brushed her hair. The absurdity made her feel like laughing and sobbing in turns.

Samira wore a composed expression, but they had known each other too long for Naime not to recognize the hidden pain.

"You know I will do everything in my power to ensure it is not Cemil," Naime said softly, looking at Samira in the mirror. Samira gave a single quick nod but said nothing. They both knew there was only one outcome for today's proceedings. Her betrothal to the Grand Vizier's son would hobble Naime as surely as a fat and useless pony in a field and destroy Samira.

The Wheel's balance sometimes struck like a viper.

"If you wish to be dismissed from service..." Naime let the words hang between them. How could she ask Samira to stay? There could be no greater cruelty.

"I love you most in all the world," Samira said without expression. *Except Cemil.* Samira no longer acknowledged it out loud, but still, Naime heard the words. "Do not take that from me as well."

Naime felt the tremor in Samira's hand as she worked the brush. Naime reached for her, but Samira shook her head. Touch might open a floodgate she did not wish unlocked. Naime clasped her hands together and tried to think of something else.

She had still not seen Ihsan, though she knew he would be at the ceremony. Even his presence would not be enough to comfort her in this disaster. Samira set down the brush and held up a white, silk entari embroidered with gold peonies. Naime stood and Samira helped her shrug into it, then circled around her and buttoned it closed. It remained open above and below the waist, revealing the cream caftan and salvar beneath. Next Samira wrapped a long, pale pink scarf embroidered with more gold peonies around Naime's hips, arranging it so the gold tassels at each end hung in front.

"Which jewelry do you wish?" Samira adjusted the sleeves of the entari so the cream caftan was shown to better advantage. Naime stood on a platform in front of the full-length mirror. The frame was silver with vines and flowers set with sapphires and emeralds. A wedding gift from her father to her mother.

"None. There is no one I will see today who is worth the sight of them."

Samira clicked her tongue. "I'll choose some."

"Mother's pearl-drop earrings then," Naime conceded, Wheel forbid she be seen in public without earrings and necklace. Diamonds and a teardrop sapphire adorned her diadem. The pearls, a nod to the Second House, would complement, if not balance, the stones of the First.

Samira obeyed, bringing the earrings from Naime's jewelry cabinet and setting them carefully in her ears. Next she brought the diadem to place atop Naime's head, so the sapphire hung over the center of

Naime's brow. She artfully arranged and pinned Naime's burnt umber hair to both hold the diadem in place and sweep back from her face. She divided the hair into two twisted plaits, which she then wound together and secured with pins. Last she affixed a gauze veil to the top. It covered Naime's hair and down her back.

Naime normally eschewed the custom of covering her hair, but a princess' betrothal was a thing of tradition, and anything she could do to ease tempers was necessary now. Though if all her plans were ruined, why should she still care about upsetting them?

"Forgive my boldness, Efendim—"

"Stop," Naime said. "I keep you near me for your boldness."

Samira smiled coyly and tipped her head to the side. "I see your troubled heart." She brought a small ceramic pot of kohl forward from the dressing table and used it to outline Naime's eyes.

"Of course you do. It is practically hanging in the air for anyone at all to see." Naime flicked her fingers. "I have never been so transparent in all my life."

"Feelings are not failings, as I have told you time and time again," Samira said impatiently. "I know you will turn this to your advantage. You always have. Have the same faith in yourself that I have in you." Samira set the kohl aside.

"I have faith in myself. It is everyone else I am worried about. The entire rooster-headed lot of them. So busy pecking at each other they can't see the fox stalking the pen." Naime turned away from Samira and stepped down. "That will do. I will not become more ready to face them by cowering in here applying makeup and jewels."

"No," Samira agreed. "Your attendants are gathered outside, shall we depart?"

Naime didn't answer, but swept toward the door, flinging it open and striding through the gaggle of attendants. They were momentarily surprised, stumbling out of the way in uncharacteristic clumsiness. She paused, allowing Samira time to exit the room. Samira clapped her hands for order, and the six escorts fell into a loose formation, with Samira at their head. She cupped her hands together over her stomach, one over the other, her back as straight as a lance, her expression serene, and ducked her head to Naime. The others were not as composed. It was difficult for anyone to live up to the standard Samira set, but they did well enough.

Naime adopted the same serene expression. Samira had learned it from her, after all. Serenity was not a natural part of a Fifth House mage's temperament, but an innate gift of every mage of the First House. Inside, she pressed her power to the very edge of her physical body, as if donning a suit of armor. Air buffered, both in its natural state, and in its nature as a magic House. There was not a single person who waited in the main palace courtyard that Naime would allow to see her inner turmoil. To them she would appear as she always was, cool, composed, and restrained. If she had to pretend until it was true, she would, no matter the tempest inside.

The walk from the living quarters to the main palace and courtyard beyond was interminable. They always held the choosing ceremonies for betrothal in the courtyard so the public could attend if they wished, though they were limited to gathering outside the Morning Gate. No one outside of the officials and attendants to the ceremony would be allowed in the courtyard. The palace guard was engaged in maintaining order in the crowds that had made the trek from the city to see who their next Sultan would be.

When she appeared in the doorway to the palace, the crowd erupted into cheers, the sound so forceful that Naime felt as if she'd walked into a physical wall. The noise, coupled with the sudden brightness of pallid sun, left her momentarily stunned at the top of the steps that led out of the palace. From this vantage point, when she had blinked the sting out of her eyes, she could see the crowds gathered outside the palace walls stretched several blocks down the broad street that sloped toward the city.

"There is your proof that the hearts of Tamar are with you, Efendim," Samira said over her shoulder. "Even if the Council is not."

Naime swallowed back a reply. It would be lost in the cacophony. She was thankful the onlookers would not be allowed close enough to hear the proceedings. She could navigate the intricacies of interacting with the Council and their offered sons; she could not direct the emotional uncertainties of what appeared to be half the city.

Ihsan met her at the bottom of the palace steps and offered his arm. In his formal caftan and ferace, white embroidered with turquoise and silver, he cut an uncharacteristically royal figure. The colors set off the warmth of his skin and the pale hazel of his eyes. The right side of his face bore a slash of red, streaked scars that rose from his neck, across the hook of his jaw, and stopped just below his right eye.

"I might call you late," he said, though his gloomy expression did not reflect the teasing nature of the statement.

"It is impossible for me to be late to my own ceremony," Naime said. The corner of his mouth threatened to tick upward, which made Naime smile. She was glad to have him at her side, even if his mood was no better than hers and he could offer no solution. He offered Samira a polite, if not warm, smile.

The day was brisk, but not uncomfortably chill. She wished it were miserable and raining, to reflect her mood and to irritate Kadir and his son. Fire mages did not care for the cold and it seemed only fair they suffer in tandem with her and Samira. Though she doubted very much Cemil supported himself as future Sultan. There was little time for drunken ennui when one was running a sultanate.

"Sultan Efendim," Naime said when they reached the benches and seats that formed a circle in the center of the courtyard. Her father sat on a carved wooden bench topped with a velvet-covered pad. The legs were curved, the spindles modeled into fluid palmetto leaves. He had also dressed in white, the color of both his royalty and his magic House, but the hems of all his garments, as well as the collars and sleeve cuffs, were embroidered in gold. The salvar beneath the caftan and his slippers were also gold, and he wore a white turban, whose lower band was embellished with intricately knotted pins of gold and gems. His eyes were clear and bright when he greeted Naime with a subdued smile, and it buoyed her. If he was in his right mind, she might yet be able to turn things in a more favorable direction as Samira had suggested.

"Daughter," Sultan Sabri said, gesturing to the smaller seats beside him. She and Ihsan sat to either side of him, and her attendants blended into the mass of his. Her father and Ihsan shielded her from view of the Morning Gate, which suited her well. So many eyes on her would only be a distraction. The Viziers stood across the circle of chairs from her father. The four candidates for betrothal sat in chairs in front of the others, with their fathers seated beside them.

Naime cast a fleeting glance over the lot of them and then up at Samira, who stood just behind her left shoulder. Her hands remained cupped one over the other at her belly, her expression blank. When Naime nodded at her Samira joined the other attendants behind her father.

Naime had carefully schooled Samira, because she trusted her. She could only afford to have people close to her who could control themselves, their tongues, and their faces. The last thing she needed was to have her secrets revealed by someone who could not manage to hold an expression. When Samira moved away, another of Naime's attendants set a tray with pitchers of juice and water between her and the Sultan on a low table reserved for the purpose.

"Efendim." The girl poured him a glass of his favorite—pomegranate juice. Then she poured water for Naime and placed a wedge of lemon in it.

"Please offer some to the Viziers," Naime said. The girl bowed and obeyed.

As she carried the tray around the circle, the Grand Vizier stood. Behram Kadir wore his most audacious finery, caftan and ferace in shades of blood and fire, woven with gold throughout. Beside him, Cemil had dressed in a similar fashion. Kadir and his son shared only their House in common. Many said Cemil favored his mother so much one could not even tell the Grand Vizier was his father.

Kadir bowed low, lifting his upturned palms in deference to the Sultan, and his magic. In his prime, her father had been a formidable mage of the First House, as was Naime, but as the dementia waxed, his magic waned. Still, there had been a time when he could have outmagicked his entire Council, including the Grand Vizier, who was the most powerful fire wielder in Narfour, by any account.

"It is our honor to present the finest sons of Tamar for your consideration, Sultan," Kadir said.

"And my pleasure to receive them," the Sultan replied in his deep, strong voice. The tension that held Naime's jaw taut eased. Her father had been her friend through her entire youth. It was only since her mother's death that she had been more parent than child, more protector than protected. He was himself in this moment, and she allowed her guard down a fraction. "Name the bride price."

Kadir swept his arms behind his back and bowed slightly to the Vizier farthest from him, Sakir Esber, whose son, Aref, was the kindest of the four, but also a weak mage and weaker politician. Naime could count on one hand the number of times she'd had a conversation with the man, and none of them had lasted more than a few moments before descending into tiresome silence. That might be preferable to a drunk and puppet of the Grand Vizier, though. Naime avoided looking at Cemil as she thought it.

"When the Wheel stops turning," the Sultan said under his breath. Naime inclined her head in feigned appreciation as Esber Pasha announced his offer.

"At least he would do as I tell him to," Naime responded, only half joking.

He cleared his throat. "That is not always a blessing in a marriage, my dear," he said back. Ihsan chuckled.

"Our estate in the southern valley, to include the orchards and vineyards. Our estate in the Earth District of the city as well, to include our shops…"

Naime tried to maintain her focus on the man, but she cared not a single wit for anything any of them had to offer. She was not in need of houses, or land, or money. None of them could offer her power, because she outstripped them in both political and magical competence. If she were a son, this entire exchange would be laughable. She wouldn't be expected to marry someone who could offer her nothing, she'd be able to choose at her leisure.

But she was not a son. And despite that her father had succumbed to pressure from her, and her mother before she died, and promised Naime could take the throne in his stead, he was forgetting. From day to day she didn't know which Sultan he would be, the powerful, confident man who had trained her as he would a son—with the expectation she would take his place—or the fearful, ghost-plagued man who wished to cower in the easy safety of the traditions of his youth.

The next Vizier stepped forward, offering similar meaningless things. Naime did not let her gaze stray from the man as he spoke but did allow her mind to wander. In her peripheral she could see the Kalspire, the great mountain and its foothills that formed the backbone of Tamar and the eastern edge of Narfour. Snow dusted the top. Perhaps if Sarkum had sent a delegate they had been delayed at the pass. It snowed more deeply there than anywhere else. The thought that they were delayed was easier to stomach than the idea they were ignoring her attempts at reaching out.

It mattered little now. In a few marks the death knell of her plans would sound, masquerading as the name of the man she was to marry.

The last Vizier had ceased speaking and Yavuz Pasha was just finishing listing his bride price offer. Kadir smiled the particular smile he wore when things were going according to his own plans. It made the hairs stand on her neck and arms and her magic stir restlessly.

Vile serpent.

"Efendim, we have nothing worthy to offer in exchange for the brightest jewel in Tamar," Kadir said after Yavuz Pasha sat.

Naime was certain she heard Ihsan snort. It almost brought a smile to her face. Beside her the Sultan shifted, tapping his knuckles against Ihsan's knee in rebuke.

Kadir continued, either ignoring or unaware of the exchange. "Yet all that is ours, is yours for the honor of the Sultana's hand." He began to list his properties, but a commotion in the crowd outside the gate distracted Naime. It seemed far away, whatever it was just beginning to cause a stir in the people nearer to the gate as they became aware of it. It was subtle, but Naime was gifted with air, and sound's distance had never been an impediment to her. While she could not lean to see around her father and interrupt Kadir or seem to be ignoring him, she could listen, and there were eyes besides her own to use.

Naime breathed a command for Samira to investigate the cause of the stir, so quietly not even her father could hear her. She sent the command to Samira's hearing with a push of her magic. Cloth rustled as Samira turned just enough to whisper to one of the other attendants. The younger woman slipped backward through the crowd of servants and attendants belonging to Naime and her father, to find her way to a guard nearer the palace wall.

Naime concentrated on Kadir again, although her eyes had never strayed from him. He was still embellishing the gravity of his offerings, so she shifted her mind, and her magic, to the gate. What had been only the indication of disruption, raised voices, a change in tone, more speakers, became words when Naime commanded them with her magic. If she had wished, she could listen to ships out in the bay or to the goat herds up on the Kalspire, but she rarely had need of such a drain of her power. This was a simple working, amplifying sound and voice.

Riders. People repeated the word. *Did you see?* Naime pushed her magic, and her awareness, farther out. *Who are they?*

Kadir held his hand toward his son, who stepped forward and bowed. Cemil Kadir was considered by many to be unusually handsome, and Naime frequently heard the servants and noble daughters speaking of him. He was aware of this interest, and sometimes even cared enough to keep his appearance to the standard of a noble's son. Today he favored them with good grooming, his dark, curly hair cropped short and his beard neatly trimmed. He had a square jaw and prominent cheekbones and his eyes were the color of hammered gold.

But the smile other women found charming appeared smug to her, and the brightness of his eyes reminded her of the fire that took Ihsan's peace. After Ihsan's tragedy, Naime could never look at Cemil and see anything but a monster, despite Samira's insistence he had nothing to do with it.

He was smiling now, but it held none of its usual arrogant boredom or taunt. The uncharacteristic tension in his expression drew her attention completely away from whatever disturbance was growing closer outside the palace wall. One day, she had vowed, she would see Behram and Cemil Kadir in the Cliffs, if she did not steal the air from their lungs long before that. Her latent anger swirled up in her belly, filling her with its heat and irrationality.

"What say you?" the Sultan asked her as Kadir stepped back and put his hand on his son's shoulder, who bowed toward the Sultan.

"What need have I of estates and farms, Sultan?" She pitched her voice so the Viziers could hear her, keeping her expression neutral. "You have given me all I could ever need or want. I would choose someone who has something to give to Tamar, and none of these have offered any such thing," Naime said, carefully, watching her father from the corner of her eye. The line along his brow deepened.

Over her shoulder, Naime's attendant returned and whispered into Samira's ear. Naime tipped her head a fraction to indicate to Samira that she was listening. Samira raised a hand as if she were covering a cough and whispered into it. Naime's magic captured the sound and gave it to her as if Samira were speaking directly into her ear.

"Two riders entered the city and have been attempting to reach the palace. The crowd has been blocking them, and now they are being questioned by the palace guards. One has been injured."

"Injured by our guards?" Naime ducked her head to hide the movement of her lips, sending the sound over the distance that separated them. She could hardly believe that—Commander Ayan's men were too disciplined for unnecessary violence. Those who did not belong to Kadir, that is.

"On the road. They claim to be from Al-Nimas, here by the Sultan's invitation." Samira lowered her hand, resuming her posture of attentive waiting.

"Bring them to me, now."

"Daughter?" the Sultan said, more in irritation than curiosity. Naime lifted her head to smile at him.

"Forgive me, Sultan."

"Has something upset the Sultana?" Kadir said, and when Naime met his eyes she realized he was so focused on closing in on what he wanted that he had not noticed the commotion in the crowd outside. It should not surprise her, to him the common people of the city were of no more consequence than ants.

Naime smiled at him, allowing it to show nothing more than politeness, despite the frantic pace of her heart. "Nothing has upset me, Grand Vizier." She need only stall long enough for the guard to bring her the Sarkum delegate. Surely that would be enough to persuade her father to postpone a betrothal. "I am overwhelmed by the generosity of my father's Council."

She leaned nearer her father, and said quietly, "Do you find these bride prices suitable, Sultan?"

"You do not?" His eyes had begun to take on the vacant look that accompanied a lapse into confusion. The ceremony was taking too long; the attentiveness demanded of him had taken its toll. He was always at his worst when he was tired. If she could keep him present a few more moments, it would be enough. She hoped.

"We had discussed that marriage would only distract me from more important work," Naime said, with all the humility she could muster.

"We did," he said, but whether it was affirmation or question, Naime wasn't certain. She could hear that the guards had reached the gate, but to everyone else it was just commotion within commotion. All of the Viziers were focused on her and her father. Just a moment more.

Kadir spoke. "I fear it would be unwise to forestall a decision, especially after your daughter's careful preparation for today." His apologetic expression reanimated her girlhood desire to claw his eyes from his face. "If you are concerned about the business with Sarkum interfering with a marriage, I do not foresee that will be a problem. Since a delegate has yet to send word, we can only assume your attempts at alliance have failed."

"Grand Vizier, I'm not certain what you mean by failed." Naime widened her eyes. Kadir's brows drew together, and he hesitated. Naime tilted her head toward the gate. She could not see, it was indecorous to lean around her father to gain a view, but Kadir turned in the direction she indicated. All the Viziers followed suit. Then they stood, surprised and straining to see. Naime had the pleasure of watching Kadir's expression contort and warp briefly to rage and back again.

"Father, the delegate from Al-Nimas has arrived."

"Al-Nimas?" He twisted toward the gate. Naime took the opportunity to peek around him at Ihsan, who also watched the gate, his expression like a stormy sea. Three palace guards escorted two men, who led their mounts behind them. They were filthy, covered in dust from traveling, and their mounts appeared moments away from perishing. Neither man wore caftans with colors reflecting their Houses, nor were there tiraz around their upper arms to indicate anything of their magic affiliation. Naime struggled to even determine that beneath the dust they wore drab shades of grey and black.

They had the appearance of soldiers, not government officials arrived to negotiate. Her feeling of triumph had all but disappeared by the time the Viziers had shuffled out of the circle of chairs to make room.

The taller of the two handed his reins to his companion before making his way to drop to his knees in front of her father. He prostrated himself, instead of offering his upturned hands as was customary, and as he sat back up he faltered as though he might tip. Alarm bolted through her, and Naime started to push to her feet at the same time the man's companion moved as if to rush to his side. He waved him away and sat back on his heels, and Naime relaxed marginally into her seat.

Now that they were in front of her, Naime could see they were beyond exhausted, and the one kneeling before her father was bleeding. The right sleeve of his ferace had been ripped through all the layers, the fabric around the gash wet with dirt stained dark by his blood. Blood had dried along his fingers. They needed rest and care, not the interrogation they were certain to undergo if she allowed things to progress.

"Sultan Sabri Efendim," the injured one said in a weary, hoarse voice, "I am Makram Attaraya Al-Nimas, Agassi of the Mirza's janissary and sipahi forces in Sarkum. The Mirza has sent us, at your bidding, in hopes of negotiating an alliance between Sarkum and Tamar."

They wore yataghans at their waists, and the one holding the horses also carried a bow and quiver. From what she could see of them, they had the build and coloring that reflected Sarkum's brief alliance with the east, the Odokan plainsmen, their hair long and bound in clips against the backs of their heads. Their faces were scruffy with beards, but Naime could not tell if that was purposeful or simply a matter of days of traveling. They appeared oddly wild and ferocious among the bright, polished colors of the backdrop the Viziers made behind them. Men in Tamar did not openly carry weapons of war, but Sarkum was a martial state. Magic was no longer their greatest weapon.

Her father made a thoughtful sound. "I welcome you, Agassi—"

"How dare you appear before the Sultan of Tamar bearing weapons," Kadir said, interrupting anything else her father might have said as he strode forward to stand nearer the Sultan's seat.

The Agassi's gaze sliced toward Kadir with enough venom to wound, but he did not turn his head. He stared straight ahead as he tore open the buckle on his belt. He grabbed the sheathed yataghan and tugged, pulling the belt from around his waist, and threw it on the ground in front of him. His companion did the same with his sword, as well as his bow.

Naime glanced at her father, whose greying brows were furrowed, his eyes twitched closed. He curled and uncurled his fingers, growing more restless. She needed to end things now, before he gave himself away to the Sarkum men and they had knowledge of his weakness to use against her. Or before Kadir recovered from his shock and managed to turn the situation to his favor.

"Forgive me, Sultan Efendim," the Agassi said. "We encountered bandits on our trek through the barrens. The weapons were necessary for travel and in my haste to arrive I did not think to stow them."

"Hide them, you mean." Kadir pointed at the two. "Guards! Hold these men in prison until they can prove who they are."

Makram tensed. The man in red had puffed up like a disturbed field grouse, and it was Makram's experience that men like that were all too happy to ask questions after they'd hanged you from the gallows. He shifted his gaze to the Sultan, who seemed uncertain how to handle the situation. He could not blame the man. He could easily have been mistaken for a beggar, at the moment. It had been a gamble to take the northern route with so few men, he'd known the risks but chosen it for speed. They'd only endured one attack, but it had eaten up valuable time. He'd had to separate from his escort and leave their heavy packs behind, with all their clothes, to make it to Narfour.

"Agassi," Tareck warned, eyes on the guards who had brought them and who were now looking between the man who had shouted and the table where the Sultan sat. Makram didn't dare grab for his sword, and he absolutely did not plan on using magic here. The courtyard would be a blood bath.

"Grand Vizier." The woman beside the Sultan stood, shifting the attention of everyone in the courtyard to her. Until now he had noted only that she was there, nothing about her, assuming she was a consort. It was never a good idea to take interest in someone else's woman at a first meeting. It tended to set a bad precedent.

The barest movement of her hand set the guards at ease. "Imprisoning them will not be necessary." She folded her hands in front of her and gave a polite smile. "These men traveled in haste at our behest. I will vouch for them." She said the words to the Grand Vizier, but leveled a look on Makram that pierced straight into him and left no doubt she was displeased. Void and stars she was stunning. He'd never seen a more beautiful woman in all his life. She seemed young to be either Queen Sultana or consort, compared to the aged man beside her. A daughter?

The Grand Vizier turned his back on Makram to face her. "They have interrupted your choosing, Sultana Efendim. Surely we can deal with them after—"

"This man is bleeding, Grand Vizier." The flash of disgust in her eyes was the only emotion she had shown until now. He wasn't certain if it was disgust at the man she addressed, or at the audacity of Makram bleeding on the gravel of her courtyard. "The Sultan, and therefore I, must extend hospitality to our guests. It wouldn't do for delegates of Sarkum to return and spread tales that the most powerful Sultan in the world could not be bothered to extend simple courtesy." She gave the coldest smile Makram had ever seen.

"Sultana Efendim, that is impossible. The decision must be made today." The Grand Vizier spoke in a tone that was restrained but underlined with outrage. The special kind of anger that came with the failure of a political maneuver.

Makram closed his eyes. The bandit attack had been refreshing, in that it had reminded him how things outside of a palace could be so clear cut and easy to navigate. Now he was weaponless and bleeding between two people who clearly despised each other. At least in Al-Nimas he knew all the players.

"I am certain you did not mean to indicate you dictate when the Sultan makes a decision?" The woman, who was either a very young queen or the Sultan's daughter, by the way she was being addressed, smiled again, and accompanied it with a slow blink that mesmerized Makram. If Kinus laid eyes on her he'd fall over himself to marry her in alliance. Perhaps the offer of a beautiful woman would succeed where common sense had not.

"Of course not, Princess Sultana." The Grand Vizier ducked his head, in what appeared to be deference but was actually a concession of defeat. The daughter then, if she was Princess.

"Sultanim." The young woman turned to the Sultan and bowed, spreading her hands. An Old Sultanate custom, honoring the power of another's magic. "I ask your leave to attend to our guests. I will meet with you as soon as possible to hear your decision."

"Why is he kneeling? Are they Odokan?" the Sultan asked. Makram kept his eyes down, head bowed, but the tone of the Sultan's voice and the odd question set him on edge. There was something not as it had seemed from his distant appraisal in Sarkum.

"He only means respect by it, Father. They are not Odokan, they are from Sarkum. Please, let the Sehzade take you to your quarters. I'll have these men taken care of, if it pleases you."

"Yes, yes. And bring them to speak with me," he said. When the Viziers behind Makram began shuffling off, Makram stood. The Grand Vizier lingered, frowning.

Makram smiled, bowing low, then straightened. "Grand Vizier," he said.

The elder man's mouth thinned and then he watched as the Sultan rose from his seat and moved for the palace. Once the Sultan had reached the stairs to the entrance, the Grand Vizier gave Makram one last look of appraisal before following.

Tareck came to Makram's side, leaving the horses to stand as they were outside the circle of chairs. They were too near dropping of exhaustion to run off without sufficient impetus. They watched the procession ascend the stairs, first the Sultan and his many attendants, then the Viziers. There appeared to be twelve of the officials, though with all the colors of caftans and ferace Makram thought he might go blind trying to understand who was who, or what their rank might be. In Sarkum magic was not flaunted with such…fervor.

The Sultana watched the others leave before she focused on Makram again. Only one attendant remained with her, who stood just behind her and to the side and kept her head bowed. He supposed it was safe enough for a woman with strangers, with the focused attention of the entire guard force on him.

When the group of Viziers, attendants, and the Sultan disappeared beneath the arches that framed the palace entrance, she beckoned with her hand, and a guard approached. Makram eyed him in appraisal. The man was a monolith and dwarfed the Sultana in proximity.

"Make certain the crowds have been dispersed. Rumors will spread quickly," she said.

The guard, who Makram suspected was the commander based on the braids on his uniform, ducked his head. His gaze swept Makram, assessment but not dismissal. He left to obey, and the Sultana moved around the table to cross the gravel toward Makram and Tareck. Her attendant moved quietly behind, silent as she stopped. Silence was not a trait typical of a fire mage, which the attendant was, if her gold and orange clothes were any indication.

The Sultana inclined her head to him, and her servant bowed low. "Forgive our rudeness, Agassi. The Viziers can be quite cross when interrupted." She offered a fleeting smile. "I am Princess Sultana Naime Sabri ilr Narfour, Sival of the First House. Please allow me to attend to you in my father's stead. He has been ill with the change of seasons."

Makram had to take a moment to sort through all the titles. Not only a princess, but a powerful mage. She wore a white ferace embroidered all over with gold flowers and embellished along the hems and sleeves with gold braids, and the caftan and dresses beneath it were cream and pink. He might not have cared a wit about the colors she wore except it was striking against her honey skin and near black of her braided and coiled hair. It was wrong of him to think the hardship of the fast-paced ride had been worth it just to meet her. But think it, he did. A man who did not appreciate a beautiful woman was hardly a man at all.

"I do not believe you were the one being rude," Makram said, trying to sound cheerful, despite that more than anything he wanted to lie down and sleep right where he was. He wasn't entirely sure what manner of ceremony they had interrupted, but she had seemed all too eager to end it.

She held his gaze, serene, the slightest smile curving her full lips. There were not many people in the world who could meet the eyes of a death mage and not instinctively look away. Even his father and brother were unable.

He had an inkling he was going to like this woman, when he had all his faculties back.

"I will endeavor to continue to be inoffensive." She used a cool, flat tone. Yet he knew she was jesting, and he grinned. She appraised the weapons they had left on the ground, then the horses where they stood with their heads hanging, their coats caked with sweat and dust. "I cannot decide if you have the worst timing in the world, or the best."

"There is far too much in that statement to dissect before I've had a bath, Sultana. And perhaps seen a physician, if you have one to spare."

One corner of her mouth lifted. He was going to have to stop looking at her, Wheel help him. "Several. Are you in danger of dying?" she asked. If she meant the question, she seemed disturbingly untroubled by the prospect.

"Would that please you?"

She glanced from him to Tareck with a once-over that somehow encompassed them both and made clear she was unimpressed.

"I am in the unfortunate position of needing you alive." She tipped her head to her attendant, who bowed at the waist and hurried toward the palace steps, the same way the larger procession had gone moments before. "Come. I will have servants assigned to you who can show you the baths. The physician will see to your wounds and you may rest and recover. I will attend you in the morning to discuss how we will undo the poor impression you've made."

Makram glanced at Tareck as the Sultana swept past them. Tareck lifted one shoulder.

"I have more men coming. Six of them."

She stilled. Her lips moved as if she were speaking, but he could hear nothing.

A moment later two guardsmen sprinted toward them from the wall and bowed to her. Only a mage of the third order, Sival, as she had titled herself, or higher could cast magic without a spoken or written spell. His brother was a first-order mage of the Fifth House, an Aval, and had to use spoken spells to perform any magic. He was capable of only a handful of the most basic of fire spells and would have been called a Lightbringer if he were not Mirza. This woman had just cast a whisper all the way to the palace wall with her will alone. The rumor that Tamar was home to an abundance of high-level mages was proving true, so far.

"A handy skill for ordering people about without having to exert oneself," Makram said, softly. Tareck grunted a laugh.

"Store these weapons and have their horses seen to. Send an escort to the main road entering from the Kalspire. They have six more men coming. See that they are fed and shown the bathhouse and quarters in the barracks," the Sultana commanded with decisiveness he found himself grateful for.

"Yes, Efendim," one of the guardsmen said, bowing and spreading his hands before him. Both men turned, heading for the horses. Tareck jogged to meet them, to prevent them causing the two geldings to bolt across the courtyard.

"Thank you," Makram said when she faced him again. The woman was as unreadable as marble. His brother could learn scads from her, if only he would deign to.

"This way," she said, turning once again toward the palace.

Six

STITCHES TO HIS ARM, a bath, and a full belly. The only thing missing in the complete reversal of his comfort today was not knowing how Kinus had taken news of his departure. But he could do little about that at the moment, so best to turn his thoughts to the situation at hand.

Makram could not fault the Sultana. When she extended hospitality, she did so with alacrity. The physician had been waiting for them when they arrived in the guest rooms, and moments later a slew of servants had arrived with trays of food, a bottle of arak, and attendants to show them to the bathhouse. He hoped the men he'd separated from in the barrens before the Engeli had not encountered any other attacks, though it was unlikely. They'd made it through the worst of the barrens before parting. Even the most desperate of bandits did not spend their time waiting to ambush travelers in the knee-deep, sometimes hip-high, snow in the pass or where guards at the Engeli Gate might use them for target practice.

The day was only half done, but Makram considered taking advantage of the time to catch up on the sleep he'd missed while traveling. While he was accustomed to sleeping outside and in less than comfortable conditions, he didn't like it. And the couch he currently occupied was more than pleasant enough to nap on.

"I don't like it," Tareck said, without preamble, from where he stood observing the garden that lay outside the trio of windows and doors. They took up nearly the entire wall of the sitting room in the suite, two arched windows flanking a set of matching doubled doors, the entirety of it set with panes of glass so the view was not obstructed.

"The garden?" Makram prompted without opening his eyes. He didn't feel like discussing any of it. There was too much to examine in even that first short introduction, and the prospect of delving in to schemes and intrigues of a foreign court made him more tired than he already was.

Makram had the distinct impression he wasn't going to enjoy their next encounter with the Sultana. There was a woman who demanded control, if ever he'd seen one. At least she was a pleasure to look at. He'd endured tongue lashings and lectures before, but never from someone beautiful.

"The palace. Everything in this damn palace is First House," Tareck said, distaste coloring his tone.

Makram cracked one eye open. Earth and air were in opposition on the Wheel. Makram had hardly noticed, but once Tareck mentioned it he took stock of the surroundings. The colors were subdued, blues, whites, silvers. They were the colors of the Sabri family and royalty, of course, but also of the First House, the realm of air. Their walk through the palace halls had revealed a place of soaring ceilings and walls made entirely of arched windows or lattice to let the light and air in. Galleries that opened to gardens, halls that passed through atriums of plants and more windows.

Makram chuckled. Perhaps he hadn't been troubled because he found the design calming. He liked light and constant reminders of the outdoors, in contrast Tareck would live in a cave if he had his druthers.

"The stables might be more to your liking," Makram suggested, closing his eyes again. Sleep called to him and he was of a mind to heed it.

A knock on the door prevented Tareck's reply and Makram groaned, staying as he was while Tareck crossed the room and opened the door.

"Good afternoon, gentlemen. I am Mahir Balik, steward to the Grand Vizier. He has come to ensure you have everything you need."

Broken Wheel he had. He'd come to take their measure and recruit them to his cause before the Sultana made her attempts at the same. At least she had the decency to give them until morning.

Makram opened his eyes and stared at the ceiling. The back of the couch prevented his view of the door from where he lay. He'd left all his assets behind in Al-Nimas, particularly his spies, who were necessary to navigate the Sarkum court. It seemed they might have been a good addition to his traveling company. Too late now. He would have to do his best to salvage the situation and get the Sultan to tell him his terms, so he could relay them to Kinus. Along with his apology.

As Elder Attiyeh had told him time and time again upon his reintroduction to the palace after a decade and a half with the janissaries, "You will never find a battleground more relentless and exhausting than a royal court in transition."

"Send him in," Makram grumbled as he sat up and rubbed his hands over his face. He stood and turned as the Grand Vizier made his entrance, an assault of red, purple, orange, and gold on the subdued decor of the room. The Sundering War had left Sarkum with a distaste for the divisions inherent in the Wheel, and so they did not hold to the old traditions of flaunting their House in every conceivable aspect of their lives. Clothes, titles, paint, decor. Makram had always been grateful for that, for a variety of reasons. The one most prominent in his mind at the moment as he gave the Grand Vizier a bow, was that fire mages could never do anything in half measures. That included color. He could barely look at the man without a throb of pain behind his eyes.

When Makram straightened, the Grand Vizier gave him a sweeping examination from head to toe and seemed to take amusement from what he found. They'd been given clothes to replace their own, ruined by travel and their skirmish in the barrens. But they were the brown and tan linen garments of servants. He'd be glad when his men arrived with his own clothes and they gave him some modicum of authority back.

Tareck moved as if he might speak, his brow furrowed with irritation that the Grand Vizier had not bowed in return. Makram suspected, based on the reactions in the courtyard, that they did not realize he was a prince of Sarkum. He was a second son, and so bore his mother's surname and not his father's, apparently another tradition they did not share with Tamar. He shook his head at Tareck, who obeyed the command for silence.

For now, he would rather tell them less than more, until the disposition of players was known to him. That there was no love lost between the Sultana and her father's Grand Vizier had been obvious even in his compromised state of mind, but which of them would be more valuable to him was yet to be determined. And he had no idea whether the daughter and the father were aligned. The last letter had indicated the Sultan and his Council might not be in agreement. No one was likely to offer him a chart of alignments and oppositions, so he would have to navigate the breaks himself.

"It is a pleasure to see you again, Grand Vizier. To what do I owe the honor of your visit?" Makram said.

"I see you have already eaten. Would you care to join me for coffee?"

"Of course." Makram gestured to the chairs that surrounded the table, turning to hide his grimace.

"Mahir, coffee. And…?" The Grand Vizier looked at Tareck in question.

"Captain Habaal," Makram answered.

"Ah. Take the captain with you," the Grand Vizier said.

Tareck looked to Makram for guidance, and Makram nodded. When both men had left, the Grand Vizier moved to sit in the chair Makram had indicated. Makram sat again as well.

"I have come to apologize for this afternoon. I was caught off guard and behaved poorly."

"I am certain the manner of our arrival was a surprise." Makram leaned back against the couch and crossed an ankle over the opposite knee. The Grand Vizier raised an eyebrow in disapproval but said nothing. Makram repressed a grin. Though he did not always enjoy that he was a prince with little power, he did enjoy being a soldier with freedom to offend anyone he chose. "It seemed we interrupted a ceremony of some kind."

"The Princess Sultana is of age to marry. The Sultan was being presented with suitors."

"I see," Makram said. "I apologize for our poor timing." She had seemed pleased to end the ceremony before its natural conclusion, perhaps she found her choices lacking. Maybe she'd prefer a man about to be Sultan himself? Perhaps that was what the Sultan intended, when he sent the offer of alliance. It would explain him urging their haste in arriving.

Makram wished he wasn't so entirely blind to the situation, that he knew what terms the Sultan intended to offer.

"Odd that you were not informed about the proceedings." The Grand Vizier smiled. "Have you had time to consider the Sultan's terms?"

Makram stretched an arm along the back of the couch and did not respond immediately. The question indicated the Grand Vizier was unaware the Sultan had not offered terms in his correspondence. Had he been aware the Sultan had communicated with Sarkum at all? Surely the Sultan would have informed his Council about his intent to negotiate with Sarkum—he could hardly make such an enormous move without at least a majority approval. If not, he would risk civil war.

The lack of knowledge of the Sultan's communications suggested they were kept a secret from the Grand Vizier, which in turn suggested he was not aligned with the Sultan. If he was not, then Makram suspected he would be a powerful influence in steering the Council in opposition of an alliance. A man not to offend too terribly, then.

The Grand Vizier shifted, apparently displeased with Makram's lack of response.

"I have not," Makram said.

Tareck and Mahir returned with a tray of coffee, which they set up amongst the remaining plates of food. Mahir cleared the table, transferring empty plates to trays and moving them out of the way. He was an actual steward, probably a noble son trained to the task from a young age. Tareck was just pretending to be one, and so had not bothered to put order to the room. He did feign servitude long enough to pour coffee from a copper ibrik into tiny cups and set one before Makram and the Grand Vizier. It was not a bad act, considering Tareck was far more accustomed to pouring arak for comrades than coffee for nobles.

"Take Captain Habaal for a tour of the palace. We want them to feel at home," the Grand Vizier said to Mahir as he lifted his cup.

Tareck glanced to Makram with raised eyebrows, already tired of being ordered away. Makram ducked his head in acknowledgment and command. Tareck barely suppressed a roll of his eyes before he bowed then followed Mahir into the hall. Tareck did not have to feign quite so much decorum in Al-Nimas. He would be in a poor temper if he had to continue to do so for the entirety of their stay in Narfour.

Kadir set his cup down without drinking, and so Makram did the same.

"I am told Al-Nimas suffers from rifts in its Elder Council, just as Narfour is burdened with the same in the High Council?" The Grand Vizier said it conversationally, as if he had not just revealed he likely had spies in Al-Nimas. That was interesting. Who in Sarkum would spy for a Tamar mage? Were his spies among the voices for or against Kinus assuming the throne?

"I represent the Mirza alone and am afraid I cannot speak to the disposition of the Elders in Al-Nimas," Makram said.

The Grand Vizier gave a small smile of concession.

"I look forward to your talks with the Sultan. It will be most interesting to see what Sarkum has to offer the seat of the Old Sultanate." The implied insult did not sting, as perhaps the Grand Vizier intended. Tamar had flourished after the Sundering War, if missing two of the Houses was flourishing. Sarkum did not. At least where magic was concerned. But even in his short and distracted ride through the city Makram had been able to make an assessment he would stake negotiations on. This was a place accustomed to peace and prosperity. Even their poor appeared better fed and clothed than those in Al-Nimas. Tamar was not prepared for war.

They might have powerful mages, but those were not enough to combat the vast army of the Republic. The Sultan wanted Kinus' army, of that Makram had no doubt. What else he might want, or be willing to offer, Makram wouldn't guess.

"When will the Princess Sultana's intended take the throne?" A change in rulership would aid or hinder any negotiations that began with one Sultan and ended with another.

"Ah, the Sultana." The Grand Vizier reached for his cup of coffee, finally, and Makram gratefully did the same. He needed the jolt of energy. "I would hope it would happen soon, at least the marriage. But I am, unfortunately, not in command of the situation." He sipped at his coffee. "She is an intelligent girl, but I am afraid her father has indulged her too often." He frowned as if it pained him to assess her so. "She is not eager to marry and have her freedoms stripped away. I believe if she had her way, she would stall indefinitely. I do not believe she means harm by it, only that she does not realize the effect it has on the people, not knowing who will rule after her father, how the uncertainty can cause strife and allow divisions to grow."

He took another sip of the coffee and set the cup back on the table.

Makram took a drink from his cup and set both feet on the floor as he returned the cup to its saucer. A spoiled daughter as an ally was a complication to a situation already difficult to navigate.

"Perhaps we should marry her off to the Mirza and be done with the negotiations and the uncertainty of rulership in one stroke," Makram suggested in jest. The Grand Vizier chuckled and shook his head.

"Until I know whether Sarkum is friend or enemy, I would not resign the Mirza to such a fate." He continued to smile, but Makram thought it had taken on more calculation than humor. Makram had not thought the woman quite so unbearable as the Grand Vizier was suggesting, but then, he had only spent a few moments with her.

"Do you know when I might be able to engage the Council and the Sultan under more appropriate circumstances? I cannot be away from Al-Nimas indefinitely."

In fact, he needed to return as soon as possible with negotiation terms. Otherwise the risk he had taken in defying Kinus to travel to Tamar would leave his brother in no better disposition than he had started. This alliance would serve to silence those who claimed his brother was unfit to rule. Those who had fed the idea that Makram should take the throne, fools they were, would quiet to know they had Tamar's power to help stave off the Republic.

"I will see to it that it is within the small turn," the Grand Vizier said. "Now I shall take my leave. I wanted to be sure you were taken care of. If you want for anything, please make your needs known to me. "

"Of course." Makram stood. "Thank you." He gave an abbreviated bow, then walked with the Grand Vizier to the door, trying not to show his relief by sprinting or urging him into the hall with too much enthusiasm.

His head ached, the slash along his arm burned and throbbed, and sleep tugged at him relentlessly. When he shut the door behind the Grand Vizier he almost slammed it for the finality, but managed to contain himself.

He took his small cup of coffee and stepped out to the garden for a few steadying breaths of bracing winter air. Winter was not as far along here as it was in the mountains and the high plains of Sarkum, but he could feel it in the air nonetheless, and the chill cleared his head.

The garden was narrow, situated between two long sections of rooms. He suspected this to be the living quarters for the palace and recognized the inspiration for the design of his own home in Al-Nimas. The western half of the palace stood between him and a view of the sea, which he had not had time to enjoy on their ride through the city. He'd been half afraid the crowds in the street were going to drag them from their horses. Credit was due to the guards who had lined the main road to the palace. They had managed to maintain order without the bullying to which Kinus allowed his own guard force to be predisposed. He suspected that bulwark of a commander he'd encountered briefly upon arrival to be the cause of their discipline.

Makram's breath fogged before him as he took another drink of the bitter black coffee. He did not wait well. That was one reason being a soldier had suited him better than being a prince, there had always been something to busy himself with. Sword battles, hunting bandits, and marauding groups of Odokan riders was a cut-and-dried business, in which it was possible to decide when and where to take action. In the palace, battles were fought with pen and paper, with whispered subterfuge, with the endless torture of waiting for someone to make a move that exposed them. He was not made for such things.

Tareck tromped through the sitting room and joined him in the garden upon his return. He gave a dramatic shudder. Makram smiled. He was not immune to the cold, simply more comfortable in it. Tareck's House aligned him with heat and summer. Winter and its cold made him cross.

"What do you think?"

"Mahir is a pompous ass," Tareck said. "I do not see what pride there is to be had in admitting you've been wiping another man's ass for half your life."

Makram laughed, trying not to spit his last sip of coffee as he did. "Did he say that?"

"Not in so many words," Tareck conceded. "And the Grand Vizier?"

"He limps." Makram squinted up at the afternoon sun. "I wonder if that is a battle wound? He bears a scar as well." Makram drew a line down his cheek, mimicking the scar on the older man's face.

"Tamar hasn't had any significant battles in recent enough history that I can think of." Tareck shrugged. "I take that to mean you discovered nothing useful during the encounter."

"You are correct. I know only that the Princess Sultana does not like her Grand Vizier, and he holds a rather low opinion of her in return. I also cannot help but notice where we are."

Makram dumped the coffee grounds lingering in the bottom of his cup onto the ground. Tareck gave the garden around them a quick glance and raised his brow in question. "This is the living quarters for the palace." Makram handed Tareck the cup. "Not the guest wing. They have a guest wing in a palace of this size, I'm certain."

"Your point?"

"Well, why might a princess put delegates of an enemy state so close to the Sultan, instead of consigning them to a distant wing of the palace?" Makram rolled his neck from side to side, trying to alleviate some of the tension in it.

"To keep watch on them, in case they are dangerous?"

"Bah. Their guard force is obviously capable enough of managing two men. No, I think we're being shielded," Makram said.

"From what?"

Makram focused in the direction the Grand Vizier had gone and squinted as he considered.

"Influence."

Seven

THE DAY AFTER THE choosing ceremony disaster and the arrival of the Sarkum delegates, Ihsan approached Naime as she left her rooms. He strode from the direction of her father's rooms at the end of the hall, where he had spent the night. His brows were drawn down, his posture stiff as he approached.

"Sultana," he said as he reached her and bowed.

Naime glanced at Samira. "Find out if the Sarkum delegates have eaten breakfast, and if not, have it brought."

Samira ducked forward a fraction in acknowledgment, then turned and gave directions to the other attendants. They scattered down the hall and toward the kitchens. Samira remained, watching for anyone who might approach, so that Naime and Ihsan could speak in private.

"This is the worst I have seen him in some time. He's been ranting about death mages and Sarkum invaders." Ihsan grimaced.

"Is he in his rooms?" She had to keep him away from Kadir until he had calmed down. The oddity of the delegates' arrival had obviously stressed her father beyond his ability to cope. The last thing she needed was the Grand Vizier feeding her father's irrational panic or seeing him in the full grip of his mental deterioration.

"His quarters. I have posted a guard and his steward and attendants are with him."

"I must meet with these men before Kadir does." She nodded toward the two rooms. "I am sorry to ask, but can you stay with him a bit longer? I do not want Kadir anywhere near him."

"I don't like you meeting them without me, or at least someone." Ihsan cast a harsh look down the hall.

"I have a half dozen attendants, San. You saw those men. They were nearly dead on their feet. They pose no risk to me."

"Don't be arrogant"—his eyes narrowed in accusation—"you know nothing of their magic or intentions. And they have since rested."

Naime had neither time nor patience for a flareup of Ihsan's protective nature. "I need you with my father. I will be careful."

"Fine. But come see him as soon as you can. It could help if you talked with him." Ihsan cast one more disapproving scowl toward the room.

"I will."

He bowed again, for show to the servants watching, then returned the way he had come.

Naime gestured to Samira, and they continued down the hall. It was early, which would either serve to irritate her guests or find them still muddled with sleep and in a more suggestible state. When they reached the doors Samira strode forward to knock. Naime took a moment to make certain she was in order, smoothing her hands over her blue and gold entari. Samira had put Naime's hair in braids that morning and wound them into a coil against the back of her head. Men seemed to take her more seriously when her hair was bound up, instead of loose, one of the many little details she kept in mind.

The doors opened after long moments, revealing the shorter of the two men. In the brief moments she had spent with them the day before he had appeared deferential to the other. He was dressed in a servant's linen salvar and caftan, with a brown cloth wrapped several times around his waist as a belt, and cotton slippers. His face was difficult to age, rugged and weathered but with a generally youthful countenance. There was nothing in his build or appearance that would set him apart from a Tamar man except for the style of his hair and the slightly more angled features. His skin was a shade darker than the average in Tamar, his hair deep mahogany and untouched by grey. It was longer than was fashionable here, with occasional small sections wound into braids away from his brow and the whole of it pulled tightly back and secured within a leather clasp. His face was newly clean-shaven, another difference. Goatees were currently in favor in Narfour, but no matter the style most men wore beards.

He also looked unabashedly grumpy, his eyes still half closed with sleep, the mark of a pillow against his cheek. Good. Every disadvantage of theirs was an advantage to her.

"The Sultana seeks an audience with the delegates of Sarkum," Samira announced, and bowed.

"Please, come in." The man returned the bow, and Samira stepped to the side so Naime could enter first. The man left the door open behind her, a fact Naime thought would please Ihsan and his grandfatherly sense of propriety.

"Forgive me, Master. I do not know how to address you," Naime said when she had entered the room and turned to face him and the door, putting her back to one of the two bedrooms that lay on opposite sides of the central area.

"I am Tareck Habaal, former Captain of the janissaries and now steward."

"I see. And what title is appropriate for you?" She had researched Sarkum titles during the night but found little to go by. Some were titles shared in Tamar, some mixed with or replaced with terms from the Odokan. In Tamar it was a simple matter to order people by their titles, which were given upon initial introduction. But when the other had introduced himself he had given only a title for himself, and no House for either. Her lack of knowledge would put her at a disadvantage if she did not correct it.

Tareck smiled, bowing slightly. "The Sultana honors me with her question. Most still refer to me as Captain."

Had the Mirza intended to make a point by sending soldiers as delegates? It seemed an odd choice.

A protracted silence stretched between them during which Tareck stood staring at her.

"Is the Agassi here?" Naime said, finally. His gaze flicked away from hers.

"Yes, Efendim," Tareck said, "but he is not accustomed to rising so early."

"And I am not accustomed to being made to wait," Naime replied, baffled by the man's casual attitude toward his master, and her. Tareck's lips pressed together, and he cleared his throat. Footsteps sounded behind her.

Naime turned abruptly and nearly ran into the Agassi as he came to a stop at her back. Barely a handspan separated them, and he was still in the process of adjusting his caftan, as though he had just finished putting it on. He regarded her with grim amusement. She gave a moderate bow, and when he only nodded in response, she raised an eyebrow.

Even if he were the general of an army, she outranked him. It had been her hope to deal with the Mirza himself or a delegate who would not treat her with the same dismissal that so many of her father's governors did. But as a child she had also wished for wings, and the Wheel had yet to provide her with those.

When she attempted to meet his eyes to convey her disapproval, he glanced away. Naime had held his stare the day before, when they arrived. It had been immensely difficult, and she pondered the reasons through the night. For one, his eyes were the color of black coffee, and once they held hers, appeared to darken more—dark enough to swallow her whole—and her magic whispered and writhed. No mage of any House had ever affected her own magic in such a way, and it made her suspicious of what power he carried inside him.

For another, he was striking, his features an unusual blend of Old Sultanate blood and the Odokan of the east, who had gifted him broad, high cheekbones and hooded, downturned eyes. He shared his companion's hair style and freshly shaven face but was taller, his hair true black, his skin honeyed gold. In the courtyard, even bloodied and travel stained, she had battled her desire to continue studying him. It was not a difficulty she ran into often, not since she had aged from adolescence. As an adult she had never met a handsome man who did not believe it gave him the right to act however he pleased.

And he was already proving the rule to her yet again.

"If you make a habit of showing up in my rooms"—he glanced out to the garden, where the sun had not yet spread its light—"before I can see the sun, then I am afraid you will grow very accustomed to being made to wait." The hoarseness of the day before had left his voice, allowing her to hear the vocal rhythm of his Sarkum ancestry and the warmth of the humor he inflected.

Voices were as informative as books, and to an air mage, to whom hearing was their most powerful sense, an invaluable tool. His sat the line between bass and baritone and felt to her senses like a smooth stroke of velvet. At least his voice would be a pleasure to listen to in negotiations, even if his words were not. Was it possible he was a water mage? Second House mages were known for their alluring voices.

"Forgive my intrusion, in Narfour business begins early," Naime said, resisting the urge to step away from him. Was he trying to intimidate her with the nearness? Bully her into conceding something by stepping back? Or perhaps he had observed her staring at him overlong and thought that gave him license to crowd her.

Naime sought the cool swirl of magic inside her to tame her discomfiture.

"In Sarkum is it common for men to stand so close to a woman without her permission?"

A muscle jumped along the length of his jaw, and the humor faded from the slant of his mouth. If he meant to answer, it was prevented by the remainder of her attendants entering the room. Naime turned to watch the women place plates of fruit, nuts, flatbread, and labneh on the table.

"Forgive me, Princess Sultana. I did not mean to cause you offense."

Naime took a deeper breath as soon as he moved away from her and sat on the floor cushions that surrounded the low-slung table.

"I hear congratulations are in order," the Agassi said, with a look like he was about to sweep the board in chess. Naime wrapped her power more tightly around herself, schooling her expression, her thoughts, and her emotions. His choice of words gave away both that Kadir had managed to get to him before her, and that he had spoken of marriage. "You have an impending betrothal."

Naime tipped her head. "Until our business with Sarkum is concluded, it is not my father's intention to betroth me to anyone. Whoever gave you that information was misinformed."

"I see. Would you care to sit?" he asked. "Your Grand Vizier at least had the manners to share coffee with me while he attempted to divine my intentions."

Naime looked askance at Samira, who gave her head the slightest shake to indicate she'd heard nothing of Kadir visiting them. It infuriated her to know he had come and gone from the Sultan's wing without her hearing so much as a whisper. That damned steward, Mahir, must have cast a dampening to hide them, and Naime had been too preoccupied with her father to sense it.

It was her own fault. She should not have waited to come speak with them, but they had been exhausted. Her father had warned her that consideration and mercy were often more weakness than weapon when it came to the games in the court. When she returned her gaze to the Agassi, he wore a darkly amused expression that indicated he knew she was troubled by Kadir's visit, no matter that she had not let her displeasure show.

"Surely you haven't eaten yet?" He gestured at the food. Naime hesitated, then knelt amidst the cushions on the opposite side of the table from him, tearing off a small piece of flatbread. He eyed her in disapproval. "Are you such a powerful air mage that you need only air to eat?"

Naime raised her eyebrow and popped the bread into her mouth. No soldier she had ever known would so boldly tease a noble, let alone a princess. He was arrogant, or something more than a soldier. Perhaps both. Why was he hiding it?

"Air. And men's tears," she said. The captain made a sound then started coughing, pounding his chest. Naime leaned forward and poured a glass of water, which she held up to him. He nodded thanks before taking it and draining the glass.

"I have no doubt," the Agassi said, dryly, though amusement also played in his voice. She admired his profile when he looked at Tareck then ripped her gaze away to the garden.

Handsome and prone to teasing. She could guess what all her attendants would be talking about for the rest of his stay.

"And have you come to induct us into polite society, Sultana? Or are you simply here to keep us company until your father can see us?"

"You are quite rude. That seems an odd trait in a delegate." Naime reached for a slice of cucumber.

"No, I am blunt. They are two different things. I have no patience for games." He sat languidly, one leg folded on the floor cushion, one bent toward his chest, his arms stretched across the seat of the couch behind him. If it were anyone else, sitting like that would have been a grave insult, but she knew little of Sarkum customs, and nothing of this man. In an odd way, she found his ability to relax disarming. She credited it to him being a stranger, and perhaps to his bluntness. That could be a refreshing change.

"You are not the first soldier I have met who speaks of his inability to navigate polite society as if it were a virtue."

He lowered his face to hide his grin, turning his head as he wiped a finger over his eyes. She was glad he found her pseudo-criticism amusing, instead of insulting. She relaxed a fraction more.

"I rarely find society polite," he countered when he lifted his head, "even if their words appear to be."

"Fair enough," Naime agreed, noticing Tareck again as she tore another piece of flatbread off. "You needn't stand at attention like that, Captain Habaal. I did not come here to prevent you from breaking your fast." She gestured to the cushion between her and the Agassi. Tareck took it, swinging a look between her and his master, as if he didn't trust either of them.

"Samira"—Naime indicated the cushion to her right—"if it does not displease you, Agassi?"

He peered up and over his shoulder as Samira skirted the couch and knelt where Naime pointed, appearing surprised by the invitation.

"It does not. So, explain this poor impression I have made on you by heeding your father's request for haste in my travels."

"Not on me, on polite society." Naime thought she could match his lack of formality at least until he proved himself something other than an ally. "When you meet with my father to discuss alliance, it is imperative the Council respects you, which they will not if your conduct is not impeccable."

"I see." He peeled a dried date open and pulled the pit free. His eyes followed the movements as Samira slathered a piece of flatbread with labneh, laid pieces of cucumber over it, and handed it to Naime. Naime narrowed her eyes but Samira didn't look at her, only repeated the process for herself.

Naime switched her gaze to the Agassi and found him watching her. She could not look away without appearing weak, and so she held his stare as she nibbled at her food. He glanced away abruptly, his gaze seeking purchase somewhere else.

"I was given to believe not everyone in Tamar wants alliance," he said in low tones that suggested distraction. It was little surprise he knew. Her second letter had laid out the tension in the Council for the Mirza, and he had obviously seen fit to inform his delegate. And he seemed intelligent enough not to miss the rift between her and the Grand Vizier.

"Show me the panacea where people rush happily toward change of any kind," Naime replied.

His eyes settled on her face, and he gave his head the slightest tilt to indicate concession. A smile pulled at the corners of his mouth, but he fought it. The expression faded completely when Tareck held out a sloppy replica of what Samira had handed to Naime, a flatbread with labneh and cucumber. The Agassi turned a withering look on him, and the captain shrugged, taking a large bite out of it himself, eyes wide. Samira choked a little but bowed her head to hide it. Naime hid her own amusement with a lingering drink from her water glass.

"If"—the Agassi gave Captain Habaal another warning look then turned to her again—"the Sultan's High Council does not share his desire for alliance, how will he navigate that?"

"That depends on what Sarkum can offer, and how persuasive you can be." All Naime needed were terms sound enough to convince those with level heads and the rest might be swayed. If only she could pry them loose from Kadir's influence. She had hoped someone with power might have come from Sarkum, had hoped for someone with charisma enough to sway her Council to at least read and consider the terms of alliance she and her father had worked out.

Naime reached for a dried apricot. She *was* hungry. She often forgot to eat, lost to the endless lists of things to do that fluttered and spun in her mind.

Tareck leaned toward her, framing his mouth with a hand. "He can be very charming, in fact—"

"Do you want to go on another tour of the palace?" the Agassi said casually, hooking a thumb toward Samira. Tareck appraised her, which Samira returned with the silent, smoldering irritation that only a fire mage could do justice to. Tareck pressed his lips together and shook his head.

"I apologize, Princess Sultana, my companion was born in a cave and raised by wolves," the Agassi said.

They were baffling, yet their lack of decorum was also innocently amusing. Whether they were the norm for men, officials of Sarkum, or not, her power, combined with a lifetime of observing, rarely failed her in taking the measure of a person. These men read as genuine. Or at least as genuine as they could be for strangers in a strange court. It was indeed a nice change to be with people with whom she was not gambling everything with each word she uttered. She wondered what her Grand Vizier thought of them.

"And you?" Naime asked.

"Born in a palace," he said, his rich voice taunting her, "and raised by those same wolves." Hints. Playful games, not dangerous ones. When his full attention was on her, the intensity of it was mesmerizing, drawing her in, holding her in place, making her feel stalked, but not threatened. She found it exhilarating and unsettling. It was a rare person who could worm their way into her mental and magical armor.

Again she wondered about his magic, why they did not wear anything indicating their Houses, why they did not speak of it. Because of that she would not risk asking and insulting them.

His phrasing hinted her suspicions had been correct. He was not just a soldier. He was informing her of her miscalculation without abrading her for it. That suggested she had not offended him too much. It also suggested he was a man of more moral generosity than most who resided in the palace.

"Born in a palace? Then the janissary no longer practice the slave tax," Naime suggested. The janissaries of the Old Sultanate had been formed primarily of the children of conquered nations. In exchange for their *comfortable* lives, the conquered were forced to give up their eldest sons to the military. A barbaric practice she hoped was indeed no longer the norm.

"We abolished slavery after the Sundering," he said. "Enlistment is voluntary now." The words carried a complex weight and rhythm that told layered stories. Sadness, lingering resentment, and resignation.

"Not completely voluntary," she said, carefully, picking through a bowl of olives so her observation did not make him feel dissected.

"Why would you say that?" he asked, just as carefully.

Naime selected an olive and stripped the meat from the pit with her teeth. She buried her observations for future use.

"No reason." She set the pit aside. "Only that sometimes those of the First House hear more than just words when others speak." She offered him a smile.

He studied her in silence, and Tareck constructed another flatbread with labneh and cucumber.

"This is quite good," he said, with a little too much enthusiasm. As if the man had never had a cucumber. Samira ducked her head graciously, but her mouth tightened to prevent a smile. The Agassi shifted, folding both legs in front of him and setting his fists against his knees.

"You heard correctly then. I was sent to the janissaries, not by choice. In Sarkum, traditionally, a prince commands the armies.

I am brother and adviser to the Mirza, as well as his commanding general."

Naime closed her eyes—it was the only thing she could do to contain her mortification. Of course she had researched the Sarkum royal family. But the Mirza's name was Kinus Rahal Al-Nimas, descended of the man who pulled the tattered refugees of the Sundering War into alliance. If the Agassi was a prince, his name did not indicate so.

"Forgive me," Naime said, and tipped her head forward in apology. "I should have been better informed." She would not hold out hope he might apologize for keeping the secret. "Is Agassi your proper title, or do you prefer another?"

"Agassi, or Prince, if you must. But I think in either case you should have to bow to me when you insist on waking me in the sunless marks. In Al-Nimas, princesses bow to princes."

Samira gave a breathy huff, though she disguised it by taking another bite of food.

Naime raised an eyebrow, momentarily put off by his comment. But when they looked at each other, the lines around his eyes had deepened with his humor, and she realized he was playing. Naime folded her hands in her lap, caught off guard by his teasing and her giddy reaction to it. She was not a little girl to be charmed by men and their play. His company was lighthearted, and she found herself enjoying it, but that did not mean she could allow herself to be comfortable in it. Who knew what agendas he hid with his warmth and humor?

Naime was accustomed to having to constrain herself far more than the men around her. He could play and be at ease, she could not.

"I will not bow to you," Naime said.

"The Grand Vizier warned me you had been overly indulged." His rich voice continued to hold strains of amusement. Naime let her breath out slowly to tame the surge of fury at the idea that Kadir had the audacity to belittle her to strangers. He noted her reaction, his gaze shifting across her face.

"You are not Mirza," Naime said. His eyes narrowed, his expression tightening. Perhaps he heard that more often than he cared to.

"Which means you are not the firstborn. I, however, am. I am the only child of Sultan Sabri. I still outrank you, and so I will not bow. I hope you do not find that overly indulged of me."

He gave his head a little shake. Beside him, Tareck appeared to fight back a smile as he raised a glass of water.

"I have taken enough of your time, I think," Naime said, rising. Samira did the same. The Agassi got to his feet in a rushed scramble.

"I thought you wanted to discuss meeting with your father and the Council?" he said.

Naime moved to the doors and he followed. Tareck stood as well, stuffing a too-large bite into his mouth as he did. He wiped his hands off on his caftan.

Samira pulled the doors open as Naime stopped and faced the Agassi. He was close again. Naime took a step back so she did not have to tip her head. His brow notched.

"I came to discuss repairing the impression you made, in preparation for meeting the Council. And now I know you are a prince. If you conduct yourself with care in the palace and err on the side of too much formality, I believe things will go as smoothly as they can."

"That"—he raised an eyebrow—"does not sound encouraging."

Naime smiled in apology. "You are an outsider. From Sarkum. I think that is the best we can hope for. I will do my best to assist you."

The notch in his brow smoothed, and he appeared surprised for such a brief moment she doubted she'd seen the expression once it was gone. He ducked his head. Naime returned the gesture. Behind him, Tareck bowed.

"Good day to you, Agassi," Naime said as she stepped into the hall. Samira shut the doors behind them and hurried to catch up to her.

When they were a sufficient distance from the rooms, Naime ordered her, "Tell Bashir to put guards on them." She should have done so after they arrived but had not wanted them to feel like prisoners instead of guests. And it had allowed Kadir to attempt to plant the seeds of his lies. At least the Agassi seemed to have resisted the attempt. Or he was a gifted liar.

"Will you go to see the Sultan now?" Samira strode briskly beside her.

"Yes."

"If he is unwell, then you will need to stand in for the mid-turn audience with the guilds. Perhaps it would be wise to arrive early, before the Grand Vizier takes the seat."

Naime slowed then stopped, lifting a hand to press against her eyes. The last thing she needed was to battle Kadir for the right to hear and respond to the guilds' grievances. But she could not neglect her father, not when he was so upset. She needed him in his best state to deal with negotiations.

"Perhaps I should just do as they wish. I'll marry Aref Esber and let them have the simpleton while I spend all my time in my rooms reading and eating sweets."

Samira's honey-brown eyes crinkled at the edges and just the corners of her mouth turned up. "You do have a gift for allowing people to punish themselves with their own decisions. It would be a fitting end," Samira said. "And if you were in your rooms so often, perhaps he would forget about you and you would not have to endure his clumsy hands." She shuddered.

Naime agreed silently, starting again toward her father's room. If she had to endure anyone's clumsy hands, it would be because they believed in what she did. Marriage, however, was not in her plans. Ruling Tamar was what she wanted, what she was meant for. The Wheel had gifted her privilege. She would not squander that gift in idleness. She was meant to keep her people safe.

EIGHT

MAKRAM STOOD IN THE garden outside the suite of rooms, sipping at the terrible coffee Tareck had brewed for him as he examined a fig tree some distance away. Despite the slight warmth of the late-morning sun, the fig was a misshapen skeleton against the rest of the carefully groomed garden of dormant roses and vines. It appeared dead, considering its utter lack of leaves. Tamar's winters, especially this close to the Sun Sea, surely did not get cold enough to kill a tree like that. If he brushed it with his power he'd know for certain, but that was a flagrant waste of magic and would put him at risk of being perceived by another mage.

"Why would they keep that there?" Makram asked, conversationally, as Tareck came from inside to join him.

Tareck followed his line of sight. "What? That tree? Does it matter?"

"It is dead. Of course it matters." Makram sighed.

"You only remark on meaningless things when you're angry," Tareck observed.

"Shall I enumerate the reasons why I am angry?"

Tareck held up the ibrik he'd brought out of the rooms with him, offering it to Makram, who nodded. Tareck poured more coffee into the tiny cup then set the ibrik on the gravel path.

"You may, if it helps," Tareck said, blandly.

"It would help to strike something. Are you volunteering?" He downed the coffee, hissing when it burned his throat.

"Aren't you injured enough already?" Tareck grinned. Makram rolled his eyes.

"Fine. I will make a list. First, there are obviously divisions here and I am at a distinct disadvantage in the face of them. Second, I am not certain I will be able to explain myself to my brother without some proof that defying him was not a pointless display of will, but the Sultan has yet to announce he will even see me. And my arm hurts." He punctuated himself by taking a drink. The steam from the coffee left condensation on his face and he wiped it off. The physician they had sent to him had done a fine job of stitching the wound but had warned that Makram had done himself no favors by waiting to treat it. There hadn't been much choice but to keep moving after the ambush, in order to reach Tamar as quickly as possible.

"Besides all of those things, that damn tree is a travesty. Why would they just leave a dead tree in the garden?" In Sarkum, death was not something the people cared to be reminded of. Perhaps it was different in Tamar, although its history of genocide would not suggest so, he thought with wry, black humor.

Tareck chuckled. "Well, I thought the Sultana at least seemed—"

"As warm and forthcoming as a marble column?" Makram said. The truth was he had been as intrigued. She had handled his initial, early morning rudeness with an impressive amount of decorum. Intelligent, quick witted, and she adapted quickly to Tareck and himself, which was no small feat for someone he suspected was accustomed to the most proper of behavior in her presence.

How did she keep herself so unfailingly composed and controlled? Makram had only seen a hint of temper or emotion on her face when he'd revealed his birthright to her, and the rest of the time she'd delivered every word in the same cool, measured tone. An air mage gift, perhaps. He might not have been so caught off guard by the exchange if she hadn't flustered him so. Everywhere he looked he found some little detail to admire. If the ceremony the day before had been for suitors, he was surprised every man in the city wasn't packed into the palace. The woman was breathtaking.

"Mmm." Tareck gave a grave nod, then said into the demitasse of coffee, "I liked her. "

"Of course you did. She has the same traits as the horses you choose."

Tareck choked, then tried to gasp for breath, then began to cough violently.

Makram gestured vainly at nothing. "Pretty to look at and personalities like ground glass. They all bite too."

"I don't think you should speak of the Sultana like that," Tareck said gruffly. "She never bit you, and with her magical ability she is probably listening to you right now."

"I was talking about horses, Tareck." Makram sighed as he tried not to picture the Sultana biting him. She was much too proper for biting, surely. "I also think she might suspect my House." She had no qualms about meeting his gaze, and he was certain she had sensed his magic. Her eyes saw so much.

Wheel. He was supposed to be the one who could strip people to their core with a look, but she seemed to see right through him.

His skin prickled.

"Did you intend to keep it a secret for the entire stay?"

"If I can. I do not care for the idea of being chased out of Tamar by torches and acid."

The stories of how Tamar had purged itself of Sixth House mages had been the cause of all his nightmares as a child. Although, if he did not negotiate something that would make his brother happy, he might as well let them light him like a celebration torch. He certainly would not be welcome back home.

Someone knocked on the doors, loud enough they heard it in the garden. Tareck went inside to answer and Makram tried to steel himself for another encounter. He caught just a glimpse of Kadir's steward through the distance and the windows, then Tareck returned to his side.

"The Grand Vizier has invited us to join him as he attends to the guild tradesmen. He thought you might be interested in observing Tamar governance." Tareck sounded as if they had just been invited to watch plaster being laid.

"Better than remaining caged up in here, don't you think?"

"Not by much. Merchants and their whining," Tareck grumbled as he followed Makram through their rooms and into the hall. Makram was surprised to see two palace guards outside his room, who bowed to them and fell into step behind as they walked.

He had thought the Sultana had seemed, if not charmed, at least amicable. So, were the guards to manage him, or to keep others away? She had been displeased to hear the Grand Vizier had visited. Makram needed to know in what manner the two of them disagreed, and where the Sultan fell in their game.

By the time Mahir led their little procession through the palace and to the receiving hall, Makram was exhausted by pondering the daunting task of sorting through political turmoil. When they arrived and the hall was empty except for the Sultana and the Grand Vizier, Makram considered returning immediately to his rooms. How could he possibly navigate their game if he was given no time to think without them vying for his favor?

As they entered, his assigned guards set themselves to either side of the entrance doors. The receiving hall was a long, broad room with colonnades stretching the length toward the dais. A broad, velvet-cushioned chair with a back carved intricately into a gaudy representation of the Wheel sat upon the platform. A latticework, gilded frame surrounded it on three sides and above. The Sultana sat straight-backed and stone-faced in the chair, her hands folded in her lap. The Grand Vizier stood in front of her, at the base of the dais, with his back to them.

Upon seeing the two of them, Mahir paused, and his furrowed brow suggested he had not expected to see the Sultana sitting where she was. Had she taken the seat from the Grand Vizier? She had said the day before her father was ill with the change of seasons. Apparently ill enough that petty infighting had already begun in his absence. If they had nothing better to argue over than who would oversee the minor quibbles of tradesmen and guild politics, then Tamar was a prosperous country indeed. If Kinus took ill Makram quite expected there to be murders within the first days.

"You may sit anywhere in this section." Mahir gestured to the unpadded wooden benches nearest the doors. Makram noted a variety of potted palms that seemed placed to shield the two corners nearest the door from the Sultan's view at the head of the room. This was where they consigned the undesirables, then. He grinned. That was perfectly fine with him, he did not want the notice of the Grand Vizier or the Sultana for the time being.

Mahir left them to join his master, and Tareck immediately took up a bench that allowed him to lean into the corner of the wall and closed his eyes.

Odd to be in a room with so much history pertaining to the Sundering War. According to the account of the Battle of Narfour, there was a passage between this room and the prisons that had allowed Makram's ancestor to murder Sultan Omar Sabri the Third and take the palace. Albeit briefly. Perhaps he would have time to search for it before he returned to Al-Nimas.

The Grand Vizier tapped his staff against the floor. "Shouldn't you be with your father, Sultana Efendim? Surely your time would be better spent there than here, dealing with day-to-day complaints and claims of infraction?" he said, not loudly, but it carried in the cavernous space.

"I have already been, Grand Vizier. He is resting, thank you for your concern. I am certain it will comfort him to know you asked after his health." She smiled. Makram thought the expression particularly frosty. Yet she had smiled when they had spoken, she was capable of warmth and humor. Not for the Grand Vizier, it seemed.

"These are matters for the Council. I would rather not have to forcibly remove you from the hall, Sultana," the Grand Vizier said. Makram raised his eyebrows. That was a bold threat to make to a ruler's daughter. If anyone dared to threaten Kinus with such a thing it would likely be the last time they ever saw daylight.

"I will remind you, again"—she said the last word with tired force—"that the Council exists to advise the Sultan, not rule him. I am his heir and will stand in his stead when he is unable to perform his duties. You know that is his wish." She stood with all the hauteur of someone utterly unafraid or intimidated.

She continued, "I will, for the moment, assume your mention of removing me forcibly was simply a jest in poor taste. And if for some reason the desire to say such rises in you again, I will remind you that the commander of the palace guard, and his lieutenants, are loyal to me."

"Ah yes, your slumdog. Of course he is loyal, you certainly paid enough for him to be," Kadir said, with an ingratiating smile.

"My mother's scholarship paid a talented mage's way through the University, based on his performance at the testing, as it has done for a dozen others. He arrived at his position in the guard through merit." She punctuated the matter-of-fact declaration by returning to her seat on the bench.

"I appreciate you coming to the audience, Kadir Pasha, and your willingness to take on extra duties during my father's hopefully brief illness. But I will conduct today. You may remain if you wish. I am always willing to consider your wise opinion."

Her artfully executed verbal checkmate raised her in Makram's estimation by several degrees.

Kadir spun on his heel and stalked to the far-left side of the dais, where he planted his staff of office against the floor with a resounding crack. The Sultana did not so much as blink an eye at the shocking noise. Instead she turned her head toward her attendants, who formed a half-circle at the back of the dais, behind her bench.

"Samira, you may have the guards escort the guilds in." She shifted her attention forward as she said it and saw Makram. Her lips parted and her chest rose as she drew in a deep breath. Composure snapped across her like a curtain she had drawn shut. Had that been surprise? Disappointment? He had just witnessed an argument with the Grand Vizier, it might have been embarrassment.

Her handmaiden swept down the hall and out the doors, breaking Makram's line of thought and pulling the Sultana's attention away from him. When the woman returned, a parade of merchants and tradesmen followed.

Makram took a seat beside Tareck and leaned his head against the cool tile of the wall. They wore clothes no less colorful than those of the Viziers he had seen so far. It made him think of his own clothes, packed away with the men who should be arriving by the end of the day. If they did not, he would request a few riders to search for them, to make certain they had not been lost in a snowstorm or hurt somewhere.

The guilds and tradesmen crowded the hall nearly to capacity, though they did congregate together in groups. Closest to him, five men had circled together and were discussing a shipment of iron delayed by winter storm. Smiths. Beyond them, a mixed group of older men and women erupted into laughter, the young man in their midst gesturing wildly and grinning.

Across the hall the front half of the room was dominated by the largest group, who Makram hazarded to guess were the merchant guild. They were the largest in Sarkum as well, encompassing many of the other guilds. They went first, their spokesman an elder gentleman who wore his silver hair combed back from his high brow and a neatly trimmed goatee that still held more black than grey. Makram stroked his fingers over his own jaw. He had yet to see a man besides himself and Tareck who went clean-shaven, which was customary in the janissaries.

Makram listened to bits and pieces of the discussion with the Sultana. Nothing out of the ordinary—boundary concerns, taxes that were not being applied where the guild thought they should be, an ongoing dispute with immigrant merchants who were not beholden to the guild. The encounter was enlightening in that it highlighted the similarities between Tamar and Sarkum.

His thoughts wandered to his brother and back again. The guilds and tradesmen at home had brought the same grievances before Kinus. The Sultana feigned interest, and better than Kinus did. Or perhaps she wasn't feigning at all. When she spoke, she chose her words carefully, and even for matters that did not require a ruler's attention, was respectful in her comportment. She favored her father in that, her discourse very reminiscent of his letters to Sarkum. The men and women who spoke to her did so with deference, and openness, as if they were familiar with her and trusted her to engage with them fairly. It was a far cry from the chaos of such engagements in his brother's court, men shouting over each other to be heard, Kinus often reacting with dismissal or disdain, or even allowing the Elders to answer on his behalf.

Makram glanced to the Grand Vizier, struggling to see him through the shifting crowd of people as they greeted each other and chatted idly while waiting their turn to speak. He stood at the bottom edge of the dais and spoke into his steward's ear. Mahir bowed, then wove his way through the crowds toward the back of the hall.

Makram watched the steward until he had left the hall, then looked to the front of the room again. The groups were beginning to shift to the edges of the room. Beside him, Tareck occasionally let out a soft snore, his head periodically dipping forward off the wall then jerking back when the movement woke him. Makram stood to ward off his own sleepiness, leaning against the nearest of the columns. He did so in the lull between speakers, and the movement caused the Sultana to look toward him once more. It would have been flattering to believe she looked at him because she found him interesting, but he suspected she was only continuing to size him up.

She was distracted from her scrutiny by the entrance of a quartet of men in uniforms. They were not the uniforms of palace guards, which had been unrelenting shades of sand and stone. These wore steel grey and sky blue, belted in more grey, and in their midst they led a man chained at the wrists and ankles. Makram looked to the Sultana for her reaction.

The Sultana's lips pressed together as the group approached her. The prisoner's chains rang against the stone tiles with each step. The merchants and tradesmen parted, shifting toward the sides of the hall to give the guards and prisoner plenty of room. The incongruous procession came to a stop in front of the Sultana. Makram caught a glimpse of the Grand Vizier's steward as he slunk into the room, skirting the wall, behind the gathered guildsmen.

"Why is this man here?" the Sultana asked, temper crackling in her eyes. Makram felt the faintest shift in the air around him, a thread of magic she used to give her voice volume. It had the intended effect, silencing the onlookers.

The Grand Vizier stepped up beside the Sultana, and bent half over to whisper something to her. She turned her head, slowly, and tilted it to look up at him as he straightened beside her. He smiled down at her benevolently, and she gazed back with malevolence. The air shifted again, and Makram swore tendrils of her hair shifted in a breeze he could not feel. Some of the people began to stir, names, and the words *murdered* and *ransacked* were said several times. The Sultana scrutinized the man who led the group of guards and prisoner.

"This is not a tribunal, Captain Akkas. Return this man to the Cliffs," the Sultana said, and by the way she regarded him, Makram suspected he would not be a captain for much longer.

"He was brought up from the Cliffs last night, Efendim. I was told it was on the Sultan's order, that you had decided to forego the trial. "

Fury ignited in her eyes and was whisked away by the winter that claimed her countenance. She lifted her hands from her lap and set them on the arms of her chair, her fingers tightening against the wood. Beside her, the Grand Vizier rapped his staff twice against the dais.

"There has been some confusion, I see," he announced into the hall.

The man in chains began to laugh. It came in broken spurts, in a high pitch that grated against Makram's nerves and sent his magic into a swirl of smoke and ink. He imagined he could smell the madness in the man's mind, but it was just his magic, sensing decay.

"I want to confess," the prisoner chanted, "I'll do it for your hands on me." The hall erupted into chatter, and to her credit, the Sultana ignored the man's foulness. Even Makram's skin crawled at the tone and suggestion, and he had to subdue the urge to stride forward in some misguided sense that he should intervene on her behalf. Had the Grand Vizier sent his steward to cause the man to be brought? The timing was suspect, and Makram could not guess what he hoped to gain from such a thing.

Tareck had roused and moved to stand beside him.

"Who told you the Sultan ordered this man brought to the palace?" The Sultana ignored the Grand Vizier and addressed the captain.

"A missive," he responded, uncertainly. His men shifted, glancing at each other.

"Give it to me." The Sultana's severe tone and clipped speech suggested suppressed anger.

Makram folded his arms across his chest. This man's presence in the room felt like seeping poison in the pool of his magic, and he did not think he could stomach being any closer to him. How was she bearing it? Even the Grand Vizier appeared ill at ease.

"It is in my office," the captain replied. The prisoner giggled.

"They don't like you, Princess. But I do. If you want my mind, you can have it." He lowered his head, as if he meant to charge toward her. One of the guards yanked hard on his chains to stop him, and he yelped.

"Stop," she commanded. "Return this man to the Cliffs and bring me the order you received. For the future, Captain, neither I nor the Sultan would ever bring a prisoner to the palace during audience. Do you understand me?"

"Yes, Sultana." Captain Akkas bowed.

"Hold." The Grand Vizier stepped forward from beside the dais. "Efendim. A moment of your time now, and this vile creature will never bother our citizens again. Think of the comfort it would give them"—he gestured at the gathered men and women—"to see justice served right before their eyes."

"I will not sentence a man without a trial, and certainly not for public entertainment," she said ferociously, glaring at the Grand Vizier.

"He's a killer!" someone shouted nearby Makram, and he glanced sideways. The mood in the hall wavered, taking on the flavor of an angry mob. Expressions that had been bored or jovial before the prisoner's arrival were now angry or confused.

"I slept through the interesting bits." Tareck yawned as he rubbed the back of his neck. Makram made a sound of agreement.

"Sultana Efendim, he has all but confessed on several occasions. I do not believe a trial is necessary, in this case," the Grand Vizier said. "Simply sentence him and be done. It is what a decisive leader would do, for the peace of mind of his subjects. Your father would have stripped his memories for the truth."

It took a moment for Makram to fully grasp the meaning of the Grand Vizier's last words.

"Void and stars," Makram breathed. The Sultan was a Veritor? He hadn't heard of one since the Sundering. Some of the most powerful magic of the Wheel had been lost when it was broken by the war, but even before that Veritors were rare. The First House governed the mind, and its children were thinkers, problem solvers, and often thought in black and white. The weakest of them commanded air and sound, could hear and speak over distances that would normally be too far for a human. The most powerful could manipulate wind and turn it into a weapon.

More rare, their power manifested as an ability to delve into a person's memories. Historically, they were used to strip unwilling confessions from the worst of criminals. Makram knew very little about the process, but he did know there was a high risk that the person stripped of their memories could be irrevocably damaged, or the Veritor driven insane by another's mind.

The Sultana's composure faltered, her lashes lowering, her mouth thinning. She recovered and said, "The laws promise a fair trial by tribunal, Grand Vizier."

"This man is insane, Sultana. Surely the law does not apply in such severe and obvious cases." The Grand Vizier smiled as murmurs of agreement ran through the room.

"I am," the criminal said, "mad as a monkey." He shrugged as if in apology then laughed when she cast him an arctic glance. What was the Grand Vizier thinking, bringing an obvious madman into an audience? Makram lowered his hand toward his sword hilt, but it wasn't there. Stored instead in the guard barracks. He curled his hand into a fist and tapped it against his thigh.

"Sentence him!" a man yelled from somewhere in front of Makram. Another called out in agreement, then more voices, until commotion and cacophony dominated the hall.

Tareck elbowed Makram in the ribs and jerked his head toward the doors, suggesting they escape before it became a true mob. But Makram shook his head. He both wanted to see what she did and had a desire to be at hand if the situation became dangerous.

"That"—the Sultana's clear voice sounded as sharp as a hammer against an anvil—"is enough." Restless silence shivered in the room.

"Sultana Efendim," the Grand Vizier said, drawing out the superlative as if patiently scolding a child in the midst of a tantrum. Her mouth tightened, and she silenced him with a sharp look. The quiet deepened, anticipatory, the kind of soundlessness that preceded chaos.

"Very well," she said, her cool voice filling the room with winter. She leaned back in her seat, propping her elbow against the armrest and rubbing her thumb across her folded fingers as she studied the prisoner.

A tide of satisfaction swept over the room and withdrew under the pull of unease. The prisoner shifted, taking a step back that made his chains slink against the tiles. The Sultana appraised him with an expression carved of ice. She lowered her hand to the armrest again.

"If that is what you wish." Her voice ascended over the undertow of conversation. "But why stop with this man? I might do the same for anyone who crosses me. Anyone whom I suspect is against me. *Anyone* who displeases me."

She stood, visually browsing the attendees. When she chose a subject, she pointed.

"Master Nalci, you questioned how the Sultan uses your taxes. That feels suggestive of rebellion to me. Shall I sentence you to prison to prevent the spread of your ideas?" The man she addressed blanched. She turned to the crowd once again. Her gaze brushed Makram's, and though he was too far away to see every detail of her expression, he could feel the push of her magic, loosened by her controlled temper, swirling against his own. The feel of it called to mind winter wind and sunlight. He felt held in thrall, watching her, waiting for her trap to slam shut.

Her expression grew thoughtful as she surveyed the gathered people, her gaze flashing from one person to the next. The men and women touched by her look recoiled, shuffling to avoid her notice.

"Mistress Ozil," she said to a woman who glanced around as if she meant to hide, "you accused merchants outside of the guild of undercutting you. It would take far less time to imprison you both than sit through a guild inquiry or have you spreading undesirable rumors." The woman made a choking sound, her hand curving over her throat, her eyes wide.

The Sultana sat down once again, tapping a finger against the wood of the armrest. Even where he stood at the back of the room, the sound of her fingernail against the wood reached him in the deep silence.

"That is what you are asking for, a ruler who eschews justice, and law, for convenience." She paused, fixing the Grand Vizier with a stony look. "A decisive leader."

Makram realized he was grinning like a fool. He schooled his expression and had to peel his stare from her to the Grand Vizier, who stood stiff and silent in his defeat. Heat poured off him, distorting the air around him, his lack of restraint even more egregious for the stark contrast to the Sultana's composure.

"He keeps smoldering like that, those pretty curtains are going to catch fire," Tareck said under his breath. Makram grit his teeth against a laugh.

"Do you wish me to begin sentencing everyone I find suspicious, Grand Vizier?" The words held threat as sharp as daggers.

"No, Efendim," the Grand Vizier answered, and bowed. The Sultana's magic winked out, its touch retreating from the edge of Makram's senses. Makram fancied every person held their breath. The prisoner let out a giggle. Then gave a theatrical bow.

"Captain Akkas." Her voice sounded hollow in the silent space. "Your men will return the prisoner to the Cliffs. He will stand before a tribunal on the designated date. Is that order quite clear?"

"Yes, Efendim." The captain bowed and tapped an open hand against his heart.

"For those of you I have not seen today, I apologize. I have other matters to attend to. Please return at the next audience"—she rose, folding her hands together in front of her entari—"and I will hear you then."

She lifted a hand as the guards guided the prisoner out, and her attendants surrounded her. She shared a look with the Grand Vizier for another moment before she strode down the aisle and out of the room. Makram shoved away from the column to follow her. He had to jog to beat the crush of the others as they moved for the doors, and to make his way around the half-moon formation of her attendants.

"Sultana," he called. She stopped, turning to him, her expression wavering between surprise and wariness before it disappeared behind a mask of indifference. Makram stopped beside her, wondering how in the world he could get her to stop doing that, hiding behind her magic.

"Good afternoon, Agassi. What a pleasant surprise it was to see you in attendance," she said as she bowed to him. He couldn't help but laugh a little at her lie, and it seemed to ease a fraction of her irritation. She glanced around him and took a deep breath. "Pardon me for a moment," she said, and skirted him to meet the captain as he exited the hall.

"You will report to the City Watch for your new assignment," she told the captain. Makram flinched in sympathy.

"Sultana Efendim, I had no way to know it was not the Sultan's order," Captain Akkas said. "I will bring you the document I received. It bore his seal."

"You may trust me when I say you will not be able to find it," she said bitterly. "And I am sorry, Captain, but you should have known immediately that neither the Sultan, nor I, would order such an absurd perversion of the law. I will check in with the City Watch commander for his opinion of your progress, but I cannot have someone in charge of the Cliffs who is not dependable."

"Dependable? I followed an order!"

"Whose order?"

The man's face darkened in anger, and he gave a stiff bow before he stalked away.

"That was masterfully done," Makram said, quietly, when she returned. He wanted to be effusive, to purge himself of the static energy of his admiration, but this was far too public a place. The men and women exiting the hall were already staring, examining him, commenting on why they might be speaking to each other. Perhaps he would have a chance at another time.

"Thank you," she said, her brown eyes warming. "I would have preferred you not have witnessed it."

He offered her his arm, because he could tell she was restless to get away from the room and the people exiting the hall and slowly enclosing them. They stared, and their focus pressed like a weight against his back. The Sultana hesitated, her hands curling into the gold and blue brocade of her entari, but gave in, twining her arm around his. Her hand barely curved against his forearm. The pressure of her arm around his felt foreign for a heartbeat, small and too light. It had been some time since he had escorted a woman.

"Where?" he asked. Winter and roses filled his nose at her proximity, and he wondered if the rose was a perfume, or her magic. Magic often had a unique scent, or taste, and if one paid attention and the mage was powerful enough, they could identify a caster by it. He had never experienced magic to have an off-putting scent, but if that was her signature, it was particularly alluring.

"My father's rooms. The same hall as yours."

The people around continued to stare, some turning to each other to speculate, others stopping mid conversation to watch as he led her through their midst. Ah yes. The rumors would begin, now that he had dared to touch her arm. By the end of the small turn he suspected there would be stories that she carried his child, or that he had designs on her father's seat, no matter that he had not even been in Tamar for a day. He glanced down at her, and she returned the look, her eyebrows raising and her eyes widening in feigned shock. Makram smiled as he looked forward. At least she could be amused by it.

"Is that man guilty of the crimes he's accused of?" Makram asked, after they had cleared the crowd.

"Undoubtedly," she sighed, "but he is also completely mad. I do not believe I have the right to decide he deserves less decency than anyone else."

"Your father is a Veritor?" Makram wondered if she was too. Though he had trouble reconciling the calm, serene beauty of her with the abhorrent idea of having one's mind invaded. Her arm tightened against his, and her expression shuttered. Makram resisted the urge to grip her hand in his to offer apology for disturbing her.

"Yes," she said, directing them around a turn in the hall.

"Did he verify often?"

"Only in the worst of circumstances. When evidence was difficult to collect, when someone would not confess. When a tribunal was divided." The tone of her voice stained the words with regret.

"And you?" he asked. He watched, but she revealed nothing more.

"I will happily speak of my magic with you, Agassi"—she glanced at him from the corners of her eyes—"if you would care to speak of yours."

"Magic is a more private thing in Sarkum than it is in Tamar," he said, which was not entirely a lie.

"I have gathered as much. I would be interested to know why. There are many questions I have about Sarkum." She pressed her lips together as if that were the only way to stop her words. Air mages were renowned for their insatiable curiosity. He found the gesture endearing.

"About Sarkum? Or about the Sixth House?"

They had reached the hall where his rooms were, and she continued past them, toward the end of the hall and a set of gilt double doors tall enough for him to walk through with Tareck sitting on his shoulders. "If you answer my question, Sultana, I will answer one of yours."

"You first," she said, and when he looked at her she smiled a knowing, secret smile that lit her beautiful face with mischief. Did she understand the power of that smile? He suspected she knew a great deal of her own allure.

Makram stopped before the doors, examining the mural that surrounded them. Battles and magic lay across a depiction of the Wheel. He was perplexed to see it appeared to be the Battle for Narfour, which had been in his mind recently. He supposed he should be glad it was not a mural depicting the murder and torture of hundreds of Sixth House mages. That mural was probably somewhere, prominently displayed for the masses as a reminder. He wondered what the narrative was in Tamar, to turn a battle that ended in defeat and the death of the Sultan into art that crowned the Sultan's door.

"Do you know why mages of the Sixth House are called death mages?" he asked, disappointed when she slid her arm free of his. The coolness of her demeanor and her magic were calming, quieting the restlessness that plagued him.

"It seems obvious, which suggests to me that I am mistaken," she replied, examining his face for some clue to the answer. He suspected she was capable of divining a great deal simply by someone's expression. Air mages.

"If you believe it is because the Sixth House and destruction are synonymous with death, then yes, you are mistaken. In ancient days, it was common to employ Sixth House mages as executioners. It was a kinder death to have your heart stopped by their magic, or sleep that became death, than to be hanged, or burned alive, or beheaded. It began as mercy," he said, trying to keep the resentment out of his voice.

Her soft gaze and rapt silence made him want to bolt. He was not accustomed to that kind of focus. Most people in Sarkum knew he was a Sixth House mage, and a powerful one. They didn't look at him directly, as if that would somehow unleash his magic.

"But, as things often are, it was taken out of context. They began by calling only those employed as executioners death mages. Eventually it spread to encompass the entire Sixth House."

"I have never heard that," she said, sadly. "I have studied everything I can find, which is not much. Many of the texts were burned after the Sundering. The entire palace library was almost lost."

"A historian *and* a student of law. Admirable." He grinned to disguise the depth of the emotion behind the comment. "Now I have shared a fact. So, it is your turn." It would be an easy and pleasant thing to stay exactly where he was, conversing with her for the rest of the day. There were so many questions her statements raised. The most burning of which was why she was studying the Sixth House. If it weren't for the half dozen of her attendants watching with razor-sharp concentration and trying to appear as if they were not, he might try and coax her to walk with him longer.

"I am not a Veritor," she said, "and am glad for it."

"It could be a powerful tool and weapon to have that capability at your disposal," Makram said.

"As with a blade, the edge can cut the wielder just as easily as the opponent." There was a tone in her voice, a distracted kind of cadence, that suggested she had seen such an occurrence. Her father?

"A wise point," he said, his admiration and curiosity rising with each word she uttered.

"In my case it is the lack of that magic that cuts. Every past generation of Sabris have born a Veritor. Neither I, nor my cousin, are one. Some consider that an omen." She spoke with words devoid of emotion, but her hands tightened together.

"An omen of what?"

"The end of the Sabri Sultanate." There was more to her statement than the words, and he thought she let him see that on purpose, allowing her expression to reflect suspicion and dismissal. Baiting him to ask, so she could ascertain something of his character or angle.

"What do you think of omens?" He did not mind obliging her, hungry as he was to continue speaking with her.

"That they are a method used by those in power to blind others with fear. Endings are also beginnings." She smiled, with an edge to it that dared him. "And you, Agassi? What do you think of omens?"

He returned her smile in kind, and her gaze flicked to his and away. Even such a brief connection felt as bracing as winter wind. "I prefer to be the reason for them than to be ruled by them."

She gave a soft, subdued laugh. "Thank you for escorting me," she said. "If you'll forgive me, I need to attend my father. But perhaps we will have another chance to talk, soon."

"Of course. Relay my hope for his swift recovery, if you would."

"Certainly." She dipped her chin to him in farewell before knocking on the door.

Makram shifted, knowing he had been dismissed, but lingered while she waited for the door to be answered. It opened, revealing a man Makram remembered seeing when he arrived in the courtyard the day before. The corners of his mouth tightened as he took the two of them in, side by side. Because of where Makram stood, to the left of the doors, he could clearly see the scarred, puckered skin along the man's neck and the right side of his face. Burn scars, surely.

"Sehzade Ihsan Sabri ilr Narfour, Sival of the Second House." The Sultana held a hand up to indicate Makram. "This is Agassi Makram Attaraya, delegate from Al-Nimas."

A water mage. Interesting. Free fire could not burn a water mage, and it would take a formidable fire mage to burn a Sival of the Second House. Houses in opposition on the Wheel usually canceled out each other's magic. There must be quite a tale behind the burns, but judging from the expression on the Sehzade's face, he was uninterested in conversation.

"Sehzade is Prince?" It was not a title they used in Sarkum.

Ihsan nodded once, his gaze flicking from Makram to the Sultana and back.

"This is your cousin?" That would mean Ihsan was roughly equivalent in rank to himself.

"Yes," she said. "His father was brother to the Sultan. Sehzade is second in line to the throne."

"It is a pleasure to meet you, Sehzade," Makram said. Interesting that the male heir fell in line behind a princess.

"Don't make hasty judgments," Ihsan replied in a dry tone. "Few people find it a pleasure to meet me."

"San," the Sultana said under her breath.

"The Sultan will not be able to see you, I'm afraid, Agassi," Ihsan said.

"He only accompanied me from the receiving hall. There was a bit of a stir," she said, and entered the room. "I will have news for you on a meeting as soon as I am able, Agassi," she said as she took hold of one of the doors to close them. Only her head attendant followed her in, the rest remained in the hall, staring at Makram with eyes like owls' as she closed the door.

He spun toward the hall as Tareck rounded the corner.

"The men are here," Tareck said as he came to a halt in front of Makram. Tareck glanced sideways after he took note of Makram's hunched shoulders, and his brows rose in amusement.

Their two guards were not far behind him, which made Makram even more tense. "Causing a stir already?" Tareck accused.

"Not on purpose." He smiled politely at one of the girls as he and Tareck passed. The servants collapsed into a tight huddle thick with giggles and whispers. Even after a few more steps he could feel their stares against his back.

"You should have seen all of them after you walked away with her." Tareck grinned. "You'd have caused less uproar if you stripped naked and ran through the palace, I think."

"I'll consider that next time." Makram heard one of their guards snicker at Tareck's words.

His thoughts chased themselves in circles, leaping from the Sultana to the Grand Vizier, from his brother to negotiations. There wasn't a single productive thing he could do to resolve anything until he had met with the Sultan, and he couldn't bear the idea of sitting in the rooms to wait.

"Get me out of this maze so I can talk with the men. One of them is going back, to carry a letter to Kinus," Makram announced. Tareck muttered something under his breath that sounded suspiciously like, "let the man rot." Makram chose to ignore it.

He'd inform his brother they had arrived safely and were due to see the Sultan. Perhaps that would ease his temper.

Nine

NAIME WATCHED HER FATHER pace. His steward stood with Samira by the doors, and they occasionally engaged themselves in murmured conversation. They were all waiting for the Sultan to speak so they could assess his mental state. Naime had been with him since the Agassi had delivered her to the room the afternoon before. She'd sent Ihsan home soon after; he had reached his limit for remaining in the palace. He preferred the solitude of his own home, and came to the palace only when she needed him or he was required at a Council meeting as Vizier of Agriculture.

Rest and solitude had done a great deal for the Sultan's state of mind, but Naime feared she had pushed him back into agitation by speaking about negotiations and the Agassi. He would need time to relay any terms to his brother in Sarkum, and if he had to wait too long without even seeing her father she would not be surprised if he gave up entirely and left.

In the time since they had spoken, he had come into her mind often. Not only because he was integral to everything she planned, but because she had enjoyed speaking with him. It was not often she engaged in a conversation that did not feel like verbal fencing, in which the slightest mistake might cost her something. She recalled in perfect detail the resonant quality of his voice, the way his nearly black eyes lit when he grinned at her, the genuine admiration she had detected when he complimented her. How many men did not take her strengths as challenges and her faults as weaknesses to attack? She had been comfortable in his company as she rarely was in anyone's outside her family.

"San told me you stood for the guild audience in my place," her father said abruptly. He stopped pacing. There were moments when he seemed only an older, less hale version of the man he would always be in her mind's eye, someone tall and broad-shouldered, dark-haired and imposing. With warm brown eyes that laughed even when the rest of him was deadly serious. There was some of that in him now, the only change the streaks of silver in his hair and beard. Physically, he was still in good health.

"Yes," she said. She sat in a large, hideous armchair that had been in these rooms since she was a child. She had spent many happy times sitting in his lap in this chair as he read her history and spun tales of magic and bravery. It remained the same, threadbare and musty smelling, and so was often more comforting than he was.

"It went well?" he asked and turned his back on her.

"Yes." There was no reason to tell him anything out of the ordinary had happened. She could not prove Kadir had anything to do with it, not to the Council anyway. What he had hoped to gain by it, she could only guess. Perhaps he had planned to sentence the man in her father's absence, as a bid for popularity with the guilds. He was, she loathed to acknowledge, a more flexible thinker than she, one willing to take calculated risks to achieve his aim. When she had taken the audience instead of him, perhaps he had seen a chance to make her appear weak or indecisive to the Agassi.

In either case, Naime had come out ahead. At least if she were to gauge by the way the Agassi had regarded her. All night her thoughts had circled back to the look, which she thought indelibly blazed into her memory. Fascination. Fervor. No one had ever looked at her like that. It made her face warm every time she thought of it, which irritated and alarmed her.

"Of course it did. You've been sitting with me since your legs were too short to reach the floor from the bench." Her father chuckled.

Naime smiled, some of her anxiety flitting away at the normalcy, and his praise.

She wanted to tell him what had happened. But she could not talk to him about Kadir. Naime could never understand why. Her father had always been so rational, so unemotional about things, except Behram Kadir. They had been closer than brothers, friends since boyhood. It had been the source of some of the only arguments Naime ever witnessed between her mother and father.

Behram. His name shouted back and forth. Her mother trying to make her husband see that his one-time friend was an enemy stalking the Sultan's seat.

"The delegate from Sarkum sends his wishes for your health," Naime said, experimentally. Her father's smile faded, his salt-and-pepper brows coming together in concentration. "Makram Attaraya, brother to the Mirza of Sarkum. He traveled a dangerous road to arrive in haste. I believe he is very interested in our offer of alliance. Would you like to meet with him?"

"Sarkum," her father pondered. Naime took a steadying breath. His mind was not just damaged by decades of opening the minds of others, it contained their memories. A single word was sometimes enough to send him into an entirely different life, and fear or exhaustion were both keys to open the doors for such episodes.

He began to nod, slowly, returning to his pacing. "Yes," he said, finally, and triumph spread excitement through her limbs. "Tomorrow. Call the Council together."

Her elation faded. "Would you rather meet him alone, first? You have always been such a gifted judge of character, I thought you might like to speak with him without the distraction of the Council." Without Kadir feeding him lies and twisting the truth.

"No. They'll have to be consulted eventually and will have to agree to the terms. You know how tired I am lately. Better to get it all out at once."

"Of course, Father," Naime said. He nodded but continued to watch her. How could she ever convince them to agree with the terms if the fools would not even read them?

"What troubles you?" he asked. Even two Turns ago the question would have been answerable, but now, it was not. He had once been the one she told all her troubles to. Now he was the cause of most of them and could not be trusted with the rest. Loneliness descended heavily on her shoulders.

"The past few days have been long," Naime said, truthfully, "and I am very tired."

"Because you do not eat as often as you should, or rest when you need it," he scolded. At least this speech was a familiar comfort. "Go do both now. I do not need you to sit here staring at me and wringing your hands." He waved a hand in dismissal and Naime rose and crossed to him.

She kissed his cheek. "At least let me open the curtains. You are not a burrowing earth mage. You need the sun."

He gave her a cross look but nodded. Naime gestured to his steward, who left his post by the door and walked the length of the sitting room, tugging the curtains open as he went.

"I will return soon," Naime said. Her father nodded before he faced the window. The view was dominated by an ancient, dead fig tree. It had been her mother's favorite place in the garden, sitting beneath its shade to read. They had celebrated sorrows and triumphs underneath its branches. The tree had died when she did, and neither Naime nor her father could bear to cut it down.

Naime left him to his thoughts, and Samira joined her in the hall as the steward shut the door behind them.

"What is really troubling you?" Samira asked.

"Everything," Naime said. "Let us go inform the Agassi that my father will see him tomorrow. I suppose we should send someone to inform the Grand Vizier as well."

"You've forgotten to inform him before," Samira suggested.

"I do not believe that would be wise, this time. I'll send someone else to do it, so I don't have to look at him." She had seen more of Kadir in the last few days than she normally saw of him in a half-season, and she found it exhausting.

"But you'll deliver the message to the Agassi," Samira said, slyly, "so you *can* look at him."

Naime glared sideways at her. "I am allowed to look," she said crisply. She wasn't the only one. She had witnessed her attendants and other women in the receiving hall staring or failing at their attempts not to. Half of it was because he looked a great deal different than anyone else, with the Odokan lineage evident in his features. Some of it was because he was a new face. But the simple fact was the man was darkly handsome and magnetic. And a great deal more pleasant to look at than anyone else in the palace.

"Yes, but I'm not certain I've ever seen you look with quite so much…dedication." Samira laughed when Naime bumped into her in rebuke.

"I find him interesting," Naime said. "He is easy to speak with. Besides, even you must find him worth looking at?"

Samira gave the small, sad smile she did when her heart wasn't in it, and Naime regretted mentioning it at all. A Fifth House mage's love was often consuming, and that was true of Samira, even if the person she loved did not deserve her and was forever out of reach.

"He thinks you're worth looking at as well," Samira changed the subject, her honey eyes crinkling at the corners. "He couldn't take his eyes off you at the guild hall. You should have seen his face when you finished with the Grand Vizier."

"I saw." Warm, reluctant pride spread through her chest. Not because he looked at her, but because if felt as if he had actually seen her. Men looked at her. They always had. She knew she was beautiful, the way she knew she was a woman, and a princess. It was not something she took pride in, it was something to be used as a tool. Her mother had taught her that. She had also taught her it would be fleeting; that she must have other assets and tools at her disposal when the beauty inevitably faded, or risk losing her belief in herself, which was the only gift she truly had. He had recognized something other than her appearance, and that, in her experience, was rare.

"The guards are gone from the Agassi's room," Samira said, pointing down the hall. "Perhaps they're outside? I overheard the rest of their men had arrived last night."

"We'll check, and if they are not, I will send someone to hunt them down." While she would enjoy a chance to speak with him again, she had not lied about being tired, and she did not feel like combing the palace grounds searching for someone.

They made their way to the public rooms of the palace, where the receiving hall opened to the palace foyer and the main courtyard and entrance gate beyond.

The late-morning sun shone bright, but not warm enough to banish the threat of deepening winter. The sky held patches of grey clouds, and the distant sea was a mess of white-tipped, steely chop. A brisk wind gusted through the courtyard, adding to the barren feel as she and Samira descended the steps.

Guards were stationed to either side of the Morning Gate and one at the entrance to the guard barracks. Voices, a clash of swords, and muffled cheers reached them from the direction of the arena. Commander Ayan had his men sparring, it seemed, which she occasionally found entertaining to watch. The distinct outcomes of sparring were a relief from the machinations of the palace, in which no one was ever truly a winner. She enjoyed the physicality of it, a stark contrast to all the time she spent in her head.

There was no sign of the Agassi or his companion, nor anyone else who might be one of his men.

Samira made a sound of dismay. She had fixed her attention on the arena entrance. A man strode toward them, which was what Samira had exclaimed upon. His languid gait, as if he owned the entire world, and short, curly black hair gave him away. Cemil Kadir.

Naime had warned him once already to stay away from Samira. Apparently, the arrogant bastard did not feel the need to heed her. He came to a stop before them, gave the most cursory of bows to Naime, then turned his gold gaze on Samira. There was only one positive thing Naime would ever say about Cemil—when he looked at Samira, there could be no doubt in any observer's mind he thought she was the most beautiful creature on the Wheel.

"Hello, Spark," he said. He appeared sober, for once, at least.

"Cemi," Samira greeted and pleaded with him in one word. "What are you doing here?"

"Enjoying the show." He tipped his head toward the arena. "But it becomes dreary when the same person wins again and again."

"Who is winning and at what?" Naime resisted the urge to step between Cemil and Samira, who would be miserable for at least a day for having to be near him. Did he not care how he hurt her?

Cemil turned an apathetic look on Naime. "Your new Sarkum friend and his men have soundly embarrassed the majority of your guard force over the course of the morning, and he, at least, does not show signs of tiring." He eyed her in silence, giving her time to absorb his words and their implications to raise her ire. "The Viziers who have wandered into the arena do not seem to enjoy the spectacle quite as much as I did."

Cemil rarely smiled, but he did now, taunting. "I am sure he is giving them nightmares of being overrun with marauding Odokan."

Naime barely suppressed a curse.

The Council had already seen him bloodied and disheveled when he arrived, and now they were treated to the sight of him brawling with her guards. Perhaps she had been too quick to judge him as different. If he gave no thought at all to his comportment.

Naime hooked her arm through Samira's and took a step to walk away. Samira balked, and when Naime glanced at her, Samira's expression asked permission. Naime would have liked to order her to come, but Samira was a grown woman. She could make her own decisions.

"As you wish," Naime said, and left them alone. She glanced back only once on her way to the arena. Cemil stepped close to Samira and said something Naime did not hear. Samira turned her head away. Anger ignited over Naime's skin and she looked forward again as she strode beneath the arch in the wall of the arena.

Stone formed a curved ceiling above her, painted with murals depicting the arena's bloody history. It had once served as a coliseum, but when slavery had been outlawed, gladiator fights stopped as well. Now it served as training space for her guards, the City Watch, and eventually Tamar's army.

When she emerged from the tunnel beneath the arena seats, the walkway continued in both directions and circled the central, open pit. It teemed with guardsmen leaning over the low stone wall that separated the arena from the stables and walkway, some scattered through the risers cheering and calling taunts.

Cemil had reported correctly, five of her father's Viziers stood together on the walkway to her left, muttering to each other and casting scathing looks upon the activity in the center of the arena.

Naime's eyes narrowed on a small group of her attendants clustered several paces to her right, staring in feminine appreciation at the two men currently sparring. When she came to a stop between two groups of cheering guardsmen, they looked at her once, then again, and without a word from her they scurried toward the archway behind her and back to the palace grounds.

"Stop," Naime said, as the last one tried to slip past her. He obeyed, his eyes round and his jaw set. "Where is Commander Ayan?"

"Off duty," he replied. Then added, "sleeping."

"Get him now." She could send him a command with her magic, if she wished, but to do so to someone she could not see was a large drain on her energy, of which she had little after a long night keeping vigil in her father's room.

"Yes." The guardsman ducked away.

The two men fighting were stripped to their waists, which was likely the cause of her attendant's shameless ogling and the Viziers' outrage.

Despite her own anger at the immodesty and spectacle of it, she could not blame her women for watching. The drills and sparring that Commander Ayan taught were much more structured, and certainly required his men to be in uniform. Tamar had been peaceful since the Sundering War, and with their focus on bearing children with powerful magic and putting resources toward training them, they had moved away from the martial arts.

She had meant to only watch long enough to confirm it was indeed the Agassi in the ring. Instead she could not take her eyes away. He drove the guardsman mercilessly across the arena, moving with grace and surety, something wild and fierce and beautiful. She would have been happy to watch him longer, but he had his opponent on his back in moments, the point of his yataghan against the man's throat. A cheer went up and the Agassi hoisted the guard to his feet.

The defeated guardsman saw Naime as he stood, and must have said as much, drawing the Agassi's gaze to her. His expression contorted just before Tareck barreled into him at full speed, wrapping his arms around the Agassi's waist and driving him back. They grappled, the Agassi trying to get his arms under Tareck to leverage him away. But the janissary twisted and hooked a leg around his, slamming him into the sand.

Cheers and laughter went up like a howling pack of schoolboys. Naime pressed her fingers to her forehead. The Viziers had apparently had enough, as they moved toward the tunnel and Naime. They bowed politely as they passed her, but disdain at the perceived affront lingered in their expressions. Her anger rose at the same time her hope sank. If they didn't respect him, they wouldn't want to negotiate with him.

Tareck pulled his master to his feet. The Agassi held his hands up to silence the crowing guards.

"It is hardly a fair win if I was distracted," he announced as he pointed at her, which directed everyone's eyes in her direction. The arena fell silent, as if someone had cast a dampening spell.

As he walked toward her across the sand she tried to appear as if his state of undress did not ruffle her. She had to affect a glare, lest she simply stare at him in hungry awe despite her anger. He was perfection no matter where she looked, his warm golden skin slicked with sweat, his body muscular proof that this kind of exercise was common for him, a careless grin dismissing the exertion. His hair was out of its clasp, half pulled back from his face in small braids and bound at the back of his head, the rest left free. It fell to the back of his neck, much longer than Tamar men kept theirs.

He sheathed the yataghan in a quick, practiced movement as he approached. Naime had forgotten about his wound, but was reminded by the bandage, spotted with blood, that wound around his upper arm.

"Sultana," Bashir Ayan's deep voice said from behind her, pulling her attention away from the Agassi. The guards, trying to find an escape, shoved at each other, shuffling toward the exit, where Naime and Bashir stood. Bashir was red-eyed and mussed. His clothes were also in disarray, which was not like him. Naime felt a twinge of remorse. He held up a hand and the men trying to sneak past him stopped, milling together.

"Commander. End this," she ordered. "I expect it will not happen again."

"Of course," he said, his voice already laced with power, dark lines fissuring through his irises. He bowed then moved past her to stand at the wall and shout orders, the magic he put into his voice making the entire arena shake, sand shifting. The Agassi stopped in alarm, bracing his feet as the arena moved beneath them. He eyed Bashir with respect.

"Agassi," Naime said with all the imperiousness her mother had gifted her, "might I have a word with you?"

His grin faded. He vaulted the low wall into the walkway. She glanced to her right, where her attendants huddled, shamefaced and staring at their feet. "You may redeem yourselves by scrubbing the receiving hall floors," Naime ordered.

They bowed in unison, then left with haste, appearing almost relieved. Perhaps she should scrub floors with them, to remind herself about appropriate conduct.

Bashir's men had quickly formed up in the arena and he strode in front of them as he commanded them through a series of excruciatingly slow pushups, while the sand shifted and rolled beneath them. Naime turned, denying her urge to look at the Agassi once more, and strode through the tunnel to where it opened into columned arches that led to the courtyard and stables.

His boots scraped against the sandy stone as he jogged to catch up with her. Naime stopped in the archway, where pillars and walls blocked the guards' view of the two of them.

"It's subtle," he said, "but I get the sense I've upset you." His midnight eyes were bright and wild with energy from his fighting, his face flushed, his breath still quick. He was close enough to touch, and she clasped her hands in front of her. That was the extent of her self-control, and her gaze slid from his fierce expression to his bared torso. Naime had never been so close to a man who wasn't fully clothed, outside of Ihsan while he was recovering from his burns.

She had seen men without their caftans, in the fields, at the docks. But this was wholly different. He was different. A warrior, attested to by the hash-work of scars on his golden skin. Naime wondered at them, a thin one across his chest, a thicker, short line over his ribs, and a long, curved one that disappeared into his salvar. The entire expanse of her skin felt as if it were on fire.

Naime cut her gaze away from his body and caught sight of the Viziers, huddled just outside the walkway that opened into the main courtyard. They were watching the two of them together, expressions pinched with suspicion.

"Do you have clothes?" Naime said, appalled that she'd been so preoccupied ogling him that she hadn't considered the fact she was lurking in an archway with a half-naked man.

"I am wearing clothes," he said. Her gaze whipped to his, and her shame deepened to see the pleased expression on his face. Of course he was aware of her attention, she had been as obvious in her staring as her handmaids had.

"More clothes." Naime tried not to sound desperate, but the weak timbre of her voice gave her away.

"I do." He reached up to swipe a hand across the back of his neck. A shower of sand fell to the stone floor between them and they both peered down.

"In the future, wear them. And refrain from such inappropriate displays." Naime managed to find some composure once she wasn't looking at him.

"What exactly do you consider an inappropriate display, Sultana?" He almost laughed, but it came out as an impatient exhale instead.

"Tamar is a place of restraint and decorum, Agassi. You are more than welcome to spar with the guardsmen as long as Commander Ayan oversees it"—she pointed to Bashir—"and I would expect that you would not humiliate yourself by doing so half-clothed again. Certainly not in front of the Viziers. It will do you no favors in the Council Hall."

"Humiliate myself," the Agassi said, his voice flat with disbelief.

"It is offensive." Naime gestured at him in a lame attempt to indicate his half-clothed state, then at the lingering Viziers.

"Only in a place full of weak-bodied, self-important pacifists would sword practice count as humiliating. You find me offensive," he said, "fine. There are few things I find more tiresome than someone who puts too much stock in pageantry and pretense. And you worship at the altar of pretense."

He glanced at the Viziers, who seemed to feel a sudden urge to head for the palace. She almost spoke to correct him, that she did not find him offensive, but stopped herself when he said the last. "You want our military but cannot even bear the violence of a sparring match or the sight of a man's bare chest. You don't have the spine to send men to war." He made a dismissive sound.

"I don't? That is not…" The words twisted in her throat, her gaze caught, held, and pulled by the spreading black in his eyes. *Devour.* She felt the insistence as a ripple upon the surface of her magic. Not words, a sense. The way fire feels like heat and threat. Her magic twisted and writhed, slips of wind stirring across her skin.

Naime frowned, yanking her magic back under control that felt eaten away, ripping her gaze from his face. When she focused instead on his shoulders, she blinked. Was that…smoke, swirling under his skin?

Naime breathed and wrapped her magic around herself again. The signature of his magic, the evidence in his eyes, wiped away almost all doubt. The man before her was a Sixth House mage, and a powerful one. Magic did not flux for Aval and Deval, the weaker mages of the Wheel, was not unleashed by strong emotion, did not show in their eyes or dance in their skin. He must be a Sival.

"You are in flux. Control yourself," she ordered, "or I will do it for you." To twine her magic around his without permission would be grossly out of line, but she could already feel the push of it, and if he advanced he would begin to visibly bleed it.

"You couldn't. And I am perfectly in control." He sucked in a breath, realization dawning in his expression. Wariness replaced it, and he stared at her, anger hardening the lines of his face as his fist curled around the hilt of his yataghan. He was waiting for her to react to the fact that he was a destruction mage or attack him. But she cared far less about his magic at this moment than she did the perception of her Council.

"Allow me to strip things of their pretense, *Efendim*," Naime put mockery in the superlative, "so you find it easier to understand. You mock us for our restraint and our pretense, meanwhile you almost reveal yourself because you lack such restraint. You understand we are a country of powerful mages but have not considered what that means. We are polite, we are reserved, because passion and power are tied to each other. If we brawl, if we let ourselves do as we please, if we give in to our passions, we lose control and people die. These traditions are the lock and key that contain our violence and keep us human. I should not have to tell you that."

He stared, and his shoulders rose and fell with a single, deep breath. His eyes closed, and when they opened the deeper darkness was gone from them. The press of his magic retreated from hers, and the trace of smoke and shadow she had seen in his skin swirled away.

"No, you don't," he said, sounding tired instead of angry.

"Whatever freedoms you enjoyed in Sarkum to do as you please cannot be indulged here. You might be a prince there, but here you are considered little more than a barbarian. If you came because you want an alliance, then I will warn you, despite whatever the Grand Vizier might have told you, the Council is aligned against you. Even the smallest things you do to turn them away from you become the bricks to build a wall that prevents you from reaching whatever your goal is."

"First you find me offensive, and now I am a barbarian." He appeared miserable instead of angry, now. It did not seem prudent to tell him she did not find him offensive, or that she would have been happy to continue watching him, or staring at him exactly as he was. She wanted to, because she had spoken more harshly than she meant to, but it would strip her of any authority or respectability he attributed to her. Besides, she had to consider how many of her attendants would happily tell him the same thing, and that he was likely accustomed to such attention.

No, she had to remember that her plan's success depended on him making a good impression on the Council. Not a good impression on her.

"I do not think you are any of those things," Naime said finally, which seemed a reasonable compromise between fawning and insulting. "But I know exactly what the Viziers think, because I have to. If I worship at the altar of pretense, as you accused me, it is because I have to. I am not a son. I am not even held in the regard of a second son. My High Council will only listen to me if I make not a *single* mistake. I will only be heard if everything I do is impeccable, my dress, my manners, my method of speaking, the words I use and in what order I use them—and even then I am judged lacking. They will treat you the same, because you are different, and they abhor difference."

"Agassi," Tareck said from behind them. When Makram turned, Tareck held out a bundle of cloth Naime hoped was more clothing. The Agassi glanced at her and strode to his friend, taking the clothes.

"Tell the men I will return shortly. If the Sultana approves, we'll go for a ride to get out of this"—he looked at her in accusation—"place."

"Yes." Tareck gave a quick bow and left them.

The Agassi laid his clothes over a hook meant to hang a lamp from, turning so his side was to her. The distance did not hide his clenched jaw and tense, sharp movements.

He unbuckled his sword belt, the action drawing her gaze to his hips, to the scar that cut a line over his belly and into his salvar. There was a trace of jet hair below his navel that followed the scar lower, but none on his chest, a testament to his mixed heritage and yet another thing that set him apart from Tamar men. Naime watched the flex of muscles in his back, stomach, and arms as he pulled his caftan over his head. Her palms itched, her fingers tingling with her desire to touch him, to know what it felt like to stroke golden skin and sleek muscle. She mourned the loss when the caftan fell loosely around him, hiding his body from her.

"Is that all right with you?" His tone was more jab than question as he buttoned the caftan in quick, irritated flicks of his fingers. Naime forced herself to look at his face. How much of her admiration was obvious to him now?

"Is what all right?" she asked, her voice catching. He tugged his entari off the hook, shrugging into it then grabbing his sword belt before he strode back to her.

"I would like to take my men for a ride through your city. We do not suffer cages well." He hung the sword over the low wall beside them.

"You could at least acknowledge that you have heard and understand what I just told you. If you will not apologize."

"I won't apologize for something I don't believe was wrongdoing," he said, and the movement of his fingers as he hooked the clasps on his entari drew her gaze, "but I will heed your words. Action is better than the little lies we tell with apology, isn't it?"

His hands dropped to his sides, and Naime found him watching her when she averted her gaze from the buttons. Her pulse thumped harder. Mages could look at people with intensity fueled by magic, but this intensity was different. His coffee-dark eyes swept her face, but not her body, as she was so accustomed to, but it didn't matter.

The perusal felt as intimate, as suggestive. A swirl in her belly twisted lower, heating her thoughts with more lurid images.

"You could come with us," he suggested, the anger gone from his voice, the coaxing velvet warmth back. Naime shook her head, slowly, her stare locked to his, her voice refusing to come to her call.

"Not even a short ride?" He stepped closer, and she had to tip her head to keep her eyes on his. The scent of male sweat, and something else…the warm, spreading scent of dusk swept over her.

No. Being alone with this man was not a good idea.

"I cannot," she managed.

"Some other time then," he said, his eyes growing somehow darker, brown morphing to black. "Any time."

"No," Naime said, though her voice betrayed the truth. If it would not ruin her to do so, she would happily go anywhere with him.

"Decorum?" he said too casually, reaching for his sword belt and slinging it around his hips. "Or, is there some other offense I have committed you have yet to mention?"

"Surely in Sarkum it would be just as unseemly for a princess to go riding about with a soldier." Naime watched his competent hands as they buckled his sword into place and adjusted its position against his leg.

"I am also a prince," he said. "But do as you see fit, Sultana. Why did you come out here in the first place?"

The question jolted her back to herself, startling her into remembering where she was and that she had been standing with him alone for far too long in sight of far too many people.

"I came to inform you my father has agreed to meet with you tomorrow, with the Council."

"Good." He glanced toward the arena, where his men were gathered, watching Bashir put his own men through exercises. "If that is all you require of me, may I have your permission to take my men out of the palace?"

"Commander Ayan will arrange an escort for you," Naime said. He exhaled slowly, curled his hands into fists then flexed them open.

"Then I'll see you tomorrow, I assume?" He did not look at her.

"Yes."

He gave a sharp nod, and left her, striding back toward the arena. Naime took a deep breath and denied a desire to shake her head or rub her face in an effort to clear her mind. She could only vaguely recall the last time she had been so affected by a man. And even then, not like this, not until she couldn't seem to keep any of her wits about her.

"Sultana?" Samira called, standing in one of the arches that demarcated the courtyard. Naime joined her, grateful for the distraction.

"Are you all right?" Naime asked, searching Samira's face for signs of sadness. "What did he want?"

"We are friends. He wished to talk." Samira's lie of omission told Naime the subject had been intimate. Naime did not press. Samira leaned toward Naime to murmur, "The Agassi is watching you."

"We should go," Naime said. But she glanced over her shoulder as they started walking. Her eyes met his without effort. One side of his mouth lifted in a smile, and he glanced to one of his men to answer something they asked, then back to her, his head tipped forward as he listened, his gaze fixed on hers.

Naime looked away. Trouble. A handsome man who knew he was handsome, who knew he'd caught her eyes. It was nothing but trouble.

Ten

THE MORNING OF THE Council meet, Makram watched the Sultana as she strode beside her father toward the Council Hall. Was it because of her affinity to air that she seemed to float more than walk? He'd observed it at the stables the day before as well. Her cousin walked on the Sultan's opposite side, but Makram only gave Ihsan a passing glance before focusing on the Sultana again. Her expression was closed, a far cry from the stormy mix of temper and discomfiture that had been on her face when he left her the day before.

Makram sighed and rubbed his eyes. She was, once again, cool and composed, her hair and clothing in perfect order. He, on the other hand, felt as if he were standing on the edge of a cliff, waiting to see if she would push him off. There was no doubt she knew what he was now. But she had not announced him or even spoken of it. No, instead she'd tortured him with lingering looks that somehow held wanton heat and oblivious innocence. The sparring and subsequent loss of his temper at her accusations had done enough to unravel his restraint but pretending to be ignorant to her unabashed appraisal had almost driven him mad.

Makram ripped his thoughts from it, from the image of her lovely, dark eyes, lashes lowered as she tried to hide her glances while he dressed. Her eyes…warm, brown-tinged carmine. Like cinnamon, or…

He cursed under his breath. Tareck glanced up at him, and Makram gave no explanation, forcing himself to look at the Sultan instead of her. The Sultan dipped his head to say something as the trio passed the alcove where Makram and Tareck waited. Makram couldn't hear him, but neither his daughter nor his nephew appeared pleased by what he said.

Tareck leaned on the wall opposite him, both of them tucked into an alcove across from the Council Hall. He was using a curved dagger to clean beneath his nails, and the nearly imperceptible sound of it was about to drive Makram insane. When Makram glanced sharply at him for the tenth or eleventh time, Tareck flicked his gaze to Makram's and raised his eyebrows.

"Still fuming, Agassi Efendim?" Tareck tipped the knife point in Makram's direction.

"Put that damn thing down before I use it to stab you," Makram said.

"Don't be an ass to me just because you made foolish decisions. I'm only here to haul your bags, remember?"

"Maybe I'll relieve you of your duties when we return."

"No one else would be willing to take my place but do whatever you like. You know I prefer the barracks to the palace. Also, I think you're being unreasonable."

"It is not unreasonable to do away with a steward who is not a very good steward," Makram said. The Sultan entered the hall, and Makram pushed away from the wall of the alcove. Their two guards stood several steps away, discussing the finer points of drinking arak in quantity.

"I mean about the Sultana. She was trying to help you." Tareck sheathed the dagger in the wrap at his waist.

"Help me? She called us barbarians. She said I was offensive and had humiliated myself. Humiliated myself by besting her palace guard." Makram's voice faded to a mutter. "Unbelievable." Her appreciative glances had not been enough to soothe his ego at her comments.

"You're angry because she is beautiful and she doesn't fall all over herself for you the way you're accustomed to women doing." Tareck sighed. "Which is yet more proof that she is intelligent."

"Thank you for your assessment." Makram turned a baleful glare on his friend. Women didn't fall all over him. Many thought him handsome, some even mooned, but none thought him handsome enough to make up for the magic in his blood. She had kept looking, even after she learned what he was. Even after he'd been foolish enough to lose his temper and his control right in front of her. Void and stars the way she'd stared at him.

Makram gripped his hands into fists then shook them out, trying to rid himself of the excess of energy and frantic thoughts. He had never lacked control before. Never until she'd stripped him of it with a reasoned tongue lashing and greedy stares.

Tareck shrugged. "I think you should listen to her. She knows the court better than you, the Viziers, the divisions and alliances. Why navigate such dangers without a guide if you do not need to?"

"Because she is controlling and arrogant." And beautiful, and intelligent, and he could not allow himself the things he was thinking. He'd invited her to ride with him as though she were some simple village girl. She made him into a fool without even meaning to.

Tareck's breath rushed out in a soundless laugh. "Your wounded pride is showing. That probably isn't allowed in Tamar either."

"Have I ever mentioned how much I hate you?" Makram said under his breath.

"Frequently. Shall we?" Tareck gestured at the Council Hall. "Imagine the stripping-down she'd give you if you were late to meet her father." He sauntered past Makram, tossing his dagger to the guards when one of them pointed at it.

Makram walked beside him as they entered the Council Hall. There had been a great deal of chatter just before they entered the room, but it quieted as everyone turned to them. Makram counted twenty men, the Grand Vizier among them, scattered around benches that lined the walls in three rows from the door to the dais where the Sultan sat. The only person standing was the Grand Vizier, but as Makram and Tareck reached the middle of the hall, the Sultana rose and bowed to her father. Makram took that as a hint to stop where he was.

"Sultanim, Grand Vizier, gentlemen of the Council, it is my honor to present Sehzade Makram Attaraya Al-Nimas, younger son of Sultan Ediz Rahal Al-Nimas, Agassi of the Mirza's janissaries and sipahi, and delegate of Sarkum, as well as Tareck Habaal, Captain of the Janissary."

The Viziers shifted and muttered to each other, and Makram enjoyed seeing a flash of surprise on the Grand Vizier's face when the Sultana named him a prince.

Makram and Tareck knelt and bent forward, as was customary in Sarkum, when the Sultan stood to acknowledge them. Makram thought he appeared hearty for someone who had been ill enough only a day before that his daughter had to take over his duties. He was tall and carried his shoulders in the way a man accustomed to authority often did. Age had dimmed some of it, but he assessed Makram with a familiar unreadable mien, and Makram glanced sideways at his daughter.

She stood prim and silent, her hands folded against the skirt of her caftan, her gaze directed at the middle of the floor between her and the Grand Vizier. Ihsan sat on the same bench as her, but closer to Makram. He appeared bored and disinterested in the entire affair.

"I appreciate your humility," the Sultan said, gesturing with his hand as he sat, "but kneeling is unnecessary."

"As it pleases you, Sultanim." Makram sat back on his heels and rolled to his feet, and Tareck did the same. "I hope the disturbing rumors I've heard about your health are exaggerated."

"It is likely," the Sultan said, and smiled a little, humor bright in his eyes. The same eyes as his daughter. "You have come a long way, gentlemen. I have been informed you endured an attack and braved the pass and the Engeli in winter. Your dedication impresses me."

"The Mirza was intrigued by your suggestion of alliance, Sultan Efendim." He thought better of mentioning the second letter that pleaded haste as being the reason for his speed. The Viziers shifted, almost as one, tension shrinking the room, as if they thought with one mind instead of twenty. Benches creaked in the hush. Awareness sizzled up his spine, like he felt the approach of an enemy, but it was only simple fear and aggression ramping up around him. At least in Al-Nimas he was allowed his sword. He felt exposed without it now.

"Who would not be interested in alliance, with the Republic prowling their borders?" the Sultan said, without a trace of humor. Makram grit his teeth.

"Sultanim," the Sultana said quickly but calmly, one of the fine muscles in her neck tensing. "Perhaps we should offer our terms to facilitate a discussion."

"The High Council has not agreed to this negotiation, nor have they agreed to the terms of an alliance," the Grand Vizier said. The three Viziers behind him nodded sage agreement, and the tension drifting through the room tightened a notch.

The Sultana lifted her head, her gaze lighting on the Grand Vizier's face, then her father's. "Shall I speak, Sultanim, or do you wish to?"

He lifted his hand and flicked his fingers at her, and she turned to address the others.

"The Council will recall the Sultan does not require their approval, for anything." She waited while their indignant chatter dissipated. "The High Council has been offered the chance to review the terms on numerous occasions and refused. I could only assume my father's governors are too busy to be distracted by matters that are ambiguous, so I have made them unambiguous."

She faced Makram. If any emotion lingered from their heated interaction the day before, nothing showed on her serene face. He hadn't imagined her staring, had he? The curiosity, the heat? Or had she been manipulating him? Surely not manipulating. All she need do was threaten to expose his magic, which she did not seem inclined to do. Some of the tension unwound from his chest, and he took a breath.

"Agassi, the Sultan is aware of the press of the Republic on your borders, and that if they were to take Sarkum, Tamar would be soon to follow. As you have seen," she said with a trace of dry humor, "Narfour retains its ancient heritage as a place of magic. Our peace since the Sundering War, however, has fostered a lack of military power."

Loud protests issued from several directions at once, as if she had divulged the most precious of secrets. Makram almost laughed.

"Grand Vizier," the Sultana said, "I understand the Council has concerns, and they will be addressed, but I must insist they allow me to discuss the Sultan's terms first."

"How many of our weaknesses do you plan to divulge over the course of the discussion, Princess Sultana?" the Grand Vizier replied, lightly, his gaze flicking over the Council and eliciting a few tense chuckles.

"Behram," the Sultan said, tapping his fist against his leg as he eyed the Grand Vizier in warning.

The Sultana said, "Our lack of military is not a secret, Grand Vizier, just as Sarkum's lack of mages is not. We cannot share border, heritage, and centuries of history and believe such large deficits are not known to the other." Her gaze had focused somewhere in the vicinity of Makram's chest, her face blank as she spoke. Wheel how did she bear it? The way the man tested her? He barely knew the Grand Vizier and he wanted to strangle him on her behalf. But this was her battle, and her weapons were decorum and control. As she had said so eloquently the day before.

"The lack is well known in Sarkum," Makram said, "and the only reason we have not overrun you is because of your magic superiority."

The Sultana's eyes widened, a warning look of censure flashing across her expression just before the room erupted. Tareck hissed beside him, and gave an admonishing click of his tongue as Viziers lunged to their feet, shouting. Wheel and spokes, even when he tried to contain himself he ruined everything.

"That was ill planned," Tareck said as he stepped between Makram and the rest of the room. The Sultana turned her head toward her cousin. He gave a martyred sigh and stood.

"This is preposterous," the Grand Vizier said, loud enough it carried over the others' frantic voices. Makram almost turned to him, but could not look away from Ihsan as ice scrawled away from his feet, across the floor, and up the walls. It frosted the benches, and Makram's boots, and Tareck cursed, trying to lift one foot and finding it frozen to the floor.

Ihsan tipped his head as the room changed from angry chatter to shocked outrage. Pale blue light imbued his eyes, shading them with the flux of his magic, and blue, frosted swirls blazed over his exposed skin as ice shot across the ceiling. The voices died back.

"Sit. *Down*," the Sultana said, her magic-infused command booming in the room and dislodging some of the ice crystals that blanketed it.

Slowly, the men obeyed, and Ihsan's ice receded, though the sound of dripping water punctuated the tense silence. "I expect you to control this room, Grand Vizier. It is, after all, your duty," she said in disdain.

"Control them? When you bring barbarians into the palace and threaten us with a conquering army?" the Grand Vizier said, directing a glare at Ihsan as he sat and returned it with a tense, toothy grin.

"I did not threaten them." The Sultana turned a malevolent stare on Makram. He grit his teeth. Tareck retreated to his side so he had to bear the full intensity of her displeasure. Better to keep his mouth shut. Even without his magic's help he seemed unable to sow anything but discord. "And I am certain that is not what the Agassi intended to do either."

"No? The man has shown nothing but a predisposition to violence and disrespect from the moment he appeared. Do you really mean to negotiate with him? To bring bloodshed, violence, and death mages back to Tamar?"

"Yes," the Sultana hissed, and turned to her father. Makram had not looked at the Sultan again since arriving, distracted by his daughter and the shifting energy of the room. When Makram had entered he had appeared as one would expect, a man in his sixtieth turn of the Wheel, or more, composed like his daughter, possessed of authority. Now he seemed confused, as if he wasn't certain how he had arrived at where he was.

"Sultanim." She bowed again, which Makram found odd, but forced the Sultan's focus to her. "May I continue?" He stared at her, his brow furrowing, and nodded, though he seemed unsure of his decision.

"Sultana," the Grand Vizier said, having regained his level tone. "The Council was not consulted in the drafting of the terms, and they cannot be expected to go along with an ill-thought-out alliance."

Makram resisted the urge to scoff, or speak, or leave the room. This had been a waste of his time and he had risked Kinus' ire for nothing. These men weren't going to listen to reason. They were probably direct descendants of the men who had decided to break the Wheel in the first place. He enjoyed a brief fantasy of unleashing his magic on the entirety of the palace on his way out.

"Allow me to elucidate this ill-thought-out plan, Grand Vizier." She strode to stand at her father's feet and face the room, as though she meant to shield him.

"By all means," he replied, a smile flitting over his mouth.

"Agassi, it is our intention to unite Sarkum and Tamar by trade of military power for magical." Her eyes fixed on Makram's chest instead of his face. "In that exchange, I would include that any knowledge you have of the Republic, their capabilities and weaknesses, their most recent movements, be shared with Tamar. In return, I would like our University and the Academy in Al-Nimas to combine libraries and assets, in order to regain knowledge lost to both of us after the Sundering War."

He had expected the military, knowledge of the Republic, but the rest was a surprise. Surprise enough he couldn't conceive a response before the Grand Vizier spoke.

"Outrageous. You cannot truly mean to give access to the University? The Sixth House is alive and well in Sarkum and handing them knowledge they may not have had will only increase the threat of their magic. You intend to give Sarkum's army and their death mages free run of Tamar?" He shook his head as he spoke.

Makram leveled his expression. They were not fears he had not heard, again and again throughout his life. Yes, destruction mages existed in Sarkum. They were alive, but they were not well. Superstition still surrounded them, they never knew if they would be treated with courtesy or suspicion. Even his own brother occasionally slipped and revealed his discomfort with Makram's power. They had an academy to train mages, but it was largely empty of gifted instructors. So much knowledge about the Sixth House was lost that Makram had spent just as much time experimenting to learn his own magic as he had training with bow and sword.

Why he had thought things might be different in Tamar, just because the Sultan wanted an alliance, he could not fathom. Fool that he was.

"I said nothing of the kind, Grand Vizier, and your exaggerated assumptions only serve to reveal your alarmist tendencies." She dismissed him with a flick of her fingers. "I expect more rationality from you. Or at least, my father has indicated you are capable of it."

Impatiently, he replied, "I am speaking in the interest of the people of Tamar."

"No, I am. I am speaking about an alliance that will protect them from annihilation. *You* are speaking from fear. Something I would not have expected from a Sival of the Fifth House," she said in dry mockery. The Grand Vizier responded by narrowing his eyes and pressing his lips together. "I will remind you that the Wheel is comprised of six spokes, not four. That it is our greatest endeavor in life to seek balance. A broken Wheel cannot be balanced."

She let her gaze drift across the other Viziers. "My family, because of the same fear you are slave to now, destroyed our chance at balance. Innocent mages were hunted, tortured, murdered." She bestowed the same cool look across the other side of the room. Makram wished she would look at him, so he could judge her truth in her eyes. Did she believe these things, or was this a political game?

No, he could not believe it was a game. She was too forthright, too passionate beneath that shield of air magic.

"Innocent? Their very nature makes them killers, Sultana. You are romanticizing," the Grand Vizier dismissed her, but Makram could see other faces in the room, watching her and considering. Perhaps there were cooler heads that might see reason. How could he help her turn them? He was useless, standing in silence while she verbally battled her way up a mountain of opposition.

"They are no more likely to be murderers than any other mage." There were a few scornful laughs, but she ignored them. Makram held his breath, afraid he'd miss a single word, and he couldn't take his gaze from her, waiting. "You can be burned, drowned, buried beneath the earth, and the air siphoned from your lungs just as easily as your heart stopped or your body eroded. And frankly, of those options, I might choose to have my heart stopped."

Someone cleared their throat to cover a laugh, and the Grand Vizier's expression hardened more.

"They were not always called death mages." Her gaze finally met Makram's, and her mouth curved, just barely, as she said it. Twin arrows of pleasure and surprise pinned him. She'd listened to him. She cut her gaze away from his before he could even acknowledge her with a smile.

"Destruction is a necessary part of the Wheel, and of life." Her words sliced through the air and the Viziers' quiet conversations like a honed blade, leaving a hush in its wake. "Everything dies. Everything decays. Walls are reduced to rubble, bones to dust, experiences to memories. These feed and sustain new life. That is the turning of the Wheel, from beginning to end, dawn to dusk, life to death. We are not as strong without all six of the Houses, and that is evident in the slow receding of magic from the rest of the world. We do not feel it because Tamar has always been the heart of magic, but we will. It will come to us."

She paused, her expression growing taut, her hands curling into fistfuls of her entari as her surveyed the room. "Balance will come to us, it will shatter the peace you sit so comfortably in, decay the prosperity you guard so jealousy, destroy the life you love. And it will not be destruction mages who bring it, but the Republic."

She looked to her father, who appeared almost in a trance, though some of the confusion had left his face, replaced by a flush of fervor and pride.

Makram released his breath, standing as silent and dumbfounded as the rest of them. Admiration filled him, the same that had engulfed him after her handling of the guild audience gone awry. How could these men not see what a gift she was, what an incredible queen she would be? Some looked as if they had begun to realize it, staring thunderstruck, glances shared between them, a few nods. Others wore outraged or contemptuous expressions as she spoke.

"You speak of balance, yet there is no Third House to balance the Sixth. You ignore the fact there are no mages in opposition to destruction, no creation magic left in the world." The Grand Vizier tapped his staff against the floor in punctuation.

What fervor had blazed on her face disappeared behind a shield of composure.

"Because the Wheel is broken. I do not merely intend to align with Sarkum, I intend to balance the Wheel. If we bring the Sixth House back to Tamar, right the wrong inflicted by my forefathers, I believe we will see the rebirth of the Third House," she said. A shiver raced over Makram's skin, and he glanced at Tareck, who watched the Sultana with rapt focus. "The Wheel responds to intention. To action."

"You say that, but you have never met a Sixth House mage. What will you do, Sultana, when you are forced to look death in the eye for the first time and know you have no means to stop its rampage?" the Grand Vizier said. But he was losing his Council, the mood had shifted. Makram could feel them under her thrall, taken by the calm, soothing tone of her voice, the controlled ferocity of her belief.

"I will welcome them home." Her solemn gaze touched Makram's. "Tamar is their birthright, just as it is ours, and they will be governed by the same laws that have kept Tamar safe for generations since the Sundering."

He could not unravel here, in front of them all, but his throat was tight, his breath came short, and he wanted a chance to replay her words, her acceptance, until they shone their light in every shadowed place inside him that festered with a lifetime of rejection and prejudice.

He was not allowed to bask in the truth of her declaration, or enjoy her attention, because Tareck tapped him on the back, and gave a sharp nod of approval when Makram eyed him sidelong. His friend's face reflected approval. Approval he had never shown for Kinus.

Before Makram could do anything else, the Grand Vizier sighed, loudly. "Your desire to bring balance and power to Tamar is a lofty and admirable goal, Sultana, one I think you and your mother shared." The words were a firebomb on the spell she had cast over the room. The Sultana's back stiffened, her father's face tightened, and Ihsan turned in his seat to observe the Sultan.

The Grand Vizier continued. "We can hope that whoever your father chooses as his successor shares those goals as well. For now, it seems we are at an impasse. You are unmarried, and do not have the authority to override the Council. And I do not believe"—he rotated to face the Sultan—"that my dear friend would so easily disregard the consensus of the Council."

The Sultan's expression pinched, glancing from the Grand Vizier to his daughter.

Makram frowned. His moods were too mercurial.

"I have the Sultan's authority in this matter," the Sultana said. "Whether the Council agrees or not. Sultanim, please assure the Grand Vizier that an alliance with Sarkum is your wish." She stepped close, touching her fingers to her father's hand, so his gaze went to hers.

"Sarkum?" he said, his expression growing troubled.

Makram clenched his hands into fists. How had he missed the signs? How had he not felt the faint tremor against his magic, the taste of rot and change that coated the roof of his mouth when he concentrated on the man?

The Sultan's mind was breaking.

They needed more time to get the Council on their side. Makram took a step forward.

"You speak of Sixth House mages as if they have unchecked power, Grand Vizier, and forgive me, you are misinformed," he said, quickly, to distract them. Perhaps he could stall long enough for her to calm her father. The Sultana turned to him, her gaze flicking to his, not in censure, but he thought, to try and assess his aim.

Makram spoke the next carefully, so she might ascertain his intent. "There are very few mages left in Sarkum, of any House, and those that are, are rarely born with more than a Deval's power." He twisted the truth a degree, for now was not the time to reveal himself completely. He already risked himself by defending the Sixth House. "They are governed by the same need for spells or energy to power their magic."

"Sarkum's strength does not lie in their destruction magic"—she glanced to him and he ducked his head in agreement—"but in their military."

Makram picked the thread back up, taking a step forward to draw their stares, giving his voice the same timbre he did when commanding his men. "Our sipahi and janissaries train from boyhood to their profession." He let his gaze roam the room, hunting for the men who appeared most likely to argue. "They spend their lives stationed on the Odokan borderlands and cut their teeth on the bandits and highwaymen who plague the barrens and the trade routes north and south."

Of course it was the Grand Vizier who responded first. "Those require the tactics of raiders and defenders, Agassi, not the discipline and broadscale strategy that would be necessary to counter the Republic were it to move." His words brought to mind the mural over the Sultan's door. A half-formed idea came to Makram.

"A tactician might argue the strategy of the former is more difficult than the latter, Grand Vizier." Makram smiled. "Perhaps you and I will find time to debate the Battle of Narfour, during which the palace and Sultan fell to the first Ediz Rahal." That earned him a ripple of movement and irritation, focusing them more intently on him.

The Grand Vizier laughed. "It fell for two days, and was retaken."

"But it fell, Grand Vizier." Makram strode forward, and they all turned, following his movement, listening. "Two days cost Tamar the death of their ruler and two decades of turmoil." He stopped a few strides away from the Sultana. "And those who did it were barbarians." He caught her gaze and the corner of her mouth twitched. "Men who'd been driven from their homes, in tenuous alliance with the Odokan, with whom they shared no language, with almost no magic between them. It fell to a force of raiders, as you called Sarkum's army."

When the Grand Vizier opened his mouth to reply, the Sultana spoke first. "It was only retaken by the efforts and magical strength of what remained of the Circle of Chara'a. Imagine the capability of that force, honed over two centuries by conflict, augmented with the power of Tamar's mages."

The room erupted in chatter, the Viziers turning to each other. One man pointed to Makram, another to the Grand Vizier. Two others nodded to each other as if their sage opinions were the pillars that held the ceiling above their heads. The Sultana had removed her hand from her father's, though she still stood in front of him, and folded both together in front of her caftan. She ducked her head to Makram, the smile that had twitched at the corner of her mouth now warming her eyes. That small approval should not have buoyed him so immensely.

"You speak like a man accustomed to rallying troops, Agassi. And I can see some of my Viziers have fallen prey to your talent for it," the Grand Vizier said. That earned a few chagrined expressions, and Makram knew he'd just been maneuvered into a corner. "It is easy enough to see, just by a stroll through the city, that Tamar is a place of power. But we have only your biased word that your sipahi and janissaries are capable."

"The fact that Sarkum, stripped of their magical power, has stood against invasion from the east for two centuries is not proof enough?" Makram replied.

"Perhaps the Viziers who watched the Agassi and his men spar Commander Ayan's men yesterday can attest to their prowess," the Sultana suggested, and Makram wondered if he imagined the slight discomfort with which she smiled. In response, a Vizier on the opposite side of the room from Kadir, to Makram's right, stood.

"I can—"

"Sit down, Esber Pasha," ordered the Grand Vizier. Esber Pasha obeyed. "Maintaining a border against disparate tribes is not holding off a Republic. And a sparring match is not war, Sultana. We cannot even consider such an alliance without better information. The numbers of sipahi and janissaries, their current disposition, supply lines, capabilities, their command structure. How can we know they will not march on us the moment the ink dries?"

Makram could no longer suppress his impatience with the man, and his words came out too sharply. "We have not been waiting for Tamar's permission to march, Grand Vizier. As I said only moments ago, our military is outstripped by your power and that will not be changed by an alliance. I can give you any of the information you wish, however, I would only divulge those kinds of details to an ally."

Makram glanced at the Sultana, who continued to watch him intently. Some of the fervor he had seen in her eyes before was there, a tiny, burning spark that fired one inside him as well. It made him feel fierce and invincible.

"As for our competence, if I can prove it to you, will the Council agree to send terms to Al-Nimas?"

The Sultana shifted, began to raise her hand to stop him, but clasped both together again. A mask of indifference obscured her thoughts. He was going to prove himself to her, secure an alliance, and perhaps show them all that being a barbarian in the eyes of Tamar was not such a useless thing.

"By what means do you intend to prove yourself?" the Grand Vizier asked, his words searching the way one might toe the high grass where they suspected a tripwire.

"I am going to take the palace," Makram said. He glanced at the Sultan, afraid his words would upset him. The Sultan sat, hands folded, gazing at his daughter. And Makram felt the briefest swirl of magic, only perceptible to him because of his greater power. The Sultana was shielding her father, holding him together the way she held herself.

"Take the—" The Grand Vizier gave a short, sharp laugh, then turned his humor toward the room, who responded in kind. The Sultana would not even look at him now, her entwined fingers clenched so tightly they were bloodless across the knuckles.

"You have seven men, Agassi," the Grand Vizier said, as if Makram needed reminding.

"And you have somewhere in the realm of…" Makram glanced back at Tareck.

Tareck rubbed his hand up his jaw, his eyes narrowed, posture stiff, but he answered Makram's unspoken question. "Six score."

"Six score of palace guards." He paused only because some of the Viziers acted with surprise at what he assumed was an accurate number. "One does take note of these things, when they are accustomed to fighting." He smiled. "Seven men against a hundred and twenty palace guards. "Ediz Rahal's forces were outnumbered twenty to one in the Battle of Narfour. So"—Makram shrugged one shoulder and grinned—"I have a slight advantage over him."

One of the Viziers chuckled, off to Makram's right. Someone uttered something about obscene arrogance just loudly enough to carry over the room. The Grand Vizier appeared thoughtful. The Sultana's lips pressed together, her eyes blazing at Makram in a silent plea to cease.

"Agassi," Tareck growled in disapproval.

"You must be afraid I'll do it, if you are this troubled by the notion." Makram met the Grand Vizier's eyes, continuing to grin. It felt good to goad the man, and he rewarded Makram's efforts with an expression of burning fury. The Sultan chuckled, and even Ihsan straightened, interest lighting his face. The Viziers glanced almost as one from the Sultana to the Grand Vizier then to Makram. The man sitting nearest the Grand Vizier raised his eyebrows, looking from the Sultana to the Grand Vizier.

The Grand Vizier schooled his expression and made a bid for command of the room yet again. "You think taking this palace with seven men will prove your military to us? That is absurd."

"At the Battle of Narfour, Sultan Omar Sabri the Third was killed in the Council Hall, where he and his Viziers had hidden themselves," Makram said. "If I can recreate this victory in downscaled proportions, will the Council agree to send terms with me to Al-Nimas?"

Tareck breathed a curse. Makram glanced to the Sultana, and under the heat of her steady, malignant glare, some of his triumph shriveled. Why wasn't she pleased? They could hardly say no to him if he succeeded.

"Agassi," Tareck started, but Makram held his hand up. Tareck exhaled forcefully through his nose, putting his hands on his hips and tipping forward briefly before dropping his head back to stare at the ceiling.

"I will not accept an alliance based off a child's game of soldiers," the Grand Vizier said, with a tone of dismissive humor.

"You are not the only man in the Council, Kadir Pasha," the man sitting next to him said, and stood, earning him a look of acidic disdain from the Grand Vizier. "You asked for proof of the Sarkum military capabilities, and the Agassi has responded." He glanced around the chamber and added, "I for one think it sounds intriguing, and a most effective training exercise for our newly promoted Commander Ayan and his men. If a force of seven can take the palace, then imagine what their entire army could do? The Sultana is right, after all. The Republic is threatening. It will do no harm to see Sarkum soldiers at work, to better inform our decision about an alliance, and if not an alliance, then the competence of our enemy."

The Viziers responded with nods and some excited chatter, some even appeared gleeful. Makram found their excitement concerning. It was a war game after all. No wonder they did not take the Sultana seriously, they did not take war seriously.

Yavuz Pasha folded his hands behind his back and dipped his head toward the Grand Vizier.

"Yavuz Pasha," Kadir said, as if Yavuz had made an attempt at a grandiose jest.

"When shall we hold this contest?" Yavuz Pasha said, earning him yet another black look from the Grand Vizier, who was not apparently accustomed to the others speaking against him.

"Three days from now?" Makram suggested the first number that came to mind, to prevent the Grand Vizier interrupting. "My men and I will attempt to take the palace from Commander Ayan and his guard force. If we successfully reach the Council Hall with half my men, then it is a victory. The High Council will review the Sultan's terms for an alliance and send them with me to Sarkum." Makram bowed toward the Sultan. "Is this acceptable to you, Sultanim?"

The Sultan peered at him for a long moment, distracted, rubbing one hand over the back of the other in broken rhythm. He started to nod, then frowned.

"Sultan Efendim," Makram said, striding up the aisle and bowing to him, "allow me to prove the worth of my men, so you are assured an alliance is necessary and worthwhile."

The Sultan nodded again, his eyes brighter suddenly, with humor. "Hot blood," he said. "Good, good. Don't have enough of those around here, not your kind anyway." In answer, the Sultana gave a harsh sigh, cutting her gaze away from them both.

"We have not discussed what will happen when you are unable to take the hall," the Grand Vizier interrupted. "A forfeiture of the alliance terms seems fair." He smiled dully when Makram straightened. Doubt plunged through Makram's surety like a stone in water. He glanced sidelong at the Sultana, who raised her eyebrows in accusation.

"Grand Vizier," Yavuz Pasha admonished.

"The stakes must be equal for winning or losing, as they would be in war. And if the Agassi cannot complete this task, then I should doubt his ability to win against the Republic and the forces he acknowledges outnumber us all, therefore making an alliance nothing more than an intellectual exercise. Those are the stakes. If you succeed, we will review the terms and send them to Sarkum. If you fail, then discussions of negotiation are over, as it will be clear you have little to offer us. You will leave Tamar."

He paused, and some of the excitement drained from the room as those Viziers in support realized it was not just a game. "Is this agreeable to you, Efendim?" The Grand Vizier turned to the Sultan, who paused for a beat too long before answering. He ducked his chin in agreement, his gaze growing distant, then sharpening, then fading again.

"I am tired," he announced, rising. Ihsan leapt from his seat to offer the Sultan his assistance. All the Viziers rose and bowed. "Let us end it for today."

"As you wish, Efendim," the Grand Vizier said as he bowed.

Makram moved to the side as the Sultan passed, his steward opening the Council Hall doors and falling in behind as the Sultana and Ihsan led the Sultan from the room. Makram and Tareck followed, but once outside the hall they stepped aside to allow the Viziers room as they streamed past, Makram watching until he could no longer see the Sultan and his daughter. He wanted to run after her, to speak to her and convince her that he could do what he claimed.

The Grand Vizier was the last to exit the room, and he stopped in front of Makram, leaning slightly on his staff. He smiled, and Makram considered meeting the man's gaze and stripping him of all his barriers, mental and magical, to see if it would wipe the smug expression from his scarred face. But that would mean revealing his power, and he had been careless enough already. He doubted the Grand Vizier would be anywhere near as discreet as the Sultana.

"I might warn you, Agassi," the Grand Vizier said, quietly, "the Sultana has had a lifetime of practice at trying to outmaneuver me, and still she fails. Her mother was the most brilliant woman I have ever known, and her daughter is cast in the same mold. Were I you, I would not waste my effort in an endeavor at which even the best and brightest cannot succeed."

"Mmm," Makram said, the craving to unleash his power and watch the man piss himself in fear was so strong he had to bite the inside of his cheek to refrain. "Consider that she plays a fair game, and I never have. That she abhors violence, and I was raised in it."

"You do not want to make yourself my enemy, Agassi." The Grand Vizier smiled, but the tenseness of his jaw and brow put lie to it. "I control the Council. And trust me when I tell you that though her charms are many, she will betray you at the first opportunity she sees to attain what she wants." His eyes glittered quite literally with fire, its flames lashing against the confines of his irises. The heat of his power enveloped them, making sweat bloom across Makram's skin. He had never known a fire mage that was not a bully.

"And what is it she wants?"

"Her father's crown."

Makram thought he did an admirable job of hiding his surprise. "Thank you for the advice, Grand Vizier, but I am here to make allies, not enemies."

"Choose both very carefully, Agassi," he said, as he turned and limped away.

"He and your brother would get along well," Tareck said.

Makram frowned. His brother was a fire mage through and through. A bully, temperamental, often unwilling to listen to others. Makram had always forgiven his flaws, they were brothers after all, and no one was perfect. They were things that could be fixed, that might settle out of him with age.

That he only just realized his brother had more in common with the Grand Vizier, who Makram disliked, than with the Sultana, whom Makram admired, troubled him. He and his brother had always butted heads, trying to push Sarkum in different directions, trying to win a battle of wills and steer the other.

But the Sultana…they had butted heads, but at least they were pulling in the same direction. In fact there had been moments, when she had followed his line of thought before he'd even spoken, that had been perfect, harmonious confluence.

"Explain to me how we're going to capture a palace the size of a small city with seven men. I am breathless with anticipation," Tareck said, after Makram had stared pensively in the direction the Sultana had gone for far too long.

"You read Ediz Rahal's book."

"Fifteen Turns ago. Is it going to help us?"

Makram clicked his tongue in admonishment. "What point is there in reading books if you don't bother to remember what's in them?" In all fairness, he'd read the book several times since it was first assigned for them to study. He admired the man's tactics, his brashness, his ability to turn poor situations to his favor; that when necessary, he was perfectly willing to cheat. Which was exactly how he took the palace during the Battle of Narfour.

"That day we observed the guild audience, you remember the prisoner they brought up from the Cliffs?"

"I do." Tareck shuddered.

"They brought him up the night before because it is a long trek to the palace from the Cliffs," Makram said. "That means I know something they do not."

Eleven

SAMIRA WALKED BRISKLY IN front of Makram and Tareck, leading them into a section of the palace Makram had yet to see. They were in the western half that sat on the edge of the cliff that ran the length of the palace and beyond, where the prisons, unimaginatively called the Cliffs, were dug into the rockface below the palace. Samira led them to the end of a hall and arched doors inlaid with mother of pearl in spirals representing the Wheel.

The doors opened to a vast circular room, the interior of one of the domes. Books hid the walls from view all the way to the dome, whose verdigris showed its age. Makram suspected it predated the Sundering, like most of the palace. A narrow wooden balcony ran the circumference of the room above them, and ladders were placed intermittently on both the lower level and the balcony, to allow access to the shelves and innumerable books.

The Sultana had said the library was nearly lost, many books burned. He wondered how there could possibly have been more books than there already were. Sarkum's royal and academic libraries seemed like small personal collections in comparison.

Opposite from the entrance, a row of arched windows surrounded a matching door, all set in glass, and the doors thrown open to the setting sun. The sea was visible, steely and darkening, the sun a smudge of ochre across the horizon. A stone balcony jutted away, hovering over the cliffs below it.

Makram followed Samira to the far side of the room. Benches were tucked between each set of shelves and in front of each one or two bookstands. These were not tables, but wooden slats jointed together to form an X, meant to cradle a single open book. The one Samira stopped in front of had several books open and laid on top of each other. A stack of books leaned precariously on the floor beside it, another book lay on the bench, pages of notes beside it.

"You may wait here. She will return shortly, please help yourself to the coffee and food." She held a hand open toward a central table where trays were laid with both.

"Thank you," Makram said as Samira bowed. He sat on the bench in front of the stand as she left. Tareck stopped at the table and examined the tray of food. He selected a fried patty of falafel and made an exclamation of appreciation as he took a bite. Makram began lifting the books from the pile, examining their covers and interiors for titles.

"What are you looking for?" Tareck asked as he approached.

"Nothing," Makram said. He wanted insight, anything that would tell him more about her. He could pretend it was to know his potential ally better, but Makram had never been very good at pretending.

Tareck grunted noncommittally and picked up a book from the cradle.

The books stacked on the floor were an odd assortment that had nothing to do with each other. The first three were small, bound in goatskin, their titles inked by hand on the inside pages. Law books, all for the Tamar Sultanate, the Wheel depicted within their pages only encompassing four Houses. He set them aside.

The one beneath them was older, covered in aged, cracking leather, a gold-embossed, six-spoked Wheel on the front cover. He opened it carefully and flinched when the age-weakened spine gave a little snap. This one held not just laws, but cases studied under each, which were used to justify the laws in every chapter. This was a book that predated the Sundering, as the complete depiction of the Wheel indicated.

The Grand Vizier had said she wanted her father's crown. Was that why she was studying law? Makram set the old laws with the new then reached for the next book. He had no idea what its stiff, black cover was made from, but when he opened it there was no title or author. It was a personal journal of some sort. He read a few paragraphs in the middle, and his brows drew down.

"...it has been our experience that in every case in which a Veritor liberally utilizes their power, their mind grows weaker."

"Makram," Tareck said. Makram shook his head and kept reading.

"The boundary between their minds and those of the mages they confess begins to erode, so memories intermingle. In extreme cases, the Veritor will switch from mind to mind as the madness progresses, the memories becoming indistinguishable from their own."

He flipped a few more pages, read passages that grew more troubling. Veritors who lost control of their powers, who became other people, and the more depraved the minds they had opened, the worse their decline. Some became lost in the memories of murderers, of madmen.

Makram set the book down hastily and wiped his hands on his caftan. This was what was happening to the Sultan. She was studying her father's decline. Magic always had a price, and in this case it was high.

"Makram," Tareck said again, holding a book down to him, "look."

Makram took one last glance at the black journal, then took the book Tareck held out. The cover was deep blue, supple, and had a buckle to close it, which Tareck had opened.

"What is it?" Makram flipped it open. There was no title, only an illumination, rendered in all the colors of the Wheel, depicting the Wheel itself in shining gold. He wanted to touch the extraordinary painting, but did not, turning the page instead.

"The evolution of Houses," Makram read without waiting for Tareck to answer, "and the turning of the Wheel, are a misunderstood—why am I reading this?" He squinted up at Tareck. Old religious texts bored him to mutinous fury and Tareck knew it.

Tareck took it from him and flipped through thick sections until he found the place he wanted, marked by a loose page of notes, and handed it back to him. The first thing that caught Makram's eye were the handwritten notes. He exhaled as weight slid into his belly. He knew that writing, had read it, repeatedly, noted the particulars of the hand, the perfect spacing, because it was so unlike his own, so unlike his brother's. The handwriting of someone careful, thoughtful, and reasoned.

The Sultan hadn't written to his brother about an alliance. His daughter had. It made sense, in context with the black journal, that she would have to. Did her father support her in wanting to take the throne under her own power and not a husband's? Both her Council and Sarkum's were split on the idea of alliance, and Makram suspected the Grand Vizier had more influence in the Tamar Council than even the Sultan, especially with his erratic moods and failing mind. And though he thought she should have influence in the Council, based solely on what he had seen of her, the truth was she did not have much. How did she hope to win them over?

He read the notes.

Wheel turns from dawn to dusk.

What is a focus? These were her musings. Apparently she was a student of religion as well as law. If he could just bottle a fraction of her drive for knowledge and give it to his brother…

The notes went on, texts she wanted to locate, some of whose titles he recognized because they were in the libraries in Al-Nimas. No wonder she wanted to combine their assets. Perhaps if he convinced her to come with him to Al-Nimas to speak with his brother, he could gift her a book as thanks.

"What is she studying this for?" Makram rifled the pages, trying to find more of her notes, consumed by the desire for more glimpses into her thoughts, into her mind. He wanted to know who she was beneath the armor of magic and composure. He wanted to know what she cared about, so he could make her look at him again as she had in the stables the previous day.

"Would you look at the book?" Tareck tapped the page impatiently.

Makram set her notes down and stood, taking the tome from Tareck. On the left, another illumination had been painted, the facing page a parable told in the cryptic poetry common before the formation of the Old Sultanate. The painting was an interesting portrayal of the Wheel. Instead of the typical Wheel with ornate spokes, this one was comprised of faceless figures, one for each spoke or House, walking around what appeared to be the sun to represent the Turning. The figures were each painted in halves, with two colors. The First House figure was white on the left half, and turquoise on the right. The Second, turquoise on the left, and green on the right. Makram's eyes instinctively focused on the Sixth House. Black on the left, white on the right.

"I've never seen mages depicted as broken between Houses," he mused.

Mages were born into a single House. They did not cross over, did not share powers from the Houses that preceded or followed. An air mage had First House abilities and nothing more. And Houses bred true. Air mages bred air mages, and parents of differing houses had children of one or the other, not children that were half of each.

"Not just mages. Chara'a. The Circle of Chara'a. Did you read it?"

The Circle. Before the Sundering, the Old Sultanate had been ruled by a Sultan, but governed by a Circle of the most powerful mages, Chara'a. Chara'a were the exception to the "Houses bred true" rule. There was always a chance, a very slim, perfectly random chance, that a child of two parents in the same House was born of the next House. That child was always a Charah.

Aval mages were first tier, needed words or movement to cast their litany of weak, short-lived spells. Deval were the next, who could incorporate sigils into their casting to hold their power or amplify it, expanding their capabilities. Sival, like the Sultana and the Grand Vizier, could cast a variety of complicated workings, and used their internal energy as their currency, their intention as their spell. But

Chara'a could use any of those methods, as well as channel the energy of others to fuel workings of enormous complexity and power.

Makram was a Sixth House mage born to parents of the Fifth House. He was the first Charah, that he knew of, born since the Sundering. His power was known in Al-Nimas, it was impossible to keep such a secret. It was, however, never spoken of directly. Perhaps in another time the birth of a Charah might have been celebrated, but that was not true of Makram's birth. His parents had pretended he did not have magic, had shipped him off to train as a soldier as soon as he could lift a sword.

"This book suggests that Chara'a are the evolution of the Houses, Makram. That you are not just a destruction mage, but the bridge between Houses—see how these figures bridge three Houses? The preceding, the birth House, and the following House? You bridge the Fifth, Sixth, and First Houses."

"This is interesting," Makram said. "But ultimately useless." He did not want to discuss his power. Outside of battle, it was a liability.

"This is important," Tareck demanded. "Here, this. Look at what she wrote." He tapped the description on the right-hand page.

It is believed Chara'a of each House are born to the same generation.

Makram sighed, glaring at Tareck. Tareck swiped her page of notes and shook it in Makram's face. He snatched it back and continued reading.

References Emer Saban's books on the interplay of the Houses. Copy in Al-Nimas?

"Tareck." Makram closed the book, but Tareck shoved his hand in between and flipped it open again.

"This." He pointed to the parable, the poem, which she had transcribed onto her notes. Scribbled in the margin of her page, it read:

Find the First House Charah to start the turning of the Wheel, to stand the Circle.

Makram's impatience evaporated. He read the words again.

Something in him opened up, shifted, and began reaching, searching. It was subtle, a change in his magic, a twist that made him feel unsettled, energetic, pulled. The feeling was so faint that he lost his hold on it when he considered the ramifications of what he was reading.

"I thought she just wanted to bring the Sixth House back to Tamar. To balance the Wheel."

"No," Tareck said, staring fiercely at Makram, "she wants to stand the Circle. You have to help her."

"I can help her by doing what I said I would. I cannot help her with this, how would I explain that to Kinus? Tell him I am going to abandon him to come here and play Circle mage to an old enemy?"

"Damn Kinus. This is more important and you know it. If she stands the Circle it will restore power to the Wheel, to Sarkum, Tamar, and beyond."

"Tareck." Makram closed the book and set it on the bench. "Even if I wanted to help her with this, I cannot. Kinus needs me. And we need to spend our energy on this exercise, or there will be no alliance and certainly no Circle of Chara'a."

"You are a prince of Sarkum, a Rahal. You are a Charah. You are not just Kinus' obedient sword and I am tired—"

"Put this back just as you found it."

It was not the first time Tareck had erupted into the rant. Makram used to argue with him, with Elder Attiyeh, with all of them who preferred the idea of him as ruler to his brother. They smelled war, and they thought a soldier would make a better ruler than the man raised for the position. They wanted a mage with more power to lead them.

Tareck tugged the book out of Makram's grasp and replaced it, then took another bite of falafel, chewing it vigorously, as if that would make a point.

Makram turned his mind from revelations and questions by sorting through the remaining books on the stand. There was no way to make every man, woman, and child happy. A ruler was popular with some, a tyrant to others. Those who had what they wanted rarely wanted to change anything, and those who did not feel they had their share were certain someone else would be better.

It was never better, only different. And Makram was not made for the palace. He was made for war, by blood, by magic, by birth.

He picked up a few more pages of notes laid on the bench in front of the bookstand. She was studying so many things, so many subjects, holding the reins of too many horses, as the Odokan often said.

Regents: Sultan Haytham Sabri's eldest stood as Regent, the notes read.

Makram felt the Sultana's approach like a cool breeze and looked up as she arrived at his side and plucked the papers from his hand.

"Good evening, Sultana," he said, smiling. He was determined they would not argue. They would talk like allies. And he would not think about how she had looked at him, or how she was the perfect height to fit neatly beneath his chin if he held her.

Twelve

"DO YOU NOT EVER think before you act? Before you speak?" Naime demanded, dropping all facade of composure or calm. He looked at his empty hand, at the papers she brandished at him, and turned toward her, brow furrowing. "Or have you come only to ruin any chance at all at alliance?" She nearly crumpled the pages he had been holding in her fist. Tareck stood near the bench, halfway through eating a falafel, chewing methodically as he glanced from her to the Agassi.

"Leave us," Naime said to him, and when he obeyed, she regarded the Agassi again. He flinched when the doors closed with a thump. "This is a game to you, or you are a fool. You have pitted the lives and welfare of every person in Tamar and Sarkum in a game of ego."

He shook his head, lifted a hand as if to brush it over his hair and then dropped it. "That is not—"

"Ediz Rahal knew the palace inside and out, Agassi. He lived here, before the war. The Rahal family had served as Grand Vizier to the Sabri Sultanate for generations before the war. You have been here only days. You cannot replicate what he did with hundreds of men with only seven."

"You have no idea what I can do. You could trust me, instead of attacking everything I do at any given moment." He was managing a very calm voice, and Naime resented his calm when she felt nothing but frustration.

"Trust you?" she scoffed. "I have spent the last full Cycle planning this alliance, and you just gambled it away on a whim and half-conceived idea!" Wind stirred her hair, whipping some of the loose strands against her face. She shoved her power down, glaring at him.

"I did not." He held a hand toward the doors, facing her fully, forceful but not aggressive. "You know just as well as I that your Grand Vizier had them stalled. Nothing was moving forward. You would prefer I had done nothing and let them refuse to even consider an alliance? I can do this." He tapped his chest and lowered his hand again.

He wasn't wrong. She had felt the Council slipping from her grasp. His brashness irritated her, but there had been little hope of salvaging the chance at negotiation with reason and discourse, not with Kadir blocking her at every turn. If the Agassi hadn't stepped forward and caught their interest with his insane suggestion, he would be on his way back to Sarkum without any hope at all, and she would be standing in front of a betrothal circle. She owed him thanks, and she didn't want to thank him or owe him anything.

"Plans go awry. Sometimes you have to take what you want. Sometimes"—he lifted a shoulder—"you have to cheat."

Naime pressed her fingers between her brows, where a headache was beginning to throb. Makram shifted, and his hands moved up, then fell to his sides.

"If you win a sparring match by attacking an opponent's back, have you won?" she asked. Had he intended to reach to her? They were standing so close, her desperate irritation was not enough to erase the awareness from her thoughts.

"Of course not. But this is not play-fighting, this is the fate of all the Wheel's mages." His hand moved toward his hip. Reaching for a sword that was not there. A movement of habit.

"And in real battle, would you trust someone who had attained their position by cheating? Would you follow them?"

"I would follow you," he said. Suspicion blossomed at the bald, ardent declaration. Was he trying to curry favor? Make up for calling her spineless when they had argued in the stables?

She dismissed him with a shake of her head. "No you wouldn't."

"No?" he said with exaggerated surprise. "You know me better than I know myself. Why wouldn't I, then?"

"I am beautiful, which makes men mistake me for a conquest."

Naime watched his face for his reaction. His jet brows rose and then fell, his dark gaze darting from hers to her mouth and back. His lips parted to speak, an expression of denial telling her just as much as his words would have. Then he clenched his jaw.

"Then they mistake me for an adversary because I am intelligent. When I rise up they are angered, because they believe I contrived to push them down. Men do not follow women, no matter what their ardor might trick them into believing for the moment."

She did not think it was *his* ardor that was going to be especially troublesome. He had been unmoved by her blatant staring the day before, and she was still confused and flustered by it.

"It does not sound to me like you know very many men at all," he said, his eyes flashing anger. "The Grand Vizier told me you take after your mother."

Naime stood silent as answer.

"Did your father treat her that way?"

"No. He worshiped her." Loved her, adored her, thought of her as his equal.

"That is the example I think you should judge men by. The Grand Vizier and his minions are no better examples of rational men than the worst of court gossips and schemers are of women." The tone of his voice caught her off guard, the offense in it, making her consider his words more carefully.

Naime lifted her eyes to his, searching his expression for truth, and when she found it, felt unmoored. Of course he was right. Bashir Ayan was an honorable man, and he followed her, not because he wanted her or wanted to best her. But because he was loyal. There were good men in the Council. Sometimes she forgot, because it was so difficult to see past Kadir and his manipulations.

"Forgive me," she said. "We needn't speak about these things any longer. They have no bearing on our current problem."

"It is not a problem. I have a plan," he said jovially. Except when she angered him by insulting him, he seemed perpetually in a playful mood. It was disarming, and she wondered if that was the entire point of the act.

"What is your plan?" she asked, her temper cooling marginally.

He said nothing, only gave his head a slow shake, an incremental smile curving his lips.

"Are you mocking me?"

He sighed, brushing his palm over his hair. "I cannot tell you my plan, Sultana, because it will not work if anyone else knows." He dropped his hands to his sides. "You *can* trust me. I want this alliance as much as you do."

Right now she needed him and his mysterious plan, and she despised it. She did not care for needing anyone. Adding elements she could not control put her at a great disadvantage.

"I hardly know you. Most of our interactions have not inspired trust, yet you want me to trust you alone with something vital to my people. What proof do I have that you are worthy of that?"

Before he could answer, a whisper of magic brushed across her skin, as if she had just stepped through an unexpected spider web. Its strands wove through the air like wisps of breeze. A listening spell. She held up her hand then touched a finger to her lips. His brow furrowed.

"Mistress Banu," Naime said, her temper rearing up again, "tell your master that if he wishes to know what the Agassi and I are discussing, he is welcome to join us. Release this spell, or I will have you in the Cliffs for espionage."

Naime gripped the front of her caftan until the spell faded away. "Clumsy harlot," she snarled under her breath. The Agassi snorted a laugh, staring at her with wide eyes.

Kadir employed a number of capable mages whose loyalty could be bought with coin and threats, but the two who had proved Naime's bane were Mahir, his steward and an earth mage, and Banu, a Deval of the First House with a singular talent for listening spells.

"Every time I think I begin to understand you, you show me something new," the Agassi said. Naime eyed him, trying to determine whether he was complimenting or insulting.

"The Grand Vizier will be here shortly, so if you have something to say that you wish for only me to hear, I suggest you do so now. You could begin by answering the question—why should I trust you?"

"You have a secret of mine, Sultana, that I have been forced to trust you with." The suggestion of a smile that curved his mouth was not the true, teasing smile she had seen before. This one held tension.

Naime sighed, picking at the embroidery on her cuff. "Hardly. It is in my interest as well that no one knows. It would be difficult to negotiate terms with someone who is being pursued with torches."

He snorted again, his eyes crinkling at the corners as his smile became true, making her aware of how deeply etched those lines were on a young face. Someone who laughed frequently. It made her realize how infrequently she had laughed since her father's illness began to take root, since her mother had died. Sadness erupted inside her, again, and she buried it, again.

"Do you know," he said idly, bending to retrieve the small, black journal written ages ago by three physicians studying Veritors, "that grief is mine? The Sixth House owns it the way the Fifth owns passion. I can feel it in others." He handed her the book, and Naime hugged it against her chest. "I sense it in you"—he brushed a hand through the air in front of her—"but you aren't grieving. You aren't allowing yourself to."

"How can I?" Her throat tightened, everything he spoke of threatening to well up out of her control. Acknowledging it would give it life, freedom, something she could not do.

"Yes," he said, regretfully, "how can you? Your father is deteriorating, leaving you alone, and you are trying to hold his sultanate together, even strengthen it. Yet there are enemies every direction you turn."

"He has secrets that could ruin everything," she confessed. Secrets that would put her in danger, make her hold on the throne even more tenuous. She was so afraid for anyone to use her father's illness against them both that she felt cut off from her grief. As if she could not risk mourning the loss of the man she loved so dearly. It was a knife twisting in her heart that she could neither reach for nor remove.

Naime chanced a look at the Agassi's eyes. There was nothing but truth in them, simple, human sympathy. And a swirl of midnight magic that courted her, coaxed her open, whispered, *break*.

She sucked in a breath, her eyes burning. "Stop," she ordered, taking back control of herself. Whether he was using magic to break her apart or she had not realized how fragile she was did not matter. She could not bear his recognition. His face softened.

"I am not an enemy. I am not here to trick you or hurt you. I swear it." He tipped his head back to look at the dome above them. "You and I"—his voice deepened because of the awkward angle—"we like things to go our way. Yes, we have argued, but we can work together, because we share a goal." He leveled his gaze at her again. "Not conflict, harmony."

Naime's fingers tightened on the book and she swallowed. Why did those words make her feel desperate? She wanted that. An ally. Someone who wanted what she did, someone who could help pull in the same direction.

A slow, teasing grin spread over his mouth again.

"I don't even mind if all they see is you, and I simply help in the background." He lifted one shoulder as if he had not just offered something no other man she knew would have. "I'm just a soldier after all. You are the queen."

"I do not take credit for the efforts of others. And I am not a queen yet."

"You are something, or you are not. A title that someone else bestows upon you does not make it more or less true. You," he said, "are a queen as I had never dared to hope might exist."

"Praise is cheap." She set the black journal on the table, warmed by and suspicious of his compliment.

"Mine isn't," he said. "It is earned. This cost one public tongue lashing against a prince, and two incidents in which you verbally demolished opponents of your ideas."

She suppressed a smile and lifted an eyebrow instead. "I will give you credit, you may be the first man to compliment me for something other than my beauty."

"I will happily compliment that as well, at no cost, but I think we both know that would be a waste of breath," he said, his eyes slipping over her face then away.

"Yes." Though, she might like to know that he found her as magnetic as she found him. A thread of awareness swept through her magic, an instant before Kadir traipsed through the library doors.

"Good afternoon, Grand Vizier," Naime said. He bowed, glancing from one to the other. She had not realized how at ease she was in the Agassi's company until Kadir entered the room and sucked the air and calm from it.

"Efendim, I must insist that the two of you not spend time alone together like this, unescorted and hiding away in secret corners."

"The library is hardly a secret corner, Grand Vizier," the Agassi said. Naime wished they were not standing so close, as if to provide proof of Kadir's accusations. "And we are not alone, there are guards and half a dozen attendants just outside the doors. Did you not see them on your way in?"

Kadir's lip curled. "You are disrespectful of the Sultana's reputation, Agassi. I would hope you would be more interested in maintaining people's good opinion of the Sultan's daughter."

"That is quite enough," Naime cut in. "I am unable to play games today, Grand Vizier. All three of us know the only reason you care who I spend time with is because you do not wish me to assist the Agassi in his endeavor. We have spoken of nothing more covert than my father's health, as I am certain your pet air mage can attest to."

Kadir pressed a hand to his chest. "I resent the implication—"

"You think I cannot feel a listening spell? You think I do not know she is yours? If it were your son instead of the Agassi, you would be perfectly happy to have my reputation ruined by hiding away in corners. Let us stop pretending, shall we? If you wish to sit in here to ensure I do not hand the Agassi the keys to the Morning Gate, then please feel free to do so." She could not remember the last time she had snapped at him in such a manner, and his eyes were wide with surprise.

"Sultana, you are to be betrothed. You cannot risk any rumors that you have been sullied."

Bile rose in her throat, and the Agassi made a wordless sound of warning.

"How dare you speak of such things in front of a stranger and guest of the Sultan's." Fury whipped her power into a cyclone inside her. "You will *never* speak to me, or of me, like that again."

"Sultana," Kadir said, smiling as he did when he believed he was in command of a situation. "Your reputation is the Sultan's."

"Get out," Naime ordered. He reeled as if she had struck him. "Get out of my sight. And if I feel your mage put another listening spell on me, this game between you and I is over. I will put her in the Cliffs along with you for the rest of your miserable lives."

Heat burst around them. "You wouldn't dare."

Naime scoffed. "I am not my cousin. Do not think your temper intimidates me. Fire will not burn without air, and your magic is impotent in the face of mine."

"You arrogant little girl," Kadir snarled.

"Shall I escort you to the door, Grand Vizier?" the Agassi said, in a friendly tone that somehow still raised the hair on the back of Naime's neck. Kadir she understood. He would never attack her openly, risk losing his popularity by harming her, though he might flaunt his power. The Agassi…she knew neither the extent of his power nor the disposition of his temper.

She found his gaze fixed on Kadir the way an eagle's fixed on a rodent. "I wouldn't want you to lose your way." The Agassi smiled, threat overt in every tense muscle and slowly spoken word.

Kadir spun and left, as fast as his limp would allow.

Both of them stared after him. The moment was dominated by the thunderous pounding of Naime's heart. Her hands shook. She mentally tallied all the ways her outburst might cost her, what she needed to do to mitigate the effects.

"I did not think it was possible to admire you more."

His whispered compliment sank over her skin and into her, like the heat of a fire, and remained burning in her cheeks. Naime looked at him. His gaze stayed fixed on the doors for a moment longer before sliding to hers.

Night coiled in his irises, pulsing outward in time with what she suspected was his heartbeat. What would his magic look like, fully unleashed? Would it be terrifying? Her breath stilled, and he smiled sadly, glancing down at his hands, which he flexed open from fists as he lifted his gaze to the door once more.

"Do not admire me most when I lose control," she said, irritated that she had lost her temper. "Thank you for that"—she gestured at the doors—"and for stepping in during the Council." She pushed power through her skin to check her reaction to Kadir. "I am not accustomed to help and can be ungracious about it when it is offered." But it had been very nice. To have an ally, even if only for a moment.

"I maintain hope we might find our common ground and become friends," he said, tentatively.

"I would like that, Agassi." She smiled.

"Makram," he said. "Call me Makram, when it is appropriate."

Naime gripped handfuls of her caftan, trying to weigh the ramifications of such an invitation, and whether it would put her at a disadvantage. The only people she called by given name were Ihsan, and her attendants.

"It gives me no power over you if you call me by my name," he said, amused.

"I cannot. It is too familiar, and the Grand Vizier was not completely wrong about allowing rumors to spread."

He shifted his weight, folding his arms over his chest. "You do not have to play the games they force you to play, not with me. I will be a real person with you, and you can be a real person with me. But first you have to make me a person, and not an obstacle," he said. "Call me by my name."

"I cannot allow you to call me by mine." Though she decided she would like it if he did. The sincerity of his proclamation made her believe him.

He dipped his head. "As you wish."

She hesitated, a foreboding sense of giving away too much rooting her in place.

"If you do not wish to…"

"I do," she said, and was surprised by her own vehemence. "I do wish to." But what would it do? She had already discovered she had a weakness for the man. If they became familiar, would she only become more foolish for it? Take more liberties than just looking?

While his motivations for saying it were misplaced, Kadir was not wrong about Naime's reputation.

Makram grinned, raising his black brows. "I did not anticipate it would be so difficult for you. Don't worry, with practice it will come more easily."

"It isn't hard," she said too quickly, and tried to make herself end it with his name and failed.

Now he chuckled, clasping his hands behind his back.

"Mak…ram," he said, forming the syllables with exaggeration as he leaned toward her. His eyes were crinkled at the corners with his amusement and his mouth curved in a smile. Her thoughts staggered, tripping and tangling, upset by the wicked warmth of his voice, the proximity of him, and her inability to turn her stare from the movement of his lips. She liked his smile, the way it seemed to hint he was always holding back something else, something satirical.

"You are such a child," she managed, "Makram." She had not meant to say his name with a breathy sigh, nor let him realize she was staring at his mouth. Nor did she mean to let her thoughts wander to what it might be like to be kissed by someone. Someone she was drawn to, someone who was not just kissing her for the benefit of others, as she suspected any future husband might.

Would he want to kiss her?

"No," he said, his voice taking on a purr that did not aid her in the least, "I am a man."

"I meant figuratively." Naime tried not to think of him, with half his clothes gone as he had been in the arena, his golden skin, moving with the strength and grace of a fighter. She failed. She was well aware he was a man.

"I know what you meant," he said. His dark, dark gaze slipped from hers, to her mouth, then lower, and back, quickly. His jaw tightened, and he straightened, turning his head away. "Don't do that."

"What?" Naime felt as if she snapped awake.

"Don't." He grimaced, swiping a hand over his face. "Just don't look at me like that."

"I wasn't…" She flushed. "It's your fault."

"See? You were looking," he said, and Naime marveled at the absurd turn of the conversation.

"You could not have been closer, where else was I supposed to look?"

"I could have been closer," he said, almost like a threat. His lips pressed together when her eyebrows rose, and he rolled his eyes toward the ceiling. "Unbelievable," he breathed. "I am not a babbling simpleton, despite evidence to the contrary."

"I have never thought you were," Naime said, confused.

"You make me feel like one." He stepped away from her and to the high table, where coffee and food were laid out. He poured a cup.

"I don't intend to," she said. He gave her the demitasse of coffee he'd poured before preparing a second.

"I know that," he said, adding a curse under his breath. He gulped his coffee in one tip of the cup. Naime smiled.

"I can call for something stronger, if you're feeling the need." She sipped at her own cup.

He laughed a little. "I don't think that would benefit me."

"So." Naime set her cup down in its saucer, deciding a change of subject was desperately needed. "You will not tell me your plan. What do you need from me?"

His initial glance at her was startled, as if he thought she were joking. Then he turned to the table, setting his cup carefully on its surface, and shook his head.

"I am sorry to say, there is nothing for you to do but wait."

"If we are to be allies, you do not have to accomplish this by yourself." She touched her fingers to his arm. It felt easy, to connect with him this way. Though once she touched him she realized how odd it might seem, how she could not think of another man she had ever reached out to in such a way, besides those in her family. That was the danger of names. They were more effective at removing barriers than even destruction magic.

He reacted to her touch by not reacting at all. She could tell he forced himself not to look, not to move, his body tense, his eyes narrowed. Naime wondered if she'd offended him, and pulled her hand back, but he spun, catching her wrist. He laid his thumb against her palm, holding her hand up between them.

"I am accustomed to being left to my own devices," he said. "We will both need to adjust to this, yes? To being allies?"

Naime nodded mutely. His thumb circled lightly against her palm. Some of the simple easiness of his presence in her space left. In its place, expectant tension made her hyperaware of how their spaces interconnected, where their skin met, the roughness of his calloused thumb against skin that was unexpectedly tender and sensitive, how much distance there was between every part of her and every part of him. There was a pull she had not perceived before, as if the most natural thing in the world would be to step closer.

"There is one thing," he said, his voice taking on the same purr it had earlier. Naime felt too vulnerable without the shield of irritation she had kept between them before. Without something to focus on that took her mind from the fact he was attractive, that when given the opportunity, he was kind and playful.

"What?" Naime was appalled at the weakness of her own voice.

"When this is over, I would like to call you by name."

"That doesn't seem like a very good idea." She was so tempted to lean closer to him.

"No, I don't think it is," he agreed. But she wanted that, to hear him say her name, like they were friends. She had so few. In his eyes, void and oblivion leached outward in inky tendrils from his pupils.

There was so much she wanted to know about him. About his magic. About Sarkum.

"If you win, I will agree. But also," she said, "you will tell me everything I want to know about your magic." She twisted her hand gently free of his grip and reached for his cheek, drawn to and fascinated by the manifestation of his power. She stopped before she touched him, the spell broken by the suspicion that passed over his face.

"No, your name is in exchange for me winning," he said. "If you want to know about my magic, then you have to offer something of equal value." He turned his face a fraction, as if he meant to move it against her outstretched fingers, but did not.

"I am trusting you with all my dreams for the future. You don't think you can trust me with this?"

"Is your name worth that much?" he asked as she lowered her hand to her side.

"Only you can decide that." She curled her hands in her caftan to prevent herself reaching for him again.

"Well," he said, "I will have plenty of time to consider it as I prepare for this. Which reminds me that I need something else." He scooped a handful of almonds from a plate and shook them in his fist.

Naime raised her eyebrows in question. "It is yours, for your magic."

He grinned, and tipped his head in agreement.

"Rope." He tossed a few of the almonds into his mouth. "And grappling hooks."

THIRTEEN

THE EVENING BEFORE THE designated day, Makram stood in the foyer of the palace entrance, waiting for the Sultana to arrive. Most of the Viziers who had attended the Council meeting had gathered on the stairs outside, prepared to deliver the rules of the engagement before sending him on his merry way. Tareck and his men were already near the Morning Gate, waiting with the horses.

His sword was on his saddle, but he would have liked it now, to have something to do with his hands. He'd managed to avoid her the last two days, under the auspices of preparing for the exercise. Makram wanted to see her, but he wasn't a fool. He had obviously stepped over an internal line at some point, the one he feared, the razor edge between admiration and attraction.

The Grand Vizier limped into the foyer, and Makram wished more fervently for his sword.

"Good evening, Agassi," he said as he bowed. Makram nodded. "I look forward with great anticipation to the conclusion of this farce."

"Is it a farce because it was not your idea, or because you know I am going to succeed?" Makram asked, his voice dull, his gaze fixed past Kadir on the hall he expected her to appear from.

"Perhaps you have time for such frivolity, but as a governor, I have far too much work to do to waste my time with nonsense like this."

It sounded so much like something Kinus would say that Makram had to pause to find words. They were not that alike, were they? Makram shook off the concern.

"Do you? I seem to see a great deal of you for someone who is preoccupied with work." He smiled. Kadir's brows snapped together.

Makram was distracted from him by the Sultana's arrival. She walked beside her father, her arm linked through his, and when she saw Makram she smiled. It was a real smile, the kind he imagined she might bestow on a friend. Her eyes were bright with it, her expression warm and lovely. Void and stars. His chest constricted; his hands twitched.

Kadir detected his change in mien and turned. The smile disappeared, her gaze flicking to her father instantly to hide that she had been looking at Makram. He felt robbed, and tried not to glower when the Grand Vizier focused a predatory smile on him.

"She is not for you, *Agassi*," he hissed, fire in his voice and its heat in the air around them. "Do not even begin to think that Tamar will allow its only heir to be given away to Sarkum trash."

"No? Only Tamar trash?" Makram said. "Spare me your threats and speeches, please." That he had let his attraction be so obvious to someone so vile was infuriating enough. He would not also endure a lecture that told him nothing he didn't already know. "Whatever you think you saw has nothing to do with an alliance."

"I think it has everything to do with an alliance, and I will see you mounted on a pike on the Engeli before I allow it."

"I'd like to see you try that, Grand Vizier." Only by a choking grasp on his will did Makram hold his temper and his magic back, prevent Kadir from seeing how impotent his threat was.

When the Sultana reached them her gaze traveled over him, warning him. It made him realize how tense his body was, and he forced it to relax.

"Agassi, Grand Vizier." Her gaze remained fixed on Makram with concern. She extracted her arm from her father's and bowed. Makram gave a deeper one to her father, who examined him. The Grand Vizier followed suit.

"Behram," the Sultan said, reaching to clutch the Grand Vizier's shoulder, "you look as if you just swallowed purge oil." He steered him away, toward the doors. Makram watched them go with some confusion.

"He seems well today," he said quietly.

"For now. I don't intend for him to wait in the Council Hall tomorrow, I am afraid he won't remember it is a game, and not real." Her cool tone, her voice like winter sun and wind, soothed away his anger and he took a deep breath. He thought of offering to escort her outside, then decided against it. He shouldn't allow them to touch. Attraction was a dangerous spark that could turn the most innocent of things into the kindling of a fire, and then the fuel of a blaze.

Of course, the Wheel seemed to turn especially fast toward disaster for him. She slipped her hand around his arm and held his bicep. Awareness bolted through him as it had in the library, of proximity and potential. Her hand slid down to the crook of his elbow as he bent his arm up and all his worry proved true. The common, formal touch only served to set his mind to whirling, wondering things it should not, encouraging his body that she meant more than she did by it.

"Are you going to tell me why you looked like murder incarnate when I arrived?"

"I'm going to pretend that was a compliment," he said. "And I will only say that your Grand Vizier is more bold to me than he dares to be to you."

"Proof that he is more fallible than he would like us to believe."

"No." Makram liked that she said *us*. "I think he knows which of us is more dangerous, and censors himself."

"That is an attempt at flattery," she said in quiet disapproval.

"It is truth. I'll just kill him. You'll ruin him. That is a man who would rather be dead than disgraced."

"What an astute observer you are." The hint of a smile curved her mouth. He'd already failed once at preventing himself thoughts of kissing her. Now he failed again, ensnared by her smile. He could kiss her there, on that little curve at the corner, it would be a very good place to start.

"You're staring," she mouthed as her smile faded. He realized they had just been standing there looking at each other, her arm in his. He might as well be following her about drooling like a starved half-wit for everyone to see.

Makram started for the doors. "I didn't mean to."

"No?" she asked. They passed through the doors and onto the broad half-circle of the landing, the Viziers arrayed below them on the stairs. She pulled her hand away.

Yavuz Pasha stepped forward from the pack of Viziers, to the stair just below Makram and the Sultana. The Grand Vizier stood to Makram's left, with the Sultan.

"We have determined the rules to be as follows," Yavuz Pasha began. "At least four men must make it to the Council Hall. You must be one of the men that arrives."

Makram nodded.

"Commander Ayan and the palace guards will be using practice blades to mitigate chances of real injury, and have distributed the same to your men, along with chalk arrows."

Makram grimaced. Practice blades were notoriously unbalanced, weak, and unreliable. The arrows were terrible, tipped with small, burlap-covered bulbs of powdered chalk. They were meant to explode on impact, but sometimes they simply bounced off a target, and they had short range and were inaccurate.

"A man is killed if he is observed to have been struck a mortal or maiming injury that would, if real, prevent him from continuing to fight. Those who are captured or killed are to remain in place until the exercise is over. Magic may be used, but not to cause lasting harm. You are not to enter the city. Any cheating on either side will result in the other side being declared the victor."

Kadir made a noise of protest, but the Sultan patted him on the back, chuckling to himself.

"You may begin at dawn tomorrow, measured as the first light of the sun over the Kalspire, and must be in the Council Hall and present yourself to the Sultana before the sun sinks completely into the sea. Do you have questions?"

"Only a request," Makram said, clasping his hands behind his back and turning to the Grand Vizier. "When I win, the Grand Vizier will provide my men with enough arak for a proper celebration." He let the words sink in, and added, "A good brew, not the swill they sell in the markets."

Yavuz Pasha laughed, mounting the stairs to stand beside Kadir. "I think that is fair, don't you, my friend?"

Kadir gave a smile that suggested to Makram he might want to avoid any drinks Kadir provided him for the foreseeable future.

"Then, I will see you tomorrow, gentlemen." He started down the stairs and the Viziers parted for him.

"May the Wheel turn in your favor, Agassi," the Sultana said from behind him. He spun back to grin at her.

She raised an eyebrow, her eyes brightening with amusement though she did not smile.

Makram walked down the stairs. Some of the Viziers clapped him on the back as he went. He joined his men at the gate, mounted, and they rode away from the palace.

Just after they passed under the gate a breeze caressed his cheek, and her voice was in his ear. *"If he can cheat, he will."* Her magic flitted against his and then was gone. It was as if she had stood at his side and breathed the words into his ear. A shiver raced over his skin, followed by longing. He shook it off in irritation.

This was good. He'd leave the palace, get away from her, so he could remember what he was, and what he was not. He'd remember the things he could attain. And the things that would forever be barred from him.

FOURTEEN

"I DID *SO* MISS SLEEPING on the ground," Tareck announced as he came to Makram's side. Makram stared at the Kalspire, wondering how literal he had to be to interpret "the first light of the sun over the Kalspire." It was a relatively subjective rule.

"Even by liberal standards the sun isn't up yet," Tareck said when Makram called for the men to prepare. Regardless, he gave the order for the men to present all their weapons for inspection.

"We're just going for a ride, Tareck. Not a word about what we're doing or where we are," Makram ordered as the men circled around them. "There might still be Listeners."

"I'm certain I would feel a listening spell," Tareck protested as he inspected swords and bows, "which I don't." They'd allotted each of the men twenty of the chalk arrows, and Tareck gave them all a brief examination.

Makram glanced up at the peak again as the men went through their checks. Old stories said the Kalspire was the hub around which the Wheel spun, the heart of Tamar. They said there was a fire at the top that never ceased burning, the font of magic. If he succeeded in this game, there might be a day he would see for himself.

The sky beyond the layered, basalt column was fading from black to violet, the color bleeding closer as the sun crept up the far side of the mountains. Dawn was perhaps a candlemark away. They could ride and set up the ropes before light revealed too much.

"Are you going to tell me where we're going?" Tareck asked once he returned.

"Check again," Makram ordered. He had not felt the listening spell that the Sultana had, but Tareck's earth magic would be troubled by even the most skilled air mage's spells. Tareck shook his head.

"The Cliffs," Makram said. "Ediz Rahal used a passage between the Cliffs and the Council Chambers to take the palace during the Sundering War. It was the tunnel they used to bring prisoners to the tribunal."

"That's your plan?" Tareck spat. "You utter madman."

"I told you, if you'd read the book…" Makram shrugged.

"I did read the infernal book. How do you even remember those things? Reading it was like having sand poured into my eyes." Tareck growled. "That book is two centuries old. How do you know the tunnel is still there?"

"I don't." Makram swung into his saddle. "But it's our only chance."

"Don't you think they know about it?"

"No, or they would have used it to move that prisoner to the Council hall the day of the guild audience."

"Do you know where the entrance is?"

"That's what I have an earth mage for," Makram said, "so stop talking and save your energy."

"You're going to send me to an early grave," Tareck groaned.

The Cliffs were a full candlemark's trek from the palace proper, and its guards operated under their own command structure. Commander Ayan's palace guards might be informed of the exercise, but Makram doubted anyone had thought to involve the prison guards in the planning. There was no reason for anyone to suspect Makram would use the prison, and it was too far away to be casually involved in the war game.

Even he could admit this might be the most flawed plan he had ever devised. He had never seen the inside of the Cliffs. He did not know where the tunnel from them to the palace was located. The prison guards were unlikely to be prepared to participate in the exercise, so it stood to reason they *were* likely to be wielding weapons and magic aimed at killing instead of incapacitating.

A flawed plan was still a plan.

They did have a few advantages. The guards had recently undergone a command change, thanks to the Sultana's firing of their captain. That would make them somewhat less organized. Surprise would be his greatest advantage, if they managed to avoid entering in the middle of shift change, when there would be double the number of guards.

"Ready," Tareck said.

Makram pointed west and they broke into a canter. The prison lay west and south of the palace, its only access from the outside a long, narrow stairway cut into the sandstone wall. He wouldn't risk the horses on it, though if given enough time they might be able to navigate the stairs.

They didn't have time, however, because he suspected Commander Ayan would send a scouting party as soon as dawn broke. He also did not want to be stuck halfway down the stairs and within arrow range of the top and bottom. Instead, he intended to drop to the entrance from above.

They reached the cliff as the violet in the eastern sky faded to lavender, and a halo of light rose from the base of the Kalspire. The countdown had begun. Commander Ayan was probably ordering men to find them at this very moment. Though he was likely powerful enough to use a tracking spell to feel them out, the distance was enough to buy time before he pinpointed them. Besides, those were costly spells, and he would want to conserve his energy.

"Set a lookout." Makram dismounted. The stairs down were marked by a large circle of sandstone tiles set into the earth and tall stone pillars to the left and right. Makram marveled at the stairs, visually tracing their path as it switched back and forth across the stone face. The entrance to the Cliffs sat at the bottom, on a ledge that spanned half the length of the cliff itself, three times as deep as the stairs, though tucked back beneath the rock so he could see only the ledge and not the exact placement of the door or gate. The western half of the palace loomed north of them, pale spires and domes blotting out the dawn sky. The sea crashed against the base of the cliff below.

"Ropes," Makram said, pacing the cliff, searching for suitable anchors for their descent. The men didn't need long explanations to understand his intent.

"Here," he said, pointing down one of the smoother portions of the cliff face. It would drop them on the far side of the ledge from the stairs, the least likely place for the entrance to be located. He didn't want to dangle his men in front of a door where they'd be vulnerable to any guards posted outside.

"No anchors," Tareck grunted, casting about.

"We'll have to use two men instead of the hooks."

"And only take five inside?" Tareck shook his head.

"They can join us after." Makram pointed to the stairs. "We'll have cleared the entrance by the time they get down."

"Emre, Musa." Tareck pointed to two of the men and communicated the rest of the order with hand gestures and by shoving them into position. Makram peered over the edge again as the men set themselves and Tareck and the remaining three began knotting the ropes.

He ducked away from the edge when two guards exited from beneath the overhang below and began climbing the stairs. Their voices bounced up the cliffs, and all his men stopped moving, looking to him. Makram pointed away from the edge of the cliff, to get them all out of sight, then pointed five fingers at the top of the stairs. Musa and Emre jumped up to join the other three, and all five gathered around the two pillars, crouching in wait. Tareck went to his saddle and dug through one of the traveling packs, pulling out a linen caftan. He ripped lengths of cloth from it, laying them over his saddle until he was satisfied he had enough.

The two voices grew louder, and Makram lay on his belly and edged himself close enough to the drop-off to see them. The two prison guards had reached the final switchback. Makram lifted his hand to his men to warn them to be ready. He kept it raised as the two men hiked up the stairs, drawing closer. Makram flinched at every sound, afraid they would alert the two. Fighting would definitely be audible to anyone pursuing them, echoed off the palace wall.

The two men reached the place the stairs took a final, ninety-degree turn and left only five steps between them and his men. Makram dropped his hand.

"Good morning," Tareck said from where he stood by the horses, and the prison guards gawked at him in surprise, enough time for Makram's soldiers to ambush them. They were flat on their bellies on the stone landing before Makram had gotten to his feet, and Tareck handed the lengths of cloth to one of the soldiers, to gag the men.

Makram glanced at the sun. It framed the Kalspire completely now, a bright corona around the shadowed spear of rock.

"Put them and the horses over by the trees, as out of sight as you can make them," Makram said. Once that was done Musa and Emre sat side by side a few paces from the cliff edge. Tareck tossed one end of the heavy, rough hemp rope over the edge, and looped the other around the backs of two men. They gripped the rope in gloved hands and set their heels against the ground. They'd lean back into the weight to provide counter as the others dropped down the cliff.

"Doesn't reach," Tareck announced. "We'll have to climb down at the bottom, if it's possible."

"It's too far to jump?" Makram eyed the distance.

"Won't know until we're down there."

"Elders and children first." Makram slapped Tareck on the back. He was only a Turn older than Makram. Tareck grumbled, hooking his bow across his back and unhooking his sword belt. He looped it beneath his quiver and across his shoulders, buckling it so the sword hung high enough he could draw it while suspended. Without warning or announcement, he picked up the rope, faced the two men on the ground, and walked backwards over the cliff, feeding the rope between his legs and his hands.

Makram squatted on the edge of the cliff, watching his friend's descent. When Tareck reached the end of the rope, he found purchase on the cliff and began climbing down. Makram signaled to the next man, Cem, who dropped over the edge, then to Ahmad once Cem was off the rope.

Makram went next. The rock was pockmarked and worn away, so once he reached the end of the rope climbing down was not as difficult as he had feared. The final man, Demir, began his descent once Makram released the rope. When Makram was close enough for a safe drop he let go, landing close to Tareck on the ledge. Demir wasn't far behind.

All of them pressed their backs to the rock, to hide from view of the entrance. It was close to the stairs and set back into the cliff, appearing as little more than a cave mouth. There was no gate or door, just a gaping hole in the rock.

The cliff blocked what dawn light there had been at the top, and Makram was glad for that, at least they wouldn't be blind the moment they stepped into the dark of the prison.

A quick bird's trill warned them Emre and Musa were releasing the rope. It made a low, zipping hum as it fell, slapping against the ledge, its tail whipping over the edge and pulling the rest of it down and off, into the ocean below. Makram felt the sound in every bone, watching the prison entrance, certain guards would come pouring out. Tareck drew his sword and advanced on the door, Ahmad and Cem at his back, then Makram and Demir.

Two guards popped out of the cavern to investigate. Tareck knocked one out with a well-timed punch that surprised the first man, but the other had to be wrestled to the ground. They gagged him with more of the strips Tareck had made and lashed him together with his unconscious comrade. Makram glanced up at the stairs just before they entered the prison. Musa and Emre were taking the steps down as quickly as they could.

The first half of the cave was unlit, but faint mage light glowed from deeper within. He could only see the starker shadows of his men against the frame of the cave entrance. Makram grabbed Tareck's shoulder to make them wait while their eyes adjusted. Tareck's breathing was unsteady, matching the pace of Makram's pulse. He waited, listening, certain any moment he would hear the arrival of horses and they would be set upon by Commander Ayan's men.

Once they started forward again they ascended a short, paved path. It was easier to quiet his steps against the stones than it would have been the unaltered cave floor, which would have had pebbles and protrusions to give them away. They slowed their creeping pace even more, pressing tightly against the cave walls, as the light grew brighter and the sound of voices from up ahead rose and fell in conversation.

Makram took the lead, feeling for each footstep, his back pressed to the wall, one hand holding his sheathed sword to prevent it scraping, the other feeling along the wall ahead. If this were not an exercise, he'd be done by now. They'd run in, apply a healthy dose of his magic and swords, and sweep the place clean. Sneaking was burdensome and unnecessarily exhausting and he hated the way it made his whole body crawl with tension. Sneaking felt too much like waiting, too uncertain, too vulnerable.

The light poured from a circular outlet into an expansive cavern made into a room. As soon as he could see it, Makram stopped, and the others did the same. Breath held, he crept as close as he dared to the halo of light that spilled from the opening.

Desks were set around the perimeter, carpets tossed haphazardly across the stone-tiled floor, and three tunnels opened up on the far side. A giant, low-slung table surrounded by cushions for sitting dominated the middle of the room. There were a dozen men inside. Two sat at desks, three lounged near the table, picking at the remains of breakfast. A man stood beside each tunnel. The remaining five were scattered throughout, one sharpening his blade, three engaged in a conversation, and the final man stood before one of the desks, lecturing the guard seated behind it.

Makram gestured to Tareck, who strode into the room.

A dozen stares landed on him. Gravid silence permeated the space.

"Gentlemen," Tareck said. His affable tone confused them long enough for Makram and the others to get inside the room, but not enough to prevent them noticing the drawn swords, bows, and distinctly foreign look of the group.

"What is this?" A guard stood from behind one of the desks, leaning forward on his fists as he glared at them. His response, more than any one thing Makram had experienced so far in Tamar, spoke of a country at peace. He responded to armed foreigners with questions, not swords.

"We are conducting an exercise in the name of the High Council"—Makram edged toward the center of the room—"and do not intend you any harm."

"You will stand right where you are," the guard ordered as he moved around the desk. The others did the same, shifting toward the center of the room, toward Makram, trying to cut him off from his men.

Running footsteps echoed in the entrance tunnel.

"It's us," Musa called, to identify himself, and Makram relaxed a fraction. "Company on its way," Musa said when they reached him, both breathing heavy. "About twenty men from the palace."

"Find me keys to a cell," Makram ordered. They'd wasted too much time sneaking. His pulse throbbed in his temples as he shoved down his instinct to release the reins on his magic. No magic. He could not win the exercise only to be denied because they found out what he was.

"I will put you *in* a cell, I don't care who you say you're working for." The guard gestured at the others, and they drew swords.

Messy, cramped melee ensued. They advanced in a semicircle, crowding each other, one man actually bloodied his comrade's nose when he swung his sword back to hack it downward at Cem as he moved to meet them.

Chaos was as familiar to Makram as his own breath and pulse. His magic was chaos, the rapid disassembly of order, and he existed in it like a fish in the sea. It flowed around him and was him, as necessary to who he was as his heart and bones. This fast, short battle felt to some small degree like coming home. Though Makram did not like violence, he was good at it. Was made for it. He'd spend too many days cramped and muted in the palace, containing himself until he'd go mad with it.

The cavern echoed the cacophony of shouts and swords, sounds that meant nothing during the fight and echoed long after. Makram wrestled more than fought in an effort to avoid hurting anyone permanently. The first man who came for him had to do so by running behind his companions, giving Makram enough time to set himself up and step aside in time to use the guard's momentum to drive him headfirst into the stone wall. His head snapped back and he crumpled to the floor at Makram's feet.

He was immediately replaced by two more. Makram braced his back against the wall and kicked one man away, turning on the second by spinning away from the wall so the man's swing curved around his back. Makram drove the hilt of his own sword against the man's temple and stepped over him as he fell, toward the second.

The guard lunged, driving the point of his yataghan toward Makram's belly. Makram swatted the blade down but the guard recovered in a circle, drawing the curved tip of the blade across Makram's ribs. It didn't hurt, initially, and Makram lowered his shoulder and charged, wrapping his arms around the other's waist and driving them both to the center of the room and away from the rest of the fray. Makram dropped and rolled away before the guard could bring his fists and sword hilt down on his back, and lunged up, swinging his elbow up into the man's chin. He staggered backwards, his arms swinging for balance, and Makram kicked his legs out from under him. Pain arrowed up Makram's side as his opponent toppled.

"Keys!" Emre announced, which also signaled the fight was done. Makram kicked his opponent's sword away and pointed his own at his throat.

"Who are you?" the guard asked, struggling up to watch what Makram's men were doing. Makram pushed him back down with his foot.

"Proof you spend too much time sitting and not enough time fighting." Makram dug the toe of his boot into the man's prodigious belly. "Put them all in a cell," he said.

"This one will hold them," Musa said, standing just inside the middle tunnel. Tareck experimented with keys on the lock while the others dragged the unconscious guards toward him. Once he opened the cell, the ones who were awake were herded inside.

With all the guards packed together, Tareck closed and locked the door, tucking the keys into the wrap at his waist. The cut on Makram's ribs burned furiously now, and blood had soaked through to his entari. It was deeper than he thought, and the pain was coming as the fugue of battle faded.

"You're that lot from Sarkum, that's who you are," the fat one said. He spat through the bars at them. Makram sidestepped just in time and resisted the urge to retaliate.

"Quick on the uptake, isn't he?" Tareck said with face still downturned. "What about these tunnels?"

"We'll split," Makram said, feeling at his wound as he spoke. "Cem and Ahmad down the first tunnel, Tareck, take that one with Demir. You two with me." He pointed at Emre and Musa. "If it gets hairy, use your arrows to chalk the walls, so you can find your way back. You're looking for anything that could potentially be the entrance to a tunnel that leads to the palace."

"And if we find it?"

"Send a man back to me."

Makram tugged an arrow from the nearest man's quiver and cut the burlap with the tip of his blade, then started down the middle tunnel. "And hurry up. Those palace guards will be here any moment."

Musa and Emre had seen twenty scouts from the palace. They might be able to defeat twenty, if they were positioned right, but it would not be easy. Especially if Ayan's men did the smart thing and released the prison guards to aid them.

Makram led down the tunnel at a jog, Emre behind and Musa in the rear. As they ran Makram tried to listen over the sound of their boots for the arrival of Commander Ayan's palace guards.

Broken Wheel, what had he been thinking? He had no idea where he was going, what lay ahead. They couldn't possibly find a tunnel entrance even the prison guards weren't aware of before Ayan's men hunted him down. Makram quickened his steps, which sent pain radiating through his side.

Mage orbs floated, contained in stamped metal lamps every hundred paces or so, so that they passed through stretches of shadow and stretches of weak, warm light. The cells came in sets of six in the lighted regions, three to each side, with no cells where the light faded.

Musa let out a strangled shout, followed by the sound of thrashing. Makram almost fell trying to stop and turn, and Emre nearly ran into him. One of the cell's occupants had reached through the bars and grabbed Musa. Now the prisoner had an arm cinched around Musa's neck, another man held his arms, and a third was attempting to divest Musa of his sword. Musa swore, kicking and trying to get a grip on his sword.

Shouts came from the entrance of the tunnel, the room they had left behind. The captured prison guards greeting the arrival of Ayan's men. Makram cursed as he and Emre returned to Musa's side. Emre jabbed his blade through the bars, and the man trying to steal Musa's sword leapt back. The sword clattered to the stones, the man holding Musa's arms released them and dropped to his knees to try and grab it just as Emre did the same. He was too slow. The prisoner yanked the blade through the bars, then thrust it back out at Emre, who fell backwards on his haunches to avoid a wound. Musa grabbed at the arm around his neck and Makram tried to help pry it away. Musa aimed a kick through the bars but his leg got stuck and the man holding him leaned his weight into it until Musa released a pained cry.

Makram finally resorted to his yataghan, jabbing the tip into the meat of the forearm wrapped around Musa's neck. The prisoner yelped, yanking his arm free, and Makram slung Musa away from the bars. The prisoners jeered, and the one who had stolen Musa's sword waved it above his head in triumph.

Once again Makram had to pull hard on his power. He could not reveal his magic. Not even an inkling. They'd have to abandon the sword, leaving Musa injured and weaponless if they were caught by Ayan's men.

The shouting from the entrance had stopped, but sound echoed clearly in the cavern, and orders were given for men to pursue into the tunnels.

Makram yanked Emre to his feet. "Run!"

Fifteen

Samira strode into the Council Hall with two attendants treading closely behind, one bearing a tray with coffee and a pitcher of water with lemon in it, the other with fruit, bread, and sour, thick labneh along with a selection of vegetables. Naime's stomach clenched. She'd been up most of the night, unable to sleep. The library had held no peace or comfort for her as it usually did. When the sun appeared over the Kalspire she had finally moved to the Council Hall. The morning had come and gone and the only report she'd had from Bashir was that he sent scouts to find Makram and his men as soon as the sun had risen. Those scouts had not returned, and as Samira's arrival with food indicated, it was midday.

She was pacing when Samira arrived, as she had been off and on for some time. The Viziers made the trek from the Council Hall to the courtyard throughout the morning to watch for signs of the battle. By the time Samira arrived with food, many of them had returned to their quarters for their own meals.

The two attendants set the trays on one of the benches. One of them poured water into a glass and proffered it to Naime.

"Did you speak with Bashir?" Naime descended from the dais to examine the tray. She smiled at the attendant as she took the water.

"No. He is walking the wall."

"You have heard nothing else?" She wanted to know where Makram was. If he was near the palace and intended to take it by the wall, she had no doubt he would fail. Bashir's men might not be trained to battle as Makram's were, but they were trained very well to hold the palace. And their numbers were far too great for Makram to confront head to head and have any chance of winning, especially since she doubted he intended to use his magic and reveal himself. He was hobbled in more ways than one. Damn him and his mysterious plan.

Samira watched her fidget with the glass, turning it one way then the other, casting her gaze everywhere in the room and never settling.

"Efendim," Samira began with a sigh, "I think you should have more faith in him. He is brash, not stupid."

"I know." Naime closed her eyes and took a deep breath. "I know." He would not have taken the risk if he had not thought he could succeed. He knew something she did not. She had to trust him. She did trust him. That did not make it easier to have no oversight, no control.

"Eat," Samira said, gently. "You will only make yourself sick worrying like this with nothing in your stomach."

Naime scooped labneh onto a carrot stick and swept it through a puddle of olive oil. Samira watched her critically as she continued to eat. It helped lessen her nerves to have food in her belly.

"Good afternoon, Sultana Efendim," Yavuz Pasha called cheerily as he entered the room. His steward followed, along with his son, Sadiq, one of her potential betrothed.

Naime took another sip of water to concentrate on something other than the loathing that swept through her. If everything failed and she had to marry, Sadiq would be her last choice. In fact whenever she could avoid having to speak to him at all, she did.

"Good morning, Yavuz Pasha," Naime said. Sadiq bowed, and she greeted him with a quick nod but did not linger in meeting his eyes. He always stared at her so. Not in a flattering way, not in the warm, almost sad way Makram did.

Her pulse sped thinking about it. The way he looked at her the night before, looked at her so long she had to tell him to stop. Not that she had wanted him to. But he did not make her feel stalked, the way Sadiq did.

"Father tells me this Sarkum prince is reckless," Sadiq said, sidling closer and taking a fig from the tray. He helped himself to the water pitcher, oblivious to Samira's fiery stare of disapproval. When he reached for another bit of food, Samira snatched up the tray and put herself between Sadiq and Naime as she held the tray out in offer.

"I should think that was relatively obvious, considering the circumstances," Naime said, meeting Samira's eyes as she picked several almonds from a bowl. Samira stuck the tip of her tongue out. "Did you need your father to point that out to you?" Naime popped an almond in her mouth and watched Sadiq. He stared after Samira as she marched up the dais steps and set the tray of food beside the Sultan's seat.

"Yavuz Pasha, would you care for coffee?" Naime turned from Sadiq. His father nodded, and Naime's attendant poured and delivered a cup to him.

"Have you heard anything yet?" Yavuz Pasha asked, sipping at his coffee. Sadiq followed when Naime went to his father, insinuating himself between the two of them.

"Nothing."

"There is time. Surprise is the only advantage he has."

"You sound as if you want for him to succeed," Naime said, trying not to sound hopeful.

"You spoke well, Sultana"—he bowed his head in respect—"and he acted on your behalf. To me, it suggested the opportunity for a balanced alliance. But mine is only one opinion, as you are well aware, and not an opinion that carries enough weight to sway the Council."

He was being modest as Kadir would never be. Many of the Council would follow Yavuz Pasha. He was the second-most influential Vizier after Kadir. Knowing he was even considering her words felt like a victory as massive as Makram taking the palace. A thread of hope wove through her thoughts.

"Will your father be here?" he asked.

"I am afraid he is too ill today," Naime said. In fact she'd left Ihsan in charge of him, with strict orders to keep him away.

"A pity. There was a time he would have enjoyed this game more than anyone else."

She wondered how much the Council knew of her father, if they realized how quickly he was slipping. They were not simpletons; they knew the time to install a new ruler was looming. She just hoped they did not realize how unstable his mind was.

"I know," she said. It was true. Her father loved things like this, that ruffled feathers and forced change. She thought, suddenly, that her father would have liked Makram, would have liked his boldness, his easy confidence. Her chest felt squeezed by an unseen force.

"Has your father decided on your betrothed?" Sadiq had been watching the sliver of sky they could see from the Council Hall but turned back as he spoke. His father sighed and finished his coffee, turning to hand the tiny cup to Naime's attendant.

"No, Master Yavuz, he has not. The negotiation with Sarkum is the priority."

"He should not put it off for too long," he said. "You won't be beautiful forever."

"My beauty may wither, Master Yavuz, but the throne remains evergreen." She failed to keep the sharpness from her tone.

Yavuz Pasha cleared his throat and slitted his eyes to prevent rolling them. "Forgive him, Sultana Efendim. I will instruct him on more appropriate subjects for conversation."

Naime tipped her head, then strode away from them both.

"I don't see what was inappropriate about it," Sadiq said as she walked away.

Yavuz Pasha, though not always in agreement with her or her father, was always polite. Naime had only met his wife a few times, but rather suspected it was her influence, more than her husband's, that had stoked Sadiq's desire to be Sultan, as well as his arrogant way of speaking. None of the sons offered as potential husbands, potential future Sultans, had ever bothered engaging her in conversation beyond polite niceties. None of them spoke to her as an equal. None of them cared about her.

She walked outside into the garden and courtyard between the main palace and the Council Hall. Many of the Viziers had gathered there, and were broken into groups, sharing food or coffee from trays held by their servants or simply engaged in conversation. Besides their conversation, and the wet, cold breeze that stirred, she heard nothing. Even tucked away at the interior of the palace she knew she'd hear something if Makram and his men were attacking.

Naime threaded her way between the Viziers and headed for the south end of the palace and the courtyard. Samira followed, but kept silent. When they arrived near the Morning Gate, Naime surveyed the wall. Guards stood at regular intervals across the ramparts.

"Commander Ayan," Naime spoke into the wind of her power, picturing the stalwart commander in her mind's eye as she strode closer. At the top, a figure broke away from one of the groups of archers and jogged toward the nearest stair. He met her when she was halfway to the gate. Naime did not consider herself short, but Bashir made her feel so when he stood next to her. She had to tip her head back to meet his eyes.

"I know only that they went west. I have even tried a tracking spell and felt nothing. None of my scouts have returned, and I will not send more men after them." His voice always called to mind old stone and mountains, steady and imperturbable. "It might be a trap." The lines in his brow were the only indication of his frustration. Bashir hated failure.

She hesitated to order him to send more men. She did not want to interfere and have Kadir claim it had altered the exercise in Makram's favor. Nor did she want to encourage Bashir to overwhelm Makram with more of Bashir's men than he could handle. Naime considered the direction. There was nothing west but the Cliffs, and there was no easier way into the palace on that side of the wall. The cliff itself made approach impossible. What did Makram know?

She curled her hands into her caftan, reminding herself, yet again, that interfering would not help Makram. This was his game, and she only a spectator in it.

"If anything changes," she started.

"I know." A smile tugged at his mouth. "I will send word as soon as anything happens."

Though they had never had a chance to become true friends, she admired Bashir and all that he had gone through to attain his position. She thought the feeling was returned, and also knew he felt indebted to her. He had grown up in the poorer parts of the Earth District, his mother a healer to the poorest of the city. Without scholarship, he would not have been able to attend the University to master his power. He was a powerful and talented Sival of the Fourth House, and she was grateful to have him in command of her guard. He had taken over the position from the last man, who had been fiercely loyal to Kadir, and Bashir was slowly weeding out those who were more likely to follow Kadir's coin than Bashir's orders.

"Thank you." She smiled, a little sheepishly, and he bowed, then returned to the wall.

When Naime arrived back to the Council Hall it had begun to drizzle, and many of the Viziers had moved into the hall. Kadir had arrived from wherever he'd been plotting all morning, and stood with his steward, three palace guards Naime knew to be more loyal to him than to Bashir, Banu the air mage, and his son crowding around him. Banu eyed Naime, who ducked her head in greeting.

There had been some speculation that Banu was Kadir's mistress as well as Kadir's spy, but Naime doubted that. Kadir had an appreciation for beautiful things, whether they were objects or living, breathing people, and Banu was not beautiful. Striking, perhaps, but plain. She was an example of how a mage could be twisted by promises of power, when they were resentful of the amount allotted them by the Wheel. Kadir, despite his elitism, managed to curate bitter, disenfranchised followers like a shepherd acquired sheep.

"What is the meaning of this?" he asked before she even reached his little group, which dominated the center of the room.

Naime folded her hands in front of her caftan and raised an eyebrow. He gave a perfunctory bow.

"What has upset you, Grand Vizier?"

"These men report the Sarkum contingent were followed to the west."

Her belly tightened and irritation buzzed up her back. Just once she would like for Kadir to know less than she did.

"Was there something in the rules the Council decided upon that denied them from riding west?"

Someone to her left laughed, and Kadir's face twisted in rage. "You have interfered with this, I know it to my bones. This game is forfeit."

"Unless you can prove that accusation, Grand Vizier, the game is not forfeit," Naime said.

"Here now, Kadir Pasha," Yavuz said, calmly. "You did not expect them to try to saunter through the Morning Gate, did you?"

"Perhaps they are confused," Sadiq offered, and received a few laughs for his contribution.

"He was given no constraints as to how he could take the palace, only that he must. Even a novice at war such as myself knows that attacking the wall directly would be folly," Naime said.

"I still believe he's been given information from someone in this room, information that would have changed the nature of the challenge if it were known to the Council."

"Again, Grand Vizier, without proof, you cannot call for forfeit." Naime glanced at Yavuz, who nodded in agreement.

"Very well. Then I suggest we add difficulty, to maintain the integrity of the exercise."

"That is hardly fair, Grand Vizier." Naime's stomach clenched harder as irritation became panic.

"War is not fair," Kadir said, and several of the Viziers spoke in agreement. "Let us move to the throne room, where a proper Sultan would be found."

Naime forced calm into her face and breath. The throne room was even deeper in the palace, and would take extra time to navigate to, as well as allowing Kadir to place yet more guards in Makram's path.

"You cannot change the destination halfway through the game, Kadir Pasha," Yavuz Pasha said with a careful tone.

"No? A Sultan would sit idly, waiting for his conqueror to arrive? If you have so much faith in this man and his army, then let him show us how he adapts," Kadir announced to the room. And they agreed, with boisterous calls and Viziers immediately heading for the throne room.

Kadir limped toward Naime, smiling.

"He must be informed," Naime said, the last idea she had. Trying to send a message with her magic to Makram, when she couldn't see him and when he might be so far away, would take a great thrust of power. Banu would know, would feel it if she tried to do so covertly, and Kadir would use it as evidence that Naime had interfered.

Wheel save her from herself, someday she was certain she would snap like a dry reed and strangle Behram Kadir in front of everyone.

"I'll leave these guards behind to escort him." Kadir gestured at the three men standing with Cemil. Naime bit her cheek to curb her temper, then smiled.

"One man will suffice," she suggested. He did not think she was stupid, she knew that. He was taunting her. Baiting her.

"Then allow me," Cemil announced. The twist of panic in her belly spread cold through her limbs as she turned to him.

"Ah, perfect," Kadir said. Naime walked from Kadir to his son, and stopped before him, closer than she normally cared to. Cemil continued to smile, his gold eyes fixed on her face. Naime inhaled slowly, deeply. There was no lingering stench of stale alcohol, as usually accompanied Cemil. His smile flattened. For once, she was disappointed he was sober.

"Don't worry, Sultana," Cemil said under his breath, "I'll take good care of him."

She met his gaze, glittering with threat. He was a cheater, just like his father. He'd attack Makram and his men, and he would use his magic.

"The Grand Vizier's little puppet," Naime said under her breath. "Where's your spine to stand up to him, hmm?"

His eyes widened, and heat bloomed in the air around them. It was gone as suddenly as it appeared, and Cemil smiled again.

"Where's yours?" he whispered back, then looked past her to his father. "That's all sorted, Grand Vizier."

"Let us walk together then, Sultana. And speak of your betrothal," Kadir said.

Naime stared at Cemil another moment, nauseous with her loathing. When she turned, Yavuz Pasha fell in beside her. Kadir joined them, and they slowed to match his limping speed. Naime seethed beneath the quiet expression she used to hide her panic.

"Have one of the guards leave me a sword," Cemil called as they reached the doors.

Naime whirled, and Cemil grinned, showing his teeth.

"Just in case." He winked.

Sixteen

THE LAMPS HAD CEASED as soon as they left the main prison and began wandering, fruitlessly, in a honeycomb of dead ends and twisting tunnels that circled back on themselves. Musa was a Lightbringer, thankfully, but his power would not hold out much longer.

"I hear them," Musa said quietly.

"We'll run again," Makram said.

"Leave me here, Agassi." Musa stopped, leaning against the wall. "They aren't supposed to hurt me, and I'm just slowing you down." He patted the leg that had been twisted against the cell bars.

Makram considered it, listening for sounds of the palace guards. He wiped the sweat from his eyes, putting a hand over the wound at his side. It was simultaneously numb and aching. A bad sign.

They had two swords between the three of them, Musa could barely jog, and they still had not caught up to Tareck and the others. He'd never leave someone if the stakes were life, but in this case…

"I owe you a horse, Musa," Makram said.

"I'll try and slow them down," he said grimly as he unhooked his bow from his back. Emre unslung his quiver and handed it to Musa.

"Leash your mage orb to us for as long as you can," Makram said. Musa nodded, focusing on Makram as he intoned his spell. The orb drifted to float above Makram's head.

“Good man,” Makram said, touching his shoulder. Musa nocked one of the chalk arrows and pointed it down the hall. Makram and Emre turned and ran, leaving Musa in the dark. The mage orb might last half a candlemark—Makram hoped they wouldn’t need it that long. He was ready to be out of the dank maze of stone.

“Is that you, Agassi?” Tareck called from some distance away, his voice echoing. Makram didn’t call back, the noise would carry too easily to the palace guards somewhere behind them. The tunnel they ran through ended abruptly, dumping them into a cavern as large as the palace courtyard, with a vast, domed ceiling above, covered in jagged protrusions that hung like teeth. Water dripped from above. Makram slowed to a walk, and Emre gave another of his sharp bird whistles to answer Tareck’s challenge.

There were no mage orbs, but something on the walls gave a faint, pale light. Lichen or moss? Some of the wadis in Sarkum had such, if the rock walls around them had deep overhangs, lichen that glowed in the dark. In the faint, tinged light, Makram could see the floor of the cavern was occupied by a gridwork of freestanding, empty cells.

The cavern’s silence echoed even the smallest sound, the drip of water, the scrape of their boots, Tareck’s quiet conversation with one of the other men. Makram and Emre found him and Demir on the far side of the vast room, where Tareck was examining the rock wall, hands on his hips.

“Could have used your magic to get us out of that damn maze.” Makram wiped the sweat off his face with a sleeve. Tareck eyed him.

“You’re still bleeding.” Tareck’s gaze was hard and worried.

“Yes I’m aware. I’m unlikely to die,” he said. “The palace guards are on their way, and we had to leave Musa behind. We don’t have time to dawdle. Do you have enough reserve to cast a spell?”

“I was about to,” Tareck said. “I don’t know how many times I’ll be able to cast, or how far my range will be through this rock.”

“Do it,” Makram said. Tareck crouched, drawing one of the arrows and using it to chalk a sigil on the floor. “Emre and Cem, go that way, along the wall, see if you can find anything. Ahmad and Demir.” Makram pointed. “That way.”

Tareck spoke his spell, and the sigil glowed with the warm golden light of the Fourth House. Makram moved away from Tareck, between two of the cages, and listened. There was no way for him to tell time down here, and the lightless quiet warped his sense of its passing. He had no idea how long they'd run since leaving Musa.

Makram glanced back at Tareck. He had begun whispering again as the light started to fade from the sigil, his brows knit together, his fingers clawing against the stone floor. Golden lines reached from the sigil, across the floor and up the wall.

Makram noted their progress, watching for the outline of a door. Sweat dripped from Tareck's brow onto the stone.

"Don't exhaust yourself," Makram warned.

"You can change my nappy after," Tareck bit out.

Makram shook his head. The sigil flared with a new influx of power when Tareck growled another word. The crawling lines flared in response, and one shot forward across the wall, ten steps from Makram, suddenly changing from jagged to straight, tracing the rectangular outline of a door. Tareck grunted and released the spell. He fell forward on his hands, panting. Makram walked to the door. There was no indication, except the thinnest of perfect, straight cuts in the stone.

"On me," Makram ordered his men back, loud enough to cause an echo.

Tareck clambered to his feet and staggered toward Makram.

"All right?" Makram asked. Tareck nodded. A Deval's power was exhausted quickly, proportionate to the distance they were trying to cast a spell and whether their target was known or not. "Well done. Now we just need to open it."

"Either it's meant to be opened with magic, or only opened from the inside, or there is a mechanism somewhere," Tareck said. Makram made a sound of agreement as he crouched, turning slowly and examining the stones around them for a plate switch. He dropped to his knees and ran his hands over the floor. Ahmad and Demir returned at a jog.

"How about six to six?" Tareck suggested.

"What?" Ahmad asked, turning from where he was attempting to wedge his fingers into the crack in the stone.

"Old superstitions," Makram explained, searching the floor for any sort of pattern in the tiles. "The Wheel has six Houses. So, the pious believe multiples of six to be numbers that bestow balance, fortune, and general happiness. They might have used that to place a mechanism."

"Shall I just spell it?" Tareck asked.

Makram wiped his dirt-covered hand down his face in exasperation. "I'd rather save your power, just in case."

Cem and Emre jogged back, and Cem pointed toward the far side of the cavern. "We saw light. They're here."

Makram pushed a thread of power into Musa's borrowed mage orb, destroying the spell that held it. The light dimmed and the orb faded away.

"Stomp on every stone between here and those cages," Makram said quietly, indicating a rough circle between the door and the nearest three cells with his finger. The men obeyed, spreading out to cover the area, while Makram and Tareck continued exploring the wall for secret switches.

The arrival of the palace guard force into the cavern was announced by a muffled shout. Makram assumed they'd brought Musa with them and he was trying to warn them, though it sounded as if he were gagged.

"Nothing," Emre murmured. Makram watched through the cages as the mage orbs the guards carried bobbed and traced light trails through the murky cavern.

"No," Ahmad said.

"We'll have to fight them here," Makram announced, gripping the hilt of his borrowed sword.

Something gave a loud, metallic-sounding thump in the wall above Makram. All eyes went to the remaining soldier, Cem, who glanced at his feet. Makram looked at the wall, and the stone had shifted open a fraction. On the other side of the cavern, whoever was in charge gave orders to split up and weave through the cells.

"Get it open!" Makram tugged the lower portion of the stone while his men took hold of spots above him, pulling the slab open in slow, scraping increments.

"There!" a voice shouted from the other side of the cavern, having caught sight of them huddled at the wall. Makram and his men tugged and pulled on the massive slab of stone until they could each barely squeeze through. Cem shimmied between the wall and the slab, and Makram started in when Tareck returned.

"Leave me the rest of the arrows and a bow," he said.

"No," Makram said as he shifted sideways through the gap and into the tunnel beyond.

"A spell will take too long to close it, so I'll distract them and hopefully give you time to get to the Council Hall."

Emre slipped through as Makram considered.

"Fine. Ahmed, stay with him," Makram said to the last soldier. That left him with exactly the number he needed to win the game. But if Ediz Rahal's account had been true, this tunnel let out in the Council Hall, so he shouldn't need to worry about having to sacrifice any others.

"Wheel Turn for you," Tareck said over his shoulder as he grabbed the nearest cage and climbed to its top, Ahmad behind him.

"Left hand on the wall, right hand on the man in front of you," Makram said, taking the lead. He shouldn't have extinguished the damn orb, it was darker than the void in the passage.

They jogged up the corridor and out of what faint light made it through the crack between the wall and the open slab. Makram was certain they were running out of time. They'd been wandering in the caves for half a day at least, he'd bet on it. If they kept a good pace and the tunnel wasn't too long, they might make it to the Council Hall without any more fighting. But Tareck wouldn't be able to hold twenty palace guards for long.

Makram's wound had been seeping blood the better part of the day, and his limbs weren't working with quite the precision with which they should. He was weak from a full day of running. They'd had no time to stop and eat. Stopping meant allowing the palace guard time to catch up. All those in-the-moment decisions seemed poorly made, now that he was plunged into darkness and forced to examine them.

Without any light, his sense of the space was distorted. The tunnel felt vast but was narrow—if he reached out with his right hand, he could touch the opposite wall. The slope had been a gradual incline, and his legs burned. His men were breathing as hard as he was.

Behind them, there were shouts, and the scrape of stone on stone.

He cursed and broke into a jog. The tunnel flattened out and Makram extended his stride. Three strides farther and his foot hit something. He pitched forward onto a set of stone stairs. He landed on his wounded side, and one of his men landed on top of him, though the others managed to stop in time. Makram groaned in pain, forcing himself onto his hands and knees, feeling out the stairs. The muscles along his side seized as he stood, protesting, demanding he stop.

"I hope this means we're almost there," Emre said as he untangled himself from Makram.

"Agreed. I could use a drink," Makram said, and the others laughed breathlessly, though it was tense laughter.

They climbed the steep, shallow steps, as the sound of the guards grew louder behind them. He moved with one hand on the wall for balance, one outstretched, hoping any moment he'd run into something solid, indicating they'd arrived at the end of the tunnel.

And then he did.

"Wheel take me," he groaned in disbelief, feeling at the uneven, rocky pile in front of him.

A cave-in.

"Start digging."

He felt along the rocks, reaching above his head as his men began slinging rocks away from the pile.

"I can feel air," Cem said. "Give me a boost."

Makram moved aside as the others hoisted him up. Cem kicked and clawed, grunting as he moved around above them.

"There's space up here," he announced. "Barely. Give me your hands."

Makram reached up, and Cem reached down. They locked holds on each other's wrists. Cem shimmied backward, pulling Makram up and into the crevice between the ceiling and the cave-in. Makram had to clench his teeth and breathe through his nose to stifle a shout of pain. Sweat beaded his brow and temples by the time he was wedged on his belly between the pile of rocks and the ceiling.

Cem inched backwards and dropped down on the other side. There was barely enough space around Makram to draw a breath, and to move he had to grab with his fingers and push with his toes; there was not enough space to bend knee or elbow. When he finally made it through to the other side, Cem helped him down before he crawled back up to pull Emre through.

Makram collapsed against the wall, grasping his side and tipping his head against the stone. He was grateful the pitch-black hid his fatigue from the men.

"There they are!" an unfamiliar voice shouted, muffled by the wall of stone between him and Makram. Light glittered across the ceiling of the tunnel through the narrow gap as his last soldier dropped down from the crawlspace.

"Move," he ordered, and they fell into the same formation they had before as he jogged forward, feeling ahead with one hand. The wall of rock behind them gave a groan, obeying an earth mage's command, no doubt. He cursed again under his breath. His remaining men were not mages, and while his magic would have made quick work of the stone pile, he couldn't risk revealing himself. The corridor climbed again, then leveled out as the wall of rocks collapsed behind them in a sound like shattering stone.

He found the second set of stairs much as he had the first, only this time he didn't fall. They were steep, more ladder than stairs. One of the men gave a plaintive groan. Makram climbed as quickly as he could, though he had to use his hands and his legs threatened to give beneath him, burning with a Firestormer's wrath.

He forced himself to climb as fast as he could and was rewarded for his hurry by smacking his head against the stone ceiling. Streaks of stars swam in front of his eyes as he cursed and lifted his hands, feeling for an outlet or door. There was no indication of one, so he pushed. The section above him shifted.

"Agassi!" one of his men cried in warning. Makram put both hands on the stone above him and heaved himself upward. The section of stone lifted above him. Makram maneuvered it through the hole it created and popped his head up into a brightly lit room. The hole from the tunnel had let out behind the dais and the latticework screen that surrounded the Sultan's seat in the Council Hall.

An arrow burst in a shower of chalk on the wall near his feet, silencing his triumph. Makram crawled out of the hole and into the room then reached down to help pull his men after him. Demir, the last, pulled himself up and kicked downward at one of the palace guards who had climbed the stone ladder behind him. The guard lost his balance and fell with a shout, knocking two companions back down into the tunnel as he went.

"The stone," Makram ordered, and Cem and Emre slid it back into place, then all three sat on top of it to hold it.

Makram, still on hands and knees, surveyed the Council Hall in triumph. He'd been right.

His relief twisted into a hard, burning knot.

The room was empty.

Confusion warred with anger as he got to his feet. He looked to the garden beyond, wondering if he was too late. Evening was just darkening the sky, which indicated he still had a little time. Why was the hall empty?

The guards in the tunnel shouted to each other, though the sound was muffled. The stone tile his men sat on shifted as they tried to move it from below. Makram's soldiers held it, but he wasn't certain how long they could.

"Finally. I was about to expire of boredom," a man said.

Tension locked Makram's muscles, and he rotated toward the voice, drawing the practice blade they'd given him. He was too tired if he had completely missed someone's presence in the room

A figure stirred on one of the Viziers' benches on the side of the room blocked from Makram's view by the screen. He stalked around it and stepped off the dais. A man lay on the bench, his hands folded over his stomach, his near leg on the floor, the other bent up, his foot on the bench.

"What is going on?" Makram demanded. From his dress Makram could see the man was a noble, and Makram was too tired, too angry, and in too much pain to be mocked by a pampered palace brat.

The man sat up, leaning his forearms on his knees. He assessed Makram and smirked as though he had seen something that amused him.

"The esteemed Grand Vizier believed the game had been unfairly weighted in your favor. So he weighted it back into balance by moving your goal."

"Where is my goal?" Makram barely contained an explosive reveal of his power, held in check by the wavering grip he maintained. The man stood. He was about the same height and weight as Makram, dressed in the unbearable reds and oranges of a fire mage, a guardsman's sword belted over the yellow cloth that wound his waist.

"Tsk," he said. "There'd be no fun in it if I just told you." He raised an eyebrow. The tile bucked underneath the soldiers, and Makram's men cursed and shifted, trying to hold it down. "Although you look like you've had plenty of fun already." He gestured to Makram's bloodstained caftan and entari.

"We don't have time for this." Makram pointed outside, to the fading light.

"You'll have to make time." He drew the yataghan at his side. It was not a practice blade. Makram's blood sang with magic and fury. Was this an elaborate attempt at assassinating him? Why did he have a real blade?

"Who are you?" Makram demanded.

"Ah. My manners. Master Cemil Kadir, Sival of the Fifth House."

"Your family is like a scourge in Tamar," Makram blurted in anger. Cemil laughed, then charged. Makram shoved his blade against Cemil's to deflect it as he sidestepped the onslaught. Cemil moved and struck like a cobra. Makram dodged a series of quick, cross-hatched swings.

When Cemil circled away, Makram took his full measure. He'd fought fire mages in Sarkum, and many of them had the same traits, fire's speed and unpredictability. They could be phenomenal swordsmen, with enough training and practice. As long as they could contain their tempers, which was rare.

Makram had never fought a Fifth House Sival. But surely his temper was as quick as his father's.

"Did Baba leave you here like a trained dog?"

Cemil's odd, gold eyes almost glowed with his irritation and heat crackled in the air. He attacked again, driving at Makram until their blades locked against each other and Cemil tried to force Makram to his knees.

"And you're here to bed a princess. So which of us is more noble?" Cemil snarled as he leaned his weight into their locked blades. The muscles in Makram's side, already aching from his shallow wound, seized with the effort of fighting against Cemil's downward push. That answered the question about his temper. His own reared at Cemil's taunt, but Makram was not a hotheaded dimwit, to rise to bait in the middle of a sword fight.

Makram allowed one leg to give under the pressure, dropping to a knee as he ran the palm of his hand up the flat of his blade to bear the weight of Cemil pressing down. It prevented Cemil hacking his blade downward into Makram's shoulder and made Cemil lose his balance under the sudden change of position.

Makram drove his body upward when Cemil stumbled, slamming his shoulder into Cemil's midsection and shoving his blade aside. He spun out from under Cemil and rotated again to swing his sword at his back. Cemil had stumbled, half bent forward, but twisted, falling to one knee and slinging a bolt of fire at Makram.

Makram jerked sideways and the bolt shot past him, slamming into the lattice above the Sultan's seat and exploding into sparks and rivulets that burned themselves out. Emre shouted a surprised curse. Makram ran at Cemil, but he dropped and rolled out of his path, jumping to his feet in the time it took Makram to stop and spin back.

"Can't win a swordfight without magic?" Makram taunted.

Cemil lunged in, swiping at Makram's midsection, knowing there was far too much distance for it to have a chance of landing. But Makram still had to dodge it, and while he was regaining his balance, a whip of heat curved over his back. He stumbled forward with a surprised grunt of pain. Cemil went for him again, carving his blade downward at Makram's bent neck. Makram twisted, just managing to catch Cemil's blade against his own. Cemil bore down, and because Makram was twisted at an angle, he had to go down or Cemil's blade would slip free of his and catch him in the arm. He hit the floor and rolled, kicking for Cemil's legs.

Cemil leapt sideways in time to avoid Makram's kick, and sliced his blade down at the same time, opening a wound in Makram's other side. Makram swore as pain lanced up his body. He forced himself to roll to his belly and push to his feet, half hopping as the pain in his sides shot down his legs and the muscles cramped. He buried the pain beneath a surge of temper.

"That's a useful trick, burning without manifesting fire," Makram said as they came together again.

"Isn't it? I have more," Cemil said, his gold eyes glittering with reflected fire.

"By all means," Makram said, and returned the favor of the wound along his ribs with a quick, crossways swipe of his blade that surprised Cemil, "but you're still going to lose."

Cemil clutched at his side, sidestepping Makram's follow-up swing. Cemil held up his hand, bloodied by the wound in his side. Another skein of fire shot up Makram's hip and back as Cemil lowered his hand. Makram shouted, jerking away from it as if it had been a physical blow.

"Agassi!" Emre called in concern.

"Hold," he bellowed back. Then he rushed at Cemil, and the sound of their swords striking together drowned out the sound of the tile as it lifted and fell back into place under the next assault from the guards within the tunnel.

Makram was accustomed to fighting through pain, but Cemil did not appear to be. He heavily favored his side, trying to protect it from Makram's swings and shortening his own strokes to prevent himself pulling at it.

Makram swiped aside a thrust of Cemil's sword and punched him in the face. It split the fire mage's lip. Fire whipped up Makram's stomach and neck and he jerked in surprise.

"Keep burning me, little Kadir. You'll only run out of power," Makram said. The cost of such spells, even for a Sival, was high.

"I wouldn't bet on that." Cemil laughed.

Makram lunged, grabbing Cemil's right wrist, his sword arm, and slammed it down against his knee. His hand opened reflexively, the sword dropping from his grip. Heat bloomed where Makram held Cemil's wrist, until he could feel it burning his skin, blistering it as Cemil stared at him with venom and a sneer on his lips.

Makram slammed his forehead into the bridge of Cemil's nose, forcing himself to maintain his hold, despite the aching, bone-deep pain that surged up his arm from the heat of Cemil's magic.

Cemil gagged on the pain and the blood, blinded momentarily as his eyes watered.

"Damned cheating fire mages." Makram slammed the hilt of his sword against Cemil's temple. He released his wrist, letting him slump to the ground. Skin peeled away from Makram's blistered palm and he breathed a curse in pain and realization. Now he couldn't find out where everyone had gone.

He limped to the side of the room and clutched one of the benches in his uninjured hand, dragging it toward the stone where his men lay. He handed it off to the men, and went for another, every step a battle between him and the lancing pain of his wounds and the burns.

When he was helping them place a third bench to hold the tile, Cemil stirred. Makram crossed to him and caught the collar of his caftan in his uninjured hand.

"Where are they?"

"You're a vicious son of a bitch," Cemil said as if it were a compliment, touching his fingers to the bleeding knot that was beginning to bruise on his temple.

"You have no idea. Where are they?" Makram released his grip on Cemil's collar, struggling mightily to hold his magic in check, to keep it from showing on his skin, unleashed by his fatigue and temper. This game would have been nothing if he hadn't had to hide his magic. He could have walked through the front gate and been done with it all in a mark. He could show the Grand Vizier exactly what looking a death mage in the eyes was like, since he seemed so curious.

"Throne room," Cemil groaned, and clutched at his head. Makram addressed his men.

"When I say so, you're all going to get up, and we're going to run."

They nodded.

"Do you even know where the throne room is?" Cemil asked, pressing his palms against his eyes.

"No, but I have a guide." Makram grabbed the back of Cemil's caftan and hauled him to his feet.

Cemil staggered a step, laughing. "No wonder my father hates you."

They'd have to run all the way to the throne room, wherever it was. Once his men moved away from the door the benches would only hold it a few moments.

"You're coming with us, little Kadir. In case your father has any more surprises in store for us."

Seventeen

NAIME STOOD APART FROM the Viziers, facing the throne room's western windows. What remained of the sun above the water flared red and gold. A fitting end she supposed, appropriate symbolism for her hopes dying in flames. Now she found herself more worried for Makram's safety than for his victory. The victory she'd given up on the moment Kadir took them from the Council Hall. As far as she knew, Makram didn't even know where the throne room was. She'd tried to secretly send servants to the Council Hall, to guide him, but Kadir managed to prevent every one of her attempts. And there was no guessing what Cemil would do if Makram did arrive in the Council Hall on time.

"Sultana." Yavuz Pasha approached her.

"You cannot truly mean to let this stand?" she said, quietly, her gaze shifting to Kadir then back. "The Council must see this is blatant cheating. He is not even respecting the rules you laid down."

"I am doing my best, but you know as well as I that it is more complicated than that. They do not want death mages in Tamar. Some of them are relieved he has made it easy for them to deny the terms." His gaze started to slip to Kadir then stopped, meeting hers instead. "And you know better than most what it can mean to risk crossing him."

"I understand," Naime said. She understood better than any of them, or rather, Ihsan did.

She was glad Ihsan was with her father, and not with her to see Kadir cheating and getting away with it yet again. It infuriated her that she still did not have the power to get rid of him. But if she did anything to Kadir that a majority of the Council did not support, her hopes for ruling Tamar would be finished. There would be no amount of political maneuvering to prevent civil war.

"There may be other ways," he suggested.

"After we put their prince and military commander through a humiliating exercise and lied to him? I think not," Naime said, more sharply than she had meant to. "This is beyond ludicrous, and it is embarrassing for Tamar."

She had not completely given up hope. There was still a tiny, warm spark in her, hope fed by denial, by desperation, by her memory of watching him in the arena. A fierce and capable fighter. Bold enough to overcome a cheating opponent.

But that spark died too, because the sun was just a fiery line across the water when she looked again. She was so lost to the despair that opened within her, that it took longer than it should have to hear the shouting in the hall.

Naime spun to see all the Viziers had focused on the doors to the hall, which were closed. Three Sarkum soldiers threw them open, and as soon as they were in, one of them closed one side of the doors. Makram came through next, sideways, his arm around Cemil's neck, half dragging him through the door. Relief erupted like cold fire through her lungs and limbs. Samira gasped at the sight of Cemil. She'd put her hands to her mouth but dropped them as soon as Naime looked at her.

Makram kicked the second door closed on a pack of Bashir's guardsmen and his soldiers threw their backs against the doors to hold them closed.

"You'll call this finished, Grand Vizier," he announced, pointing his yataghan at Kadir, "unless you plan to make me chase you all over this Wheel-damned pile of stones like the coward you are."

The Viziers erupted into cacophony. Shouts of anger and cheers of excitement deafened her as she glanced at the setting sun, catching it as the final, paper-thin sliver sank beneath the water. Naime cut her gaze to Kadir, who had also noted the light. She smiled in triumph that roared in her veins.

Kadir turned from her in disgust, ordering, "Unhand my son."

Makram unhooked his arm from Cemil's neck and shoved him forward. Cemil dropped to his knees, then fell forward to his hands. His face was bloodied, his caftan stained with several explosions of chalk, as though Makram had used him as a shield against the practice arrows. He sat back on his heels and tipped his head back to stare at the ceiling. Makram's men exchanged looks, leaning backwards against the doors to hold them closed. Makram and Kadir faced off in the center of everything, Kadir blocking Naime's complete view of Makram.

"What have you done to him?" Kadir did not go to his son, or even look at him beyond assessing the damage. Naime glanced at Samira. Her face was washed of color, her hands clenched in her caftan. That Cemil had gotten exactly what he deserved, Naime had no doubt. That Samira was hurt by it distressed Naime.

"What have I done to him? A great deal less than I plan to do to the next Tamar noble who tries to double cross me," Makram said, loud enough to silence every Vizier in the room.

Yavuz Pasha moved to stand beside Naime, glancing sideways at her. His face was grim.

"Threats?" Kadir said.

"I have not even begun to threaten," Makram said, and his magic brushed across hers, magic energized by anger, a shadow passing over the sun. If every person in the room didn't feel it, she'd be surprised. Makram was not in control.

"I think that is enough," Naime said, stepping in before he revealed enough of his magic they guessed its nature. "This game is over. He has more than fulfilled the requirements set by the Council, Grand Vizier. Your son needs medical care." Naime touched Samira's sleeve. "Go."

Samira hiked up the sides of her entari and dashed down the aisle, dropping to her knees beside Cemil.

"You two," Naime addressed her attendants, "inform the physician that I will be sending him patients shortly." They bowed and left through a side door.

Naime descended the three steps of the dais to the marble floor. She buried a desire to run to Makram and throw her arms around his neck as joy and gratitude charged her with energy.

Kadir moved aside for her, and Naime stopped, her triumph replaced with dismay.

Makram's entari and caftan were soaked with blood around his torso, and he held his left hand cradled against his belly. She could see red, blistered skin that oozed, and recognized it as a burn that covered his palm and fingers. He wouldn't meet her gaze, his own trained somewhere behind her at the Sultan's seat, but she knew he was exhausted.

"Do you always arrive at the very last moment?" she said in tones only he could hear. Humor flashed in his coffee-colored eyes, his mouth twitched toward a smile, and he breathed a laugh.

"And dirty, and injured," he agreed.

"You may open those doors," Naime said to his men. They obeyed, revealing eight of Bashir's guards clustered outside, confused, but also weary. "Escort these men to the physician," she told them, "and inform Commander Ayan the game is done."

"Sultana, I expect appropriate measures will be taken to address the fact my son has been injured," Kadir said.

Naime turned, almost shoulder to shoulder with Makram, who, she realized in alarm, was weaving in place. It took everything in her not to lean against him, to support him.

"You put him into the game, Grand Vizier, and it appears"—she gripped Makram's left wrist carefully and he allowed her to lift his hand so everyone in the room could see his burns—"that he disobeyed the rules."

She released her grip on Makram as sounds of disapproval rippled through the room. "Guards. Escort Cemil Kadir to a cell. He can be treated there by the physician once he has seen to the Agassi and his men."

"That is outrageous," Kadir cried, and some of the Viziers chimed in to agree.

"Your son will pay the fine for illegal use of magic outside the bounds of this exercise."

Naime met Kadir's furious look as those men who supported him most strongly called in outrage. Samira, who knelt behind Kadir next to Cemil, had pulled her hands back from Cemil, the expression on her face crumpling in sorrow and disappointment. She got to her feet, and Cemil bowed his head. Samira forgave him too much, but she could not, apparently, forgive brutality. He had a fistful of her entari's hem in his hand, but he let it slide from his grip when she stood.

"How far can you walk?" Naime asked Makram when she had turned her back on Kadir.

"I'm fine." He tried to grin but it became a grimace as he moved away from her and toward his men. "As soon as you show my men to the physician," Makram ordered the guards, "you'll go back and retrieve the rest of my men from the tunnels. Three of them."

The guards deferred to Naime, and she ducked her head in agreement with his order.

Tunnels? She was unaware of any. He would explain later.

"Grand Vizier, you owe my men a drink," Makram called over his shoulder as he rounded the corner into the hall.

Three of the palace guards remained. Naime gestured them toward Cemil.

"Sultana Efendim, imprisoning my son is ludicrous," Kadir said, holding his hand up in a command to the guards as they moved to obey her. "There was no stipulation against magic."

"There was one against lasting harm. That burn is deep, Grand Vizier. It is quite possible the Agassi will lose function in that hand. And that"—she pointed to Cemil's hip as he stood, where the borrowed sword hung—"is not a practice blade."

"The Agassi used a practice sword, and my son was wounded anyway." Kadir gestured at Cemil.

"A chance Cemil was aware of when he joined the game. I will have him released when his fine is paid." She raised her hand and the three remaining guards surrounded Cemil. He waved them off, limping past Naime with a mock salute. Naime glanced at Samira, who whirled and walked back to the dais, where she might be spared the scrutiny of all the Viziers.

Naime addressed the room. "This exercise is over, and by my estimation the Agassi and his men have won. Do you agree?"

She looked at each face in turn. The last half of the day had been tense and uncomfortable. Many of the Viziers had disagreed with Kadir's decision to move, but as Yavuz had pointed out, were cowed by Kadir. Now, everyone in the room knew he would be furious. It was not his temper that worried Naime, but the calculating expression that he wore.

"Agreed," he said, in a dead tone.

"Then I will give the terms of the negotiation to Yavuz Pasha for the Council to review and seal. They will be sent with the Agassi to be presented to the Mirza in Al-Nimas."

"Yes, Efendim," Kadir said, and bowed.

Naime's elation at Makram's success, at her plan moving forward, withered against the heat of her suspicion.

Kadir straightened, and as he did, his gaze raked up her body and to her face. He smiled.

EIGHTEEN

"IT WOULD BE BEST if you rested for a turn before traveling," the physician, Ceylik, said as he packed up his supplies. "And if you keep the burns on your hand covered in the salve it should prevent it scarring so badly you lose the use of it."

Makram examined the bandage and started to flex his hand open experimentally.

"Let it rest," Ceylik said, sharply.

"Habit," Makram replied.

Tareck stood by the doors leading to the garden, his arms folded across his chest. His expression revealed concern, though he was attempting to hide it. Makram felt the same. Though Ceylik had stitched them, the nearly mirrored slashes on Makram's left and right side would scar. That did not matter in comparison to whether he would have the full use of his hand. He already had scars. The whips of heat that Cemil had employed had left other burns along his back, belly, and neck, but they were minor in comparison to Makram's hand. If he did lose any use in it, Kadir and his son would know the full power of Makram's magic, and not a thing they owned would be left intact.

"Captain Habaal will take you to see my men," Makram said. He had wanted them treated first, but Tareck had insisted all their wounds were superficial.

"I'll track someone down to have food sent," Tareck said, eyeing Makram critically as he stood from the couch where Ceylik had treated him. Dizziness came and went, leaving only exhaustion. "You're all right?" Tareck asked when Makram grabbed the back of the couch to steady himself.

Makram waved him away. They both knew he was best left alone after battle, to allow his magic to settle. Having painful wounds tended with even more painful treatments and foul-smelling creams had not improved his mood or his limits on his power. When the door shut behind the physician and Tareck, Makram exhaled loudly into the silence.

The physician had lit the brazier to warm the room, and now the heat was oppressive and exaggerated the lingering smell of the herbs and salve. Makram opened the doors into the garden and stepped out onto the patio. The night was damp and cool, and though the sun had set, light lingered enough to prevent the sight of stars.

This was his season, his time of day, and he had won his gamble. He should be completely at peace. Yet he was restless, the edge of his temper raw, his magic still in flux and barely contained. He considered whether he should return inside and go to the baths. His skin ached from the burns and the stitches, and he did not wish to add the sting of soap and water to his woes. Instead he stepped inside and grabbed his ferace. He hung it over his shoulders for warmth but didn't bother with the sleeves. The movements to put it on fully would require contortions he did not care to execute in his condition.

When he returned to the garden, he walked, and was halfway to the dead fig tree before he realized where he was going. Makram stopped, staring at the skeletal figure of it, its bark pale in the deepening evening. He had walked as if he were drawn to it, though he knew it wasn't the tree that called him. The garden path ended past the tree, at the Sultan's rooms. But the tree was planted in front of the Sultana's rooms, right in front of the windows and glass doors that led into her sitting room. Makram cursed himself for being a pathetic fool and continued walking until he reached the tree.

He pressed a hand to its gnarled trunk. It had been dead some time, he sensed that through his magic. Intuition, gut feelings… mages had to train themselves to listen to such things. They were the voice of magic, the way it spoke to its host. Some senses were more subtle than others, like this, just a fleeting idea of seasons passing across an unchanging shell. Other times magic spoke more loudly, as it did next, filling his thoughts with winter sun and breezes. That was the signature of the Sultana's magic.

He turned. She stood framed by the light of the mage orbs in her rooms, just inside the doors, holding the curtains open with one hand as she watched him. Her garments were much simpler than the ones she wore earlier, and they suited her, slim-cut silver salvar and a form-fitting caftan in the same flattering shade, which pulled over her head instead of buttoning down the front. There was no entari layered over it to add bulk, and the simple cut showed her slim figure to advantage. Her hair fell against her back in a dark cascade. It shone as rich as the mink furs the noble women in Sarkum loved so much. Would it feel as soft as those furs if he stroked his fingers through it? He wanted to.

That was why he had walked to the tree. He wanted her close, wanted to purge the violence and anger from the day with the sound of her voice, to wash away the heat of battle and the scent of blood with the winter of her magic and rose of her perfume.

The fact he should not want any of those things, and was not allowed them, stayed distant and buried beneath everything else. She opened the doors and stepped out, pausing to close them before crossing to him. Her gaze flicked to his face, but not his eyes, her expression wary, as if he were an injured and rabid wolf and not a wounded and tired man.

"I expected to see you," Makram said, only realizing how much of his restlessness was her absence when his voice came out gruff with accusation.

"I wasn't certain if you would or not. If you would blame me for Kadir's scheme at the end, or Cemil's cheating, or whether your magic might be too near the surface for company."

"It is," he confessed, "and I do not blame you." His magic was certainly too near the surface to be near her, who stripped him of sense and control without even trying. But they were alone, for the moment. She had already proved trustworthy when it came to keeping the secret of his magic.

"Will your pride be wounded if I ask if you are all right?"

"Marginally," he teased. "I would rather you thought so highly of my skill that you could only assume I was all right." Some of her wariness eased, and she smiled a little, her gaze dropping to his bandaged hand. Makram lifted it. "Your physician claims if I keep his vile salve on it that it may prevent scarring."

"It will. That was the same salve we used on the Sehzade." She stepped closer. "It is vile. It still makes me sick whenever I smell it."

"But the Sehzade is scarred," Makram said, miserable and peaceful in her company. His body ached, the burns seemed to reach to his bones, the stitched gashes throbbed and stung, but she took his mind from it. Took his mind to other things, things he wanted and could not have.

"Some of the burns were…" She drew a breath that shook, her eyes half closing before she shook her head. "Only the fact that his magic transformed to ice saved his life. There was nothing anyone could do for him."

"I've never heard of that, magic changing its manifestation."

"I have only seen one similar event recorded, but it was not as drastic as Ihsan's," she said.

He watched her take a breath and square her shoulders, as if preparing for some great trial. Then she closed the space between them and took his injured hand in both of hers, lifting it so she could press her palm against the bandage. Her magic swirled loose, breezes teasing strands of her hair and slipping over his skin. Her palm grew cold against his, her winter wind soothing the ache in his hand.

"This helped him, sometimes," she said, shyly, and lifted her face. Pale light shone in her eyes, freed by her use of magic. He wanted to see it fully unleashed, dancing on her skin.

"What happened to him?" He chanced curling his fingers between hers, and his wounded hand protested, but her magic soothed it.

"We have never been able to prove it," she said, quietly, "but you have had a taste of how Kadir deals with those who get in his way."

"*He* did that to your cousin? Burned a water mage? And there was no proof?" He had so many questions, but he did not wish to prod her. Kadir's power was formidable, if he was able to nearly kill a mage in opposition. That was, supposedly, impossible.

"No proof strong enough to turn the Council against him. He is a Charah of lies, a master swordsman whose blades are deception and charm. He is wealthy and influential, and far too smart to leave evidence," she said, tempered fury in her voice.

"Why didn't your father strip his memories for proof?"

"The Council would never stand for that. It is a brutal, vile spell. And my father and Behram Kadir were boyhood friends. My father took something from him…and Kadir never forgave him. And my father could not forgive himself either, or stop grieving the loss of a man he always considered a friend."

What about her? What would Kadir do to her if he could no longer hold her back with political maneuvering? His imagination took the thought and twisted it into the direst of possibilities then set them loose in his mind, so as he looked at her all he could see was fire.

In response his magic twisted and surged out of his hold.

"Makram," she said, gently, staring up at him, her own magic suddenly extinguished, and she pulled her hand from his. He realized too late that the bonds on his power had slipped, his thoughts seized by the horror of what Kadir could do to her. He knew how he appeared, shadows like smoke wafted beneath his skin, swirls of ink and void.

Her gaze strayed to his, then swept across his face and neck, following the dancing movement of his magic. Apprehension twisted a circle in his belly, his breath caught, waiting for her fear, her repulsion. It was too late to pull it back now that it was loose and she had seen it.

He had once used his magic to carve a ruined sculpture in his mother's garden into a bird bath, and she had been furious with him. Admittedly, it hadn't been a very good birdbath, but he had only been ten turns. His father had it destroyed, because he did not want a constant visual reminder of the son born with ruin in his blood. His mother's fury and his father's edict served as a lifetime reminder that even those he loved hated his magic.

"I suppose I could see"—her brows drew together and she lifted her hand as though she meant to touch his face, or at least the manifestation of his magic—"how someone might be terrified by you." She stepped closer yet again, so close her clothes brushed his.

"Are you?" he asked, his voice uneven as he tried to prevent the magic speaking when he did, and because she was close, and he wanted her to touch him. He felt broken open, with his magic revealed to her, and was certain her touch would mean she did not think he was an abhorrent monster.

"No." She smiled. "But I have never seen a black quite so absolute."

She was speaking of his eyes. While hers had shone with pale light in the flare of her magic, and her cousin's blue like deep ice, his opened to the void, to the absolute nothing of oblivion. The first time he had seen it as a child he had wept, because he realized no one would ever look at him and not be afraid.

"Unfortunately"—he cleared his throat to ease the tightening in it—"we do not get to choose if our magic is beautiful or not."

"All magic is beautiful," she said, "and terrible. Do you not see the beauty in yours, or the terror in mine?" Her fingers brushed his cheek. "You can stop a heart, and I can stop your breath."

She turned her hand, her thumb tracing a sinuous path over his jaw and down his neck, following the trail of magic as it moved across his skin, leaving a streak of raw heat in the wake of her touch. His breath did stop, but not because of her magic.

"I can shine like dawn, and you bring the peace of dusk." She pulled her hand away. "Beginnings and endings. That is why there must be balance. To relieve the terrible with the beautiful, to make the beautiful more precious, for the threat of its absence." She hesitated, her gaze lifting to his, meeting his eyes.

"You say the most incredible things." His power lurched, searching, scrambling toward her. Her magic answered the power of his, a faint glow emanating from her skin. Most magic manifested as a suggestion of its power, so, swirls of ice and crystal in her cousin, fire in Kadir's eyes. But she simply glowed, so beautiful he couldn't look away from her.

"May I?" She held her hands to either side of his face, and he did not know what she was asking permission for, but he didn't care, and simply grunted. Her hands closed against his cheeks and she tipped his face toward hers as she peered into his eyes. "Is it meant to do that?" She came too close, her nose almost touching his, so her words and breath touched his lips. "Draw me in as if I'll never escape?"

"I do not know exactly." He swallowed against the pull of her, the draw to kiss her until her breath and light was his. "Even in Sarkum much of the truth of the Sixth House has been lost."

Her eyes saddened, flicking from his and over his face until her gaze caught on his mouth. Heat cut a line up his spine.

"You underestimate your effect on me, I think, Sultana," he whispered, lifting his hands to grip her wrists. Pain burned through his left, a reminder that he should be eating and resting, not testing his self-control against the magnetic pull of her.

His voice broke, ravaged with the rise of emotion and memories he tried never to think about. She had passed his test, and not even realized she was being tested, and he didn't want to let her go. He wanted to keep her near him so he could feel like a normal man for a moment longer.

She made no pull to move back. "You said we could become friends." Her hands on his face were gentle and chilled, and he could feel the brush of her magic like gusts of breeze against his own. Her First House power resonating against his Sixth, harmony on the Wheel. She was cool and composed, a thinker and a planner, and he unpredictable and mercurial, someone who acted before he thought. Did she realize they were balanced too?

Balanced and impossible. He was nothing, and she had all the makings of the greatest ruler he would see in his lifetime.

"I did," he said, and nearly choked on the words for the bitterness they caused him.

"You asked to call me by name as your prize if you won today, do you remember?"

"I remember." Kadir and his cheating had stolen the joy of his victory, but anything she gave him would be reward enough. "I thought you were avoiding me so I could not collect, so I came to find you." He stroked the insides of her wrists with his thumbs, because he could not have her so close and remain still.

She laughed quietly, then rolled to her tiptoes, stretching up to press her lips against his cheek. "It is yours," she said against his ear. Her skin was cool and smooth against his, and her hair slid against his jaw, so it took all of his restraint not to tangle his hands in it and hold her to him.

"Naime," he pleaded. His body reacted on instinct, out of desperation, and he moved his face toward hers, to kiss her, but she turned and ducked her head, lowering back to her heels with a barely audible apology.

Makram released his grip on her wrists, dropping his hands to his sides.

"I am glad you came," she said, hesitantly. "Thank you. For what you risked and accomplished today. I know it wasn't for me, but I am grateful."

"It was for you." Truth forced out of him because his unleashed magic ate away his restraint, and her nearness destroyed his reason. Her wide, brown eyes met his for a breathless eternity, so he was certain she thoroughly stripped him to the truth and heart in her mind's eye. He could not see past her magic, her self-control, could not discern if she felt the way he did.

"Let it be for everyone, for Sarkum and Tamar," she said, "but not for me."

"They need to hear you. I wanted them to listen. I did it for you, because I believe in you."

Her brows furrowed as she lifted her fingers to smooth away the same furrow on his own brow. He closed his eyes, trying to take what he needed from the simple touch.

"You are a good man, aren't you?" She dropped her hands away, leaving him wanting. "Reckless." She smiled. "But kind and brave and reasonable. How lucky your brother is to have you."

The mention of Kinus chilled him. Everything fell over him like the stones of a crumbling wall. He had told her she could trust him, and he had lied. Was lying. He still had to return to Al-Nimas and convince Kinus, and she thought that was already done. What a complete mess he was making. Destruction mage indeed. He had to tell her. He could not lie to her anymore.

"I'd like for you to meet him, and when you do, feel free to tell him how lucky he is."

"Would he come here?"

"I was hoping to convince you to come to Sarkum with me when I deliver the terms," he confessed. "He is as reluctant as your Council about an alliance." This didn't seem like the time to describe his brother's complicated relationship with magic, since it was impossible to do so without revealing himself as a Charah. That was another entanglement he did not need.

"I see," she said, carefully. Her gaze fixed on his face, her expression taut with suspicion. Too perceptive by half, this woman. "Yet he sent you?"

He said nothing, but whatever of his tension showed in his face was enough to reveal the truth to her.

"Did you come on your own?" Her voice somehow carried both accusation and breathless denial. She was not going to forgive him. The thought brought on a hitch of desperation. He could not bear it if he never saw her again, never spoke to her again. If she despised him.

"He is temperamental. His first reaction is rarely his last. I knew if I gave him time, if I approach him with concrete terms, he would see reason. And I believe he will listen to you, even if he will not listen to me."

She folded her hands in front of her caftan, which he had come to realize was the first indication she was shutting herself away behind her armor. He could almost watch the protections fall into place around her, mental and magical, cool stoicism to wall her away from him, his senses, and his magic.

"Come with me." He started to reach for her but stopped. There was so much more he wanted to say but couldn't. "I believe you will succeed where I have failed."

"You waited until I was indebted to you to ask this of me," she said, with all the cold winter of her power in her voice, "to admit the truth to me."

"No. That isn't it at all," he said, reaching toward her. "I came because I believe in this as much as you do. It was the only way."

Naime stepped back, holding her hands up to stay him. "I will consider it."

He tried desperately to think of something to say to her to bring the warmth back to her expression. But he'd lost her, damaged her trust in him.

"Good night, Agassi." She strode to her room.

NINETEEN

NAIME'S FATHER PRESSED THE seal bearing his *tughra* to the cooling white wax.

They had reviewed the terms together the night before. It should have felt like a victory, but because of Makram's revelation, it felt like a battle half finished. She handed the documents to Yavuz Pasha, taking the opportunity to glance at Kadir as she did. He seemed pleased, and that disturbed her.

Yavuz Pasha rolled the documents once the wax was cooled and inserted them into a messenger tube, which they then sealed again. He presented the leather case to Makram. There were only a handful of other Viziers present in the Council Hall, and a servant had brought a small table to serve as a desk for her father. The quiet of the somber gathering felt all wrong.

"When will you be leaving, Agassi?" Kadir asked as Makram handed the messenger tube to Tareck. The Grand Vizier stood to the Sultan's right, but not on the dais, and Naime to her father's left, at his shoulder.

"A few more days, I think, before the wounds are closed enough to ride." He held his bandaged hand up, his gaze fixed on Kadir. "Though this will take turns to heal."

"Even the most unseasoned of Tamar's mages knows never to grab a Fifth House mage in a fight, Agassi, and even a simpleton would have thought to let go." Kadir smiled. Someone laughed quietly; others shifted in discomfort.

Makram smiled in return. "Is it wise to bait a man who knows secrets about your palace that you do not? I would hate for something unpleasant to happen to you in your sleep."

Kadir's smile slipped, not in fear, but anger.

"Gentlemen," Naime said, "this is a momentous occasion, marking the first real steps toward mending the past. Please do not sully it with your sword-rattling."

"I doubt the Grand Vizier would ever rattle his sword, Sultana," Makram said. "Surely he'd have someone do it for him."

"That is enough," Naime ordered, staring at Makram in disbelief. Had he lost his senses completely? "You will speak to the Grand Vizier with respect, Agassi."

Kadir smiled in surprised pleasure.

"And you will not bait a prince of Sarkum, Grand Vizier," Naime said to him. His smile disappeared. "Are there any other children in need of scolding?" she asked the room. One of the gathered Viziers cleared his throat. Her father gave a short bark of a laugh.

"Just like her mother, isn't she, Behram?" His eyes held a look in them she hadn't seen since before her mother died. Calculation. Kadir saw it too, and he tipped his head in agreement, his jaw set too tensely for words. More passed between them, but it was lost on Naime. An unattributable tension occupied the silence.

Yavuz Pasha clapped his hands together. "I believe this concludes our business, yes, Sultanim?"

"Are we not sending delegates?" the Sultan asked.

Naime avoided Makram's glance. Though she had decided that morning she would go, his betrayal lingered, the sense she had given him too much and allowed herself to be wounded too humiliating.

"Yes, Efendim. I would like your permission to accompany the Agassi to Al-Nimas to speak on your behalf." She bowed to him slightly.

Kadir whirled, addressing Naime and not her father. "Absolutely not."

Naime raised her eyebrows, and her father tapped his knuckles against the table.

Kadir managed to rein in his temper, bowing slightly, and spoke his next words more calmly. "The journey is dangerous, Sultanim, as evidenced by the Agassi arriving wounded. We cannot risk the Sultana being injured or worse. And the Sultana has only just come of age, surely there are more qualified delegates to send?"

"She has been dealing with you since she was a child, I do not know who could be more qualified," the Sultan said.

Kadir gave a polite smile, but his eyes reflected fire and insult. Makram coughed, turning his head and holding his uninjured hand up in a fist to cover his mouth. Naime glared at him and put a hand on her father's shoulder.

"Grand Vizier, your concern for my welfare is touching, as always. You will recall I am perfectly capable of taking care of myself. But to put your mind at ease, I will take Lieutenant Terzi and a guard contingent with me." She faced her father, who regarded her with lucid, grave focus. "You have put me in charge of this alliance from the beginning, and so I believe I am the best choice to represent it."

"You will take a guard contingent, and a full host of attendants. And you." The Sultan pointed at Makram. "If she is harmed, I will expect to hear you died trying to prevent it."

Makram studied her face, which she kept impassive, and bowed to the Sultan. "I swear it."

"Let it be known I do not support this," Kadir said, his hand tightening so hard against his staff that his skin rubbed audibly against the wood.

"Noted," the Sultan sighed. "You and I will speak alone, Behram. The rest of you are dismissed."

"Father," Naime protested. She didn't want him alone with Kadir. Who knew what ideas Kadir might plant or whether her father would lapse again while she wasn't around to manage it? That same fear had nearly prevented her deciding to travel. Ihsan and Bashir had assured her they would keep him protected in her absence. Even that was barely enough to ease her concern. If the possibility of alliance did not hinge on her travel, she would never leave him. But Makram had made it clear that it did.

"You may go, Daughter," he said, gruffly. Naime grit her teeth as she bowed to him, then descended the dais.

"May I walk with you?" Makram asked under his breath, as she passed him. Naime stopped, steeling herself, and faced him. The Viziers were making their way from the benches and into the aisle, and Yavuz Pasha offered his arm. Naime slid her arm into the Vizier's. Makram's jaw clenched.

"Please inform me when you have decided on the day you would like to travel. Once I have decided who will be traveling with me I will pass the information along to you. Is there anything else?" she asked.

"No," Makram said, his eyes narrowed with resignation, and maybe, resentment.

"Good day then, Agassi." Naime ducked her head and let Yavuz Pasha lead her out of the room.

Her meeting with Makram in the garden had been troublesome for far more than the revelation that Makram had lied about the circumstances of his arrival in Tamar. They were growing too close. Even a friendship would have to be carefully managed, to avoid the appearance of anything inappropriate. She was inexperienced with intimate relationships, certainly, but she wasn't a fool. Her attraction to him grew stronger with every moment they spent together, every look she cast his way, every stray, wishful thought she indulged.

Whatever he wanted from her outside of the alliance, whether friendship, the chance to bed a princess, affection…it didn't matter. It had gone too far. Until she had herself and her desires under control, she could not be alone with him.

When they reached the foyer she glanced back. Makram stood unmoved, head bowed, and beyond him Kadir stood on the dais by her father, bent forward and speaking urgently to him. Her father was watching Makram, and then his gaze shifted to hers, his expression unreadable.

Twenty

The man wore rancor like raiment. And could do so indefinitely, it seemed.

Naime looked at him for what might have been the hundredth time over the first two days of their journey. Tareck rode in the lead, and his soldiers and her guards rode interspersed around her and her attendants. Makram rode in front of her and her circle of handmaids and other attendants, so she had spent a great deal of time staring at his back.

It was not an unpleasant view, despite the mood that clung to him. The shape of his broad shoulders, the suggestion of strength beneath the layers of caftan, entari, and ferace. Even the metal clasp that bound his black hair was a better sight than the winter-ravaged mountainside that stretched endlessly before them.

Despite her attempts to prevent such thoughts, remembering how much she had enjoyed touching Makram in the garden kept her from thinking of how badly her back and legs ached. Wishing he would come to his senses and speak to her so she could look at something other than his back kept her from focusing on the questions that had chased her even in sleep.

What was Kadir planning, and what had her father spoken to him about? Was everything all right in her absence? Was Ihsan faring well? She had hardly slept the first few nights for fear of what might happen between Kadir and her father. The distance was too great for a Diviner to speak with Ihsan, even if they had carried essence water with them. So she knew nothing. She trusted Ihsan, she trusted Bashir. Samira reminded her, when she grew too agitated.

So she tried to think of something else. If she focused on pleasant things, it stalled her fearful thoughts. And it helped tame the desire to shove Makram face first out of his saddle for acting like such an unbearable ass.

His silence extended only to her, it seemed. He and Tareck spent time with both the Tamar guards and the servants, asking after their welfare and generally instilling goodwill. Their efforts did not quell all the tension. The Sarkum soldiers were resentful of the burden of men and women unaccustomed to riding long days and camping in frozen wilderness. Her people were on edge with the presence of soldiers of a longtime enemy nation, armed with swords, bows, and experience. Even Samira, whose stoicism often rivaled Naime's, showed a great deal of fiery surliness. She did not like the snow and the cold and the hard, frozen ground.

Naime didn't care for it either, but winter was shared by the Sixth and First House, and cool weather was in her blood and power, which made it easier for her to bear. Samira was happiest when temperatures baked the ground to hard clay and sweat was an ever-present annoyance. She and Tareck had traded many stories about summertime activities and food, which Naime thought only made the cold feel worse, but seemed to cheer them both.

As they descended the narrow trail from the pass and toward the Engeli in the distance, fat, heavy flakes of snow fell around them. It guaranteed that when night finally came and they camped, everyone would be wet and miserable and sleep little. The night they'd spent in the pass had been the coldest Naime had ever been, despite the fires they built and Samira and Lieutenant Terzi's combined efforts at warming the air around them.

Sarkum would be warmer, though Tareck warned the winds that swept the barrens were brutally cold.

Samira pulled her hood more tightly around her head with a muted sigh of misery. Naime glanced sideways at her friend, who only stuck her tongue out in response. What would Cemil Kadir think of his Spark trekking through the winter wilderness of the Kalspire? She doubted he had the fortitude to attempt anything like it. But then, she had always loved Samira and despised Cemil, and could not understand the bond between them.

"It pleases me that this trek has served to bring our people closer through trial," Naime announced. At the front of the formation, Tareck gave a harsh laugh, and some of his soldiers joined in with less enthusiastic chuckles. Makram's shoulders tensed, then relaxed and she thought he might turn, but he did not. This was the closest he allowed himself to her at any point. At night he made certain to keep the entirety of the camp between them even when chatting with her attendants.

Naime oscillated from feeling hurt by his avoidance to reminding herself that she had all but demanded it. He was doing what she obviously lacked the will to do. It was a good thing.

When they made camp that night, half a day's ride into the Sarkum side of the Engeli and into the barrens, Tareck sat with Lieutenant Terzi and his men and sketched out a rough map in half-frozen mud. They talked for quite some time about the route they would take through the barrens, about the bandits that sometimes prowled it, about tactics and how they would travel through it.

Their talk of ambushes and the fate of some travelers served to keep Naime awake and staring at the ceiling of her tent for the better part of the night, and Samira lay with her in mute, worried camaraderie. There had been little danger of attack in the steep, snow-cloaked mountains, but winter brought desperation, and the flatlands would be dangerous. The landscape they would travel through beginning the next day Naime knew only from studying maps.

In the morning, Naime took some time to study the Engeli while the camp was packed. The name meant wall or barrier, but it wasn't block stone or brick and mortar. At the end of the Sundering War the earth Charah of the time, Vural Tekin, had brought the Engeli into being at the cost of his life and the lives of a dozen earth mages. Razors of white and yellow stone streaked through with black, pockmarked basalt sliced toward the sky, too high to scale without ropes and a disregard for one's life. He'd built it to protect Tamar from the return of those they had cast out, to seal magic away from the rest of the world. It had remained for two centuries. There was only one place, the Gate, that allowed passage. Tamar had built towers for watchmen to overlook the dry plains of Sarkum and prevent the movement of anyone but merchants and traders.

She had seen it once from the Tamar side, as a child, just before the fire that nearly took Ihsan's life. Her mother had brought her to it to tell her the story of Vural and how he had poured his life force into its creation, after draining the Circle and a contingent of his brethren of all their power. Her mother had told her that he would not have had to die to do it, had they not murdered the Charah of the Sixth House. That a closed Circle, a balanced Wheel, bestowed power to all mages. That Chara'a fed and were fed by all mages of their House and their lives and power protected Tamar without need for a wall of stone and earth's blood. That had been the last Circle of Chara'a to stand.

If she could bring the Circle of Chara'a back, they would destroy the Engeli. Tamar was not meant to be cordoned off from the world, but to serve as a font of magic, of wonder and power.

Naime drew a circle across her palm, an ancient prayer, and a reminder of the promise she had made to her mother. And to herself.

TWENTY-ONE

MAKRAM WATCHED HER HIKE up to the rise and stand there, staring west toward the Engeli, and debated whether to go to her or not. He had chafed under his self-imposed silence for two days, and it was all he could take. He'd talked to everyone but the one person he wanted to.

He joined her on the rise and spoke before she realized he was there. "What do you see when you look at it?"

Naime let her breath out slowly as he came up beside her, as if he had surprised her or annoyed her, or both.

"Folly," Naime said.

Makram laughed, and she questioned it with a look.

"That is not what I expected you to say." He'd thought she might aggrandize the power of Tamar magic and what it could do.

"What do you see?"

"A wall," Makram said, as he curved his hand over the hilt of his sword. It was good to have it back. He'd felt vulnerable every moment he had to spend without it in the palace.

The camp stretched below them, in the shadow of the looming stone, and he watched the soldiers and attendants pack it up in preparation for the day's travel.

"A soldier's assessment," Naime said. "What does the prince see?"

"You do know I'm only a prince in the barest sense of the word, don't you?"

"I have begun to understand that, yes."

"I see two centuries of unbreakable prejudice," Makram said.

"No, not unbreakable." She pointed at the Gate, a tunnel through the rock, drilled over Turns by earth mages, only barely visible from where they stood. How did she do that? See the possibility…the brightness in things so easily? No, he couldn't bear another day of pretending that every moment he avoided her wasn't torture.

"Naime." Makram sighed. "What can I say to make you forgive me? I did not keep the circumstances from you out of spite, but in the interest of pursuing an alliance."

"I forgave you before we left. I wish you had informed me sooner, but I can hardly condemn you, considering I forged a letter in my father's name," she said wryly.

"Two," he corrected. Relief unfurled in him at her small smile.

"Very well, two. You would know I had forgiven you, if you had deigned to speak to me in all this time." Her annoyed tone made the relief burn brighter, and he wanted to gather her up in his arms and squeeze her until she understood that he had missed her. He'd only known her for a turn, and yet he could barely contain his desire to know her better, to know everything.

"You wouldn't even look at me in the Council Hall or walk with me to allow me to explain. I was trying to respect that." He shook his head. "But these may be the last chances I ever have to speak with you, to learn more about you. After this, you will return to Tamar and be married, and I will likely be fighting a war."

He was never going to see her again. Or if so, only in passing, only for orders to be given and reports to be made. The thought sent his mood plummeting into the void of his magic.

"Then the first thing you should know is I have no intention of marrying anyone," she said, with finality but little volume.

Makram tried to hide his surprise, but failed, which caused a small, resigned smile to pass across her face.

"It has been my father's intention to make me his heir in my own right, though if he will remember that when I need him to is in question."

"Is that why you sent the second letter?" Makram asked. "So we would arrive before you were betrothed?"

She ducked her chin. "I am, at the moment, your best chance at an alliance. The Grand Vizier does not think we need Sarkum. And he wants my father's seat, if it were not immediately obvious to you. His best means of obtaining it is through a marriage between me and his son, who will serve only as puppet to the Grand Vizier."

"So marry someone else."

The idea of Cemil Kadir putting his hands on her made him crazy.

She gave a soft exhale that might have been a laugh. "Spoken like a man whose marriage holds little political significance."

Makram grimaced. The comment stung his pride for its reference to his extraneous position, and because it made him feel she might view him as worthless. "People do not marry for love in Tamar?"

She looked at him crossly. "Some do, outside of the nobility it is common. But I am the daughter of a Sultan. If you think of me as a scepter of office that is bestowed upon someone, rather than a woman, you will come closer to the truth of what part of my own fate I currently control."

She continued to look at him, and one corner of her mouth curved up. "How long did it take before you thought I might be part of the negotiation terms offered by my father? A brood mare bartered for an army?"

Heat burned his face, and he clenched his teeth, wrenching his gaze away from her. It would have been humiliating in any case, but his admiration of her had grown so significantly in so few days that he felt even fouler for it.

She made a thoughtful sound, and he wanted to drop to his knees to ask forgiveness, and wouldn't that be an interesting picture for everyone watching them from down below.

"I would rather die than give my father's seat to someone who sees power where they should see responsibility. And I would rather watch the sultanate fall than marry Cemil and leave my people in the hands of Behram Kadir."

Makram considered her words, the vehemence with which she spoke them.

"I will fight it until there is nothing left in me. Until every trick, loophole, and contingency are exhausted."

"Spoken like a true warrior," Makram said. She seemed unsure about whether he was jesting.

"Of the pen and the law, perhaps. Certainly not of the sword."

"Your kind is rarer, I think. Those who believe in and care about what's right for all, and will stand for it."

"Isn't that why you fight, as a soldier?"

"No. I do it because it is all I know."

"I don't think I believe that. Not after what I've seen of you."

He wanted to know what she had seen, what she thought of him. When he'd arrived in the throne room after the tunnels, she had looked at him with fierce, bright admiration. He'd wanted to stride up the dais and kiss her, and afterward had been angry for even thinking it.

"I'm a soldier because my parents had the son they needed and didn't want another." Didn't want a boy who could destroy the palace in a fit of temper, take a life with a simple thought. Didn't want a child who was a nation's nightmare brought to life.

"From the little I have put together, I might suggest they chose the wrong son," Naime said, softly, and lifted her eyes to his. "You are the one who is concerned about the greater good of your people, if you are the one fighting, bleeding, and sacrificing for an alliance that will strengthen them. What is your brother doing? What will he do to you for this, for defying him to travel to Tamar, for bringing us back with you?"

The accusation in her tone, the disdain, rankled.

"You don't understand. Ruling was thrust upon him suddenly when our father died, and the Council of Elders bullies him and does not believe him fit to rule in our father's place. He..." Makram trailed off as her brows rose in slow increments with each word, and he realized what a callous fool he was being.

"Yes," she said, dryly, and fixed her gaze to the Engeli once more. "I could see how that might be very trying for him."

"I mean that sometimes he makes poor decisions, but he can be reasoned with." Makram chafed at the realization of his own stupidity and rubbed a hand over the back of his neck.

"Well, nothing can be done about it until we reach Al-Nimas. Then we shall see how reasonable he is."

TWENTY-TWO

THE BARRENS WERE A featureless expanse of rolling, wind-whipped misery. The mood in the group was significantly colder with fear and tension. The soldiers rode more closely together around the main group, and pairs of Sarkum riders broke away in shifts to circle them at a distance, serving as advanced warning for possible attacks. It made Naime all the gladder for Makram's company.

He rode with her the better part of the day, though he made a perimeter ride several times to speak with the farthest outlying of his riders. Each time he returned to her side Samira gave Naime a sideways look of curiosity, and she knew she'd be answering questions once they made camp for the night. What could she say? Revealing feelings to Samira would only strengthen them and make her more miserable for it.

Makram was quiet for much of the ride, though it was an easy silence, one she found comfortable rather than anxious. But during the worst of the weather, he distracted everyone near enough to hear him by telling the story of their battle through the tunnels in the Cliffs. Tareck added occasional dry commentary, which earned him laughs. That led to conversations between the Sarkum soldiers and the Tamar guards, about training tactics they shared, and those they did not. Occasionally one of them laughed when some common trial was revealed, such as Bashir's fondness for punishment involving physical hardship.

There were too many times she corrected herself for staring at Makram. Too many times she had to chide herself for the details she committed to memory. The easy way he sat in the saddle, as if he were born to it. The confident and practiced manner of his riding. She thought he had little need of the bridle—his horse seemed to respond to him as if it could read his thoughts. She saw the way his men looked for him frequently, how quickly they obeyed his commands, how he and Tareck communicated with so few words. And she could not help but notice, despite his alertness and tension, how much more at ease he seemed, now that he was away from the politics of Narfour.

There were other things. The flex of his leg nearest her, the movement of muscles beneath the fabric of his salvar, exposed because sitting bunched his caftan up. That he often stretched by raising up fully in his stirrups, that even in movement he was restless. His uninjured hand flexed open and closed when he was surveying their group. And all those restless movements ceased when he looked at her. Throughout the day their gazes locked and broke apart. When he made his relays around the circle of guards, he looked to her too often.

Once everyone had exhausted themselves of stories and conversations, the ride grew tedious. By the time they made camp that night, everyone was cold, angry, and on edge. The wind died with the sun, at least, so setting up camp was not quite the nightmare Naime had imagined it would be. Once her tent was erected, she went inside to set up her and Samira's things, and Samira joined her, with food for them both, lentils and winter vegetables. They sat on cushions and shared a piece of flatbread, using broken-off pieces to eat their food.

After a pleasant stretch of what Naime had thought was companionable silence, Samira exhaled audibly.

"Are you going to tell me," Samira asked, without looking up from her food, "about what I saw today?"

"What did you see?" Naime asked. The brutal cold and burning wind had made her hungrier than usual, so she finished her own food in a shocking amount of time. She knew exactly what Samira was asking, and set her bowl down, avoiding her friend's gaze.

"Anyone with half a wit saw," Samira replied, passing a skin with water in it to Naime.

"I know." She had seen others noticing one or the other of them staring at each other. She would bring herself under control for the remaining travel. There were enough stewards and attendants present to fill the palace with gossip for the rest of her natural life. But in the worst case, the problem would cease when they left Al-Nimas, and Makram, behind.

Something clenched in her chest, a dull ache that made her breath come short.

"Am I to pretend I have not seen the way you look at each other?"

"Yes," Naime said, coolly, standing.

Samira sighed again, picking up both of their bowls and muttering, "…could try to make it less obvious then." She ducked out of the tent.

Naime followed her, past the central fire and toward her attendants, who had gathered together to share their meal, their closeness helping ward them against the cold night. The first who saw her began to rise and she waved the action away. They resumed their meals, and Naime waited for Samira while she scraped their bowls clean with a rag and put them in the pile to be packed away the next day.

Two of the girls abruptly put their heads close together to speak quietly, and cast furtive glances behind Naime. More joined in shortly, and Naime knew they saw Makram. Wheel, did she look as besotted as they did? Their gazes tracked him as he walked, until he joined her.

"You have a number of admirers," she said quietly. His abrupt scrutiny sent her attendants into a frenzy of busywork.

"It never lasts long," Makram said, with amused disinterest. "Terror does not inspire affection, I'm afraid."

Naime pondered the implication of Makram's statement. Samira took Tareck's bowl from him and cleaned it as he chatted with her. Past them, at the distant perimeter of the camp, an odd shadow moved in a way that did not make sense.

“What is that?” She pointed. Heads turned in the direction she indicated and a hush fell. The amorphous shape coalesced and broke apart against the indigo night sky.

Makram cursed.

“Riders!” Tareck bellowed.

Then came the collective thunder of the hooves of a score of horses, though they were still some distance away, the bellows and cries of attackers and defenders, the clash of swords as the riders met the perimeter guards. An odd, numb kind of calm blanketed her, and she was distantly aware it was not the appropriate response. It wasn’t control, but a paralyzing fear.

“Arrows!”

Tareck dove against Samira, driving her to the ground beneath him.

The whip and snap of bowstrings came just before the strange, soft whistle of projectiles in the air. Naime just stood, staring at the blackened sky. Makram caught her around the waist and pulled her against him. Naime felt the reverberation in her own magic as he released the mental hold on his. He was solid and steady, contrast to the cool, insistent chaos that swept across her magic and thoughts when he released it.

Shadow burst from him like black flame, writhing through the air around them. He tightened his arm around her and swept the other in an arc over his head, drawing ink and smoke through the light cast by the fire. The volley of arrows fell all through the camp, but those that struck the black cloud of Makram’s magic disintegrated, and what was left of them rained like ash across the huddled circle of attendants.

One of them screamed, pointing at Makram as though he were the threat, her face pallid even in the light of the fire. Tareck lunged to his feet and drew his sword. Makram released Naime and went to Tareck’s side, drawing his own sword. Night’s darkness coiled around it, writhing and smoking.

Naime rushed to Samira and helped her to her feet. Riders careened through the camp, swinging swords wildly and yelling. Perhaps they meant to instill fear and chaos, rather than challenge the soldiers, and it proved quite effective on her people, who rose and tried to scatter. Makram and Tareck remained calm, only moving to turn their backs to each other, following the movement of the riders with their eyes and nothing more.

"Stay down," Naime commanded, keeping her voice calm. If they separated, the soldiers could not keep them safe. Some of them obeyed. Several did not.

Naime shouted after the runners. A rider materialized out of the night and swung down without bringing his horse to a stop, striding directly for Naime. Samira darted around her and lunged at him, and he laughed, catching her wrists and yanking her arms above her head.

"Fool," Samira snarled as she swung her arms down, turning her hands over and clasping his wrists. Sparks and fire flew from her, and the man howled in pain, yanking one hand out of her grasp and grabbing for a dagger. Samira pressed a hand to his face, glowing like an iron from the fire, and he screamed, dropping the dagger, then fell to his knees. She stumbled back, and Naime caught her arm, pulling her farther away from the man as he rolled on the ground, clutching his burned face and screaming.

The riders who had trampled the camp on their first pass circled and came again, this time organized, aiming for the huddling group of men and women.

"On the camp!" Tareck bellowed as Makram ran into the midst of the riders, wielding blade and shadow. Naime could feel the twist of his unleashed magic against hers, feel it reach and attempt to siphon power from her. For the briefest instant she was disoriented, panicked, but the searching of his magic stopped. Samira stared at her own stomach and clutched at her clothes as if she could physically stop the same feeling.

Charah. He was a Charah, and if they had been Sixth House mages as well, he could have used their power as his own.

Shock turned her to stone.

Men fell from their saddles. An attacker cried a warning about the death mage, but Makram moved through the midst of them like killing fog. Shadow twined around his blade, the magic deadlier than the blade it caressed, eroding weapons, clothes, anything it came in contact with. Naime and Samira hugged each other, Samira burying her face against Naime's shoulder, as Naime watched the battle.

Fear and awe grappled inside her. She did not want to be afraid of him, despite the senseless twist of animal panic that lunged through her. He was funny. He was soft spoken. She reminded herself. He was a mage like any other. Less capable of hurting her and those she loved than Behram Kadir was.

Naime repeated these things, again and again, as Makram unleashed horror in front of her.

Makram and Tareck stayed positioned between the riders and Naime's people, and the Sarkum soldiers and Tamar guards started at the rear of the riders, hemming them in, driving them toward Makram.

As the fighting slowed, and riderless horses escaped the fray, Makram and Tareck retreated toward Naime and Samira.

A final surge of men charged out of the milling horses, three focused on Makram and Tareck, a fourth and fifth maneuvering around them. One fell before he reached them, an arrow in his back, though Samira was well prepared for him, crackling with power. The other did not make it two steps beyond Makram. He cut his yataghan sideways across his opponent and continued through the turn, grabbing the last man by the back of the neck. The bandit gave a strange, sudden jerk. They were close enough Naime witnessed the life wink out in the man's eyes. Her heart seemed to beat too high in her chest, her breath quick and shallow.

Makram released his hold, letting the man's momentum send him toppling to the ground. His eyes met Naime's for one instant, his expression tightening with regret, then spun away.

"Perimeter clear," a soldier yelled from the direction the riders had come. Another echoed on the far edge of camp. The soldiers in camp rattled off similar reports, slowly making their way to the central fire, where Makram and Tareck had placed themselves.

"Did you know?" Samira asked Naime, her eyes wide and staring at Makram's back.

Naime's galloping heart and unsteady breath made it hard to think, to put words to all the emotions that were turning circles through her.

"I knew he was a Sixth House mage," Naime said. But not that he was a Charah. That was a lie of omission, but she could forgive it. To be a destruction mage in Tamar was dangerous enough. To be a Charah, capable of what Makram had just demonstrated, magic completely untethered, that needed neither touch, sigil, nor incantation, was a death sentence. That he had survived to adulthood, even in Sarkum, was a Wheel-blessed miracle.

No wonder he had mistrusted her when she had asked to see his magic. A Charah of any other House was a wonder, the pinnacle of magic. A Charah of the Sixth House would be seen as death incarnate. As he had just demonstrated.

From behind her, voices lowered in accusation. Samira likely did not hear them, but Naime was an air mage, and sound obeyed her.

Death mage. Killer. He was in the palace! Did she know? Did she see? An assassin. How could Tamar defeat a Sarkum army with a Charah?

"Sultana." Lieutenant Terzi jogged around the mess of horses and bodies left in the aftermath of the bandit attack, relieved when he saw her. "One of my men and one steward are injured."

"How badly?"

"Badly enough to need a better equipped physician."

She started to respond, but Samira shouted, "No!"

Naime spun in time to see one of Lieutenant Terzi's men drive a sword toward Makram's back. Makram barely twisted out of the way in time and blocked the next strike by sweeping his bent arm up and under the man's swing, then caught his sword hand by the wrist. He ripped the blade out of the guard's hand and reduced it to rusted, pitted metal in an instant, his eyes inked with endless night. The guard clasped Makram's wrist in turn and unleashed a heat spell.

"Wheel-cursed fire mages," Makram swore and tried to yank free.

Sarkum soldiers descended on Naime and her people, swords drawn, anger stark on their faces. Tareck drew his sword, and Naime knew if either guard or prince died, she and her people would not be leaving Sarkum alive.

She stalked out of the tangle of her attendants, toward the guard's back. Makram's face, painted with ink and shadow, was contorted in barely tempered fury and pain as he and the guard grappled.

"Abomination!" the guard cried.

Naime concentrated on him, on everything about him to direct her spell, to indicate her intention. Air and sound were hers to command, and he only stood a short distance away. She purged a sharp, harsh word. His back bowed, his jaw going slack and his eyes widening. He shrieked, pitching forward and ripping his arms free of Makram's grip as he dropped to his knees, grabbing at his ears. Blood trickled down his jaw. Naime released the spell and the piercing keen only he could hear, and he fell to the ground, curling around himself, hands clapped over his ears.

"Stand down," Tareck ordered his men as Makram staggered back, away from the prone guard. The edges of his coat sleeve were burned, he bore an angry red handprint on his right wrist. Fury at the sight of his wounds chased away any fear his unleashed magic had inspired in her. He saved them. He saved them from arrows, death, torture.

Naime faced the tightly huddled group of men and women she'd brought with her. The Sarkum men lowered their swords reluctantly, glancing from Tareck to Makram then her with confusion and betrayal.

"The next of you who dares to attack an ally of the Sultan, or even breathes the words death mage, will find yourselves aboard ships bound for Menei and an inhospitable welcome the moment we return to Narfour."

Unease rustled through them.

"Am I quite clear?" She spoke loudly enough she thought the guards at the Engeli Gate might hear her.

"Yes, Sultana," Samira prompted, and bowed, and the group followed suit. Naime rounded on Lieutenant Terzi, who cast glances between Makram and his own groaning subordinate, who still lay on the ground.

"I am not feeling especially generous, Lieutenant. If I catch a single word or action of insubordination from any of your men, I will leave them here to be dealt with by Sarkum law. Do you understand me?"

"Yes, Efendim," Terzi said, his expression grave, his darting a glance to Makram then away.

"That man is to be bound for the remainder of this journey. And when we return to Narfour he will be tried for attempted assassination."

"Yes, Efendim." He bowed.

Naime turned toward Makram, but he was gone. She looked around for him. Tareck caught her bewildered glance and approached her.

"Captain Habaal. The Lieutenant has informed me that two of ours are gravely injured. They require a physician."

He nodded, watching her attendants and stewards as they began to settle, checking each other over for wounds and sharing things they had seen.

"We have some supplies, but the nearest hospital and surgeon is in Al-Nimas. We'll get there tomorrow evening if we leave at first light. I'll have my men triage yours, to be certain," he said. "Sometimes excited soldiers judge wounds worse than they are right after a battle."

She knew he meant her guards, who were not as hardened to battle as his soldiers, might exaggerate out of fear. Her restless gaze slipped away from him, searching for Makram. Tareck cleared his throat.

"He'll return. He needs time, after he unleashes. Especially when his good deeds are punished." He watched as Lieutenant Terzi yanked his guard up and sat him on his haunches, then bound his hands and feet with rope.

"I can apologize for them, but it feels hollow," Naime said. Tareck studied her face, one corner of his mouth turning up with wry humor.

"Apologize? For being the only person to ever defend him publicly or punish someone who attacked him?" He shrugged. "If you like."

"The only one?" Anger and sadness wrestled for a place in her heart. "Not even his parents?"

"The only one, Efendim." Tareck took a step away from her and dropped to his knees, then bent forward at the waist and placed his hands on the ground.

"Please get up," Naime said, as her men and women broke into excited chatter and some of Tareck's men approached to do as Tareck, dropping to their knees in the mud.

"That is unnecessary. I am not the one who saved us. In fact," she said, "I am appalled that every person in this camp did not fall to their knees in gratitude to the Agassi the moment they realized they were still alive and well thanks to him."

Her stewards and attendants, huddled together near the fire, grew quiet, some of them appearing chastised. A few faces were angry, but all were silent.

Tareck sat back on his feet and rose and she thought he repressed a grin before he gestured to his men, who got to their feet.

"Lieutenant Terzi." Tareck ducked his head to her as he moved away. "Bring your wounded over there with ours." The two of them moved past the dying fire, which a Sarkum soldier tried to coach from coals to blaze. Naime watched him. She needed to remain and see to her people, but she wanted to search for Makram.

Samira stepped beside her, studied the soldier who poked at the fire, and then held a hand toward it and whispered a spell. The fire blazed up, startling the soldier so he gave a shout and fell back on his haunches. Samira apologized, but the soldier kept an eye on her as he fed the fire more wood.

"You have perhaps missed your calling as a battle mage," Naime said quietly.

Samira flushed. "Do not praise me yet, Efendim. I was just as frightened as the others when I realized what he was."

"But you did not try to kill him."

"I know him a little," Samira said. "I do not believe there is evil in his heart. But they might."

She gestured behind her at the others. Naime had never thought it would be a simple thing, to bring destruction magic back to Tamar, but this was a bleak reminder of what she faced. If they could still hate someone who had put himself at risk for them, had saved them, the road was much longer than she had hoped.

Several of her guards carried one of their own past the far side of the fire. She and Samira followed to where they laid him. Even with poor light and the mess of clothes and bloodstains, Naime could see he was gravely injured. She knelt beside him as a Sarkum soldier sat on his other side, preparing supplies to treat him.

"Guardsman Onan," she said, slipping her hand into his. He grinned fiercely, though sweat glistened across his face and his skin was pallid.

"Efendim." He grimaced as the Sarkum soldier pulled his torn clothes aside to examine the gash in his side.

"This will hurt," the Sarkum soldier said at the same moment he prodded the wound. Onan flinched, gasped, and passed out. Samira put a hand on his brow, watching the Sarkum soldier's hands as he worked.

"Will he be all right?" Naime asked. The soldier eyed her with misgiving. He unbuttoned Onan's ferace and entari, working quickly to expose the wound.

"If he fights it," the soldier said.

Naime had to turn away to suppress her nausea when the open gash across his side and belly were exposed. Hot copper and something darker soaked the air. Samira made a low noise of distress. More wounded were consolidated in the flat patch of drier ground, their comrades working over minor and major injuries, of which there were only three, thankfully. Naime found her wounded steward, who apparently had been one to run during the assault. An arrow protruded from his thigh. He wore a wild-eyed expression of pain and barely held panic.

"We'll be in Sarkum tomorrow, and you'll be treated by a physician there." She knelt at his side.

"All right," he groaned, gritting his teeth and falling back on his elbows. The soldier placed a hand against his wound to hold the arrow then snapped the fletching off. The steward sucked a sharp breath, his skin pale as linen.

"You'll not want to stay for the next, Efendim," the soldier warned in gruff tones.

"I'll check on you again soon." She touched the steward's hand as she rose. Tareck did the same from the side of one of his soldiers. He wove his way through the little cluster of the injured toward her.

"Here." He took her hand, placing a small pouch into it. "In case you encounter any soldiers who haven't come to be treated for their wounds," he said, one eyebrow hitched up. When he left, Naime pursed her lips. She examined the package in her hand, medical supplies, then looked sidelong at Samira, who did an admirable job of pretending she didn't know exactly which soldier Tareck meant.

"Let's check on the others," Naime said to Samira, squeezing the pouch in her hand and wondering where he was. Did he want to be alone? What if he'd been injured more than just the burn from the guard? What if his other injuries, from Tamar, had reopened?

"If you are worried, go find him," Samira suggested.

"I'm not worried." Naime clutched the pouch harder.

"Lie to everyone else, but not to me."

"He chose to be alone; it is what he wants. I'll let him have his peace." They stood together between the fire and the group of servants, and Naime could feel how they watched.

"He was just thanked for saving all our lives by someone trying to put a sword in his back. He didn't choose to be alone, he has to be."

"I cannot go to him," Naime said.

"You're a queen. You can do anything you want," Samira protested. Naime glared at her in exasperation.

"I am not a queen, and you know better than most that I cannot do whatever I want, go to whoever I want." She had never resented those constraints more than she did now.

Samira took a sharp breath, her brows drawing down.

"Forgive me," Naime said, appalled at her own self-centeredness.

Samira nodded, but looked away. "I'll join you at the tent shortly, Efendim." She bowed.

Naime watched her join the other attendants, wanting to apologize again, to soothe the hurt she had caused. Instead she left Samira alone, and returned to their tent.

TWENTY-THREE

THE TENT HAD SEVERAL new holes in it, and a gash where a sword had been dragged along its side. When she ducked inside there was only a faint glow of light from the embers left in the brazier, and even less heat. The coals cast just enough light to see arrows lodged in some of their belongings. Naime went to the nearest, pulling it out of one of the sitting cushions. She studied the brutal barbs and wicked point. Designed to rip through a man, the barbs to hold it in place and tear upon removal. She shuddered as she laid it aside, then moved to the next, trying to dislodge it from one of her bags. She ended up breaking the fletch off and pushing it through, as the Sarkum soldier had done with her steward.

Something rustled at the back of the tent, and when she whirled to look, a shadow came through the back wall.

Terror froze her in place, seizing the scream that jumped from her belly into her throat. The shape grew taller, a man, facing her.

Naime recognized Makram. She pressed her hands over her chest, taking a steadying breath as her heart continued to pound. When he twisted away to tie the flap closed again she crossed the space between them and shoved both hands against him. He staggered a step and gave a surprised grunt.

"You frightened me," she accused. "What are you doing here? What if I hadn't recognized you and used magic on you? You never think—"

He caught her around the waist with one arm and pulled her against him, cupping the back of her neck with his uninjured hand and tipping his forehead against hers. Naime sucked in a breath and held it, uncertain what to do with her hands. She finally lifted them and pressed her fists against his chest. This close he felt bigger, broader, stronger, even with so many layers of clothes separating them. Naime swallowed down a surge of nervous energy that made her think of all the things she shouldn't do.

His eyes were closed but magic still danced on his skin and lifted away from him in shadows as though he were a smoking ember. He pulled breaths sharply through his nose and released them through his mouth, tension leaving him with each exhale.

"Are you all right?" She hesitantly cupped his face, closing her eyes and allowing herself to relax into his presence. She'd never felt destruction magic until the night in the garden when his magic danced for the first time between them. She'd felt earth, air, fire, and water. Each had their own signature, each engaged with a feeling or state of mind. Makram's magic was surprisingly peaceful, like the embrace of a soft bed at the end of a terrible day, a sense like letting go.

But he did not reflect the feelings she took from the aura of his power. His grip on her was not tender, but desperate, as though he were holding onto something to keep from being swept away.

"I am not a monster," he pleaded. "I am not…I do not kill for the joy of it. Please don't"—he took a shuddering breath—"please don't think I'm a monster."

"You are not a monster." Naime stroked his cheek. He sounded so broken. She didn't know how to help.

"I was waiting for you," he sighed. "Talk to me. About anything."

"I worried for you." She stroked her thumbs across his temples and held his head as she pulled away enough to look at him. His eyes opened, still black like night. "I didn't know where you went." Naime drew her thumb over one brow, and he dropped his head against her shoulder. Her words failed for an instant, at the vulnerability of him, at the closeness, the foreign and somehow perfect weight of his head against her. "Tareck gave me some things for you—are you wounded? I know that guard burned you."

"What did you do to him?" Makram mumbled into the curve between her shoulder and neck. The coat and layers of clothes muffled his words, the fur on the hood and collar of her ferace shield against his touch on her skin. It was wrong that she'd like to be rid of it, immediately, and feel him more closely. He smelled like cold winter air, like wood smoke, like dusk.

"I damaged his ears with sound." It was a vicious and painful attack, and she had only practiced it, going so far as to cripple someone with the pain of it, never as far as she had to the guard. She'd never damaged someone. But there had seemed few other options besides one or the other of them being killed or more dangerously wounded. Naime inched her fingers up his neck, thinking to dig them into his hair, to hold him harder against her, to cling because she could not bear the thought of his pain. Because she had been afraid for him.

"A Sabri defending a destruction mage," Makram said in a gravelly voice, "that should be in the history books." He rubbed his face back and forth against her coat, as if he meant to burrow closer, wanted her skin as much as she wanted him to have it.

"I am sorry I did not do so before he hurt you, or called you—"

"I've been called worse." His hand relaxed against her neck, and he lifted his head, nuzzling his nose and mouth against her braided and coiled hair and inhaling. The gesture unmade her and reshaped her into something needful. His breath was warm but made her skin cold, the suggestion he made with the intimate touch new and more magical than any Charah's flux. It was sweet in its innocence, and obvious in its claim.

"You smell like roses even out here."

"I think you're imagining that," Naime breathed, shaken. Instinct demanded she turn her face toward his, as it had in the garden, when he had tried to kiss her. She forced herself not to and the desire instead manifested as her fingers pressing harder to his neck. This not quite embrace, this nearness, was something she had imagined. Being closer, their bodies aligned, the shape and strength of him encompassing her. Yet, now that she was here, in it, it was not enough.

"If I were going to imagine something"—he lowered his mouth to her ear—"it would not be the smell of your hair."

Shivers skittered down her body, and her breath left her in a rush. The sense of wanting more became distinct. Skin and heat and breath, touches. There was no mistaking the suggestion in his words, in the warm velvet of his voice, the way his lips hovered near her ear without touching. She did not need personal experience with such things to know they were dangerously aligned in what they wanted now.

She'd allowed his initial embrace because she knew he was only trying to regulate his magic. Instincts, and emotions like fear, anger, passion, and love, fed magic and were amplified by it, leaving a mage in flux also in the grip of feelings that often overpowered them. He'd been worried for her, he'd been fighting, he'd been attacked by a supposed ally. That he was not entirely in command was understandable.

But now the desperation had faded, and she could feel his magic withdrawing under his hold once more. She should step away from him, send him to have his wounds treated, anything but what she wanted, his arms around her. Intimacy of touch and words. To divulge all the things she felt so he would know he was cared for. Who had made him think he was a monster? A thread of anger braided through her desire.

Naime called upon the tenuous self-control that remained to her and held his head firmly, separating them. "Sit. I'll see to your burn." With him so close, she struggled as the distinct idea of what she wanted most—to be respected, to rule—wavered, taking on the shape of the man that let out a soft groan as she pulled away from him.

"Why are there so many fire mages in Tamar?" Makram grumbled, following her as she directed him to the trunk.

"A topic of endless debate." There were numerous half-joking explanations for why fire mages were so prolific, most referring to fire's connection to passion. None seemed particularly appropriate at the moment, when the subject of passion felt too suggestive. He unbuckled his sword belt and set it aside before he sat.

"Is that your blood?" Makram said in alarm, almost bolting to his feet when the light cast by the brazier highlighted the dark stains on her clothes.

"No." Naime pressed her hands to his shoulders to keep him in place. She wrenched her thoughts away from the flex of his muscles beneath her hands. "I spoke with some of the wounded, I could hardly avoid the blood. Between this and the mud from traveling I will appear much as you did when you rode into Narfour."

She arranged the contents of the pouch on the trunk lid beside Makram, then knelt in front of him. There was a length of bandage, a piece of leather pierced with needle and catgut, a rolled tube of oiled canvas she thought might contain ointment, bits of chamois. She lifted his hand into his lap and gently pushed back the sleeves of his ferace and caftan. His left hand was still bandaged from the burns Cemil had given him, and now his right wrist bore burns as well. They were much more superficial.

"Did you do this for Ihsan when he was burned?"

She nodded. Day after day. Bandage after bandage. Who else would have done it for him? Suddenly alone in the world. The smell of the special salve still made her sick. The ointment Tareck had given her smelled different, thankfully.

Makram only flinched once while she applied it to his wrist. She wrapped the bandage carefully, then moved his right hand aside and brought his left into his lap, unwinding the other bandage.

"Thank you for putting yourself at risk for me and mine. For revealing yourself to people who do not understand."

"You already thanked me," he said. Naime glanced up at him in question. "I am not accustomed to others coming to my rescue." The magic had receded from his eyes, so she could see the mirth in them, and the tenderness. The tenderness was hardest to resist.

Naime focused on his hand, swallowing the lump in her throat as she applied salve to the burns. They appeared to be healing well, but slowly. She used the rest of the bandage to rewrap it, doing her best to fit it between his fingers and thumb to allow him some movement.

"Are you hurt anywhere else?"

"Not that I know of"—he shifted—"but do feel free to examine me thoroughly. Sometimes the pain of wounds does not make itself known for some time."

She made a soft sound of rebuke, and he grinned before he tipped his head back.

For a while after she remained silent, staring up through the hole in the tent top that served as chimney. The black winter sky was streaked with silver clouds, and she occasionally caught a glimpse of stars between them. Somehow it reminded her of his cloud of magic, so potent that arrows could not penetrate it.

He was a Charah. She had thought she needed the Air Charah to stand the circle but had stumbled upon the Sixth House first. Would he listen to her? Would he be willing to stand in the Circle? Naime did not even know how to go about asking him. There were so many things to say, and asking him for favors, enormous favors, was not the place to start. There were other things she wanted him to know and was afraid to say. But then she thought of Samira and Cemil, and that she might never again have a chance to tell Makram all that she felt and thought.

"You are extraordinary," she said, softly, her cheeks heating as she did, embarrassment making her entire body hot despite the chill air in the tent, "to watch. The way you move." She took a quavering breath. She could not look at him as she spoke. "I never seemed to find a chance to tell you that. When I saw you in the arena. I would have watched you all day if I could have. And here…"

She forced herself to look at him. "How can you do all that? Wield blade and magic, and track so many opponents at once? Horses, men, who is enemy and who is not?"

"Practice." Makram's head was tipped back as he watched the stars through the hole, and he swallowed sharply. "It is not so different than navigating a Council full of men with different motivations and goals, different habits and expectations. How you know exactly what to say and when, think so far in advance. I admire you fiercely."

"It is different. There is far less bloodshed." Naime clasped her hands together to prevent herself reaching to touch him again. His compliment made an entirely different heat warm her skin.

"Not from what I have seen of Narfour. The place is strewn with dead parents and mangled nobles."

Naime's eyes widened in shock, and she giggled at the absurdity of it. Makram grinned, but kept his head tipped back.

"I can leave you here for a time, if you'd like to be alone." She lifted her hand to reach for his, but pulled back before she actually touched him, uncertain. Touching was such a nuanced communication. The same touch could mean so many different things to different people. She knew when she touched him it was different than when she touched anyone else, but she could hardly stop herself, despite the warning in her belly that every contact edged her closer to a precipice from which there would come only pain.

"I like you at my side, Naime."

"I am the firstborn, so I believe you're at my side, by rank," she teased. Makram opened his eyes and ducked his chin, a slow smile spreading over his mouth.

"All right, Sultana. I am at your side. Command me."

She could not speak, at first. That he would say such a thing to her, even in jest, was difficult to assimilate.

"I have never known anyone like you, who does not demand to be first. That is so brave and forceful, and so humble." She could not understand why everything he said and did made her want to touch him so badly. To connect physically as she felt them connect emotionally.

He picked at the bandage on his hand. "You're mistaking recklessness for bravery."

"I don't think I am." Naime brushed his fingers away from the bandage.

"I am reckless. You are willing to stand for a belief that goes against lifetimes of hate and prejudice, that caused a brutal and bloody war, to challenge the most powerful men in Tamar with nothing and no one at your back. Not for some personal gain, but because you believe it is what is best for all." He tipped his head back again. "That is the bravest thing I have ever witnessed."

Naime studied him as he watched the sky. Clouds drifted over the moon, dropping the tent into deeper shadow. She had never stopped to think about it in such a way.

"It doesn't feel brave, it feels necessary, as if I sat back and did nothing I might cease to exist."

"A sentiment exactly opposite to how most live their lives. But I understand. That is why I left Al-Nimas without my brother's say. Because it felt necessary. I thought if I could begin momentum toward an alliance, he would hardly be able to stop it, and by the time I returned his temper would be cooled and his thinking more reasonable." Makram sighed. "It was never my intention to hurt you or put your plans at risk in the process."

"You are so loyal to your brother." Naime laid her palm over his left wrist and swept her magic around it, to cool the burn. Makram's chest rose, the sound of his inhale highlighted by the silence, and the fog of his exhale obscured his face for a moment. He wrapped his fingers around her wrist, loosely.

"He is ten turns older than I am, was often more father to me than my actual father." Makram shrugged. "I owe him. He was brother and friend to me when almost no one else was. It is not as true now as it once was, but I do not want you to think I wander the palace halls alone, unwanted and maligned."

Naime smiled. "I am glad to hear it." His words only confirmed her fear. He would never leave Sarkum, never abandon his brother to be part of a Circle of Chara'a. Was his brother worthy of such devotion?

He burrowed his hand beneath the cuffs of her various garments, catching her bare wrist as her magic swirled over his, distracting her.

"I am very charming. People cannot help but like me."

His hand was warm, and seemed the only point of warmth in a tent that was swiftly cooling as the brazier's coals died.

"Aren't you though." Naime imagined what it might feel like if he stroked his hand up her arm, that warm grip traveling across skin that was never exposed or touched. She was cold, and trying not to shiver. "You aren't cold?" she asked. "I could relight the brazier."

"Don't. It will cast our shadows on the tent, and they might come hunt me down."

Naime closed her eyes. Because she could threaten them all she wanted and it would not change the fear and loathing with which they viewed him. She heaved a sigh. "I wish I could make them see you as I do."

He released her wrist and skated his hand down her arm, over her sleeves.

"How do you see me?" He held her hand and brought it up, nudging it with his nose and mouth, so that she uncurled her fingers and brushed them over his cheek.

"I have wanted to tell you and did not think you would listen."

Makram shifted, leaning his forearms on his thighs so his face was almost level with hers. Naime needed to touch him, more than she already had. More than careful touches that could be labeled as warm friendship. More than she should. His stubble was rough against her palm, his skin warm against her chill fingers, his gaze fixed on hers.

"I'm listening now," he said.

"I see a man who is loyal even when others may not deserve it. Someone who stands beside those he believes in with humility, without diminishing or being diminished. I see"—she swallowed back her trepidation—"shadow like dusk, the peace at the end of struggle, magic to break down barriers that imprison us."

His brow furrowed, and he lifted his hands to her face. The bandage on the right was soft in comparison to the calluses on his left.

"You are necessary." She mirrored his touch by lifting her other hand so his face was caught between her fingers. "Your magic is necessary. And beautiful, like night."

"Naime," he said her name in supplication, ducking his head toward hers. He stopped before he reached her, his gaze catching hers, pleading.

Her breath shuddered away, desire snapping through her, followed swiftly by dread that made her want to pull away.

But wouldn't she always wonder? She did not want to live a lifetime never knowing what it felt like to be kissed by someone who she actually wanted to kiss. Naime rose up on her knees and pressed her mouth softly to his, her breath held, slipping her hands to rest on his shoulders. She pulled immediately away, unsure.

"I don't know how."

Makram slid off the trunk, landing on his knees in front of her, wrapping his arm around her waist to draw her against him.

"I know you don't." He brushed his mouth over the bridge of her nose, then her cheek, then her brow, burning her with the tenderness of it. "I know I shouldn't touch you or let you touch me. I shouldn't speak to you, I shouldn't look at you."

"But I like all of those things," she protested breathlessly, her mind fogged.

"I can't stop," he said. "I am trying and failing."

"Then," she began, tingles of anticipation and shyness arcing across her lips and down her throat, "teach me."

"Yes, Sultana." The pupils of his eyes broke open, spilling black night across the irises.

Her pulse roared, her mouth went dry, and she breathed a halfhearted murmur of apprehension. Her parents had loved each other, but Naime had never expected that to be her fate. She had always imagined any kiss she experienced would be two people who barely liked each other pressing lips together for awkward moments of silence and the benefit of others.

She had not imagined she would feel the clutch of desire that stole her breath.

His first kiss was brief and fierce, the softness of his mouth laid over hers, warmth and little shocks of sensation bursting all over her body, not just where his lips touched hers. Then he pulled back and rubbed his mouth over hers before concentrating first on her lower lip then her top with gentle, coaxing pressure. Naime gave the same in kind, trying to match his pace and focus on him without being made useless by sensation.

He tipped his head, pressing the same kisses along her jaw, and her throat, and the shivers that slipped across her skin were indiscernible from those caused by the cold. She gasped, her arms sliding around his neck to prevent herself falling backwards under his ministrations, and he returned his mouth to hers, less gently. His stubbled jaw abraded her skin, a shocking contrast to the wet, warm stroke of his mouth, then his tongue.

She had never understood when she saw people lurking in corners and alcoves, had thought it all unseemly and nauseating. But now she understood. She did not know how she would ever stop thinking of this, of sharing breath and longing and touches so intimate they were unbearable and yet not enough. Naime's hands flew to his neck, her nails digging against his nape, clinging as much as she was pleading, afraid and enraptured by every emotion and sensation that swept over her. Her entire world collapsed in and existed only in the places they touched.

Makram parted from her but did not draw back, only tipped his face to nuzzle hers as his breath slid out in a slow stream.

"You aren't finished?" she said against his jaw. "I was just beginning to get the hang of it."

He breathed a laugh. "I am finished. You've ended me."

Naime closed her eyes, trying to find her calm in the raging swirl of fading desperation. No one had ever written in any history book that a destruction mage's kisses might be just as devastating as their magic. Or perhaps that was only Makram.

The skin of her chin and cheeks burned in the absence of him, the cold air making her realize how rough his several-days-long stubble was. Naime released his neck to press her fingers against her cheeks, and Makram made a face.

"You are too delicate for me," he murmured, brushing his thumb along her jaw, and kissing her skin along the line he drew.

"I do not expect it will kill me," she said.

"But others may notice."

Naime pondered that, grateful for the pause that allowed her to claim some sense and reason, and also hopeful that he intended to come back to her for more.

She slid her fingers to his neck again, tracing the bumps of his spine, tucking her fingers into the collar of his clothes and around, reveling in the warm, smooth skin. Imagining touching him more intimately had been a pale, lifeless shadow of the joy that spilled over her at the actual act. Even just this simple, stolen touch, her fingertips against skin she could barely reach for the constriction of his coat and caftan, was enough to fill her with greed. She wanted more. She dipped a fingertip against the hollow of his throat.

"Naime." His voice was magic, dark longing.

She touched her mouth to his with hesitant pressure, half afraid he would pull away, and mimicked his tongue against hers, drawing it over the seam of his lips. Naime drew back a fraction to gauge his reaction.

"You learn fast," he said, starless night in his eyes and swirling smoke drifting beneath his skin. Was that her effect on him? His magic breaking from his control, because of her?

"I always have…but the pleasantness of the subject makes it easy to learn."

"Let us review, then." He twisted to sit, folding his legs in front of him before lifting her sideways into his lap. He guided her arms around him and cradled the back of her neck with his uninjured hand as he kissed her. She liked it better, sitting at level with him, able to push and pull, give and take in equal measure.

"Still pleasant?" he asked breathlessly. Pleasant, and torturous. What had begun as wonder and surprise became aching and need, the burn beneath her skin radiated through her whole body, her pulse beating a rhythm between her thighs that threatened to turn her mindless and savage. His hands had not strayed from her neck but to grip her shoulders and hold her for his deeper kisses, but she wanted them to. She wanted his hands everywhere, especially where her body felt empty and desperate, the places her skin felt taut and sensitive.

"If I say I don't know, will you understand?"

"I understand." He tipped his head to graze her neck with his lips then flick his tongue against the hollow of her throat. An unsteady, quiet sound escaped her as the winter cold claimed the wet spot left by his tongue. Makram buried his face against her neck and shifted beneath her. His hands slipped downward to clasp her waist.

The grip, new, intimate because it was the first time a man had held her so possessively, distracted her for a moment so she did not discern the new ridge of pressure against her leg. When she did, her cheeks flamed, and she went rigid. Should she pretend she didn't notice? Get up immediately? Surely she shouldn't move…what if she hurt him or…the opposite?

Makram lifted his head to look at her, perhaps concerned by her sudden change in demeanor. Naime could not meet his gaze. He made a sound, like a purr, and traced her cheekbone with the tip of his nose. When he looked at her again, one corner of his mouth lifted.

"You don't like that?" His hands on her waist snugging her more tightly against him, and the evidence his body wanted hers, as well.

"No, I…" She did meet his eyes then. "I…" She liked it. Should she tell him that?

"You are a charming creature, Naime. You are more afraid of my desire than my magic." He grinned at her and she frowned.

"I am not afraid."

"No? Then keep touching me." He ducked his head again, into the crook of her neck. She curved one hand over his head to hold him as he was, his warm breath caressing the small amount of skin exposed by her high-necked ferace, and used the other to pull open the etched metal band that held his hair back. She set it beside her, then slid her hands up the back of his neck and into his hair. It was coarser than she expected, thick and as black as the oblivion that colored his magic. Only the hair that framed his face was braided, so she combed her fingers through the back, and he tipped his head into her caress, baring his throat to her.

Her body was hot and slow, as if she'd been drinking too much wine. She leaned in and kissed his neck as he had kissed hers, tasting the salt of his skin, smelling the heady combination of dusk and male, feeling the harsh thrum of his pulse against her lips. She was not brave enough to lick him, as he had her, uncertain what he would like or want, but she did nuzzle his ear and breathe his name.

A violent shiver tensed his whole body.

"Enough," he said, "that is all I can bear."

"Forgive me." She pulled her hands from his hair and set them in her lap, swallowing back embarrassment. "I thought you were enjoying it too."

"Look at me."

She obeyed, flicking her gaze up to his face, and her breath rushed out. "Oh," she exclaimed quietly, confronted with the severity of his flux. Shadow pulsed in the air around him, magic bleeding from him, aroused and unleashed by his desire.

"Yes, oh," he mocked gently, "you are murdering me by degrees."

"I didn't mean to." She smoothed a hand over his face, and down his neck. "I have wanted to touch you since I saw you…" Her memories of his half-clothed body snuck up and tyrannized her thoughts at the worst possible moments.

"You have touched me," he said, his voice like shadow.

"Not like this. Not like I wanted to."

"There is a great deal more of me to touch," he suggested in a voice like cascading silk, catching her mouth in a lingering kiss.

"I know," she said, trying not to lose herself to the flare of longing he inspired, "but you said to stop."

"You make me forget myself, and I do not want to forget myself too much, and push you too far."

"If I promise not to let you push me too far, will you kiss me again?" She touched his lips. He nodded gravely. "Then I promise."

He kissed her again. Naime hummed approval, sinking happily into the heated stupor the touch of his mouth and hands inspired. Their brief exchange had apparently cut a cord of reservation, because he touched her as he had not before.

His hands skated down her back, encircled her waist, twisted her more toward him. Then one slid over her hip and to her thigh, gripping her through the layers of clothing, and stroking down to her knee. His hand slid back up, curving toward her inner thigh and beneath the layers of caftan, entari, and coat. It was the most intimate touch she had ever received, with just the fabric of her salvar between her skin and his. She could feel the heat and pressure of his hand, how his fingers curled against tender, sensitive flesh. His hand was only halfway up her thigh and his touch sent her tumbling headlong into desire, raking through her control like knives through gossamer.

Her magic burst around her.

Makram cursed, wrapping his arms around her and laying her on the floor, covering her body with his and tucking her beneath him, circling his arms around her head and ducking his against them.

"You're glowing like a mage orb," he accused. "They'll see you through the tent walls."

"What did you expect to happen when you touched me like that?"

"I barely touched you at all." His voice dropped to a throaty growl she thought held more surprise than irritation.

"I have never been touched…*there*." Her voice faded and she had to force the rest of the words out. "I will try to restrain myself in the future." She fought her magic and herself, breathing until the glow faded from her skin.

She realized what she had said, might have inadvertently promised. There wasn't any future for them. There wouldn't be more chances to touch him, to kiss him, to see his magic unbound by his desire. Naime felt wounded for it, for what she had given him and the realization she could not imagine giving the same to someone else.

The only light left in the tent was from the moon that shone through the vent in the top, but it was enough to see resignation and disappointment on his face.

He brushed his lips over her cheek and up the curve of her earlobe, reigniting the shiver of longing across her cold skin.

"I admire your control," he said in a voice like wicked night, "but were I ever to have you alone again, restraint is the last thing I would want from you. You surprised me, and I do not want half the camp trekking over here to investigate your glowing tent." He nipped her neck, sending a tiny shock of surprise and pleasure straight to her belly.

Naime's body arched of its own volition at the touch. It curved against his and he yielded, pressing his weight onto his right forearm and sliding his left hand under her low back, urging her harder against him.

He pressed her back to the ground, hitching one leg up by her hip and burying his face in her neck to muffle his groan. The sound of it, longing and need, filled Naime with pulsing desire. He lifted the weight of his hips off of hers and dug his hand beneath her ferace, lifting up her entari, then tugged up on her caftan.

Naime wasn't entirely certain what his goal was, but her harsh desire demanded she assist him. She squirmed, trying to help, and he finally rolled to his side and off her, freeing her clothes enough that he could shove his hand up under her caftan and belts. He dug his fingers against the waist of her salvar and the sliver of skin he could access with the constriction of her clothing and belt.

Naime jerked with a sharp gasp because he grabbed more than stroked, and it tickled. He tried to pull his hand away, but the bandages on his wrist caught against the cinch of her belt, making the problem worse and sending her into a fit of writhing giggles.

"Would you hold still," he demanded, though he was grinning, and managed to get his hand higher, flattening it against her ribs and belly. He didn't do more than that, but it made her laugh harder, and she put her hands over her face to stifle the sound. Makram nipped the back of her hand.

"Ow!" she gasped, slapping his shoulder, and he used the opening to kiss her, hard.

Naime curved her hand over the back of his neck as she met his kiss, still giggling. His fingers moved against her belly, but her body decided his touch only tickled, and she gave a little squeal of laughter against his mouth. He managed to grin and kiss her, his eyes open, watching her as he did. The joy in his face, the sweet adoration in his eyes as he watched her, wrapped cords around her heart. Her laughter faded, and his smile dimmed, and they stared at each other in silence that roared with words held back.

"Naime?" Samira called, and neither of them could move fast enough to untangle before she ducked into the tent, one of her mage orbs bobbing obediently behind her. "Why haven't you lit..." She stopped, staring. "...the brazier." She held an ewer of water and a basin.

Makram rolled across Naime's body, hiding his hand as he extracted it from beneath her clothes, and sat up. Naime did the same, the skin of her face on fire with her humiliation.

"I will"—Samira's gaze flicked around the tent, trying to find something to fix on besides them—"I'll come back." She executed a slow, stiff about-face and ducked outside. The mage orb continued to float by the tent door, like a large, accusing eye.

Makram let his breath out between his teeth. "What do you need me to do to prevent this becoming a problem?" he asked, staring, unseeing, at the tent door.

"Samira is not a gossip." Thank the Wheel it had been her, and not one of the others. Naime felt like a complete and utter fool, giving into her desires instead of listening to her common sense and restraint. She patted at her hair, trying to even her breathing.

"Small favors," Makram said, pressing a hand over his eyes and bowing his head. "Forgive me. I shouldn't have come."

"No. I am glad you came. But, we cannot let it go any further. If I avoid you in these coming days, if I do not look at you, or touch you, if..."

"I understand," he said, his voice desolate. "I am not unaccustomed to being denied the things I want. And neither are you." He turned, rising to one knee as he did, and caught her chin in his fingers. He gave her a gentle, chaste kiss and ducked his head when he pulled back. "You are the most beautiful thing to ever happen to me."

He stood, grabbed his sword and belt, and left.

The cords he'd unwittingly tied around her heart tightened until they hurt.

TWENTY-FOUR

MAKRAM RODE IN THE lead of the perimeter, as far from Naime as he could get. Scanning the horizon and the hills and wadis around them as they traveled that day kept his mind from her, for the most part. When his thoughts would stray, he'd pull them back to his brother, to the words he would need to convince him. Or he'd think about his men, and how many reports he would need to read through to be caught up. But the thoughts would stray again, and he'd catch himself mentally recounting the moments he'd spent with her. The sound of her warm whispers, the soft, cool touch of her hands, the hesitance of her inexperienced kisses, the eagerness of her touches. He'd be lost in the earnest, gentle words she'd spoken about him, his magic, or the way her fingers felt against his skin, and have to rein his mind under control like a horse bolting toward its stable.

The one thing he wouldn't think of, couldn't, was her laughter, and the look in her eyes at the last moment. The way he'd burst with the awareness that all he wanted in the world was to make her laugh like that, make her forget her discipline and her burdens. And the choking, bitter realization he never would. It would be someone else. In a few days, a turn at the most, they would part.

They reached the main, broad road that led into Al-Nimas in the late afternoon and Tareck joined him to report on the state of the wounded. The only one whose recovery Tareck was unsure of was the Tamar guardsman, whose entire left side had been laid nearly open by a bandit's sword. It was not the first time Makram wondered what it would have been like in the time before the Sundering, when creation mages lived, when their magic could be used to treat such catastrophic injuries. In their absence, medicine had come a long way, but could not make up for the lack of healing magic on the Wheel.

His mind flipped to thoughts of Chara'a, of the Circle. She hadn't asked him. Hadn't even mentioned it, though there was no doubt she had realized what he was the moment he cast the cloud of destruction over the camp. Perhaps her notes in the library had been just musings. Maybe she had no intention of standing a Circle, or realized it might prove impossible. Or she knew, as he did, that he could never leave his brother's side.

"What do you want to happen when we arrive?" Tareck asked.

"Get the Sultana and her people settled. I'll find Kinus." He simultaneously dreaded facing his brother and was eager to have it over with. The weight of his decision to defy Kinus had been heavy, and he was ready to make amends and move forward.

"Perhaps the Sultana would be more comfortable at Elder Attiyeh's estate?" Tareck said in the bland tone he used when he was trying to maneuver Makram into something.

"Why?" Makram sighed. Tareck and his conspiracies would turn Makram's hair grey before he reached his thirtieth turn.

"I fear your brother will not be in the proper frame of mind to receive the daughter of a nation he believes to be an enemy. And I'm afraid there will be movement in some of the quarters that have remained quiet, about his ascension. You don't want the Sultana to bear witness to that, do you?"

"What are you suggesting, exactly?" Makram assessed Tareck from the edge of his vision.

"I just assumed you would want to keep her as comfortable as possible," Tareck said dismissively, "which would not be around a man who despises mages more powerful than himself."

"I'll see him alone, when we get back. Once he's had it out then I'll arrange for a time to bring the Sultana and the terms to him."

"So she will hardly be missed if she isn't at the palace," Tareck said.

Makram knew he was on edge because of his time with Naime, because of all the emotions he was trying to manage. So instead of snapping an angry reply at Tareck, he remained silent. Tareck was not a man prone to hysteria. If he saw fit to warn that he was concerned in any other endeavor, Makram would listen to him without question. Except about Kinus, because Makram understood his brother in a way Tareck could not.

But there had been moments, times when he could easily have fit Kinus in place of Naime's Grand Vizier. Was Tareck right? Was his brother so unreasonable that he might pose a risk to Naime? Makram struggled to believe that.

"Bringing her here and sequestering her with an Elder who is not fully aligned with Kinus will only cause him more affront," Makram said after a long time spent pondering. Tareck quietly watched the horizon. He reached up and scratched at his stubbled jaw.

"Do you remember when that boy Jabr found that wild dog pup in a flooded-out burrow?"

"The one he wanted to train to be a war dog," Makram said. He'd always regretted that he'd stood by and let Jabr keep the poor beast.

"That one. He was afraid of it, thought it would bite him if he didn't show it that it belonged to him."

"I remember," Makram said, wondering if Tareck was coming to a point, or if he had decided to move on from the subject of Kinus and Naime. Jabr had been an atrocious animal-handler. In fact it was his handling of the dog that had made the sipahi commander at the time decide he was unfit to be around the horses and sent him to the janissaries. The poor beast hadn't known up from down; half the time Jabr coddled it, praising it and feeding it scraps. Then he'd beat it for perfectly normal behavior, like when it chewed up all the leather in sight while its teeth were coming in.

"He finally did attack him," Tareck said, "because of the rabbit."

"I'd forgotten the rabbit," Makram said. One of the other boys had taken pity on the dog, having to sleep outside alone, and given it an old, straw-stuffed toy rabbit. It was an ugly thing, ragged and missing a leg and one ear. But the dog carried it everywhere. Jabr hated the rabbit, because he wanted his dog to be fierce and frightening. So he took it, and beat the other boy for interfering. The dog nearly ripped Jabr's arm off for it.

"What was the other boy's name?"

"Zayn. He took the dog. They're both on the border outposts now. The dog gets more accolades than Zayn does." Tareck grinned. Makram glared at him from the corners of his eyes.

"Why don't you just tell me what point you're trying to make?"

"No point. Just conversation. But I'll be off now, check on the rear."

"Tareck," Makram said.

"No point. We were talking about your brother"—Tareck started to turn his horse around—"and it brought Jabr to mind." His horse broke into a trot, then a canter.

Makram watched him until he had to twist uncomfortably to do so. Before he faced forward he searched the central group of riders for her. Riding in the very center of everyone, her attendants, stewards, and palace guards forming concentric circles outward from her, so she appeared to be the hub of a chaotic wheel. The center of everything. He wrenched his gaze forward, giving his horse's sides a squeeze to order it faster, and farther away from her.

TARECK REJOINED HIM WHEN they reached the edge of Al-Nimas. They skirted the city—Makram did not want to deal with the crowds that would impede their progress. He was ready to be out of the saddle, ready to find a distance from Naime that allowed him to breathe. Every part of him felt pulled to her, his breath, his body, his heart. Avoiding her in every action and thought would drive him completely mad if it didn't first kill him from exhaustion.

Every man and woman in the group was just as ready as him to be out of the saddle. Tempers were high, and when they reached the city they were forced to ride in closer proximity, which made little squabbles break out. Each time someone snapped at someone else, or a horse squealed in anger, his temper unraveled a bit more. Tareck's silence said he was of a similar mood, and they did not speak to each other for the last two marks it took them to skirt the city to the northern end, where a road ran the length of the squat, thick wall that surrounded the palace.

A winter storm had been chasing them for the second half of the day, and the cold wind that preceded it found them as they made it to the palace gates. Flakes of snow whipped through the air as his men, augmented with more from the palace guard, ushered the Tamar travelers inside.

Tareck stayed mounted, circling through the chaos to oversee things. Boys came from the stable to take the horses, and his soldiers worked with the Tamar guards to set up the wounded out of the wind until they could be taken somewhere to be tended to.

Makram only stayed mounted until he found Naime in the shuffle. He handed his horse to one of the stable boys and made his way to her. The courtyard into which they arrived was not gardens and gravel paths, but tiled stone, black basalt alternated with white limestone to form patterns of lines, squares within squares, and visual labyrinths. The face of the palace was striped with the same black basalt bricks and white limestone, with a central stripe halfway up the outer wall made of large squares of mosaics, each a different collection of repeating geometric shapes, running across the face of each building that surrounded the courtyard. A fountain large enough for swimming sat in the center of the courtyard, directly in line with the stairs that led to the palace entrance. The Rahal family had always favored fire, and the water fountain stood in balance to that.

"Agassi." Samira stepped into his path and bowed. "Please tell me the details of where the Sultana and her people will be accommodated and I will see to it. You needn't be troubled with such trivial matters."

When she straightened she stood stiff-backed and smiling, her hands clasped together in front of her, eyes directed somewhere in the vicinity of his chin. Remarkably composed for a fire mage. The cold wind dampened, and the snowflakes began to come in short, heavy bursts.

"What a fierce guardian you are," Makram said. "One wouldn't expect it, from the look of you."

She ducked her head in acknowledgment.

"She's done a remarkable job of training you to be just like her." Makram looked past her to find he'd lost sight of Naime. He'd like her to be inside before the storm descended on them, and that would be very soon.

"Thank you, Efendim," Samira said. "I could not ask for a more generous compliment."

"Has she assigned you to this task, or have you taken it upon yourself?"

"I am her servant, Efendim. It is my duty to know what she needs, even if she does not."

"She is the daughter of a Sultan and the first delegate of Tamar to step foot in Sarkum since the Sundering. If you do not allow me to welcome her, as a prince and official of this palace, you disrespect her."

Her eyes flashed to his, her smile taking on a sharp note. Sparks drifted in the honey-brown irises, like the kind that flew away from a fire in the dark. "Better my disrespect than she be wounded by someone who cares only for what they want, and not at all for her."

His frayed temper snapped, unleashing a whip of black rage through him. He was home, and did not need to hide who and what he was anymore. If she wanted to play brave soldier and taunt him, then she could suffer the consequences of it.

Her eyes met his, where magic had opened to the void. Her composure slipped, her face paling, her eyes widening.

A hand slipped beneath his arm from behind, small, but firm in its grip. Cold power swept around his magic. Not a threat, or a binding, but a reminder. Its touch was somehow warm and comforting in comparison to the storm that swept around the courtyard the way her power twined his. Makram's anger stuttered and died as he glanced down.

"I am so pleased to see you getting to know each other," Naime said, her hand stroking down his bicep. "Two people who are so dear to me." Her voice, her touch, her presence soothed him when he had thought it would only make everything he felt worse. Makram pulled his magic back.

"Efendim," Samira said, bowing, her voice slightly unsteady.

"Samira," Naime said, "I am certain the Agassi did not mean to frighten you. As I am also certain you did not mean to imply he would act with anything but honor."

"No, Efendim."

"Forgive me for letting temper and fatigue to get the better of me," Makram said. He and Samira locked eyes again, until hers flicked to Naime's hand on his arm and her lips pressed together.

"I am pleased to be in your home, Agassi, and would enjoy seeing anything of it you wish to share, but perhaps at a later time. My people, and I, are in need of rest for the moment. I would appreciate a chance to clean up before I am introduced to the Mirza." She tilted her face toward his, but her gaze fixed on the sky over his shoulder. It stung, her self-control.

"Walk with me," he said. "So I may speak with you."

"Efendim." Samira held up a hand.

"I didn't say alone," Makram snarled, and Samira relaxed as she bowed. "Tareck will see you to rooms. I'll need to find my brother," Makram told them once they had cleared the majority of the throng that milled the courtyard. "I will try to convince him to see you as soon as I can."

"Is there anything I can do in the meantime? Meet with your Elders?" Naime suggested.

"It all depends on Kinus' disposition." Makram realized how pathetic he sounded. "I have to apologize for doing what I did, and once I have done that, we can move forward."

"Are you certain it would not be better if I were with you?" She followed as he guided her toward the palace entrance.

The palace did not have steps, as the one in Narfour. It was half the size of its predecessor, built by slaves instead of mages. The architecture was similar, though in Tamar stone and plasterwork were whitewashed, giving everything a clean, stark appearance. The walls and domed towers here retained the natural golden tones of the sandstone that formed the majority of their bricks.

They walked through the arched doors of the palace as the snow began to fall in earnest and wind whipped the courtyard into a melee of miserable people and agitated horses. Naime stopped, turning to look outside, her brow furrowed.

"Everyone will be all right. My men will have them sorted in short order."

"I trust you," she said. His throat closed at how easily she said it, as though it were the most natural thing in the world. He knew it wasn't, not for her. "It rarely snows in Narfour, and I do not have much reason to travel to the valley in the winter."

She stepped back outside, sticking her hand out to catch some of the flakes. The wind blew them into flurries and swirls, and she had to grab some out of the air. "They are all little Wheels, did you realize?" She stared at them in her palm for the moments before they melted.

"My mother says each snowflake is a different Wheel, and that they represent all the ways it can turn, all the choices we could make, and how the world can be remade by them." Samira stepped beside Naime, catching more snow to examine as she spoke.

"The flakes in the mountains were much bigger and easier to catch than these," Makram chided, though watching them grasping at snowflakes as if they were little girls seeing them for the first time charmed him immeasurably.

"We were preoccupied with misery," Naime said in a crisp voice.

"Some of us," Samira added, holding her hand out again, "and some of us didn't see the snow at all." She looked sidelong at Naime, who cast her a stern look. Naime's gaze cut to his, then quickly away. Red crept along her neck and jaw. He wanted to ask what that meant, if the subject that precluded her noticing the snow had been him. But they had agreed. That was over.

Tareck strode out of the swirl of snow and bowed quickly. Naime's attendants came behind him in a cluster.

"Elder Attiyeh has requested to see you, at his estate," Tareck announced.

"Of course he has." Makram rubbed his brow with his fingers. The last thing he wanted was to go back out in the damn storm.

"You aren't riding through that?" Naime indicated the courtyard, already accumulating a dusting of wind-whipped snow. Her face was lovely in its concern, and the warmth in her eyes fed the fierce, hungry monster that had grown inside him that seemed only nourished by her care and attention.

"I know the way," he said.

"A councilman can summon a prince, in Sarkum?" she asked as if the idea were the most outrageous she had ever encountered. Makram grinned, and Tareck curbed his own.

"He is an old friend, Sultana. And the former Agassi. It would be unwise for me to ignore him."

"Captain Habaal, we are ready when you are," she said in a neutral voice as she moved past Makram. Her cool expression conveyed her disapproval. He watched Tareck lead them away down the carpeted hall, then assessed the snowstorm, steeling himself to go back into it.

"Agassi," Samira said from behind him, and he jerked, facing her.

"You are sneakier than I might have thought," he said.

"The Sultana hopes you will inform her when you return."

"That would require that I speak to her," Makram warned. "Will her gatekeeper allow it?"

"Consider sending a missive." Samira's voice came flat as her expression.

Makram smiled despite himself and ducked his head in acquiescence. Samira spun and strode away.

He regarded the slate sky overlaid with blinding snow. It would be easier to tackle the storm and a friendly face than to deal with his brother. The Attiyeh estate wasn't so far that it was a dangerous ride, and Makram doubted the storm would last long. They tended to blow through quickly. He took a deep breath and stepped out into the harsh wind.

TWENTY-FIVE

NAIME STRODE DOWN THE hall between the baths and the rooms they'd been given, Samira and the rest of the attendants treading closely behind. Their moods had much improved after a long soak in the hot, sulphuric waters of the bath. The water was apparently piped in from a hot spring within the palace compound. Though her body was more relaxed and less sore, her mind remained disquiet.

They rounded the corner toward their rooms. Tareck stood beside her door. Naime didn't pause, though she was surprised enough to do so. There were any number of reasons he might be there, but she hoped it was to tell her that Makram had returned. Each time she looked out into the storm and saw the snowfall growing heavier, she grew more anxious.

"Captain." She stopped in front of him and he bowed.

"I wonder if you might be interested in seeing some of the palace, Sultana?" Tareck asked, without rising from his bow.

"Right now?" Naime lifted an eyebrow as he straightened. He cleared his throat and glanced at Samira.

"Yes, Sultana. And it might be best, if you chose to come with me, that your attendants remain behind, in the case anyone else should come searching for you. They would be able to inform that person that you were in your rooms but unavailable."

"How illicit," Naime said, worry twisting in her gut. Was this about Makram?

"Sultana, forgive me, this troubles me," Samira said.

"She will be in no danger," Tareck said. "There are many eyes that would notice this many new women in the palace, touring around, and it would be best not to begin rumors."

"Instead there will be rumors about the Sultana walking alone through the palace with a steward," Samira said. When Naime glanced at her, her gaze was downcast and her folded hands tense.

"I do not believe the captain would risk such without good reason," Naime said, as a question, and Tareck responded with a quick nod. "Please do as he says."

"As you wish, Sultana." Samira bowed. A flick of her hand sent the others scurrying for their own rooms. With one last glance at Naime, she stepped into their shared room and shut the door. Naime waited until she heard the latch click before she spoke again.

"Just so we are clear, Captain. Making a man bleed from the ears is not the worst I am capable of."

He bowed again, but she caught the ghost of a smile before he ducked his face out of view. "Of course, Sultana. And I am unarmed."

"You are not here at the behest of your master, are you?" she asked as he straightened.

"No."

"Do you have his permission to be here?" She folded her hands in front of her caftan.

"No, Sultana."

"Very well." She held a hand out in front of her in invitation for him to lead. He did, walking with his hands clasped behind his back and adjusting his stride so she did not have to strain to keep up with him, aware, perhaps, that her legs were still quite tired from the ride.

He led her as if they were going back toward the baths but continued in the opposite direction when they reached an intersection of halls. This palace was not as maze-like as her own, but it would take her more than once through it to understand the layout.

They walked in silence until they reached a hall she suspected would lead to the receiving hall or throne room. There were doors along the wall to their left, alternating with alcoves, and Tareck stopped at the third door and knocked. When no answer came he opened the door and gestured for her to enter.

Naime did so. The room was cast in shades of grey and brown by the dim, stormy light that came in through the window on the back wall. One wall held bookshelves, which were chock-a-block with books and stacks of rolled papers. Naime drifted toward them, scanning the spines. A few had their authors' names, many gave no indication as to what knowledge they held. This was an office, perhaps they were tax ledgers. She pulled one down and opened it as Tareck shut the door.

Troop records. Old ones. The acquisition of boys from their families, slaves from traders, horses from stables. This was Makram's office. She pressed the book back into place and faced Tareck.

"I thought it would be prudent to inform you of some of the Mirza's…particular expectations."

"Yes, thank you." She was certain that was not the real reason Tareck had trekked her halfway across the palace and sequestered her in an office. However, there was rarely such a thing as too much information.

"Mirza Rahal is an Aval of the Fifth House," Tareck began. The information came as a surprise. She knew Sarkum suffered from a dearth of powerful mages, but she had not realized that was a problem within the royal family, especially considering Makram. "With all the respect he is due from me," Tareck said, carefully if not tactfully, "he is greatly bothered by the difference in power between him and the Agassi. It is best not to draw attention to it."

Naime absently traced her fingers down one of the books on the shelf to her right. "So it would also be wise to avoid the subject of my own power."

Tareck tipped his head in affirmation.

Naime examined him. "Is the Agassi aware his brother is troubled by his power?" she asked, reading Tareck's body language and the words he had left unsaid.

Tareck shifted, folding his arms and dropping his gaze as he smiled again with a soft laugh. "Yes, and no. He is aware it raises his brother's temper, but I do not believe he understands the true depth of the Mirza's resentment."

The distinctive, sinking feeling of dread stirred through her. Tareck was leading her in a direction she was certain she did not want to go.

"The Agassi is intelligent and observant. Why does he not understand?" She pressed her fingers against her temple, turning to walk to the window. She needed air. Suddenly, the room felt as though it might crush her.

"He is a younger brother, Sultana, who was shunned and cast off by almost everyone until he made a name for himself. The Mirza has kept him close, protected him when he could. The Agassi has long looked up to him. He is also a Sixth House mage of the highest order. Your people think of them as killers, which of course they can be, as any mage. But here, we also remember they sit between the Houses of air and fire, intellect and passion. Do you know what resides there?"

"Loyalty," she said. He nodded. Naime watched the snow blowing and swirling outside, trying to sort through the new information.

"It can blind him, as it has in the case of his brother."

"Why did the Mirza take care of Makram if he hated his magic?"

"At first I think he truly cared. They were brothers. It was only after the Agassi's power manifested that the Mirza began to resent magic, resent how people listened to the Agassi and not to him, how they talked about his power but ignored the Mirza's. Now, I think he does it because the Agassi is the most dangerous man in Sarkum. The only thing that could unseat the Mirza, not just because of his magic, but because the entire military is under his command."

"I do not understand." Naime pressed her hands to the cold glass of the window and closed her eyes. "How can he despise his brother and yet Makram looks up to him, believes in him?"

"Someone starved of something will take whatever they can get and make it into what they need, because they do not know there is more to be had in the world." Tareck cleared his throat and said, "He believes in rulers from stories, that are fair, and just, and do what's right by the majority. He has tried to shape his brother into that, thinking if he believed hard enough it would come to pass."

"But it will not." Naime glanced over her shoulder at him. He shook his head. She'd learned that lesson from her father. From his belief in Behram Kadir. You could not wish a person into being what you wanted them to be.

"The Mirza grows more paranoid every day. We are divided. The Mirza believes that magic and its inherent hierarchy divides the people and gives power unequally. He, and those who are aligned with him, believe the Republic represents progress beyond this."

"And what of the rest, what do they believe?" Naime said, fighting against the upwelling of despair. She thought she knew the answer. In fact she thought she had a reasonable chance of working her way to the conclusion of Tareck's admissions without further assistance from him. There were only a few logical reasons for Tareck to tell her any of this, especially considering he did so outside of Makram's sanction.

"That war is upon us, and the wrong man is in line to take the throne. They want a soldier to lead them into war. They would align with Tamar to fend off the Republic. And until now, they did not have the power to do more than bark and argue in the Council."

"And my arrival will tip the scale in favor of those who want Makram to take the throne." Naime's stomach twisted with nausea.

"Your arrival in Sarkum will be like a hammer to glass, Sultana."

Naime closed her eyes.

"Forgive me if I overstep, but, he admires you. He cares for you. You are, as a ruler, all the things he wishes his brother to be. Now that he has seen that, I believe he will not look at the Mirza in the same light. And when the Mirza sees him again, he will sense his hold has weakened. It will frighten him, and he will attempt to take control again."

"Why are you telling me this?" Naime faced him, putting her back to the windows and the storm outside.

"I fear the Agassi may have unintentionally endangered you. Though I occasionally masquerade as a steward, I am a soldier." He tapped his sword hilt. "The Agassi and I have fought together. I always protect his blind side. There is a blow coming that he cannot see, and he will not be prepared. You have proven yourself to be someone who can set aside her emotions for logic. You will be prepared, even if he is not. What you do with this information is of course your choice." He sounded apologetic.

"You want me to choose sides and embroil Tamar in a Sarkum civil war."

"I want the person with the best interests of Sarkum and her people on the throne, Sultana. I believe that would be in Tamar's interest as well." Earth mage he might be, but all his words were delivered in deadpan, as emotionless as any air mage.

"If I decide this is not in Tamar's interest and I wish to return home, will I and my people be prevented from leaving?" She had to consider that she would make a valuable hostage, and hoped she had not walked herself into such a situation.

Tareck shook his head. "I have a contingent prepared to escort you to the Engeli Gate."

Naime believed him, though she thought perhaps he left out the part where they might be running from the faction that would take her hostage. She took a deep breath to center herself and her magic, finding the place inside her that was always calm. The eye of the storm of her power around which the chaos of her world revolved.

"How many Sival or Chara'a are there living in the palace or with access to it?" She needed to know what threat she faced.

"One, Sultana, and I do not believe he would ever hurt you."

Perhaps not with magic, she thought, acknowledging for a moment the ache in the back of her throat. Why couldn't she have stayed away from him? Things would be so much clearer now if they were not entangled with her emotions.

"How many Deval of the Fourth House?" Earth mages had power to counter her to some extent, even if they were below her level.

"Three, but I am one of them, and the others are Elders of the Council. Their stamina is not what it once was."

Naime sighed. She would need time to think on all of it, time to formulate the possible outcomes and what she could afford to risk without the guaranteed backing of her own Council. Her safest option was to leave Sarkum this instant. But that would be rash, and despite what Tareck said about her foregoing emotion for logic, she had no desire to abandon Makram to a situation he was blind to.

"I will consider what you have told me."

Twenty-six

Makram had only been in the Attiyehs' home for the time it took him to stride from their entry to their library when someone grabbed the back of his shirt. A knife pricked at his back.

"That is not the proper way to greet a prince," a dry voice said from behind Makram as his fight instinct spiked and fell.

"Tsk," said the woman pressing the knife against his lowest rib. But she withdrew the blade and Makram twisted to wrap her in a hug.

"Aysel," he said, laughing a little as he released her.

"See, it makes him happy, you great bore," Aysel shot over her shoulder to her brother, who lurked in the doorway.

"Mathei," Makram said. Mathei smiled and bowed.

The two of them were a study in contrasts. Mathei was tall and handsome, with black hair and eyes, and his sister was short and plain, with wild chestnut hair tamed in braids. Mathei was a master at getting people to tell him too much, and Aysel, accomplished at sneaking into places she didn't belong. Mathei was cultured and well spoken, Aysel sharp-witted and blunt. They were as much sibling to him as Kinus was.

"Father is on his way. I wanted to come see if you had any burn marks from your little jaunt over the Engeli."

Makram held up his hands, revealing the bandage covering the left hand and his right wrist.

"And you've ruined my joke," Mathei said as his brows drew down. Aysel made a sound of disbelief.

"It's a long story, I'm afraid. But I suppose the good news is they didn't come from people wielding torches because I'm a death mage."

"So," Aysel said as she sat in one of the library's many cushioned chairs, "what was it like?" She flipped to hook her legs over the back of the chair and hang her head over the edge of the seat, folding her arms across her chest and blinking at him from her inverted position. Mathei made a disgusted sound as he sat in a chair near her.

"Sit like a person, you cretin," he said under his breath.

"It was beautiful," Makram said, and smiled to himself, "and terrible."

"Are there as many mages there as everyone says?"

"I met three Sival the first day I was there. Everyone in the royal family is one, the Sultan is even a Veritor."

Aysel's mouth opened in a little *o*, her eyes widening.

"And," Makram said, "the second in line to the throne is an ice mage."

"An ice mage?" Mathei said thoughtfully, and stood, crossing the room to one of the shelves. "That's rare. But I have a book, somewhere..." He ran his fingers across the shelves and mused to himself.

"Wheel preserve us all, he's going to read to us," Aysel groaned, placing a hand over her eyes. Makram laughed softly but was distracted by a sudden memory. Naime's notes in the library had listed books she wanted to read. Books she hoped were in Al-Nimas. About the Circle. Mathei was the most well-read person Makram knew, one of the reasons he made such an exceptional spy. He could talk about any subject under the sun with more than passing familiarity. He and Naime would probably have a great deal to discuss, were they ever to be in the same room.

"Mat, do you have any books by Emer Saban?" That was the only name Makram could recall from the scattered notes.

"Philosophy doesn't seem your subject," Mathei said absently, but he changed his direction and moved to the other side of the room.

"Not mine," Makram agreed.

Mathei paused with his hand on the books, turning to Makram with raised eyebrows, and Aysel executed a quick flip, landing on the floor with her legs folded in front of her and her head propped in her hands. They both stared at him in expectant silence. Makram grit his teeth. The problem with being friends with spies was that they too easily read into even the simplest of things.

"What an interesting trip it must have been"—Mat turned back to the shelves when it became clear Makram wasn't volunteering anything else—"that you have come back burned, bandaged, and seeking philosophy books for someone else."

"How drunk do we need to get you to pry the story out of you?" Aysel asked.

"Very. But it will have to wait."

They'd become close because Makram had apprenticed under their father to become Agassi, and they had all trained in bladework together. The Attiyeh family business was spying, and Elder Attiyeh had passed it down to his children, who swore their loyalty to Makram. He thought half because of the link they shared through their father's military career, and because the Attiyeh family were also destruction mages.

"Agassi," a warm female voice said from the door. Makram rose to greet their mother, who bowed and directed a servant to place a tray with arak, a pitcher of water, and glasses.

"Mistress Attiyeh, thank you for having me in your home."

"Of course," she hesitated, casting a glance toward the windows, "won't you stay until the storm passes?"

"Perhaps," Makram said. It had been worse than he had first thought, when he left the castle, and took twice the time it normally would have to reach the estate. She cast an officious look at Aysel. "Come with me."

Aysel groaned and stood to follow her mother. Mathei eyed him as if to discern whether it was wise to approach.

"Drink?"

"Only if it is not to soften me up for interrogation."

"I wouldn't presume," Mathei said. "That is Father's job."

Makram cast him a chastising look and Mathei smiled to himself as he poured two glasses and added a splash of water. The arak was already turning pale white as Mathei handed him a glass. Then he crossed the room to one of the squat bookshelves by the desk and crouched, extracting one. Makram sipped the anise-flavored drink and discovered he wasn't in the mood for it. He lowered the glass to his side as Mathei returned.

"Here." Mathei handed him a plain book wrapped in a tattered cover. "This is the only book Emer Saban wrote. It examines the interaction of the Houses as it applies to Chara'a. An interesting topic, though I found it dry." He tossed his drink back in one swallow.

Makram took the book, brushing a hand over the unmarked cover. "It must be unbearable to those of us with more mundane tastes then."

"Who is it for?" Mathei returned to the bottle and poured himself another glass.

"Someone I think you'd like."

"Someone studying Chara'a?" Mathei didn't look at Makram, and tried to disguise the depth of his interest with a preoccupied expression, but they had known each other too long for that.

"She studies many things," Makram said, "just like you. Have you read much about Veritors?"

"A *she*. Interesting. I think I'd like her less than you do, then." Mathei grinned over the rim of his glass. He meant, of course, that his tastes did not lean to the feminine.

"I wasn't implying you should like her more than I do."

Mathei held his drink near his chin, studying Makram with narrowed eyes and a little smirk. "Could I?"

Makram gulped the rest of his drink rather than answer, studying the paint chipping on the window frame.

Mat sipped his arak, still watching. "I thought not. I've never known you to be a gift-giver." He rolled his eyes when Makram shot him a glare. "As for your question, I haven't had the opportunity to study Veritors. If there are texts, I am unaware of them."

Mathei gestured at the bottle for Makram to help himself, but he shook his head and set his glass down.

"The Tamar Sultan is a Veritor," Makram said. "And the library in the palace has books on them. On law. A text all about Chara'a."

Mat made a sound of interest, his eyes lighting like black fire at the prospect of new knowledge. Would Naime ever trust someone else to do her research for her, to take some of her burden? He would trust Mat to it, who had such a keen mind and memory for facts.

"I have a job for you," Makram said.

"Good. I've been bored." Mathei grinned.

"The Grand Vizier in Tamar has spies, or allies, or both, in our court. Find them."

"What's this Vizier's name?"

"Behram Kadir." Makram flexed his left hand, thinking of the Vizier, and his son.

"A fire mage?" Mathei asked. Makram raised his eyebrows. Mathei went to the small writing desk in the corner of the room and sat down on the cushion in front of it. He rummaged through the drawers until exclaiming in success.

"Ask, and I am commanded." Mathei crossed the room and handed Makram a rolled-up missive. The red wax seal on it had been carefully unstuck, likely with the blade of a hot knife. The seal was not revealing in any way. Though he was not familiar with the seals in Tamar, he knew it was not a prominent family in Al-Nimas. "Aysel found that, just lying about for any common passerby to read."

"Where?"

"Do you really want to know?"

"Yes," Makram hissed.

"Your brother's desk."

"I've told her to stay away from him."

"She was following the man who put it there, but was only able to grab this page. I suspect the man she followed to be at least one of your spies," Mathei said. "I'll find out more."

Makram unrolled the letter but stopped when the door opened to admit Mathei's father, Thoman. Thoman grinned, an expression twin to his son's.

Makram rolled the letter and tucked it into his ferace, then gripped Thoman's forearm as the Elder bowed.

"Thoman."

Mathei gave them both a shallow bow and exited quietly.

"What's all this?" the Elder said, gesturing at Makram's bandaged hand.

"A game gone awry, I'm afraid." Makram sat when Thoman indicated the chairs. Thoman paced the length of the cozy room before settling.

"I was surprised by your letter," he said. "You have gone against the Mirza before, but this—"

"Was necessary."

"I agree," Thoman said with too much fervor. He and Tareck were aligned in their propensity for shoving Makram toward the throne. "And now you have brought the Tamar heir to the palace. Have you seen your brother yet?"

"No," Makram confessed. Thoman exhaled loudly, settling back in his chair and examining Makram in silence.

"The journey was troubled. We were attacked, and I wished to have the Sultana seen to before I engaged my brother."

"What do you know of her?" Thoman rose again and poured them arak, splashing water in before offering one to Makram. He drank it, though it tasted too strong and only seemed to increase the restlessness.

"That she is capable. But she faces similar struggles in the Tamar High Council that Kinus faces here—division."

"I assume, since she has traveled all this way, that she is in favor of an alliance. And her father, the Sultan?"

"He is," Makram said. The details were too many and too convoluted to reveal to Thoman, for the time being.

"There has been…movement while you were gone."

"What kind of movement?" Wheel he was tired. Every time he tried to catch his breath some new obstacle or disaster surfaced. He'd only felt relieved of it all in the tent with Naime, or rather, she'd kept him preoccupied with other matters.

Makram wiped a hand over his face to hide his expression, then over the braids in his hair. A soldier's braids. He wasn't made for intrigue.

"Your brother did not take news of your forward-thinking well, my friend. Those who were loudly in support of you have been put under guard in their homes. Some of their servants in the palace have been imprisoned."

"What?" Heaviness stole over him as he set his cup on the table beside his chair. Kinus had so few people loyal to him, he'd taken Makram's defiance as betrayal.

He propped his elbows on his knees and put his face in his hands. "I'll speak to Kinus in the morning. He can take this out on me, instead of everyone else. Once I've explained things to him we'll come to a compromise."

"Are you certain?" Thoman asked, frowning into his empty cup before he set it aside.

"Why did you ask me to come here, Thoman?"

"You took a great risk in going to Tamar. Was it worth it? Can you make an ally of them?" Thoman leaned forward, his face lit with excitement.

"With Kinus' approval, Tamar will make a powerful ally. Their Sultana wishes to balance the Wheel again. She wants to stand a Circle of Chara'a."

Thoman's expression broke apart, and his hands clenched against the arms of the chair he sat in. Makram couldn't guess what that reaction meant. He was aware Makram was a Charah. Perhaps he feared Makram would abandon Sarkum to stand in the Circle.

"What if your brother refuses? What then?"

"I'll convince him. I think once he hears what the Sultana has to say, he will consider it."

"You have this much faith in the Sultana? Whose own Council is divided?"

"You will see, when you hear her speak."

Thoman watched Makram, and Makram studied a bookshelf across the room, afraid to reveal his weakness to Thoman. He already knew it was foolish to feel as he did, to want what he did. To have anyone else chastise him for it would serve no purpose.

"I have to ask again, what will you do if your brother refuses? You have brought this woman here, to his court, against his wishes. He was upset enough by your leaving to move on the Elders. What will he do to her if he finds her presence objectionable?"

"I won't let him hurt her, if that's what you're concerned about."

"I'm not concerned. I'm asking you to think. You are more than capable of thinking several steps ahead in battle yet rarely do so outside of it. Do so now. Think of all the ways this could go, and plan for them."

"What do you want from me?" Makram's restlessness grew into concern. Naime wasn't in danger. Kinus wouldn't hurt her… couldn't.

"You know what I want, what the men your brother has confined away from the palace want."

"And I have told you I will not turn against my brother."

"What if he turns against you?"

"He won't."

Thoman's expression hardened with impatience and he sat back in his chair, clutching the arms too tightly. "Your loyalty and belief in him is admirable, and I think he knows that if he loses it he will also likely lose his throne."

"Well he won't lose it. And this discussion is over. If this is why you brought me here, to speak treachery, I'm leaving." Makram stood and headed for the library door.

"Don't be a hotheaded fool. Stay until the storm passes. You can leave in the morning." Thoman rose and put his hand on Makram's shoulder. "Eat with us. Have Mat and Aysel tell you what you've missed in court while you were gone. We won't speak of this again."

"Fine," Makram said.

"We'll inform you when dinner is prepared."

Makram left his side and moved to one of the tall, narrow windows. Thoman closed the door behind him and Makram pressed his forehead against the cold glass. The wind howled and cold seeped through the window into the space around him. It felt sinister, a bitter, blinding storm between him and Kinus. Between Tamar and Sarkum. Between him and Naime.

He knew just the threat of his power had solved many problems for Kinus before they ever really began. Few people would go against his brother with the most powerful mage in Sarkum at his side. Makram had been proud of the fact he was useful. Yet, surely he wasn't the sole obstacle between his brother and a civil war?

Or was he that blinded?

The moment he'd left, Kinus had imprisoned those who believed as Makram did. Was Makram not an astute judge of character? Perhaps it'd been hardest to assess his brother. Again he thought of Kadir, and his thoughts spun downward.

Makram closed his eyes, trying to conjure Naime in his mind, the way her magic had quelled his in the courtyard. The smell of her that seemed perfectly crafted to soothe the edges inside him. He'd hoped the thought of her might help tame the growing discord inside him now, but it only made him worry. It was foolhardy to go back out in the storm, but he did not like the idea of her in the palace without him. Especially in light of his brother's actions.

Thoman's questions had served their purpose. To sow doubt.

Makram took the letter from his coat. The same seal, three flames set with bases together so they formed an empty sun, had been stamped instead of a signature. There was no need to see the author's name, as soon as he began reading he knew.

We the High Council of Tamar, of Sultan Omar Sabri the Sixth, present the enclosed terms of negotiation for your consideration toward an alliance.

Kadir had sent terms ahead. Forged them, most likely. And he would only have done so if he had changed them—terms Naime would not have agreed to.

Kadir had reacted violently to Naime's proclamation she would be traveling to Sarkum because he feared she would contest whatever terms he had sent ahead. This letter did not detail them. It must have been sent with other documents, whatever Aysel had been forced to leave behind on the desk.

Makram swore and rolled the letter, returning it to his coat.

Damn the storm. He could not stay.

Twenty-seven

"What troubles you?" Samira knelt at the foot of the bed, working on brushing the caked dirt from the caftan Naime had worn to travel. It would need a good cleaning, but was unlikely to get it until they returned to Narfour. And even then Naime doubted the blood could be removed.

The bed was the only place for Samira to work. The room was cozy, to put a positive term on it. From the hall one entered a narrow, compact room that served as entryway and sleeping place for a servant. Attached to it was the bedroom, only bigger than the entryway in order to accommodate a bed so high Naime thought she might need a stool to climb into it. A minuscule dressing table and a short wardrobe stood against one wall, both painted in garish red geometric designs and inlaid with obsidian and marble.

"We are sitting in a den of sleeping lions," Naime stated, staring out the window at the continuing storm. They'd had their dinner, the attendants and stewards were lodged similar rooms, the wounded in the care of a physician. Everything and everyone was safe inside, away from the storm. Except Makram. Surely he would stay out of it, and not try to return tonight?

"Is that what Tareck told you?" Samira tapped the brush over a basin and resumed her short, quick strokes across the fabric.

"To warn me." Naime tipped her head against the window glass, hugging her arms around herself.

"Is that all that troubles you?" Samira spread another section of the caftan. Naime lifted her head from the window to look at her friend, who glanced at her then back to her work.

"No," Naime said.

"Do you love him?"

"Tareck?" Naime asked.

Samira raised an eyebrow, tapping the brush against the basin again. Dust puffed away from the bristles. Naime closed her eyes, laying her head against the window again.

"I think I would, given time." Or perhaps she didn't need time at all. She thought it might have begun to creep into the cracks around her logical thoughts, around her mental reminders that she would never see him again.

"What will you do?" Samira sat back on her heels and placed the brush in her lap.

"About Makram?" Naime asked, and before Samira could respond added, "Nothing. Distance will fight that battle for me."

"It doesn't help. Distance. Time. The rules that tell you no. All the lies you tell yourself. None of it helps."

"You are a fire mage. I am different, I am air. It will pass." Naime would tell herself that until it became true.

"No. Love does not belong to the First House, it is not a piece that fits into your puzzles. You cannot command it. And I have seen the way he looks at you. It will not pass for him either."

"Then why did you say such a terrible thing to him, when we arrived?"

"When I fell in love with Cemil, every moment I spent with him made me grow more fond. Every conversation, every touch, every look. And now I curse them all, because they are each a wound that bleeds. I wanted to spare you that, the thousand cuts that will bleed you of your soul, in the end."

"I cannot spare you from Cemil, and you cannot spare me from this. But you and I are together at least, and I do not intend to let anything change that." They would both be lovesick specters, haunting the halls of the Sultan's palace.

Naime moved from the window to kneel beside Samira and took the brush from her hands.

Samira sat back on her heels as Naime took over the work. "What of the other things Tareck warned you about? What will you do?"

"Whatever I must to get us out of here and safely back to Tamar. If I can salvage an alliance, I will, but not at the expense of everything else." Naime gave the fabric a little shake, examining it for more stains. "I may need your fire before the end of things."

Samira stilled when someone knocked on the door. She glanced to Naime, then rose. There was not enough space in the entryway for two people to stand side by side, so Samira had to turn and step back to open the door to the hall.

Makram stood, clasping the door frame on either side, dripping water and irritation. Naime's relief at seeing him safe faded when she realized he had ridden through the blizzard in the dark to appear before them.

"You might have dried off first," Samira said.

He straightened, ignoring her, and reached into his ferace. He pulled out a rolled-up sheet of water-stained paper. "We have a problem."

Samira took the paper as Naime stood. When Samira handed it to her, she recognized Kadir's handwriting immediately, despite the places where water had made the ink run. She flipped it over to read the back. Her heart kicked into a gallop.

"This wasn't with the terms we brought."

"No." Makram wiped the melted snow from his face. His hair was wet, dripping down his neck, and his clothes in a similar state. "Someone loyal to me stole this. It arrived before we did."

"That snake," Naime spat, tossing the paper on the bed. "You know nothing of what terms he sent?"

"I think I can guess," he said. She pressed her fingers to her forehead. He wouldn't have offered her as collateral, would he? If she married the Mirza, it would take her out of Tamar, but he would still have Ihsan in his way and no way to the throne but by force. Naime closed her eyes, trying to move the pieces, to see the path Kadir meant to take.

"Did you ride through that storm just to bring this?" Samira asked. Makram replied with a grunt. Samira gave a soft sigh of amusement and exasperation.

"Go get dry and warm. I cannot do anything about this tonight, and neither can you," Naime said, opening her eyes. "And it will help no one if you are debilitated with illness because you never think before you act."

"That is not the only reason I rode. I have lived here all my life, you may recall. I can decide the risk posed by a storm without your lectures."

"What other reasons then?" Naime said.

Samira mumbled something about towels and maneuvered her way around Makram and into the hall. Naime almost called after her not to go, her entire body seizing with awareness. No, she could not be alone with him. Not even for a moment. She moved against the wall, clasping her hands in front of her caftan and calling her power up to shield her.

"My brother hasn't…" Makram leaned into the door of the entryway, glancing through the bedroom, "come to see you? Or sent someone? You haven't been bothered?"

"I am not harboring him in the wardrobe, if that is what you mean."

He laughed a little, though it was distracted, and he leaned back to observe the hall. "I have seen no one but Tareck and the palace attendants who helped us to our rooms. Are you worried about something?"

He pulled his gaze from the hall back to her, and said nothing, but his jaw tightened.

"You should know Tareck pulled me aside today," Naime said.

Makram took a step into the entryway, and swung the door closed enough that he could lean on the wall behind it and be protected from view by anyone who might pass. Her throat was dry and her pulse too perceptible. He gave a violent shiver.

"Why?"

"Makram, please go get warm. You think I can't see you shaking?"

"I don't need you to mother me," he fumed.

Samira swung the door open from the hall, hitting him in the midsection with the handle. He bent forward with a sharp cry of surprise and pain, and Samira dropped the towels she was carrying.

"Forgive me, Agassi, I…" She glanced desperately at Naime, who moved around the bed to pick up the towels, which were scattered between her and Makram.

"Just come in here, get out of the way of the door," Naime ordered, moving aside so he could and gestured for Samira to close the hallway door. "Are you all right? Did it hit your wounds?"

"It doesn't matter. I'll have it seen to." He kept his left hand pressed to his belly, and his face had lost some of its color.

They both stood at the foot of the bed, too close. She could cross the distance in two short steps. His gaze raked her face and his jaw tightened again.

He spun, she suspected to leave, but Samira blocked his way and someone knocked on the hall door. Makram closed his eyes and released a tired sigh. Samira held a finger to her lips, tugging the bedroom door closed before she answered the hall door.

Naime didn't need a spell to hear the conversation. It was Tareck, asking if they'd seen Makram.

"You didn't even tell Tareck you were back?" Naime chided.

Makram stepped to her, pressing his right hand against the bedroom door to prevent it opening, and kissed her. Naime jerked away, her breath catching, trying to find enough strength to back away completely. Instead she grabbed handfuls of his wet clothes and tugged them together.

"I just wanted to see you," he whispered in answer. "This is going to kill me."

She pressed her mouth to his and he captured her lower lip briefly between his with soft pressure, and repeated it when she kissed him twice more, lingering in the last.

"I'm sorry." He cupped his hand over the back of her head and tipped it against his chest. He dropped his hand from the door when Samira closed the hall. Naime pulled gently out of his grasp and he opened the door to the entryway, holding it ajar with one hand. Samira cast a glance from him to her. Her gaze lingered on Naime's in silent question.

"He said that if I were to see you, I should pass on that the Mirza has scheduled to see you both during the Elder Council tomorrow." She bowed slightly. "I believe the captain suspected you were here."

"I wouldn't keep him around if he was an idiot," Makram said. "I should go."

Samira stepped out of the way and Makram turned. Naime reached out, pinching the back of his sleeve. He stopped, his hand tightening on the door, shoulders hunching. It was the most foolish decision she had ever made. Yet she could not, just as Samira had warned, prevent herself from making it. If they were going to see the Mirza the next day, whether things went poorly or well, this was, in all likelihood, the last time she would ever have to be alone with him.

"Stay," she said, so quietly she wasn't certain he could hear. He slanted his head, his brows notched over troubled eyes. "Please."

He spun toward her, releasing the door, and Samira reached in to grab the handle. She caught Naime's gaze as she did and gave her a tremulous smile and a quick nod before she closed it. Naime wasn't certain if it was sanction or resignation, but she would have all the time in the world to speak with Samira.

Naime lifted her face to his, heat pricking her skin and her heart beating an out-of-cadence rhythm. He seemed suddenly too big and overpoweringly male, and the expectant heaviness in the air oppressive.

"I don't like that look," he said, in a voice pitched to soothe her. "You aren't afraid of me?"

"No," she blurted, "of course not. I acted without thinking, and now I'm not entirely sure what to do with you."

He laughed softly and gave her a regretful smile. "I've been a poor influence on you."

"No"—she tried to smile—"but you have neglected to demonstrate what one does after they act without thinking."

"Ah," he said, and rolled his gaze up to the ceiling. "You keep moving forward."

Naime stroked his bared throat with her stare and knew what she wanted. She reached to the dressing table, where she had stacked the towels, and picked one up. He lowered his chin when she stepped to him and slung the towel around his neck. She buried her hands in it, and stroked it over his face, then released it and reached up to urge his head lower. He tipped his head against her shoulder and Naime undid the metal band holding his hair, tossing it on the bed. Then she used the towel to squeeze the wet from his hair and pat his neck dry. He stayed as he was when she reached for the buckle of his sword belt. The leather was wet and stubborn, and took her some time to unhook.

He moved as if to help her once, but Naime brushed his hands away and touched her mouth against his ear.

"I want to." She kissed the curve of his ear. "I want to look at you again." Look at him and touch him. She could not imagine she would ever have another chance.

He took an unsteady breath and nodded, touching his lips to her neck and lifting his hands to her hair. His fingers dug into the coiled braids, searching out and removing the pins. As he worked, so did she, fighting loose the wet, tight knot in the fabric that wrapped his waist.

When he'd pulled the pins from her hair and the braids fell down her back he lifted his head and leaned to place the pins on the table. She unwound the length of black cloth from his waist and tossed it beside the wardrobe. It landed in a wet heap on the rug. Makram toed out of his boots and kicked them in the direction of the cloth. Naime unfastened the clasps of his ferace, charcoal grey made black by the melted snow, and together they tugged it off him.

"There is a quicker way," he said in a rough voice that betrayed desire. Naime looked up from the buttons of his entari. Smoke like windblown clouds streaked beneath his skin, black leaching across his eyes like spilled ink. Her fingers faltered in their work. "They are ruined anyway."

"You mean your magic." She considered it. But undressing him was pleasurable and had built a steady thrum of anticipation inside her. "Just the entari. I want the rest."

He made a soft sound she couldn't interpret and dropped his head to hers for a kiss. If he had meant it to be a gentle kiss, he had forgotten, because it heated quickly. The kisses he'd given her in the tent had been slow and patient. Now he claimed her mouth with teeth and tongue, his hold on her supportive but not confining. A soft noise escaped her, and she curved into him, her fingers still on one of his entari's clasps.

His magic moved as he commanded it, and the clasp in her fingers disintegrated. Naime opened her eyes, pulling reluctantly away from his kiss. Threads and dust drifted to the floor at his feet. She rubbed her fingers together around bits of the braided clasp she'd been holding.

"Remarkable," Naime announced, and Makram grinned, some of the fog leaving his expression.

"That is the first time I've heard that about my magic."

"I hope this is not your habitual way of undressing? How expensive it must become." She smiled. He shook his head at her, gently flicking a finger against her chin.

When she took hold of the hem of his caftan he helped by grabbing it and together they lifted it over his head. Naime snatched the towel from around his neck before he dislodged it and he tossed the caftan over his shoulder. She had not forgotten he had been wounded. But the evidence of it was hard to look at. One stitched gash curved across his left side, from his navel and up his ribs. The other nearly mirrored it on his other side, though it was straighter, from hip to under arm. The blistered marks from Cemil's heat whips overlaid them. Bruises framed both wounds, angry purple and red nearest, fading to green and yellow farther out. His magic danced and swirled, smoke rising from hips to shoulders, twisting stains beneath his skin.

"I hate this." Naime touched him, following the line of the straighter gash. His stomach tightened as a rush of breath left him. His eyes were half closed when she looked to his face.

"I hope you mean the wounds," he grumbled. Naime clicked her tongue at him and lifted the towel, across her hands, rubbing it over his chest and shoulders, and patting more gently over his stomach and sides. She feared the entire time she might catch it on the stitches, but if she did he did not let on.

"I mean the wounds, you vain creature." She wrapped her arms around him and dragged the towel down his back. "Would you like to know what I think of this?" She slid a hand down the broad plain of his back, over prominent muscles and the furrowed channel of his spine.

"Yes."

"I have not been able to push the sight of you from my mind. I could barely speak to you that day in the stables. I wanted to touch you so badly."

"Do it," he ordered, grabbing her belt and tugging her against him. "Touch me."

"Anywhere?" She liked him being a little greedy, liked giving him some measure of control, because he only took a fragment, not all of it.

"Anywhere. However you want." He bent to her neck, still holding her belt, planting a kiss below her ear. "With your hands, your mouth, your tongue, your teeth. I am yours."

His words sent lances of sharp, startling heat from her breasts to her core and dulled her thoughts to a slow, illiterate jumble. Makram shivered, and she realized his skin beneath her hands was cold and covered in gooseflesh.

"I think"—she stroked her hands down the length of his arms, fingers dipping against muscles, her thumbs curving against the hollows of his elbows—"you are cold."

"I did try my best to freeze to death out there," he conceded, his gaze dropping to her midsection. "You, on the other hand, appear to be far too hot. You could warm me." His fingers made quick work of her belt, and he tossed it behind her, then removed the other, a draping of cloth, and did the same.

"Makram," Naime said as he began to flick loose the braided gold buttons of her entari. "Before—"

He pushed the entari off her shoulders and it fell at her feet. It was more decoration than shield or covering, and she had a heavy caftan, and lighter-weight caftan, a chemise, and her salvar still. But the loss of the entari made her feel far closer to naked than she was.

She grabbed his hands, gentle on the bandaged one. "There are risks I cannot take with you," she said, quickly. At the palace in Narfour she had access to the teas and herbs that would prevent complications, but it was a chance she could not take here.

The spreading night in his eyes receded when he blinked it away, as did the magic under his skin. He nodded.

"I know, Beautiful."

Naime had never heard the word made reverence, into a state of being, into the warmest, truest expression of feeling. It had never meant anything. *You are beautiful.* They said. *What a beautiful princess. How fortunate she is beautiful.* A word that described nothing of who she was or what she wanted, how she worked to be everything she needed to be. But in his voice, shaped by night and peace, it became everything she knew he saw in her. Naime's eyes burned, and she had to swallow back a breath that felt suspiciously like a sob.

"Let me touch you and hold you," he said. "Let me see you shine. I won't ask for anything else." He lifted his hands to her hair and began combing her braids out with his fingers.

"Despite your comparison," Naime had to say something sharp to strengthen the parts of her that were falling apart, "I am not a mage orb that can be commanded to glow at your convenience."

"I am never one to back down from a challenge," he said, "as you have come to know."

A soft knock came at the door.

"I have dry clothes," Samira said from the other side. Makram stepped back so the door blocked him from view when Naime opened it. Samira took in her missing entari and unbound hair with a quick glance and handed her the clothes.

"You're all right?" Naime asked. Samira gestured to the sleeping pallet that lay opposite the door to the hall.

"A hundred times more comfortable and warmer than the plains," she said. Then she smiled and cupped her hand over the back of Naime's. "When you are happy, I am all right."

Naime kissed her cheek then closed the door, laying the clothes out on the bed.

"I sleep naked," Makram said, pressing against her back, wrapping his arms around hers to pin them to her sides when she busied herself with laying out the caftan and salvar Samira had brought.

"Even in the wilds?" Naime twisted to look up at him over her shoulder. She liked how his embrace made her feel cocooned, how it made her heart leap to her throat and beat harder. He laughed.

"No. Is this the wilds?"

"It does seem like a situation in which sleeping naked might be dangerous."

"I'm not certain how you imagine that," he said. "It isn't as if a person's parts simply act of their own volition."

It was Naime's turn to laugh, and he spun her so she faced him.

"I'll wear the salvar, if it makes you happy. But not the rest. I despise being bound and tangled in sheets and clothes while I sleep."

"Very well." Naime hooked her fingers into the top of the salvar he still wore, which were wet and clinging to his skin despite how long he'd been standing in them. Again his body reacted, his stomach tightened, and he pushed his hips closer, his hands gripping her elbows. Naime lifted her hands from the salvar to draw her fingers down the flat expanse of his stomach, between his injuries. There was the faintest indentation down the center of his body, beginning at his throat, leading to his navel, where it ended. Naime traced it up, and flattened her palms to brush them across the thicker muscles of his chest and shoulders. She was mesmerized by him, by the differences of his body and hers, by every dip and swell. A night would never be enough to memorize him.

She lifted her face to his and he caught her mouth in a kiss. Naime slid her hands over his shoulders and around his neck, circling her arms around and lifting on her tiptoes to meet him. He tamed her with his kisses, finding every tender, sensitive place on her neck and throat with his lips and tongue as his fingers worked free the tiny buttons of her caftan. Once that was on the floor he pulled the simpler one over her head, so she was left in only her chemise and salvar.

He stroked his hands down her bared arms, and her skin prickled. She leaned into him. His hands tightened on her arms. There had been so many layers of clothes between them, and now there was only the chemise. Thin, soft, and completely inadequate to the task of providing a barrier of any kind.

Naime lowered her hands from his neck to his waist, the slight swell of muscle above each of his hips. His skin was cold and pebbled beneath her fingers. She couldn't look at him now, not when she could feel even the tiniest movement through the fabric of her chemise, the hard plain of his chest against her exquisitely sensitive breasts. His stomach against hers, so that suddenly every bit of her skin begged for touch, for the rough caress of his hands.

"You're all right?" he asked, his left hand smoothing down her back. Naime nodded. "Tell me no," he said, as his fingers curled into her chemise and pulled it up in fistfuls, "about anything, and we'll stop."

"Stop talking." She smiled up at him to tease him.

He grinned and dipped his head to nip her ear, then kiss the spot below her earlobe, both hands lifting her chemise to her hips so he could pull loose the knot of fabric that held her salvar around her hips. Naime did the same to his. Doing something helped to distract her from the inevitable nervousness of having a man removing her clothes for the first time. Makram was quick at it, his fingers pulling the fabric loose and pushing the salvar off her hips. They puddled around her ankles. Naime stepped out of them as she continued her less deft attempt at removing his.

"I'm counting to five," he said as he let her chemise fall back around her legs, "then these are going the same way as my entari."

Naime huffed an impatient breath. "I said I wanted to do it." The knot finally came free and she flicked the two ends of fabric aside then tucked her fingers into the front.

"One," Makram hummed.

Should she push down from the front, or the sides? The back? Naime considered. If she pushed down on the front she might inadvertently touch parts she wasn't certain she should, at this moment. And the back had the same danger.

"Two." Makram gave a soft laugh and she flicked her gaze up at him. "Three."

Naime traced the top of the salvar with her thumbs, the smooth sweep of low belly between the jut of his hip bones. She followed the line of jet hair from his navel to the top of his salvar with her finger. She could lose herself to just that portion of him, to the intricacies of muscles that crowned his hips, the muscled, scarred column of his waist, the way his skin shivered and prickled at her touch.

"Four," he rasped. "Five."

Naime slid her hands to his hips and shoved the salvar down at the same moment shadowed smoke burst over his skin as he released his hold to cast a spell. Makram grabbed her by the waist and threw her up and onto the bed as if she weighed exactly nothing. She stared up at him as he crawled up and over her on hands and knees, rising to her elbows.

"You are warm," he rumbled, lowering his weight onto her and pressing a kiss to her collarbones, exposed by the low neck of her chemise. It was a challenge to breathe with his weight on her like that, and the ephemeral material of her chemise and his nakedness combined in wicked tandem to make the hard press of his arousal perfectly obvious against her thighs, so she didn't breathe at all.

Naime was only innocent of the actual act. Her mother had been an instructor at the University; one prone to forthrightness and who loved an opportunity to instruct. On any subject. She had taught Naime in the same way, of the belief that things that were not a mystery were much less attractive to an adolescent. Still, it was mysterious enough she was tempted to push him away so she could see him, as he had not allowed her even a glimpse.

He kissed her, urging her flat on her back, his tongue slipping against hers in such graphic suggestion that fire bloomed in her belly and between her legs, pulsing. She arched beneath him, wrapping her arms around his back and tracing unthinking trails up and down his skin with her nails. Makram shifted with a groan that vibrated through his chest and hers, hiking a knee up by her hip to take some of his weight off her. Naime pulled away from the kiss and sucked in a full, deep breath, dropping one hand from his back to his thigh.

Stiff hair crinkled against her palm, and the muscles in his leg shifted and flexed as he moved, hard beneath her grip. The flat of his knee, framed by muscle and sinew, drew her focus. She drew a circle across it with her fingertips.

"Every part of you could take me a lifetime to come to know." The words felt prickly as she said them, loaded with meaning she hadn't meant to instill but neither were they a lie.

"Dissecting me already, daughter of the First House?" he said, wryly.

"A little," she said. He'd leaned onto his arm to allow her room to move and watched her with a dazed expression that suggested his body ruled more than his mind in this moment. "But only because I want so much more time than we have."

The distance left his eyes, replaced with a trace of sadness. "Yes." He dipped his head and drew the bridge of his nose along her jaw.

"I would like to see you." Naime brushed her hands back up his thigh and to his hip.

"And ruin you for anyone to follow me? That would be cruel," he said into the hollow of her throat. Naime pinched his hip in rebuke and he flinched, laughing softly against her skin.

"I think you may have already." She lifted her head to kiss his shoulder. He stilled.

"I cannot decide if it will be your sweet touches or your unbearable words that will be the end of me." He shifted, rolling to his side and pulling her with him.

"Should I not say them?"

"No," Makram said. "Say them all, so I have them when I cannot remember the way your touches feel."

She closed her eyes to dam the tears. She slid one arm beneath his neck and draped the other over it, hugging him to her. His left arm went around her, pressing her to him as he rolled from his side to his back. Naime didn't let go or ease her grip, ducking her head against his and trying to contain her emotion.

"I told you that between you and me is not the place to control yourself, and I also told you I can feel your grief," he said into her hair, which had spilled over her shoulders and around them.

"If I let go"—Naime sucked in a shaking breath—"we will spend this time picking up all my broken pieces."

"I want them," Makram said. "I can help you carry them." His arms tightened around her. An imaginary fissure opened in her chest, the pain of it real enough.

"Terrifying death mage indeed"—she touched his lips—"who can break a heart with his tenderness."

He cupped her face, lifting her head away from him, then collected her hair into one fist and held it away from her face as he kissed her. He lifted his head up off the bed, chasing her as she sat up on his legs. He claimed her more fully with each slow, harsh stroke of his mouth over hers.

"I have to stop us now," he groaned when he released her from the last kiss, "before I can no longer bring myself to." As he spoke he guided her off his lap. Naime knelt on the blankets, unable to respond with words as sensible as his, and watched him step off the bed.

He faced her as he pulled the dry salvar on. She could not help but watch him, though she struggled to choose a place to focus. First the muscled curve of his back as he bent to fit his feet into the legs of the salvar. Then the flex of his arms as he pulled them up.

She'd never seen a fully naked man. Her mother had told her what a penis looked like, but the actual organ didn't quite match the image she'd maintained for the time since. It was foreign and fascinating and erotic and she wanted to touch him so badly she curled her hands into fists and dug her nails against her palms. He stopped when he realized she was staring at him, the salvar three-quarters of the way up his legs, drawing a fabric line that only highlighted what she was already unable to take her eyes from.

"Come here," he said, with warmth and humor. Naime scooted on her knees to the end of the bed. "Do you know that sometimes you look at me as if I am the most fascinating thing you have ever seen?"

"You are," she said. His brows drew together and he let go of the salvar to snag her shoulders and pull her up and against him.

"I told you to touch me"—he rubbed his hands down her arms, taking her wrists and bringing them together between them—"however you wanted."

"But you said we had to stop, or you would no longer be able to."

"A little exaggeration. I am not a mindless animal. And I want you to," he said. "I like the way you look at me. I want—" His breath shuddered in. "I wish I could be the one to show you everything."

Naime kissed him, twisting her hands out of his grasp. He held her right in his left and guided her palm against his arousal. She closed her fingers around him and he slid his hand to her wrist as he pulled away from her kiss and rubbed his brow against hers. His erection was heavy in her hand, and seemed to move of its own volition, pulsing when she squeezed. The skin was soft and hot, the shaft beneath it shockingly hard. Makram took another careful breath, his fingers against her wrist flexing and releasing. When she moved her hand from base to tip, his whole body came toward her, but his head fell back and he moaned. The sound was different than any of the others he had made, filling her with the greedy desire to make him do it again. But she released him, thinking if he only touched her once where her need felt greatest, that it might be more akin to torture than pleasure.

Makram sighed, keeping his head tilted back as he pulled the salvar up and tied them closed around his hips. The length of him meant that when he pressed his erection flat against his belly the head showed above the waistband. Naime circled her fingers over the protruding tip. Would he allow her to touch her lips to it? The skin was soft, she could not help thinking kisses were better matched to it than other touches. But then, how could she even ask such a thing? Instead she asked something else.

"That doesn't hurt, squashing it like that?"

He laughed and shook his head, gripping her fingers and bringing them to his lips.

"Shall we pretend to sleep?" He grinned at her, but it was tight and small, not the easy one he usually offered. It was not what she wanted. Not what her body wanted. But in the dark corner of her logical mind, she knew anything else was a risk she couldn't take.

Naime slipped off the bed and circled around to pull the blankets back. Makram stood behind her as she bent to reach the far side, tugging at the covers. He pressed his hips against hers, pulling her by her hips against the hard length of him. Naime whirled, and he bent to catch an arm under her bottom and hoist her up onto the bed. He pulled her knees apart with his hands and insinuated himself between her legs. She reminded herself that they were playing a game with fire. But her body told her that was exactly where she wanted him. Between her legs. Filling her up and making the empty ache inside her stop.

"Shine for me," he said. Naime pursed her lips.

"I want to know you want me as badly as I want you," he said, forcing her to her back again as he leaned over her. "Shine for me."

Naime maneuvered herself backwards and under the blankets, and Makram climbed on the bed and fit his body against her side, leaning over her, his gaze roaming over her face, her throat. He lingered on her breasts, which were hardly obscured by her chemise, and nestled his hand between them. Naime pressed her hand over his heart and closed her eyes. She carefully unbound her magic, releasing hold enough on it to give him what he wanted, unleashing its light across the room. She opened her eyes.

His magic answered hers with shadow for her light. Smoke beneath his skin, shadowed flames twining through and around the sharp, bright light of her power. They were a swirling, ever-changing harmony, his peace for her tempest, his restlessness for her calm, his recklessness for her planning, her independence for his loyalty. Night and day, dusk and dawn, the end, and the beginning.

"I am balanced for I am broken," Naime recited, full of sorrow and joy. Did he know the Wheel's poem? It was as old as magic.

"Parts that make a whole," he murmured, stroking her hair away from her face.

"Each joy and sorrow token, paid to mold my soul." Was knowing him and losing him payment for the peace of her life? Tears sprang to her eyes and he kissed the corners where they gathered.

"For I am nothing, and you are everything," he breathed against her cheek, changing the words of the poem to suit him, so they became divulgence and revelation. He touched his lips to hers.

There was more, but she returned his kiss instead, breathing in the dusky, warm scent of him. He rolled to his back and pulled her onto him.

Naime listened to the strong, steady beat of his heart and he stroked his fingers through her hair, and neither one of them spoke again. Eventually his breathing evened out, and his fingers stilled against her. In the dark and silence she listened to the blizzard outside, the wind rushing against the window. A storm that did not pass.

Twenty-eight

Makram had to crawl out of sleep as absolute as the void. It was not frightening, it was comforting, heavy and warm and safe. But he found his way out because somewhere, closer to consciousness, he could feel a warm, soft shape against his, and he wanted it.

She'd shifted off of him at some point, though he didn't think he had moved a muscle all night. Instead of lying on top of him as she had been when he fell asleep, she was curled backwards into the hollow of his side, between his outstretched arm and leg. Makram rubbed his fingers across his eyes and lifted his head so he could see her. She lay with her knees pulled up toward her chest, one arm draped over them, the other outstretched beneath her head, her hand on his wrist. He rolled to his side, wincing as bruised pain burst over his ribs, reminding him he was not whole yet. Naime made a soft, sleepy grunt when he pulled her into the curve of his body.

Outside the window, snow continued to blow. The room was chill, but beneath the covers, curled together, they were warm. Makram buried his face in the tangle of her silken hair. Maybe the storm would never pass, and he could keep her. Maybe they could stay exactly as they were, in a room where the rest of the world didn't exist. He would not have to confront his brother, or give her up, to Kinus or to anyone. He would not have to fear for her when she faced Kadir after a failed trap. They could finish what they started the night before. He could bury himself so deeply inside her that they were no longer two people, beginning and ending in the same being.

The final thought fired his blood and the only barely dormant want from the night. He stiffened against her back, and thought he should turn away, but didn't want to wake her.

"You do not like early mornings," she mumbled, her voice sultry with sleep, "but that part of you apparently does."

"I have a feeling the two of you would get along very well," Makram said into the back of her neck. Her lingering looks and all-too-brief touch the night before had made him frantic with want. She shook with a silent laugh and rolled to face him, stretching her legs out along his. They were bare, the chemise bunched up around her hips, and Makram pressed his knee up between her thighs, closing his eyes at the silky feel of her skin against his.

"Would you like to tell him good morning?" he asked.

She laughed again, sliding her head back so she could meet his gaze, one eyebrow raised. "Is it a him?"

"I don't know what else it would be." He reached beneath the covers to stroke his hand over her thigh.

"Well, I didn't think it was a separate entity from you." She smiled in bewildered amusement. "Have you named it?"

He held her thigh, pulling it up to his hip and rolling on top of her. "Don't be absurd." He fit his hips against hers, pressing the subject of their conversation against her pelvis. "That's your job."

A short, bright laugh burst from her. "I will not name your…" Her cheeks flushed, and her gaze cut sideways.

"Say it." He grinned. "There are a variety of words, you may take your pick."

"I will not"—she sniffed, her eyes flashing to his and away again—"name your *cock.*"

That word, coarse and hard, from her soft mouth, made sharp slashes of need prickle through his body. Wheel he wanted her.

"Where did someone as polite and refined as you learn a word like that?" he mumbled, to disguise the raw need in his voice.

Her lips pressed together and she sucked her cheeks against her teeth in an effort to prevent a smile. "I have not lived sequestered in a room my entire life, you know."

"You didn't learn it in a law book?" he teased. His question made him remember that in his haste to be inside he'd left the book he'd brought in his saddle bags. "Damn me." He rolled to his side in reflex, thinking about retrieving it.

"Makram?"

"I brought you a gift." No, he couldn't get it this instant. It would be beyond foolish to give up even a moment of the time he had with her just to retrieve it. He'd be a madman to leave her alone in a warm bed to go trekking out into the snow. Makram relaxed against her again.

"A gift?" She scrunched her face, as if he had said something repugnant.

"A pile of emeralds," he said. She rolled her eyes and Makram burst into real laughter then. He would not have ever imagined he'd see cool, composed Sultana Sabri roll her eyes.

"What can I offer you that you do not already have?" He propped himself on an elbow so he could look down at her. She shifted, so she was more on her back than her side.

"The entirety of your janissary and sipahi," she said, with the particular flavor of blank expression that hid her internal humor. He wanted to roll and cover her again, tug her chemise up, and end the longing that pulsed painfully in his groin. She wanted him, he could see it. But she was right, it was not worth the risk.

"In exchange for…?"

"I thought it was a gift." She gave two slow blinks. Teasing him in turn. He pressed the tip of his nose to the tip of hers as melancholic adoration filled his heart and belly to the brink.

She touched both her lips to his top one. Makram resisted the urge to draw her into more kisses. He could not stay much longer, and it would be even harder to tear himself away if he began kissing her. Instead, he nestled his free hand in the dip of her waist, and traced the curve of her lower rib with his thumb.

"You'll have to ask my brother for that gift. I am only a second prince, all I can offer you is a book."

Surprise ruined the calm of her expression. She stared at him, as if waiting for him to take back the words. Hopeful.

He laughed at the avarice in her warm brown eyes.

"What book?"

"Emer Saban's book. His name was in your notes, in your library. They were in the blue book."

"The Book of Chara'a," Naime named it, and her gaze raked his face. "Did you read all of my notes?" She spoke in a careful, wary tone.

"You wish to stand the Circle," he said. She gave a single nod against the pillow, her gaze holding his. Makram swallowed, praying she would not ask the question he could see in her eyes.

"Do you know that only one Charah of each House exists at any given time?" She used her fingers to comb his hair away from his jaw then brushed them down the slope of his neck. The soft touch lit his skin with sensation, but he could not enjoy it.

"I know."

"I believe that without a Circle, we will not have the strength to defeat the Republic when they come for us." She traced her fingers along his collarbone, and the touch only marginally eased his growing tension.

"You cannot stand a Circle without a Charah of every House. There is no Third House. I have heard of no Charah in generations except myself."

"You are not the only Charah." She gave the revelation gently. "And I have to believe the Wheel would not abandon its children in their time of need. I have to believe if I have the desire, the drive, to do this thing, then the Wheel has turned to make it so, to make it possible."

"Naime," he said, "I cannot leave my brother. My loyalty has always been to him."

"I cannot do it without you," she said, her expression unguarded. She was not begging. Instead her face reflected something he might have named despair. "Come back to Tamar. I have reason to believe your brother is not as loyal to you as you are to him."

Cold anger pushed through his body, obliterating everything else he felt, and he sat up.

"Is Tareck the reason you believe that? Is that what he told you when you met with him?"

She did not nod or speak, but her eyes told enough truth. Makram threw the covers off and got up.

Why would she listen to Tareck and not him? She'd never even met Kinus. She sat up, slowly, watching him stalk around the bed.

"He had no right to put ideas in your head. He had no right to speak to you about any of these things." He snatched up the dry caftan and tugged it on. Naime slipped out of bed and circled toward him, but stopped near the bedpost, allowing him space.

"I believe he did it out of interest in your wellbeing, and my own. Not to betray you."

"Betrayal comes from those who think they know better, doesn't it? If you listened to his rumor mongering, then you're not as wise as I believed." Where were his damn boots?

"Is this how you wish to leave things between us? With anger and name calling?" Her voice came stony and cool. Makram straightened, his back to her, and tipped his head back with a sigh.

"I will make my own judgments when I meet your brother today. Surely you trust me enough to do that? Though your violent reaction to the idea tells me more than even Tareck did."

"Does it?" Makram faced her. Cold as winter, her magic and her composure fully, and infuriatingly in place. She wore only the chemise, which was little different than standing naked before him. His body did not seem to care that he was angry, or that she showed all the emotion of a marble column. "What does my reaction tell you?"

Her glances raked him from head to toe. He shivered, frozen to the bone by her penetrating examination. "We defend hardest those lies that protect our failings. And your brother is yours, isn't he?"

"He is my brother. My blood. We are stronger together."

"He is stronger, with you. Are you stronger with him, Charah of the Sixth House? Agassi of all of Sarkum's forces?"

She let go of the bed post and advanced a step toward him. "Are you stronger when you are ignored and mistrusted, resented for what the

Wheel made you to be? Are you stronger because you serve someone you have to lie to in order to do the right thing?"

"You think that would be different in Tamar? Land of mage killers?" he scoffed.

She exhaled in impatience and folded her arms across her chest. "Do as you must," she said, softly, "and I will do the same."

He paused as he bent to put a boot on. Gone. All of it was gone. The tenderness, the sweetness, the desire. Only moments before she'd been looking at him like she cared about him, but now that he would not give her what she wanted, she looked at him the same way she looked at any of her Viziers. As an obstacle.

"You don't care, do you?" he said. "Not about this"—he pointed between them—"just about your plans. Your Circle. The alliance."

"If that thought gives you peace, then you may keep it." She retrieved her entari from the floor and shrugged into it. "You do not care for my reaction? How should I act? Should I run crying from the room and reveal our indiscretion to everyone outside the doors?" She combed her fingers through her hair and twisted it into a knot at the nape of her neck. "Shall I weep bitterly on my attendant's shoulder that you denied me, and reveal a weakness to anyone who might be listening?"

"Always the planner," he said, catching sight of his other boot half under the bed, "never thinking about what you feel, just how everyone sees you."

She recoiled, hurt flashing in her eyes. "I must be able to think beyond the moment. To lose myself, and my discipline, is not a luxury I have ever had." She faced the window, putting her back to him, her arms hugged around her. Makram snatched the boot up and tugged it on.

"Samira," she called. The door opened a crack. "Please make certain the Agassi is completely dressed before he departs, and that he leaves none of his things here."

"Yes, Efendim." Samira bowed in acceptance.

"Don't bother. I'll see myself out," Makram said. Samira moved aside as he stalked from the room.

TWENTY-NINE

THE DAY HAD ONLY just begun unraveling when Makram left Naime's room that morning. His brother refused to see him before Naime was scheduled to stand before the Elders. He'd hoped for a chance to make amends with Kinus before they were in the presence of the Elders, when Kinus would be all too conscious of appearing weak. He'd also hoped to convince his brother the terms he'd received from Kadir were not the true terms. There might be a chance of passing it off as a mistake if he spoke to Kinus in private, but in front of the Elders he would only be encouraged to believe it was some kind of purposeful affront.

Tareck had found him that morning to inform him that Naime's wounded guard was doing better, but was not stable enough to travel. Elder Attiyeh had arrived for the meeting with the Elders but Kinus had sequestered them all in the throne room, so Makram was unable to speak with him. And as a final, killing blow, someone had stolen the real alliance terms they'd brought with them from his office.

Makram paused before he reached the archway to his brother's throne room and faced Tareck. He hadn't spoken to him yet about what he had said to Naime. With Kinus acting so unreasonably, lending truth to whatever notions Tareck had put in Naime's mind, it made it difficult to chastise his friend for interfering. He just wanted them to understand Kinus the way he did. When he spun to him, Tareck clasped his hands behind his back and stopped.

"You overstepped."

"I had no choice."

"Horse shit."

"That stench isn't coming from me," Tareck said, his eyes narrowing. "I am only willing to let you lie to yourself. Once it begins to affect others, once it begins to endanger Sarkum, I will rein the horse for you if that is what it takes."

"What did you hope to accomplish by doing this?" Makram could not understand why Tareck would drive a wedge between them.

"I'd hoped you loving her would open your damned eyes."

"I do not love her," Makram said.

Tareck flicked his gaze up and snorted. "Wheel preserve me, the lies you tell yourself." He glanced toward the arch, then leaned forward, pitching his voice low. "I warned her that your brother is unstable because you can't pull your head out of your ass to do so. I did it to protect the only ruler I believe has the interest of the people at heart. The only one who sees things clearly. I want to believe it of you, but you remain blinded by your loyalty to your brother. He might have been friend to you once, but he is no longer."

"Do not say such things," Makram rebuked, darting a look at the doors. If Kinus heard him he'd be in prison. Cold hands squeezed around his heart. Tareck stood as he was, stone-faced and silent, watching as realization took Makram and put a stranglehold on him.

Naime wouldn't even sentence a man she *knew* was guilty without a trial. Kinus would imprison a loyal man for even daring to speak words that suggested he was unjust. Makram pressed the heels of his hands against his eyes.

"Go escort the Sultana," he said. Tareck bowed and strode away.

Makram leaned back against the wall, listening to the hum of low voices coming from Kinus' throne room. He'd take the few moments he had before she arrived to try and appeal to Kinus. He pushed away from the wall and strode the rest of the way to the throne room. He'd dressed in his most formal caftan and entari, both black brocade embroidered with charcoal poppies, and left his sword in his rooms. Both were gestures of respect he hoped would help soothe his brother.

He paused in the archway and dropped to his knees as the secretary announced him, and only stood and walked in when Kinus made a sound of acknowledgment. The Elders stood to either side of the aisle, standing in what Makram jokingly referred to as their corrals. Boxes defined by gold-leafed, geometric lattice panels that stood hip-high. Some gave Makram smiles of greeting and nods, not daring to bow to him in front of Kinus. Thoman stood at the far end of the box on Makram's right and gave him a nod of solidarity as he passed. Why were they acting as if he were headed for the gallows?

Guards lined the wall behind Kinus. There had never been such inside the throne room before. They'd always stood outside the doors. There were more lining the walls behind the Elders, armed. A heavy mantle of dread drove him down as he dropped to his knees again at the dais. He bent forward to prostrate himself.

Kinus sat upon a velvet-cushioned, ornately carved high-back chair. His consort, Lady Amal, sat beside him, not in a chair, but on a small, short bench that put her head and shoulders below him. A queen would sit at level with him. But Kinus had not found a woman he considered suitable as a queen, though that had not stopped him choosing consorts for his harem. Makram could not help but try and picture Naime next to his brother, and it brought such a surge of misery that he had to quell the image immediately or risk untethering his magic.

"Greetings, Mirza," he said.

Silence descended on the hall and lingered for so long Makram risked lifting his head. Kinus stared at him, the muscles in his neck and jaw taut, his gaze set aflame. Makram let his breath out slowly. Tightness twisted his stomach, and he felt as if he shrank, becoming the boy that still lived inside him. The boy that still sought approval, still thought his magic was his fault, something he'd done wrong. The boy that could draw notice away from his cursed power by directing it elsewhere with brash decisions and reckless behavior.

"Explain yourself." Kinus did not yell, though Makram could see he was not far from doing so.

"As you said, Mirza. Tamar seemed desperate. I wished to know if what they intended to offer for alliance was worthy of your interest." Makram the man knew he was right, knew he was justified. Makram the boy huddled, chin on knees, waiting for punishment, waiting for denial.

"Do not lie to me!" Kinus jumped to his feet. Amal reached as if to touch him but then hesitated, setting her hands in her lap. She gave a tiny, frantic shake of her head to Makram, but he did not know exactly what she wished him not to do. "You went there to broker an alliance behind my back. You went there to try and take my throne from me with help from Tamar."

Makram stared at him in silence. He did not appear entirely sane. His eyes were wild, his breathing obvious and quick, his hands clenched on the arms of his throne. What had happened in his absence to put that look in his eyes? Nothing, he realized. Kinus had always been this way. It wasn't Kinus who had changed.

Makram took a deep breath, a veil lifted from his mind, the filter through which he'd seen Kinus gone. What had caused that?

A rustle of sound came from behind Makram accompanied by speculative whispers from the Elders. Kinus' gaze cut from Makram to the door behind him, as did Amal's. Her lips pressed together, her gaze flashing to Makram and back. Kinus relaxed backwards into his throne, propping an elbow on it and touching his fingers to his mouth. There was no mistaking the sudden contemplative surprise, and Makram knew Naime had arrived. Ugly, jealous possessiveness flared in his chest.

Her soft footfalls sounded on the tile as she approached Makram's back. The scent of winter and rose filled his nostrils. Makram took an unfettered breath and reveled in a mind that felt clear and sharp.

"Greetings Mirza Rahal, I am Princess Sultana Naime Sabri ilr Narfour, delegate of Sultan Omar Sabri the Sixth, of Tamar," Naime said as she came to Makram's side and knelt beside him, then bent forward until she was prostrate. She was dressed in white that shimmered like pearl, changing and shifting as she moved, with white embroidered palmettos and gold braiding at the sleeves, hem, and throat of the caftan. Her hair appeared ebony against it, braided away from her temples and loose down her back. She wore a simpler diadem than the ones Makram had seen her in before, this one a single band of braided silver the thickness of his pinky, with a small sapphire that dangled against her brow.

She was serene and beautiful, and having her at his side made him feel forged of adamant. Makram glanced again to Amal, who measured Naime with sharp gaze and temper hard in the lines of her usually smiling face.

"You were not invited, Sultana," Kinus said.

The Elders looked to each other. Even those who supported Kinus were surprised at his rudeness. Makram's pulse sped, assaulting his ears with its steady, hard thrum. She didn't know he didn't have her father's real terms. He should have gone to her immediately to warn her they had been stolen. But his damned pride…

"I know, Mirza Rahal, and I must beg your forgiveness," Naime said smoothly and calmly. "It has long been my hope that Sarkum and Tamar could come together and balance the Wheel. When the Agassi informed me that you had declined my father's offer of alliance I begged him to bring me to you so I might try to convince you in person."

She kept her gaze downcast in deference, but her voice was dry when she added, "I hope you might see fit to forgive my impetuousness."

Makram flinched internally.

"You are beautiful and apparently share my brother's knack for rash decision making. I can see why he humored your request." Kinus sounded indulgent, but Makram recognized it as a trap.

"Your words are too kind, Mirza Efendim. Our palace was more than pleased to host the Agassi. He was a great credit to you in his words and actions."

Kinus examined Naime with a look Makram found he did not care for at all. Greed. "I have reviewed the terms sent to me most recently."

"Shall we review them, Mirza?" Naime said, folding her hands in her lap and lifting her gaze.

"Sarkum is to provide its military assets toward preserving the integrity of the Old Sultanate borders against the Republic. We agree to subdue all mages of the Sixth House. A regent will govern Tamar in my name, and in exchange, Tamar has offered you in marriage to me."

Despite that he had suspected what the terms would be, anger and oblivion rushed into Makram's head, his blood pounding up his neck. His fists tightened against his knees as he clamped control around his power. When their eyes met, his brother gave him a one-sided smile.

"These are terms suggested by my father's High Council," Naime said, "but I feel they are insulting to you."

"Do you?" Kinus seemed amused.

"I cannot claim to be worth the lives of so many destruction mages, including the Mirza's own brother. I am told you are a man of reason. Surely we can come to an agreement more worthy of your reputation."

At least she could think straight, Makram chided himself. She was not losing her temper. He had to contain himself.

"If you have alternate terms, suggest them now, my patience grows thin," Kinus said in bored tones.

Naime met Makram's eyes in silent question. He gave his head a sharp shake to indicate he did not have the written terms. Her single, slow blink was all the reaction she showed before looking to Kinus once more.

"Tamar offers its mages to defend the borders of Sarkum against invasion, to study and eradicate the Blight that plagues your crops, its University and its resources to train the mages of Sarkum, in exchange for the military power of your janissary and sipahi forces."

"No marriage?" he inquired with a yawn.

Naime hesitated, and Makram attempted to catch her eye. But she ignored him, staring at Kinus instead.

"If you wish it, Mirza," Naime said, a resigned weariness in her voice. "But only in exchange for your brother to stand in the Circle of Chara'a."

Cold anger burst in Makram's chest, leaving lacework cracks in his control from which his magic spilled through him. She was not made to be a silent decoration in a palace, her intellect and acumen wasted. She was a queen, in every breath she was nothing less, and he wouldn't allow her to degrade herself by joining Kinus' harem, no matter the consequences.

"No," Makram said, his magic pitching his voice with ruin and void. The stone tile beneath his knee cracked, echoing in the hall. Amal gasped, then clasped a hand over her mouth. Kinus curled his lip, as though Makram were a cur released into his throne room.

To his right, Elder Attiyeh hitched forward, as if preparing to jump the short, lattice barrier that separated the Elders from the aisle. Behind Thoman, guards reached for their swords. Makram grit his teeth, lowering his gaze to the floor and forcing his magic back under his hold.

"My fate, and yours, are not ours to decide," Naime said, quietly. "You are King or currency."

He didn't lift his gaze, only tipped his head to meet hers. Naime raised an eyebrow. His breath left him, and something hot and galvanizing raced up his spine. He hadn't been a lost little boy at the mercy of his brother's affection for a long time, but this was the first time he'd realized it.

"You know better than to flaunt your power here," Kinus said, and the disgust in his voice helped Makram find his control once again. Naime's smile stiffened as she looked to Kinus once more.

Makram bowed forward. "Forgive me, Mirza. I only meant that I do not wish to leave your side."

"I think it is quite clear what you meant."

Makram met his glare, then Amal's, and both wore expressions of distaste. Thoman chastised him with a frown, then leaned into the Elder next to him, who said something with a scandalized expression.

To Makram's left, the five Elders in strongest support of Kinus spoke with animated hand gestures to each other.

Magic was feeling. And he had just revealed himself to everyone. Revealed the very feelings he'd denied to Tareck, and betrayed both her and himself by it.

"Command it and I will leave, if I have upset you." Makram did not want to abandon Naime, but if he could not control himself he was of little help to her.

"You may leave after I've decided the punishment for your disobedience." Kinus switched focus from Makram to Naime. "None of what you have to offer is of use to us, Sultana. I am uninterested in an alliance that strengthens magic. Look at my brother, who has so much power and can barely manage himself at the slightest provocation."

"Mirza," Naime began.

Kinus held up his hand to her and addressed Makram. "You think you know better than I do, you always have. You think you deserve this seat more than I simply because of the accident of your birth. I am the Eldest. I am the ruler." Kinus slapped his chest. "You are nothing, Makram, but a random mistake and a disgrace to this family. I am tired of cleaning up your messes."

"Mirza…" Makram said, though he barely had breath to speak. How could Kinus say such things? How could he believe such things? They were brothers.

Naime's magic brushed his. Not a comforting touch, but the pulse of an angry mage. Thoman grabbed the wooden lattice, moving as if to stand, and the Elders to his left and right held him in place. Elders across the way spat taunts to those surrounding Thoman, who were all allied in their desire for a different ruler. They would break into arguments at any moment, goaded by Kinus and his inflammatory words.

"When the Wheel was balanced, your kind slaughtered thousands at the whim of a ruler who was only a ruler because he was a more powerful mage than his enemies. You want to help this woman strengthen the magic bloodlines so all mages born are too powerful by half, so you can subjugate the rest of us. I will not allow it. Magic brings nothing but misery and abuse. It is time for it to end. Sarkum will align under the Republic and find our way into the future, not the past."

The air left his lungs as if someone had struck him in the belly with a mallet. He could not draw a breath, let alone speak in his defense. There was hatred in his brother's eyes. It was not a new expression, not a new, surprising revelation. It had always been there. But Makram had needed it to be something else and had made it so. That lie was gone, and he felt both miserable for the loss and freed as though heavy chains had been lifted away.

"Mirza Efendim"—Naime's voice swept like wind through Makram's thoughts, bringing him back to his body—"the Agassi is a loyal brother to you and a gifted warrior and mage. You do yourself a disservice by mistrusting him."

"Who are you to lecture to me? The daughter of a pretend Sultan? You are no better than him."

Kinus rose again, pacing to the edge of the dais and pointing at her. "Thinking you know what is best simply because you were favored by the Wheel. You are exactly where you belong, on your knees and supplicant, as all of Tamar should be. You and yours broke the Wheel you wish to fix, and yet you come here as if it is my burden."

"The Republic wishes to wipe out all mages. Your consort is a mage. Your Council of Elders are mages. Your brother is a mage." Naime lifted a hand to gesture at him. "You are a mage, are you not?"

"Do not mock me," Kinus snapped. Naime straightened her back but did not rise. Makram's magic whipped and swirled inside him, fed by his temper.

"I am stating a fact, Mirza. A fact which you have twisted to suit your desires. Many of Tamar's trade ships go missing when they pass through Republic waters, and the sections of the Spice Road that swerve even remotely close to Republic lands are littered with crosses and nooses bearing the broken bodies of Tamar merchants who attempted to pass through. If you think that is not what they intend for Sarkum as well, for all the children of the Wheel, then you are a truly Unbalanced."

Several Elders gasped, then burst into chatter. The discord of their protests and approval charged the hall with a sense of imminent chaos. Thoman was the only Elder Makram observed to remain silent, admiration written in his thoughtful expression. Kinus' face flushed and he stalked down the dais steps toward Naime. Makram jumped to his feet, shoving a hand to his brother's chest as he reached them. Naime remained kneeling, her entari pooled around her, her hands folded one over the other in her lap.

"I did not give you leave to rise!" Kinus burst out. "Why do you defy me at every turn?"

"I cannot allow you to harm her, Mirza. She is the heir to the Tamar Sultan, and any mistreatment cast upon her may result in war we are not prepared for." Threads of his power slipped loose once more, eroded by the sense of betrayal and protective anger warring within.

"You will allow me to do whatever I wish, because I am your ruler, not the Tamar Sultan. You left Sarkum without permission, conspired with this woman and brought her back here to try and turn my Council against me." Kinus shoved Makram's hand away.

"No. He did not conspire against you, nor did he bring me here to speak out against you. However"—Naime's voice remained cool and composed, a stark contrast to the temper his brother could not seem to master—"if he is of no value to you, then I am prepared to purchase his services from you to stand as Sixth to the Circle."

Makram stared at her, his hand falling to his side. The Elders' outrage was so great they were silent. Kinus' expression flickered from anger to disbelief and back again. And there was nothing, not a single identifiable emotion, on her face. She simply knelt there, as if she had not just offered to purchase a prince as if he were a slave or a horse. She was far too careful a planner to have done such a thing on a whim, and surely she understood the consequences of the act.

"Are you mad?" Makram asked.

"I am not the one who does not understand the value of a subject who is loyal enough, to me and my people, to defy me when I am being a fool." Her gaze slid from Makram to Kinus, accusing.

"How dare you," Amal said, standing. Naime ignored her.

"The Sultana is right!" one of the Elders barked. Some shouted agreement, while others cried in protest. The two rows of men turned to themselves, arguing.

"Silence!" Kinus bellowed. The Elders came to a troubled quiet, still milling about in their boxes like agitated ponies. "This is what you want, brother? Already she sows unrest. She would enslave you, yoking you like an ox at a gristmill."

Naime gave an impatient click of her tongue and flicked her gaze from Kinus.

"Mirza," Makram said, "I believe she only meant to offer you an alternative alliance. She did not intend to offend you or me."

"Do not defend her! Do not forget who you belong to, and where your loyalty lies. In fact, I will give you a choice. You will take her"—he jabbed a finger in Naime's direction—"and put her in a cell so I can ransom her back to her father. Then you will return to me and prepare yourself to travel as my delegate to the Republic's envoy in Eannea. Do that, and I will welcome you back to me. Do otherwise and be labeled a criminal unwelcome on Sarkum soil."

Makram felt like laughing. It felt the only reasonable response to his brother's madness.

Kinus lifted his hand toward the guards. They moved away from the wall and around the Elders. Two of the Elders closest to the doors began to inch closer, one reaching to unhook the latch that held the gate of their box closed. A guard pointed his sword at it, and the Elder retreated a step. The guard was joined by another and they closed the doors to the hall. Thoman held the arm of the man next to him, whispering and gesturing sharply with his free hand.

The guards made it around the Elders and Makram grabbed at his belt for the sword that was not there, and his magic burst through his grip, shadows crawling beneath his skin, swirling up his neck and across his hands. The guards hesitated when he aimed a warning glare on them and power inked his skin.

"I'd like to offer a third option," Naime said, mildly. Everyone stopped, compelled to do so by the cool authority in her voice. "You call off your men and allow me to leave your palace and Sarkum in peace, as a gesture of goodwill."

"Goodwill? I owe you nothing," Kinus said, gazing down at her in sinister amusement. His response tugged at Makram's threadbare temper, and he fought to keep his magic from broadcasting from beneath his skin.

"I have noted that your brother is exceptionally agreeable and mild mannered for a Charah. Perhaps because of that you have forgotten what the wrath of a high-order mage feels like." Naime rose and took a moment to carefully shake her skirts and caftan into order. When she lifted her gaze again, light like pale winter sun lit her eyes, obliterating evidence of the iris and pupil. She drew a breath and released it.

Her magic concussed outward and Makram stumbled sideways and Kinus backwards at the force of it. Power swirled around her in eddies and gusts, fragments of wind like opalescent pieces of silk caught in a whirlwind of magic of which she was the eye. She shone, pouring light like the beacon of reason and hope that she was though now all Makram could sense was fury. The Elders reacted by shuffling farther away from her, toward the door, toward the walls.

"You will release me"—her voice held her power, lifted to fill the room with the sound of her anger—"or Sarkum will find itself devoid of a ruler."

"Kill her," Kinus ordered with a dismissive laugh. The guards moved, Makram stepped in front of her, and she lifted her hand toward Kinus, palm up, curling her fingers toward her palm.

Kinus wheezed and gagged as if he could not draw breath. Makram caught him as he went to his knees. Amal screamed, and kept screaming, standing and pointing at Kinus as he clutched at his chest. Naime reached with her other hand toward the guards, stroking her fingers through the air as they reached for their weapons. Between one moment and the next they were on their knees as well, gasping for air that was gone from their lungs. The Elders erupted in panic, pushing and stumbling over each other as they headed for the door.

"Makram!" Thoman yelled but was pushed away by the tide of his comrades. Naime spun around and wind gusted away from her, flinging the doors to the hall open. She faced Makram and Kinus once again.

"Release him," Makram demanded.

"As you wish." Naime flicked her hand and Kinus suddenly drew in a gulp of air like he had surfaced after nearly drowning. He shook in Makram's grip as he continued to suck in breaths. "Stop screaming or I will make you," Naime commanded Amal, whose mouth pressed closed, her expression still reflecting her panic.

"Stay here in your ignorance and be trampled beneath the Republic. Perhaps you will serve as stumbling block enough to attrit them before they reach Tamar. But I will not be here to see it." She whipped around and strode for the doors.

"I said kill her!" Kinus jerked out of Makram's hands, staggering to his feet. Makram caught his brother by the shoulder and yanked him back. The guards moved between Naime and the door, forming a half-moon shape around the throne room.

"Hold." Destruction poured from Makram, fed by anger and betrayal, shadow bleeding from his skin and to the ground around him. The marble tiles beneath him buckled as he strode forward. He didn't want to kill anyone, but neither would he allow Kinus to hurt Naime. He aimed his magic at the guards' swords.

"Don't you dare defy me," Kinus shrieked, his eyes wild, the tendons in his neck standing out in his anger. "Arrest him and kill her!"

But Makram had already given his magic its command, woven the spell with a thought and a word, and the swords the guards held toward Naime rusted away. Hilts clattered to the tiles as guards held their hands up, backing away from her. Guards remained between Naime and the door, trapping her and the few Elders who remained, huddling in the corners of the room.

"Do you wish to begin a war with Tamar? If you do not move your soldiers and allow me to leave this Wheel-cursed place, then that is what you will have," Naime announced.

"You will go to war against an army with a Charah at its head?" Kinus scoffed, pointing to Makram. *Never.* Never would he stand at the head of an army pointed at Naime.

"Enough," Makram barked. "Enough of this madness." Makram ordered the guards, "Let her pass."

"No," Kinus snapped.

Naime met Makram's gaze and regret cracked what was left of her composure, her expression filling with it. He took a step toward her, a jolt of panic bolting through him. She whispered a word, and there was a tug in his chest then a weight, crushing his lungs. He couldn't draw breath, couldn't think. All he knew was a panicked need for air. He tried to reach for her but could not, and dropped to his knees, his magic exploding from him in a blanket of shadow and destruction.

The edges of his vision grew black, and his body left his command as he watched her stride toward the doors, everyone in the room thrashing and gasping for air.

The black enveloped him and sucked him under.

Makram woke on his back in a prison cell. The stone floor was damp and cold beneath him, and snow blew from outside, through the bars of the narrow, high window above him. A pile of it had accumulated against the back wall of the cell. He could remember being half awake when Kinus' guards dragged him down into the prison, the yelling and jeering of the other prisoners. That continued all around him, especially once he shifted to move off a stone that was jabbing him in the lower back. They knew he was awake, and they had a great many things to say about it.

"Prince," the man in the cell next to him said, "they'll give you something better than flatbread and lentils. Give me some, and I won't piss in your cell."

"Such *pretty* clothes."

"What'd you do? Grab the wrong ass?"

Makram stared mutely at the ceiling. All he needed now was a straw-stuffed rabbit and Tareck's ham-fisted analogy would be complete.

The prison reeked of unwashed bodies and feces, so much so it burned his nostrils. Ironic that he was wearing the best of his clothes on the day his brother imprisoned him. Makram lifted his arm to put his sleeve over his mouth and nose and was disgusted to find it wet. He sat up, hoping it was melted snow from the window and not something more vile, as his neighbor had suggested.

This was it, he supposed. The very furthest he could stretch his loyalty to Kinus. It should have felt more sudden, more climactic, perhaps even devastating. But instead it simply felt that a curtain had been yanked aside to reveal things he already knew were there. They were hard, ugly truths, and as he stared up at the uneven, stone ceiling above and the prisoners yelled and jeered around him, he examined them.

That he was done defending Kinus was a far-gone conclusion. What he was going to do about it was the question he asked himself.

Would he pretend the prison could hold him?

He did not want to be a ruler. He did not want to go to war with his brother. Kinus was more fanatic than he had ever allowed himself to believe, but he did not want to sever the last link he had to his family. He was not a usurper. Makram closed his eyes. The brother that had been a friend was gone, if he had ever even really existed. There was nothing Makram could do to bring him back, no service would ever be enough.

It was time to serve something else, and he had a fine example to draw from. She served her people with every breath she took, every decision she made, every battle she fought. Willing to sacrifice herself, her freedoms, her choices, because she felt compelled to do what was right for the many. How could he claim to feel anything for her if he could not even stand for something as noble as she did? If he could not even stand for his own people?

The jeers became hoots and catcalls, shouting, announcing the arrival of someone. Makram opened his eyes.

"Have you fallen quite low enough?" Thoman's voice said from the vicinity of Makram's feet, which were nearest the cell door.

"I believe so," Makram said.

"Then I suggest you get up," the older man said in disgust. Makram got to his feet. Thoman scowled at him, his face lit by flashing, wavering torch light. All around him, from the other cells, the prisoners shouted and waved arms through the bars, ready to grab for him, to ruin his finery in some small retribution. Thoman, who had served his entire youth as a soldier, was unfazed.

"I will stand with you, if you choose to oppose your brother. The majority of the sipahi and the janissaries will stand with you. But your brother will not be alone in his claim. At least half the Elders, and their holdings, support him. If you walk out of here with me, you will be at war with him."

Makram's hands tightened against the bars. "I know." He had left to strengthen Sarkum, not strike the spark that would ignite a civil war.

"I have a contingent waiting at the eastern wadi. That was the closest I dared bring them. The palace is like a hornet's nest right now, and your brother is ready to arrest anyone who he even imagines supports you or an alliance with Tamar. Tareck took a score of men to take the Sultana and her people to the Gate, but someone set fire to the stables."

Makram almost smiled. Fierce guardian indeed. Samira, the only useful fire mage he had met in Tamar.

"We can get out through the harem," Makram said. There were tunnels there, escape routes for wives and children that Kinus did not have. It would take him in the opposite direction of the main palace. He'd send Aysel to find the false terms, and if he was lucky, the letter Kadir sent with them.

"And then what?" Thoman asked, leaning close so he could pitch his voice more quietly, though it was impossible to keep their voices down and be heard over all the ruckus from the prisoners. "It will take me time to consolidate support for you, if I wish to do so without Kinus attacking preemptively. Do you think Tamar will back you in a civil war? In the interest of an alliance?"

Makram hesitated. "They will, but the cost will be high." She would. He knew she would.

"How high?" Thoman asked, suspicion coloring his voice.

"First, let's get out of here." Makram could break the news to Thoman when they weren't surrounded by prisoners and guards loyal to his brother. Thoman wanted him as a ruler. She wanted him as a

Charah. He did not see how he could be both, and he would not put it past her to swallow Sarkum under Tamar's banners to accomplish her goals.

Thoman took a step back as Makram's magic whipped loose and the entire front of the cell, bars, and door disintegrated around him. Silence fell for an instant, but as soon as Makram stepped free, still bleeding black ruin in his wake, it erupted into cacophony, calling for him to free them.

Thoman held out his sword and belt. Makram buckled it on.

"After you, my prince," Thoman said, and bowed.

Thirty

NAIME HELPED HER FATHER sit on a bench in the garden just outside his room. The weather had given them a break from the rain, and she thought it would be good for him to get fresh air despite the cold.

She was so grateful to be out of the snow. Blizzards had chased them all the way from Al-Nimas and had not stopped until they began to descend the western slope of the mountains. If it had not been for Tareck and his men guiding them nearly to the Kalspire, she was certain they all would have lost their way and perished in the snow. The fatigue of the travel combined with her near depletion of her power reserves to fuel the spells for their escape exhausted her. Naime had spent almost an entire day upon their arrival at the palace in mage sleep.

She did not know if she had made an enemy of Makram. Using her magic violently had been a last resort. Whether he still supported an alliance or not no longer mattered—whether he sided with Kinus or stood against him, Sarkum would not be a viable ally until their internal rift was sealed.

The loss of him as Charah was devastating. There could be no Circle without him. She could attempt to locate the other Chara'a, she already knew the Charah of the Second House resided in Narfour. Perhaps by the time she found the others, there would be a chance to beseech Makram. If his brother had not imprisoned him or ordered him killed.

A prison could not hold him if he did not wish to be held. Was it possible to execute the most powerful manifestation of death that lived? The fear of the possibility had kept her awake all the nights of their journey. What kind of a monster was she, to abandon him in that situation, to just leave him there like so much cast off?

Sometimes she won over her despair by reminding herself of the obligation she had to Tamar, to her people. To her own family. He would not have come with her, even if given the choice. Those truths did not stop the ache in her chest every time she thought of him. Every time she missed him, every time she remembered the sound of his voice or the way he had sometimes looked at her as if she were the most magnificent thing he had ever laid eyes on.

Naime made herself focus on her father.

"Are you comfortable, Baba?" Naime asked, pulling the collar of her father's fur-lined ferace more tightly around his neck. He smiled at her, his expression confused.

"You are so pretty. Do I know you?" He took her hands in his. She fought back tears and wrenched her feelings deeper, burying them.

"Yes, Baba. We know each other. You are Sultan Omar Sabri the Sixth. I am your daughter, Naime," her traitorous voice cracked against the words.

"Naime," he said absently, turning from her to stare across the garden. "Do I have a daughter?" he mused, dropping his hands from hers to his lap.

Naime straightened, sucking in a breath and blinking rapidly against the sting in her eyes. Pain that burned and numbed her to her bones nearly brought her to her knees.

Ihsan stepped out of the Sultan's room, through the paned glass door she'd left open, his young steward Kuhzey behind him with a tray bearing coffee and pastries. One of the Sultan's attendants followed, carrying a small table, which he set up near Naime and her father. They arranged the tray on it and poured coffee into the demitasses, then bowed and retreated to stand near the door.

Ihsan touched Naime's hand as he passed, retrieving a cup of the coffee and offering it to her father.

"Sultan, coffee?" Ihsan's voice could be soothing, when he cared for it to be. Water mages were the peace of the Wheel, though that had never been his lot. But he gave his words now the same cadence and restfulness of the lapping waves of the sea, and the Sultan smiled, taking the cup from his hands and sipping at it.

Naime felt as fragile as the delicate porcelain cup she held out to her cousin, just as likely to shatter at the next upset. Yet when a flash of blood red on the far end of the garden announced the arrival of Kadir, she could conjure no emotion but exhaustion. Ihsan stiffened before he even saw the man, the press of the Grand Vizier's magic setting him on edge. He crossed the garden and came to them smiling as though he were greeting friends.

"Sultana. I heard you had come home while I was at my estate. I apologize for the belatedness of my greeting." He picked his way from the covered walkway through the garden, trying to disguise his limp but unable to do so completely. The one bright spot in the four days since her arrival home had been the absence of Kadir. When he reached them he bowed first to the Sultan. Her father squinted at Kadir as though trying to remember someone only barely familiar to him. Kadir bowed to Naime.

Naime stared mutely at him. She was unable to invoke a single word to say to him, or the energy to armor herself against him.

"Sehzade," Kadir said, and gave a brief bow to Ihsan, who only marginally returned it before he spun and strode farther away. He could not bear the feel of fire magic, most especially Kadir's. Naime had always been certain Kadir unleashed his enough to make Ihsan feel it whenever he was near enough. It was rude to walk about projecting one's magic on everyone, but in Ihsan's case it was cruel. It usually enraged Naime when Kadir did so, but today she felt nothing but a kind of too-full numbness.

"I plan to address the High Council tomorrow, Grand Vizier. I appreciate you making an effort to come see me, but I had hoped to spend some time with my father."

"Of course, Sultana. Forgive my intrusion. I thought only to inquire as to the state of Sarkum." He smiled. They met gazes for a long moment. The letter in his handwriting, the proof of his treachery, was in Sarkum, left behind because of the circumstances of their quick leave-taking. Tareck had done well, getting them out of the city, but he had certainly not had time to retrieve their belongings, or the letter. They had been fleeing for their lives.

"I will answer all of your questions tomorrow, at the High Council meeting. But you should know"—she took a breath, steeling herself—"that even if I do not sit in the Sultan's seat, Ihsan will. No one else."

Kadir's expression twisted, and he started to speak, but her father took her hand in one of his, his brow creased with worry. The same sense of dread that had weighed her down when speaking with Tareck before meeting Makram's brother bound her in its grasp now. She covered his hand with hers, in censure, but too late.

The Sultan spoke his worry. "No, no. We've talked about this. Ihsan can't sit the throne. He's a bastard. Remember?" The Sultan set his cup on the bench beside him, but it did not settle, and tumbled off, shattering on the stones. He did not seem to notice.

Cold like the bitter touch of Ihsan's magic laced through her veins. Dizziness raced behind it. *No.*

Naime had never felt the crushing, suffocating weight of complete and utter defeat until now. Always there had been something, a way out, a turn of phrase to save her, a clever misdirection. There was nothing for this, the revelation of the dearest of secrets. It was the knowledge of Ihsan sharing her political goals that had protected her from the most vicious maneuvering of the Council. They could oust one, but not both.

Kadir gave a sound that might have been an exhale or the softest of laughs, but when he met her gaze there was nothing but vicious, hungry victory in his eyes. His eyes shifted to Ihsan's back. He had everything he needed now to take everything from Ihsan and leave Naime vulnerable.

"I suppose"—fire laced Kadir's voice, hissing and cracking—"you would prefer to address the Council with this…new knowledge."

She didn't bother answering him, only stared at him without attempting to disguise her loathing.

"Tomorrow then." His smile deepened just before he bowed. He limped back the way he had come.

"Oh," the Sultan said, "I broke my cup."

THIRTY-ONE

IHSAN WALKED ON HER left, the darker facets of his House manifesting in the storm in his eyes. Neither of them knew what Kadir had planned, and Naime had little left to use as bargaining tools or deflections. And this would be the first time she had attended a full Council without her father.

Samira walked behind her and Ihsan, Ihsan's young steward Kuhzey beside her, trailed by a handful of attendants. She could not blame Ihsan for appearing as if he were walking to the gallows. They could take everything from him. His home in the Water District that he'd bought after his father's estate burned, the garden he'd planted and tended himself over the decade since, the only oasis that brought him peace. His ability to see Naime whenever he wanted. She was his only family. They could take it all.

Outside, visible through the arches they passed, the sun was setting. The chill of evening was sinking into the stone of the palace and sweeping in on bitter breezes from outside. Two attendants moved to the chamber doors when Naime and Ihsan stopped in front of them. Naime gave them a curt nod and they pulled them open. There was no point in stalling. She slipped her arm through Ihsan's and they walked into the hall together.

Naime was not surprised to see all the Viziers present. Word would have spread like ink on wet paper, and the news that the Sehzade was illegitimate was nearly as important as what the Council would have originally gathered for—to name her husband.

They were talking amongst themselves and did not immediately observe when she entered. Ihsan fumed silently at her side as she waited. When Samira moved as if to announce her, Naime held up her hand. It was Vizier Yavuz who first noticed, and bowed, and the others did so soon after, until the last left was Kadir, who stood in his usual place to the left of the dais.

Naime met his gaze and held it. It was not nearly the challenge it had been to hold Makram's gaze. Even when his magic was contained it demanded of her own magic in a way that made it nearly painful to maintain eye contact.

Kadir finally bowed, deeply enough to appease her, and she and Ihsan walked down the aisle.

Naime took her place on the bench to the right of the dais and eyed her father's empty seat. The lack of his presence hit her suddenly, and she curled her hands in the fabric over her knees. Gone. No longer able to support or help her. No longer able to deflect the worst of what the Council could be. She was alone, truly alone for the first time.

"We welcome you home, Sultana Efendim," Kadir said as he straightened. "Shall we wait for the Sultan to arrive before we begin?" The other Viziers took their seats on the benches, with little of the usual muffled conversations that passed for silence among them. That was proof enough they knew of Ihsan's secret and her failure in Sarkum.

"My father will not be attending the Council for the foreseeable future, Grand Vizier. I believe you can understand why."

"Of course, Sultana. We hope the Wheel balances in favor of his recovered health very soon." He frowned, his brows lifting. "In his absence, I suppose I will be required to give final ruling on the Council's decisions."

The room seemed to compress around her. A ringing began in her ears. This was it, the final blow to everything she'd worked for. If Kadir stood as Regent, nothing of what she wanted for Tamar would happen. Her breath stilled. There were no plans to prepare for this, no subtle maneuvers that could stop him. This was a moment for

Makram, who would not need plans to take a step, who would simply charge his way forward. He would act.

The room opened up in her perception, the ringing in her ears stopped, and she breathed.

"No, Grand Vizier." Naime rose from the bench. She had never considered doing what she was about to, because her father had still possessed some of his faculties and she knew the Council would be outraged at so forward a bid for power from her. Keeping them in favor of her as much as possible had always seemed the steadier course to achieving her goals.

Now, her plans in tatters, her father little more than a liability, she had nothing left to lose by using a heavy hand. She climbed the dais and stopped in front of the seat, turning to face the room. Yavuz Pasha's expression slipped from troubled to surprised, and he glanced toward Kadir. Across the aisle, Esber Pasha tapped a thumb against his chin, leaning into his neighbor to exchange a few quiet words.

"From this moment forward, I will be acting as Regent." Naime sat down in her father's seat.

Ihsan stared in disbelief as the Council Chambers erupted with the noise of the Viziers' upraised voices. She folded her hands in her lap and waited. The pervasive numbness that had begun the day before remained. She was still distraught, she still mourned the loss of her chances at accomplishing what she wanted, but now it was distant, buried beneath hopelessness that felt as if it might suck her into it. All she could do was move forward. Just as Makram had said.

Naime pushed away thoughts of him, which could be examined and cherished when she was alone, but not now, when she could not be distracted.

"Sultana." Kadir stepped forward and banged his staff against the stone floor several times to quiet his comrades. "While you are much respected, you are unmarried and unqualified to sit in your father's seat."

"The eldest child is perfectly within their rights to act as Regent for the Sultan if he is infirm, which you saw yesterday is true of my father," Naime said.

"Sultana—"

"Did you or did you not witness yesterday that the Sultan is no longer in possession of all his faculties?" Naime asked, firmly, but without allowing any emotion but command to shape her voice.

Kadir hesitated. He could not deny it, or he would be denying he heard about Ihsan's illegitimacy, but he sensed her maneuvering him toward a trap. "Yes, Sultana, I did witness, but—"

"When in the history of Tamar has a Grand Vizier ever spoken for an incapacitated Sultan when that Sultan had an heir?"

"Never."

"I am very pleased you are so well versed in the history and laws of Tamar, Grand Vizier, you do your office great credit." If it would not have earned him an instant death sentence, Naime was certain he would have immolated her right where she sat. The flames in his gaze told her as much, and the silence that blanketed the chamber punctuated it.

And as they faced off, realization like cold winter brushed her skin with ice. With her father incapacitated, and Ihsan out of the line of succession, Kadir was unleashed. Where he had only been a political danger before, now he was a physical one as well.

"Those laws govern princes, Sultana. A princess has never stood as Regent."

"That is not true, Grand Vizier," Yavuz Pasha said. "Sultan Haytham Sabri's eldest daughter stood as Regent when he fell ill with the White Plague."

Relief warmed the numbness in her chest. *An ally.*

"Only because her brother, the next Sultan, was at the border fighting skirmishes with Sarkum," Kadir said, then paused, collecting himself with a long inhale.

"Soon you may find that we are also fighting skirmishes with Sarkum, considering the state of affairs there," Naime replied. "If that is the requirement for me to sit as Regent, it has been met. Until my father's illness abates, I will sit in his place."

"Are you mocking the High Council, Sultana Efendim?" Kadir snarled.

"I would never, Grand Vizier. This is not a suggestion. This is a command." Naime waited for the surprised voices to abate. "If you are unwilling to follow it, then I will appoint a new Grand Vizier in your place."

Yavuz Pasha flinched, and one of the Viziers of the northern provinces leaned forward from the bench behind him to say something in his ear.

"You cannot possibly believe this Council would stand for that?"

"It is not my choice, Grand Vizier, it is yours." Naime's pulse was too quick, her hands sweating, and she was afraid if she lifted them they would shake. But she forced her face to remain impassive and her voice to be calm, and did not so much as shift in her seat.

His expression turned stony.

"Would you care to move on to the subject of Sarkum?" she suggested.

Kadir's glances skittered around the Council Hall.

"That would be wise," Yavuz Pasha said, gesturing across the aisle to Esber, who nodded agreement. Kadir cast about for someone to voice support, but Yavuz Pasha stood.

"We had heard that negotiations in Al-Nimas did not go as you planned," he said. Naime was grateful for his assistance in steering the conversation away before Kadir could conceive of another foothold to contest her.

"Unfortunately not. The Mirza was under the mistaken impression that an alliance by marriage was part of the negotiation terms. When we could come to no agreement, he attempted to take me hostage."

The Viziers reacted in shock, and Esber Pasha lunged to his feet.

"Barbarians!" he cried, and others stamped their feet in agreement. While many of them might have designs on increasing their power or position, she could think of only one who might truly wish her harm, or who would benefit from her being locked away in Sarkum.

Naime looked at Kadir.

"The Agassi did his best to assist me in escaping, but I fear it made him appear traitorous in the Mirza's eyes. It is not entirely unlikely that Sarkum will soon be in the midst of a civil war."

"Which would make the perfect excuse for the Republic to attack them," Yavuz Pasha said, thoughtfully.

"Yes," Naime agreed, "bringing Tamar even closer to the brink of war."

"Do you intend to take sides in their war?" Kadir said each word carefully.

"Not without good reason, Grand Vizier. My priority will always be to protect Tamar."

Esber Pasha sat down, nodding his agreement, as the men around him nodded in approval. That was two allies, at least to some degree. She wondered if they would remain so once she revealed her intention to stand the Circle of Chara'a. If she still could.

"If alliance with Sarkum is no longer an issue," Kadir said, "then that brings us to the next, I'm afraid." His gaze came to rest on Ihsan, who stared resolutely at the Council Hall doors.

"Let me apologize first to the Council, it was not my intention to keep such a secret from them." Naime did not often lie outright, but this dealt with Ihsan's life, and so she deemed it necessary. "My father only recently learned that the Elder Sehzade Sabri had been unfaithful in his marriage."

Naime paused only long enough to make certain she had their attention. A marriage broken was a broken Wheel, one of the few still deeply, widely held superstitions in Tamar. "The child of that union is my cousin, and he was subsequently adopted by the Elder Sehzade and the princess."

"The adoption does not give him legitimacy as an heir to the throne, Sultana, as I am certain you are aware."

"I am aware, Grand Vizier. What is the Council's desire in this matter?"

"At the very least he must be removed from the line of succession. Surely you agree?" Kadir said, with an expression like a cat with a caught mouse.

"I would like more time to think on this, Grand Vizier. It is a grave matter and I do not wish to mishandle it." She did not have a solution. There was no solution. But she could not bear the thought of Ihsan being stripped of everything that remained to him. Left alone. He would shrivel up and die.

"Sultana, I feel we cannot grant you that. It is a simple matter. The Sehzade, no, Master Sabri, cannot be in the line of succession if his blood does not allow him to be." Kadir's feigned apologetic tone fueled a rage inside her that ate away at the numbness.

She needed time to find ways to subvert them, though she despaired of doing so. To fight for her own right to rule while also trying to fight for Ihsan's right to stay in the line of succession as a bastard was asking too much of them.

"Grand Vizier, forgive me for my weakness." Naime stood, folding her hands in front of her and bowing slightly. "My father's mind is so far gone, many days he does not remember that I am his daughter. I have recently returned from a troubling journey to Sarkum, and now a man I have long considered more brother than cousin has been taken from me. I find myself…" She let her voice quaver as she lifted a trembling hand to touch her temple. "…over-taxed."

"Which is exactly why you should not burden yourself with taking over as Regent," Kadir said, giving her a kindhearted smile that was meant to inform her he was unimpressed with her act.

Vizier Yavuz gestured at her. "Even Sultans are given time to deal with their personal affairs when they arise. I am certain the matter of a second heir to the throne can wait. The Sultana does not appear in any danger of vacating her place as the heir apparent. Surely no one on the Council objects to a bit of human decency?"

Naime could have kissed Vizier Yavuz for his mercy.

Kadir inclined his head to Yavuz. "What say you?" he asked, gesturing at the others with his staff. Ihsan looked at her, but his expression was too guarded for her to read.

"Let her be," Esber Pasha said. "No need to be at her like a pack of vultures."

"Very well, Sultana." Kadir turned to her and bowed his face strained into a magnanimous smile. "You have three days."

Yavuz Pasha let out an impatient breath, and Esber Pasha gave his neighbor a sideways look of distaste, but Naime merely nodded. She had already pushed them enough for one day.

THIRTY-TWO

NAIME CLOSED THE BOOK and set it atop the others, bracing her elbows on the table and pressing her fingers over her eyes. Samira set another cup of tea in front of her and lifted the stack of books away to return them to their shelves.

It was growing late, the light outside the windows fading quickly. She'd missed the normal dinner time, yet again. Since her father had given Ihsan's secret away to Kadir, she'd had little appetite, and had only eaten when Samira had forced her. Naime took a sip of the tea, mint, to help keep her thoughts focused. Reading the histories was never particularly exciting, but she could not afford to miss a single detail this time.

She read over the notes she had taken, laws and scenarios she thought could be used in Ihsan's favor. On a flare of anger she almost wadded the sheet of paper into a ball and tossed it into the brazier that burned not far from her for warmth. Even if it helped a little it would not be enough. Despair had come and gone in regular cycles over the three days Kadir had given her. As the deadline neared, the despair had grown to dominate, with no moments of hope in between.

Ihsan had gone home when she'd sent him. His frantic pacing and occasional bursts of ranting had been too much for both of them to bear.

"Will you take your dinner here, or in your rooms, Sultana? Perhaps a hot bath would help ease your mind," Samira said from where she stood replacing the books.

"Neither bath nor food will help me prevent tomorrow from coming." Naime sighed. She only had the barest idea of a plan, and it was nothing more than a stall tactic and a last, desperate gambit that would fail her in the long run.

The truth was, without her father, and without Ihsan, she was powerless. She'd allowed herself to believe she had garnered respect enough to earn political power in her own right, but she knew better.

Kadir was like a shark, circling wounded and bleeding prey. Yavuz and Esber Pasha's support could only extend so far with Kadir in possession of the majority of the Council's loyalty. Ihsan, despite his disinterest in being a prince or having anything to do with the palace and the throne, had been like a shield for her. Now not only would she have to guard against political assassination, but real assassination as well. If she was gone, there was no one to step up and replace her. By political clout alone Kadir would be in line for the throne after her, and he had already proved himself perfectly willing to murder.

"Meeting the Council half-starved and stinking of three days spent in the library will not help either," Samira said, replacing the last book and turning to her. "Humor me, Sultana, so that I, at least, may rest easy tonight knowing I have discharged my duties to you properly."

"I've taught you too well, if you are using manipulation on me," Naime said.

Samira smiled and ducked her head. "I'll prepare the bath and have food brought to your rooms, if that pleases you?"

"Fine." Naime stood, snatching the paper with her notes from the table. "I'll see my father first."

Samira crossed the library and opened the door for her. Silence was the fertile field in which thoughts and worries about Makram sprouted best. Naime shoved them aside. They only hurt.

Naime greeted the two guards outside her father's door. He had begun to wander, and though his steward was always with him, he could be difficult for one man to manage. Samira slid her a look. Naime stopped, facing the door, trying to steel herself. She gave Samira a nod, who then skirted between the guards and knocked on the door.

Her father's steward answered and bowed to Naime. "He is restless this evening, Sultana. Perhaps you will have more luck than I at calming him."

Naime feared she did not have the capacity to help anyone. Her emotions were too twisted, too near the surface and ready to break away from her. There was nothing else she could handle today—she had to save her strained mental control for the Council tomorrow. Yet how could she turn from him when he was also fragile and in need?

Naime stepped past the steward. Her father's rooms were expansive, half of them given over to a place to eat and entertain. He sat on a cushion in front of the low table, staring morosely at the array of food before him. Naime approached the table and bowed. Samira and the steward remained behind, near the door.

"Girl…I don't like these foods." He gestured at the table, with plate after plate of his favorite dishes. Naime knelt across from him. He'd never been a harsh or rude man, always referring to people by their appropriate title, never as he had just addressed her. But the journals she'd been reading suggested this would happen, shifts of his personality, the remnants of the minds he'd taken pushing him aside for moments, candlemarks, or days.

"You might like these," she said, and held her sleeve back as she reached to move a plate of lamb kofta in front of him. He stared at it, scowling. After her mother had died, she and her father would occasionally hide away in one of the gardens and share a plate of them as they were prepared now, on skewers and grilled over coals. They'd talk about her mother, and he would quiz Naime on the things she had been learning. Now he stared at the food as if it were offensive.

"I hate them," he said, his salt-and-pepper brows drawn down over his eyes.

Naime withdrew her hand and surveyed the table. Her eyes were burning, her throat tightening around bitter sadness. She thought it a cruel irony that she missed him more when she was with him than when she was away. When they were apart she was not confronted with the reality of someone who no longer shared her memories.

"Hummus?" Naime asked, reaching for the plate with one hand and a flatbread with the other.

"No!" he barked. Naime froze, lifting her gaze to him. He'd never yelled at her. He had been the one to teach her how to use her magic to control herself and her emotions.

"I said"—he picked up the plate of kofta and slung the food at her—"I hate these." The meat fell apart when it struck her, splattering her pale entari and caftan and the floor around her.

Samira gasped and the steward rushed to Naime's side. He began collecting bits of meat from Naime's clothes and the floor. She stood, brushing her hands over her clothes to dislodge the worst of the mess.

"I am sorry I displeased you, Sultanim." Naime gave a quick, shallow bow to her father and strode from the room.

"Sultana." Samira rushed to catch up with her, her voice full of a sadness and pity that Naime could not take. "Naime."

"Don't," Naime said. "I just…I need some time."

"Of course."

Naime left her at the doors to her room and continued on, walking quickly with no destination in mind. Moving as though she were trying to outrun something. Everything. If she stopped, if she returned to her rooms, she would fall apart. But she could not. She had to hold it together, all of it.

She started toward the library, but halfway there thought better of it. Trying to concentrate on books any longer would be futile. Her wandering brought her back to the Council Hall. The room seemed so much less threatening when it was empty, quiet, the palace in the grip of night. Still, as she strode down the aisle between the benches, she could imagine their stares, piercing her back.

They would never see her the way they saw her father.

Naime stepped onto the dais and stood before her father's seat. She sat, as she had only a few days ago, and faced the room. It was only a chair, and an empty room, yet her heart hammered, her breath quickened, and her eyes burned. She couldn't do it. She couldn't make them understand, she couldn't make them believe, she couldn't protect Ihsan or herself anymore. Her father was a stranger. It was all lost.

She was a failure.

When she tried to draw a gulp of air, a sob building in her throat, she could not. As if she had cast her own spells on herself, ripped her own air from her lungs, she couldn't breathe, she couldn't do it anymore, any of it, she was drowning in it all. It was going to kill her, she could feel the weight of everything on her chest, on her shoulders, crushing, breaking, turning hope and belief into bitter exhaustion.

Just as she slipped from the bench to the dais, her knees hitting the stone and her hands going to her face, the sound of steps sent chill stillness through her. She could not face anyone else today.

Naime drew a thin breath and dropped her hands into her lap. Her thoughts tangled in an anxious fog. She could not fashion an excuse for why she was kneeling on the floor.

Bashir stood at the entrance to the hall, to either side of him men dressed in black and charcoal grey, shadowy bookends to the brighter colors of Bashir's uniform. Black hair pulled tightly back, swords hanging from belts around their waists, tired and travel-worn.

Makram and Tareck. All three bowed. Bowed to her, the pathetic mess kneeling in front of her father's seat like a broken and discarded doll.

The next breath she drew was jagged and harsh. She could not hold it all back a moment longer, the relief at seeing him, unharmed, filled her too full. She could not stand or move or speak because it would cause the tension holding her together to break, and everything would spill forth.

Makram said something inaudible to the other two. Bashir hesitated, his gaze sweeping over her, but nodded and left, with Tareck at his side. Makram came toward her, his pace swift, the same as her fast, shallow breaths.

"You're here," she sobbed as he dropped to his knees in front of her and pulled her body to his, her arms trapped between them. Tareck and Bashir pulled the Council Hall doors closed as Makram lowered from his knees to his haunches and enclosed her in a cage of his arms and legs.

"The worst timing, or the best?" he said against her hair. Naime tried to laugh but it came out as a wet hiccup of sound.

"The worst. You're too late," she said. His arms around her felt safe, and strong. She sucked in a breath. He was not an excuse to fall apart. She could not fall apart. She knew he had come for her, and she didn't want to need him as desperately as she did. If she allowed her feelings for him, she would never know herself again.

Naime took a ragged breath, broken with an aborted sob. "You shouldn't have come. I don't need you," she told him, and herself, and the empty room.

"I know," he said. "I know you don't need me. But I need to be here." He lifted his head and pressed his lips against her brow.

"I cannot bear it," Naime said, the strength going out of her. "It's all so broken." She wasn't strong enough.

"Don't bear it. Let it go. It's broken, let it be broken," he said. "You have to let the broken go, so you can begin again. That is the cycle, isn't it? Winter to spring. Death to life, old to new."

"I won't be able to put it back together," Naime said into her hands, which were fisted against his chest, her head resting next to them.

"Let go of it." He hugged her tighter, and tendrils of his magic encircled her, shadow and smoke, whispering about rest and peace. "Break," he commanded. "I've got you."

Break. His magic echoed, filling her with the warm dusk smell of his skin, wrapping her own magic in its grip the same way Makram held her body in his arms. *It is safe.*

Naime closed her eyes, and the burning in them intensified. Damp warmth trailed her cheeks as tears finally broke loose. She tried to draw a steady breath, and instead, sadness flooded her until it was all she could feel. It was all she had ever known and would ever know, and she was drowning in it.

Failure. Powerlessness. It wasn't everything else that was broken. It was her.

She curled her hands into his caftan, holding on because if she didn't she would be swept away, her body wasn't hers to control, it belonged to the despair. Her magic whipped loose, but his gripped it, pulling what would have been an unleashed tempest into his grip and holding it around them because she could not release herself without releasing her power.

She cried. She didn't have words or coherence or capability to tell him, she only had broken pieces that were poisoning her, and they hurt to let go of. His magic moved in and around her, and its passage left nothing of her armor and mental walls. All she could do was cry, and he held her, and her magic, and said not a word. She cried until she was empty of pain, of sadness, of failure. She cried until she was empty of everything and all she could do was sit in silence, with her entire soul laid bare and raw. It felt more intimate and revealing than removing her clothes in front of him.

When the stillness stretched between them for too many heartbeats and the tears had stopped and her throat was parched, Naime drew a shaky breath. His magic retreated from her, slipping away like the warmth that left when an embrace ended.

At some point, Makram had leaned backward against the seat, and her weight was against him, his head tipped back on the cushion. She tilted her head up just enough to peek upward at him, her fists still against his chest, her nose and mouth pressed into her curled fingers.

Embarrassment found a foothold amidst the fading sadness. He did not lift his head, so his throat and jaw dominated her view. He was still holding her magic, a monumental task that did not appear to trouble him in the least. At least if she were to judge by the relaxed way he reclined against the chair and that he appeared more asleep than struggling to contain the unleashed gale of her powers.

The only evidence that he was taxed were the visible signs of his own loosed magic, which manifested as swirls of smoke and shadow beneath his deep golden skin. Naime watched their movement for a time, soothed by the randomness of it, how it coalesced together and apart. It was peaceful, the way watching smoke from a warming fire could be, tranquil and mesmerizing.

"I am perfectly happy to sit like this all night, my beauty, but you may resume command of your magic at any point," he said, without moving or opening his eyes. "It is fiendishly temperamental and cunning, like its mistress."

Naime smiled a little, though it felt wrong and out of place. A sad smile. She reached out mentally, closing her eyes so she could concentrate, and slipped mental threads around them, replacing the shield of his own magic he had constructed to contain her outburst. Naime wrapped her magic within restraints that felt far more durable than they had not even a candlemark earlier.

Makram's body loosened a fraction, as if he had released a held breath. She opened her eyes to find he had lowered his head. His magic engulfed his eyes, blackness like the grip of deepest, starless night.

He lifted his fingers to her cheek, wiping carefully at the still-wetness. He did so for both sides, and as she watched him the shadow receded from his eyes, revealing the coffee black of his irises, and the smoke swirls faded from beneath his skin. His eyes were half-closed, so he appeared sleepy, as he stroked hair away from her face and neck. The touch was gentle, and soothing, and Naime wondered if she imagined that the look in his eyes was adoration. Adoration for her at her worst, broken apart like a ferment jar burst apart by its contents, tear-stained and red-eyed. And she smelled of the kofta her father had thrown all over her clothes.

"You should tell me," he said. She felt too fragile to speak, too broken open. But Makram felt safe, he always had—as if her spirit or her magic had sensed a kindred spirit before they even truly knew each other. And in truth, what more did she have to lose?

"My father threw his food at me. He said he hated it."

Makram slid his hand from her cheek to the back of her neck, warm comfort without demand. Naime moved her hands apart just enough to give her space to lay her head upon his shoulder.

"But he doesn't hate it. It's his favorite. When he would spend time with just me after my mother died, that is what we ate." Tears threatened again. "He doesn't know me. He doesn't remember all we had planned, how much I need him."

"You miss him, but you don't need him." Makram's voice was gentle and warm, as if there was nothing he would rather be doing than sitting in an empty hall with her, holding her while she fell apart.

"I do," Naime said without lifting her head. He smelled good, and though she was stripped bare, she was at ease, just as she had the night they had spent together. "He believed in me, made me believe I could do the things I felt were right. Unite with Sarkum, balance the Wheel. Protect us against the Republic. I failed to negotiate with Sarkum, in fact, if you are here I can only assume I have managed to ignite a civil war there, which only worsens everything. Without Sarkum there is no hope of balancing the Wheel again. Kadir will find a way to take the throne, by marriage or by force, and I will have nothing to do but sit back and watch as Tamar mages slowly die out or are exterminated like vermin by the Republic."

Makram's magic pushed against hers as it surged. He had just undergone a complicated and draining working, to pull her emotions from her and hold her magic. It did not surprise her that his control was spotty.

The night took his eyes and smoke raced beneath the skin she could see like black clouds chased by a windblown sky. She wasn't certain what she had said that interrupted his hold on his magic, but she remained quiet while he wrestled it back. The muscles in his jaw tensed, and his hand on the back of her neck tightened its grip. His arm around her waist cinched her securely against him. Naime closed her eyes, breathing in his scent and relishing the rush of his magic around her. It made her feel strong, as though nothing could stand between her and what she wanted.

"Forgive me," he said, his voice rough, "could you not breathe on me?"

Naime lifted her head away from him. It was not such an odd request. Unleashed magic amplified whatever a mage felt, whether it was love, or hatred, or lust. It could be difficult to manage both, especially during or after a greater working, when magic was heightened and in flux. Still, if what he felt was lust, and her breathing was enough to test him…

Their eyes met, his black as night. "I have missed you like a drowning man misses air," he said.

The tears streaked down her face and neck. She could only nod.

Makram sat up straighter, away from the bench, and urged her head to his with his grip on her neck, his mouth capturing hers.

His hands on her were gentle, one stroking her neck, her back, the other gripping her shoulder. The kiss began the same, but quickly became more desperate, his teeth nipping at her lips and tongue. He leaned forward, bending over her, and she knew he meant to take her to the floor in the next heartbeat. She could feel the push and sweep of his power, knew it was winning dominion over his mind.

Naime pressed her hands to his chest. He jerked his head away and sucked in a breath, closing his eyes. He collapsed against the bench and tipped his head back onto the cushion.

"Keep talking," he said. She had to admire his restraint. She had seen mages of much less power be completely ruled by whatever their magic flux demanded. If she talked of something innocuous it might help.

"My father's brother and his wife were unable to conceive a child." It was hard to concentrate on her words. Knowing Makram was lusting compelled her own tumultuous thoughts in that direction, and he still held her so tightly against him that even through their many layers of clothes she was aware of his body's strength and shape. She remembered what it felt like to touch him, to be nearly naked with him, and she wanted more.

"I do not know if they had a loveless marriage, or why he did so, but he had an affair with one of the palace attendants. She conceived a child, but died in his birthing."

"Your cousin," Makram said. His voice sounded steadier.

"My uncle and his wife adopted Ihsan, and the secret was kept. Only my parents knew, and a few of my uncle's servants. When my aunt died, Ihsan came to live at the palace and attend the University."

"No one knows he's illegitimate?" Makram's hand relaxed against her neck and he stroked his thumb against her throat. Shivers raced over her skin. Naime forced herself to sit up straight, still near him, in the circle of his legs, but folded her hands in her lap.

"Not until recently. My father told Kadir shortly after I returned from Sarkum."

"And that is a problem." Makram's voice was more at ease, and he lifted his arms to hook his elbows on the chair's seat, putting a little physical distance between them.

"His nobility is only half his blood. The Council will not accept that as enough. By political weight, the next in line would be Kadir or his heir. When they believed Ihsan was an heir, it offered me a measure of protection I will not have now, as there is no one with my same ideologies to replace me were I to suddenly fall from a cliff."

Makram exhaled sharply, and she felt the reach and latch of his power once more.

"Anyone who tries to harm you is going to be reminded why, exactly, Tamar fears the Sixth House so much," he said, threat in his voice.

"Oh?" Naime said, carefully. "Would that not require your presence in Tamar? Do you not have a battle to fight in Sarkum?" She wanted him here. Not just to stand in the Circle. She wanted him at her side. She wanted the balance he brought to her. But he was a prince, and if he fought a battle against his brother and won a place in Sarkum as ruler, that would be impossible.

"I had hoped to bathe and eat, perhaps even sleep, before we began discussing politics." He sighed and lifted his head.

"Then you are here for political reasons, not simply to act as a giant kerchief for me to cry upon?" she teased, though she was still too raw to find much humor, even in her own attempts.

"I am here"—he lowered his arms to his sides, putting a hand flat against the floor of the dais—"because I am unwelcome in Sarkum after an unfortunate incident in which my brother imprisoned me, that may or may not have ended with a wing of the palace collapsing to rubble. And because I need time and help to gather an army to make myself welcome once more. The rest…"

He shrugged one shoulder. "I knew from the first moment we met that you held too much inside. You were not grieving for your father, you did not vent your frustration with the games you have to play. I know what it is like to live in a palace at the mercy of a Council of men you do not share ideals with. Yet you were always so calm and composed. It isn't healthy. If you did not break for me, you may have broken at a much less opportune moment."

"I see. You helped me to reveal my pain and failures as a favor."

"No." He gripped her waist, pulling her forward and stroking her with his gaze. "I wanted them. Every single one. I wanted you to unleash yourself on me, so that you are mine, your secrets and hurts mine to keep and guard."

Naime twined her arms around his neck, too full of him to think of anything else. He kissed the slope of her neck as she pressed her forehead against his shoulder. She clung to him. He kissed her jaw and tipped her head back with his hands so he could kiss the tip of her nose and her forehead. It was tender and unexpected, and she laughed a little to prevent the tears that wanted to fill her eyes again.

"I am yours." Her throat closed as she met his stare. Emotion overlaid his face, fierceness, which was reflected in the quick, hard kiss he gave her.

"There is so much to say," he said when he pulled away, "but not here. Not like this." He ducked his chin to indicate their embrace, reminding her they were showing their affection in a much too public place.

Naime withdrew her arms from around his neck. Makram untangled himself from her and stood, pulling her with him. She was not ready to be away from him again, when she had just gotten him back. But he deserved time to rest, to eat, to bathe, as he had said. And, if she could keep his arrival a secret, using him in the Council meeting might be a useful distraction.

"I am not certain I like that calculating look," he said, but the bright, sharp glint in his eyes told her he liked it very much.

"I will trade my thoughts for yours, once you are settled and rested."

He gave her a slow, charged smile.

Thirty-three

Even after she had bathed, changed her clothes, and eaten, Naime felt empty, stripped of emotion. It was not a bad feeling, but something akin to having been cleansed. She was not invigorated, she was too emotionally exhausted for that, but she did feel lighter, more in command.

Samira had dismissed the other attendants once Naime finished eating. She puttered about the rooms, idly straightening things, preparing Naime's bedroom for sleep. But Naime sensed her glances, the heaviness of her silence. Worried about her, about the turning of things and how they had all gone so wrong.

"I'm all right," Naime said, staring out the doors into the night and the stark skeleton of the fig tree.

"Truly all right, or pretending to be?" Samira asked in perfect mimicry of Naime's crispest tone.

Naime took a breath and let it out slowly, feeling through herself, assessing her mind and body. Broken open and laid bare. Staring at the ruin of her plans all around her. A gaping hole in her heart left by the passing of her mother and the absence of her father's strength. But all right.

"I cried," she said. "He held me and I cried until I couldn't any more. I feel emptier than I ever have."

Samira stopped what she was doing, turning to Naime with eyebrows raised and lips parted. Naime could see her in the reflection of the glass.

"It begins in emptiness," Samira finally said, placing the small piece of pottery she was dusting back on its table. "It begins in void. Purge the old and begin again."

Naime couldn't help but smile a little. The story of creation went as such. Explained different ways by different people. The Wheel was a circle, and so could be interpreted from any point. But so few ever viewed the void as the beginning. Only the end, only destruction, death, decay. Samira shared with Naime a love for some of the old poets, who often argued that in fact, endings were beginnings. That creation did not end with void but began from it. From nothing comes everything, and back to nothing, and again.

Naime had read so many books on the subject it made her head spin. But she had not really understood. Not until Makram, who was not afraid to break things, to see the new paths revealed. And how could he be afraid, who walked with ruin in his wake and dawn in his sights?

As if her thoughts had summoned him, he stood before the fig tree, waiting for her, his hands clasped behind his back. She'd put him in the same rooms he'd had before, with Tareck. He must have come through the garden. He wore only caftan and salvar, no belts, no entari or ferace. Surely he was cold, standing out in the frosty air.

"I think he'd be happiest if he were your shadow," Samira reproached as she moved to Naime's side. He already was. Dusk to her dawn.

"He wants to talk."

"Mmm," Samira hummed. "I'll leave you to your discussions then."

Naime bumped sideways against her. A tiny knot of apprehension twisted in her belly. Samira gave a soft laugh and squeezed Naime's hand. "We promised never to lie to each other, didn't we? I'll bring your tea in the morning, yes?"

"Yes," Naime said and kissed her friend's cheek as her own heated with the admission. The tea she had not brought to Sarkum. Tea that prevented the inevitable consequences of trysting.

When Samira left, Makram approached to stand on the opposite side of the glass door from her. Naime opened the doors. She held his gaze as he stepped inside, pulling the doors closed behind him. He tugged the curtains over the glass then faced her. She hadn't realized he carried a book with him, which he held out to her. She took it.

"I didn't get a chance to give you this. We've also brought your guard home, who was so badly injured. He's through the worst of it."

"Thank you. Leaving him behind made me feel like a monster." She hugged the book to her chest. "Leaving you behind…I was so worried."

"Don't worry for me. I am exceptionally hard to kill, when I am not denied the use of my magic."

"Did you really collapse part of the palace?"

He shrugged one shoulder, a furrow appearing and disappearing in his brow. "It was abandoned, but sometimes my brother needs things to be said in the most obvious of ways to understand."

Naime raised an eyebrow. Her heartbeat seemed unable to decide on a fast pace or slow, and her body flushed in alternating patterns. First her face, then her chest, and now her hands were clammy, her grip on the book the only thing preventing them from shaking.

"Why are you here?"

Makram tipped his head to one side, his gaze flicking over her face. "You invited me in," he said. The tension between them broke, and she laughed softly, turning to set the book on the table in the center of the room.

"I could hardly leave you out in the cold, staring at my window like a lost stray," she teased as she straightened and faced him. He clicked his tongue, crossing the few steps between them and catching her by the waist.

"A stray?" His eyebrows lifted. "Not a terrifying death mage? Not a foreign prince? Not a commander of armies?"

"Those things too. But you always seemed a little lost." She reached to touch his freshly shaven jaw. His lids lowered at the touch, an edge coming over his expression.

"I was," he said.

"No longer?" Her voice dipped. He shook his head, twice in slow motion.

"I have found a light to guide me." His hands tightened on her waist, tugging her to him. She'd missed it, the feel of his body against hers, the surge of longing and safety she felt in his hands. "That is why I am here. There is something in me, my magic, or something else, pulled to you. A tug, a draw. I don't know. It started the moment I realized you wanted to stand the Circle and has not changed or dimmed."

She was both fascinated and disappointed by his admission. A pull? Like the pull she felt to him? Physical attraction? A sense of balance and completion? Or was it something magical, some magnetism between their powers—

"Stop that," he said. "Watching you think is like watching a mill turn. Not tonight. Analyze me some other time."

"What would you prefer I do tonight?" Naime asked, her hands settling on his chest, near the first button of his caftan, nervous excitement swelling to fill her stomach and her throat.

There would be time to think about the new ramifications of him attempting to usurp his brother. What it might mean for them. But in coaxing her to break open, to purge herself of all her fear and grief, he had left her open. There was room in her to fully feel everything about him that she had been holding back. It swelled outward until she thought she would burst with it.

"In Al-Nimas," he said, "you said every part of me would take a lifetime to come to know."

She remembered, lying in bed with him, touching him and feeling the time they had slipping away with speed that made her heart ache.

"One never knows how long a lifetime is," he murmured, "so we should begin now."

Naime smiled, a soft laugh escaping, and nodded. "Such a practical thinker," she purred, flicking open the top button of his caftan. He gripped her hips and steered her backwards, through the sitting room and toward her bedroom door. She worked her way through the buttons as he did, so that when they reached her room, he released his grip on her hips and shrugged out of the grey material.

"Are these things dear to you?" He tugged at her clothes as he lowered his head and brushed his lips along the slope of her neck.

Her eyes slid closed. "Why?"

"It would be so much faster—"

"Don't you dare magic my clothes to dust," Naime said. Mischief brightened his eyes. "I have never been with anyone before. Can you not find the patience to take your time?"

"I will take my time," he said, his fingers working the buttons of her caftan, "on every part of you. I only meant to get the clothes out of my way."

"You'll have to do it the old-fashioned way," she said, and his eyes lit with humor.

"Magic has been with us since the dawn of man, but using it isn't the old-fashioned way?" He pushed her caftan off her shoulders.

Naime slid her hands up his hips and waist, pushing the second, lighter-weight caftan up and toward his arms. He tugged it off and tossed it aside.

The stitches were out of his wounds, the bruising nearly faded. The bandages on his hand and wrist were gone. She slid her fingertips along his collarbones until they met below his throat, then down, fanning them to touch as much of him as possible. His skin prickled as she painted a slow stroke down his body, her ring fingers brushing his nipples and making him jerk, then down his belly. Warm golden skin lit by the fading light of the mage orbs Samira had distributed in the lamps, he was the most beautiful thing Naime had ever seen.

She kissed his shoulder, running the backs of her fingers along the waist of his salvar, then circled his hips with her fingertips. Finally, she raked her fingertips up the middle of his back. His breath shuddered out and he gripped her shoulders. He pulled her closer, then pushed her back, lowering his head and catching hers in his hands to tip it back so he could kiss her. Naime gripped his wrists and curved against him, surrendering to the heat of his body and his kiss. Her eyes were closed, so she did not see his magic burst over his skin, but felt its thrum against her own.

His hands made fists in both the short-sleeved caftan she wore and her chemise, and tugged them up to her hips, breaking the kiss only long enough to pull them over her head. She touched his chest again, and his went to her bared back, one between her shoulder blades, the other in the curve of her lower back, and molded her to him. She gasped, breaking the kiss. He tipped his head into hers, kissing the hook of her jaw, then tracing the curve of her ear with the tip of his nose.

Naime stood still, locked in place by too many sensations. Her belly pressed to his, her breasts against his chest, his warm skin, the press of his hands on her naked back. Shivers raced over her before warmth took their place, and her nipples hardened against him. Little shocks raced from them to her belly as he shifted against her, his hands sliding to her waist.

"You feel like silk," he breathed across her neck, his hands tightening.

"You're so warm." She tucked her head into the curve of his neck and kissed his throat. One of his hands traced the curve of her spine up to her neck, beneath her unbound hair. Naime placed a circle of kisses along his neck, and he dug his fingers into her hair, both hands curving over her head as she moved. His breath sounded shallow and uneven, and he tipped his head back a fraction to give her room.

Naime stood on tiptoe, acutely aware of the weight of her breasts against him as she kissed his chin, and the curve below it. She lowered to her heels, and he made a growling utterance as her skin slid over his. She kissed the hollow of his throat, and tasted it with the tip of her tongue. Makram grunted, his hands gripping her hips, pulling them hard and tight to his own. The firm line of his arousal pushed against her hip, turning the tug in her belly into an insistent throb between her thighs.

Naime continued planting soft kisses across his chest and shoulders, one hand circling his waist, the other slipping between their hips. The first time she'd seen him naked she had been reluctant to torture each other with intimate touches. But now there was no such restriction. She gripped him through the salvar, and fell immediately in love with the way he filled her hand, the ripple of tension that went through his body and his hands on her, the soft, groaning exhale her touch caused. She wanted to discover every touch that caused that sound. She wanted a lifetime. To make him hers, to be his.

Overwhelmed with the sudden upwelling of want and emotion, she released her grip on him and reached up to tip his head down to hers. She kissed him, frantic with the sudden feeling that she couldn't bear to be parted from him ever again, wanting to be connected, wanting to forget where she began and he ended.

Makram wrapped his arms around her, hitching her up against his body, meeting her kiss with teeth and tongue and just as much emotion. His magic swept around her, calling to hers, which responded in a blaze of light and a rush of wind and he shivered under its assault.

When they parted from the kiss he set her down and untied her salvar, pushing them off her hips, and she did the same in kind. He stepped out of his and held her hips, pushing their bodies a step apart so he could look at her. Naime's skin prickled under his gaze, and she resisted the urge to hug her arms around her breasts or cover her lower parts with her hands.

"Don't be shy of me." He pulled her back to him. "You're the Wheel's own perfection. I could look at you for days and never have my fill."

"You should do more than look," Naime said. Her skin felt stretched too tight, longing for the touch and warmth of his hands.

"Yes, Sultana," he said with a soft laugh, and stepped to her so he could hoist her onto the bed. "Where shall I start?" he asked himself, his gaze, night black, dropped over her. He bent, putting his hands to either side of her hips, and gave a little thrust of his chin to indicate she should move. Naime slipped backwards and he followed on all fours, looking predatory. It sent a sharp thrill into her belly, and when she reached the top of the bed he urged her onto her back with a kiss.

"It is not entirely fair that you are so beautiful, so pristine," he sighed as he moved his kisses from her lips to her throat and shoulders.

She traced the scar on his arm, the wound he had obtained on his first journey from Al-Nimas to Narfour, racing to make it to her before they betrothed her. Before he even knew her, or knew why she had asked him to hurry. Because he believed in what she did. It was still reddened, but would lighten, as some of the others—older ones—already had.

Naime slid her hands up his shoulders, his neck, and into his hair. Only the braids were pulled back, the rest loose, and she tangled her fingers in it. Shadows swirled under his skin, chasing her fingers, coalescing under her touch as she traced the furrows between the muscles of his shoulders. He was not pristine.

Naime pushed gently on his chest, urging him off her, continuing to push until he lay down on his side then rolled to his back. His hands held onto the parts of her he could reach as he obeyed her gentle urging, first her waist, then her arms, and stroked down her back as she straddled him.

Being naked with him was a conundrum of sensations. Every place they connected, she was aware of their differences. She sat on his thighs, and his were strong and hard with muscle, hers soft and yielding against them. His skin was hot to her touch, hers cold in comparison. His grip when he touched her strong and confident, hers soft and hesitant. Naime lay down on top of him, her belly on his hips, and his erection pulsed against her.

She kissed the scar on his arm. Then she drew a fingertip across a thin, short scar over his chest, one of those she had taken note of when she had seen him half-clothed in the stables. She followed her finger's path with her lips. Then did the same to a thicker one along his ribs, above the newer, still-healing wounds. Each touch and kiss was a claim, giving in to what she had wanted for so long, and declaration that she did not ever want to share him. Slipping lower along his body, she drew her lips across a long, curved scar that began at his ribs, went down the right side of his lower abdomen, and stopped at his hip.

Makram's breath hissed between his teeth, and his hips tightened and rose beneath her, pressing his erection between her breasts. Naime reached up with her hands to skim them down his torso, then traced the long scar again, this time with her tongue. Her pulse pounded in her neck and wrists as she did it. She felt both brave and unsure of what she was doing, and glanced up at his face to assess his reaction. He reached down as she did, and grabbed her arms, pulling her up him as easily as if she were a blanket.

"Hello." He caught her mouth with his for a slow, hungry kiss. "My turn."

"But," she protested, "there are more scars."

"Many," he agreed, putting her gently on her back and covering her again. "We can save a few for next time."

"What if there is no next time?"

He pinned her hands to the mattress, making a slow examination of her beneath him. She shuddered at the languid expression on his face, made hungrier by eyes painted in absolute black.

"I've decided there are going to be many next times." He lowered his head and kissed her skin. He dotted a line of soft kisses between her breasts, his hands still holding hers against the bed.

"You've decided?" She closed her eyes. His kisses veered left, making a slow spiral around her breast, closing in on her nipple. Her entire body tightened in anticipation, the sensitive tip hard and aching for touch. But he didn't, instead he stopped just short and kissed a line across her chest to her right breast and did the same thing. Naime gave a mewl of protest, arching toward him and trying to pull her arms free of his grasp.

"I've decided," he answered during a short break from his kisses. Pulses of sharp, aching want throbbed in her breasts and between her legs, where dampness slicked her thighs. She pressed them together, trying to quell the empty ache and having very little success. Makram ducked his chin, watching her rub her legs together, and shifted, planting a knee between hers.

He moved his grip from her wrists to one hand and stroked his other down her side, her hip, and his hand came to rest over her pelvis, the heel of his palm pressing just above the place she wanted it. Naime made a little sound of complaint, lifting her hips in an effort to force him to touch her there. She was certain it would ease the ache, the longing, if he would just…

Makram descended, gripping her ankles. He grazed his hands up her legs, his strong fingers urging her legs up and apart.

Naime propped herself on her elbows, watching him as he pressed a kiss to her bent knee, one hand holding her leg steady. His hair brushed her skin, a silken caress juxtaposed to his more carnal touch. His skin was a beautiful contrast to hers, warm and golden next to her paler complexion. His midnight hair and magic-painted darkness to the pearlescent pulse of her own power.

He moved slowly from her knee toward the apex of her thighs. The kisses were coaxing and lazy against her skin. Though his magic told a different story, about raw desperation and need, whips of shadow and smoke occasionally breaking loose across his shoulders. His magic was as tangible on her power as his touch was on her skin, little shocks and caresses, awareness that came and stayed, even when he lifted his mouth away. His hands moved from her knees, down her inner thighs, and stopped. His thumbs stroked up the crease of each thigh where it met her pelvis.

She dropped to her back, her pulse jagged across her entire body, her skin on fire with sensation.

"Why are you torturing me?" Naime protested.

Makram turned his thumbs inward, so he caressed the outer folds of her, and she shifted her hips, urging him to touch her where the throbbing and need seemed most concentrated.

"Am I?" he said in a low, gravelly voice, just before he kissed the skin above the triangle of hair. Naime gave a soft sound of encouragement, reaching to tangle her fingers in his hair.

"You are," she said, gripping fistfuls of his hair and guiding his head so his face was above hers. She glared at him. He narrowed his eyes in mockery of her glare, barely stifling a grin as he moved down again.

Makram pressed another kiss to her, just the pressure of his lips, against the tiny bundle of nerves and need that ached so desperately.

She gasped then moaned in disappointment as he kissed a trail back up her torso, his hands following along, up her waist and ribs.

"I'll not be rushed." He lowered his head to nudge her cheek. "I have wanted this too long to let it be ruined by haste." As he spoke, his hand wandered to her breast, his fingers cupping the weight of it, sliding up. His fingers plucked at her nipple gently as he said, "I don't want it to hurt for you."

The words were lost in the shock of pleasure. She'd barely drawn a breath when he lowered his head and caressed her breast again, this time capturing her nipple in his mouth. She squeezed her eyes shut. The bolts of fire and lightning arcing through her were too much sensation when coupled with the soft sound of his pleased rumble and the sight of his head against her body.

His hips moved over hers, the blunt tip of his erection grazing against the seam between her legs, slipping against her wetness. They both groaned, his sound vibrating on her captured nipple, and she arched, clenching his shoulders. He lifted his mouth from her breast and pressed his forehead just below her collarbones, letting out a languid exhale.

Makram held still for a long moment, his hands curled into handfuls of the bedspread. Naime stroked her hands, one after the other, down his back, sensing him trying to restrain his magic and his urgency.

Makram closed his eyes as her gentle, measured strokes calmed the beast of his magic. She gave a little shift beneath him and drew in a breath, which she held for just a moment before she spoke.

"I've thought of a question," she said, and he was glad she couldn't see his exasperated smile. "Your magic…"

"Harms only what I tell it to," he said, surprised it had taken her so long to think of, or ask that question. It was usually the first question women asked him, if they stayed around long enough to ask any questions at all once they knew what he was.

"Even in flux? Even"—she stroked her fingers down his side, strumming his ribs like the strings of a komuz—"even when you…"

He lifted his head. She watched him, wide-eyed, her cheeks bright, light pouring out of her eyes so he could just barely distinguish the mahogany ring of her irises behind it. Her fingers twitched against his hip, stroking across the rounded bone, seeking entrance between their bodies. He didn't grant it. It had been a long time since he'd been with a woman, and his body was threatening revolt already. Her little, curious fingers would not help his cause. The talking did, though.

"Even when I…?" he prompted.

Her eyes closed halfway as she examined him from beneath brown, thick lashes. Makram scooted up enough to kiss her, because he could not look at her without wanting to. She met him eagerly, and her legs circled his, rubbing in rhythmic suggestion of what her body wanted.

Kissing had been a bad idea. He pulled away, burying his head next to hers, breathing in the rose and winter of her scent. There were other smells, warmth, her arousal.

"I have heard…that at the moment of climax a mage loses their grip completely on their magic."

"Not every time." Makram nipped her earlobe and was rewarded with a shudder of her body beneath his, a quick hitch in her breath. The sounds she made were so sweetly feminine he didn't think he needed anything else to be fully and painfully aroused. There was no doubt in his mind he would lose control of his magic this night. "Only the best times."

"Oh," she said, caution in her voice. "And the best times—"

"My magic will never hurt you."

There had always been that sick twisting in his gut before. They never believed him. The fear was too strong. If the question came up, they never really wanted an answer, they wanted an excuse to leave. So he always let them. But not Naime. She was not ruled by emotion, but by logic.

"Just as the wind that comes when you release your magic does not harm unless you shape it to, fire does not burn unless commanded, earth does not break unless made to."

"Then hurry up." She giggled softly when he snorted against her ear. His heart filled with warmth and joy at her easy dismissal of something that had caused him so many hurts in the past.

"And here I thought you were so patient," he said, moving up so he could give the care to her other breast that he had lavished on the first.

She didn't answer, only tangled her hands in his hair again, holding his head to her as she arched up, pushing her hips to his. His cock lay between her lush thighs, caressed every time she moved, slipping against the ready, slick heat of her core. For the hundredth time he denied himself the screaming urge to plunge inside her. He didn't want her to feel even the slightest, shortest moment of discomfort, and that meant patience now. He could lose himself later.

He propped himself on one arm, reaching between her legs, sliding his fingers down, across the slippery, silken place between her thighs. He groaned and she gave a sharp, high gasp, one hand gripping his forearm, the other still clutching at his hair. Makram watched her face as he explored her, petting, circling, stroking. Her eyes were squeezed shut in concentration, her teeth digging into her bottom lip, her neck arched. Beautiful. He kissed the hollow of her throat, flicked his tongue against it, easing a finger inside her.

Naime's body stilled at the invasion, while his mind spun at the grip of her inner muscles, at the heat of her.

"All right?" he asked. She nodded, turning her head to meet his gaze, and gave an experimental wiggle of her hips.

"I have never known what being all right was until now," Naime moaned.

He huffed a laugh, leaning over to kiss her as he circled the tiny apex of her pleasure with his thumb, carefully slipping his finger against the inside of her. She gave a surprised cry, and her teeth clamped on his lower lip. It was only a quick bite, and it hurt, but it fractured him, and his aching cock informed him it could do a much better job than his finger.

"Oh no," she gasped, "I'm so sorry." She cupped his face, pressing her thumb to his lip.

"We'll discuss your penance later," he mumbled, rolling fully on top of her, settling his hips between hers. Pale magic lit her beautiful face and her lips parted when he moved, her breath hitching.

"Breathe," he commanded, gently.

She obeyed, and Makram smoothed a hand down her inner thigh, resuming his intimate strokes. She gave a moan that ended with a high-pitched break in her voice. He thought of the most monotonous, mind-numbing tasks and chores he could, listing them mentally. They only helped marginally to temper him, but it was better than nothing.

He fit himself against her, continuing his touches as he slipped just the head of his erection inside her. Sweat broke out along his back and brow, and he had to think hard of something else to add to his list, the muscles in his legs cramping with his effort to wait for her. Makram withdrew, entering again, slowly, only a fraction further. Her legs spread wider, her breath became more shallow, and she lifted her hands to grip his arms, her nails biting against his skin.

"It's good," she said breathlessly.

He didn't like good. It was perfect. It was ecstasy and agony, waiting, going so slowly when his body could only conceive of fast and hard.

"I know there's more of you than that," Naime said, with a sharp tone of impatience.

Makram laughed, collapsing on top of her and kissing her, cupping her face and lifting his weight onto his forearms. He withdrew and pressed in again, deeper, and she made a tiny sound of encouragement into his mouth, nipping at his tongue. He repeated, slow withdrawal, slower push, gaining depth then giving it up with each careful thrust. She asked him to stop only once, and it took everything in him to hold still. Because her internal muscles squeezed him, pulling him deeper, pressing wet and warmth around him that made his thoughts and restraint scatter like dust motes in a breeze.

When he finally buried himself in her, he waited, more for himself than her. She clung to him, arms and legs, her head lifted and pressed into the slope of his neck, her breath shuddering across his sweat-slicked skin. He pressed his head to hers, burying his face in her hair and her scent, and slid all the way out and all the way back. Relief tangled with pleasure, heat filling his core. She tilted her hips up, her legs squeezed, and he did, for a moment, lose track of their beginning and ending, which soft, noisy groan belonged to who, whose magic gusted and whose smoked.

"Again," she said into his skin, and gave his neck a tiny, soft nip. Cold fire blazed over him, in his thoughts, and he let go of the white-knuckled grip he had on himself. Whips of power reached away from him, each with a core of night and a trail of smoke. He moved, a few slow, even strokes, but she was ready and he was dying a slow death, and when he sped his pace, she nodded. Her hands gripped his neck as she pushed her head back against the bed, her body finding rhythm with his. She planted her feet, her bent knees cradling his hips, and her hands reached down his back, one, then the other. She dragged her nails up his skin, her breath coming in surprised little sounds each time their hips met.

It was too much, watching pleasure and surprise and joy war for her expression. She was so bright in her unleashed magic he had to slit his eyes to look at her. His own magic cut through hers like blades of shadow, a stark and mesmerizing contrast.

When he was certain he'd run out of dull things to concentrate on, and his body threatened to take command from his mind, he thought about stopping. He could help her to her climax first, then come back to finish his. When he slowed, readying to pull away, her nails bit against his shoulders and her breath came in a desperate cry.

"Please don't stop," she pleaded, when it felt like he meant to pull completely away from her. Was she doing it wrong?

"You need time I don't have in me," he said, the warm velvet of his voice tattered and uneven.

"I don't." She wrapped her legs around his thighs to hold him in place. "Don't go. I think it's close." Close to a precipice, close to breaking, every time he moved she thought she was going to shatter apart.

"Naime," he said, digging deeper into her with a little push and making all the hard, shimmering sensations burst over her hips and thighs again. She moaned his name in return, and he began again.

"Don't be afraid," he said, and she didn't understand, until his magic burst open around her, blanketing them in nothingness like a silent, starless sky.

She couldn't see anything anymore, only feel Makram as he moved. It was neither warm nor cold in the grip of his magic, and everything else but his breathing and hers was silenced. She could feel him, every touch, every kiss, every movement of him against her amplified tenfold by the lack of every other sense.

"I could never fear you," she said against his mouth. "You are etched in my heart."

He kissed her savagely, until she had to tear herself away for breath. His arms squeezed more tightly around hers, and his rhythm changed, his hips rolling against her. Stars lit behind her eyelids and her breath left her in a cry, but the sound was lost to the void of his magic.

"What do I do?" she gasped, trying to hold herself together and not succumb to the rush of feeling and need.

He gave a soft, strangled grunt and fumbled in the dark for her hands, bringing them above her head on the bed and circling his arms over hers. He kissed her.

"Let go." He pushed hard against her hips and she moaned into his mouth. "Give me everything."

Tendrils of shadow and smoke, warmth and peace, slid through her, slicing through her grip on her body as he continued to move. Everything inside her, beginning at their joining, shattered in great bursts of pleasure and release and she breathed his name in wonder. He buried his head against her neck as the light from her magic burst outward from her, piercing the void of his. Ripples of pleasure cascaded away from his movement, until she lost control of her muscles completely and all she could do was gasp for breath as short bursts continued to pulse as he moved.

"Come with me," she demanded, wanting to pull her hands from his grip to touch him.

Makram said a harsh, course word, and she felt his teeth clench together because his face was pressed to hers. His movements shortened then stopped. His hands closed like vises on her wrists and the hard sound that escaped him bled into a low moan. A shudder wracked his entire body, and he relaxed his weight into her.

His magic receded, light beginning to bleed and run through it as he called it back to himself. His breathing grew more even, and he loosened his grip on her wrists. She twined her legs around his hips and tucked her head to his, feeling the thunderous beat of his heart against her body.

Once his magic retreated the room appeared too frenetic. All the shapes and pale colors burned her eyes, in contrast to the simple nothingness of the moments before.

"My hands," she said, and he released her. Naime dug her fingers into his hair, holding his head as she pressed her cheek to his. She closed her eyes against everything else.

Makram stroked a hand down her side, riding the curves of her body, until he came to her hip. He shifted off of her, to his side, and tugged her against him. She obeyed the gentle guidance of his hands, relaxing back into exhausted euphoria. The aftermath was… stickier than she might have imagined. Though she found she did not care in the least.

Makram patted around them until he found the edge of the blankets Samira had drawn back, and pulled them up to ward them against the night chill that was creeping through the rooms. He brushed a hand over her hip, weaving his legs between hers.

The air sat heavy in its stillness, and Naime opened her eyes and tipped her head back. His brows were pulled together, his lips pressed thin, his expression reticent.

"Tell me to stay," he said.

She took a slow, audible breath. "I did. You're here."

His gaze hardened on hers. "No, not the night. Ask me to stay with you. Ask me to stay forever."

"What?" she asked. "How can I? How could that possibly work?" She wanted him to. She never wanted to leave the moment they were in. Never wanted to be without him.

"Command me, and I will make it work."

"Makram." Naime touched his cheek. "Your people need a ruler."

"Not me. I was not born to rule, I am not made to. But you are." He took her hand and brought it to his lips. "I am made and born to serve. You are the one I want to serve, the one I wish to stand beside."

Naime drew back, her throat tightening. "I will not leave Tamar."

"No," he said, and kissed her brow. "Think about it, my beauty. I know you can solve it."

"I cannot, there isn't—"

He silenced her with a kiss, a deep, hungry kiss that shot vigor and heat through her limbs. She sighed a halfhearted protest, trying to concentrate on what he'd said. What he'd meant.

"Say it," he ordered when he withdrew from the kiss. "Say it and we will find a way."

"Stay." She surprised herself with the desperation in the word, with the emotion that welled up and broke free of her relaxed grip on her mind and her magic.

"Yes, my queen." He cupped her face in his hands. "My heart."

THIRTY-FOUR

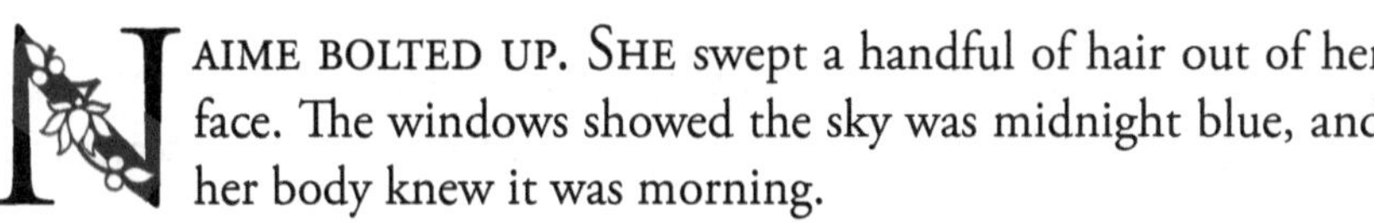

NAIME BOLTED UP. SHE swept a handful of hair out of her face. The windows showed the sky was midnight blue, and her body knew it was morning.

She twisted to find Makram. He sprawled on his stomach, one arm and one leg hooked over the edge of the mattress, as if he fell asleep halfway out of the bed. Thoughts whipped around her mind, caught in a whirlwind. If she did not get them ordered, write them down, check her ideas against her books, she might lose them. It was hard to leave him there like that.

Beautiful, perfect, his warm golden skin beckoning to be touched again. She stared at him for a long time. He'd kicked the blankets away from him at some point. It was so easy to lose herself in staring at him. She couldn't stop herself. Shouldn't their trysting have quenched the desire to look at him? If anything, it had only inflamed it.

She knew if she hesitated even a moment more, or dared to brush her fingers over his muscled back, she would not be leaving the bed at all. Carefully, she slipped off the side opposite him, picking up her chemise from the floor and pulling it over her head as she tiptoed into the sitting room.

It was morning, but far too early for any but perhaps the kitchen staff to be up and about. Samira had her own rooms in the palace, and

Naime did not expect she'd come until breakfast time. She picked up the book he'd brought her, and the Book of Chara'a, its bright blue cover belying its age. Holding both books in her lap, she sat on one of the couches, reclining against the arm and stretching her legs out. Her body was sore in ways and places it had never been, reminding her of how she'd spent her night, and heat flushed her cheeks as she opened the blue book to the last third. It was there that laws governing Chara'a had been written out by Sultan Omar the First.

The Council meeting was this afternoon and she still had no solutions. In fact she had more problems. Makram wanted to stay. She wanted that too but wasn't certain how to make it work.

Makram strode out of the bedroom, naked still, and obviously unworried by it. He crossed the sitting room and bent over her, assessing her position with a mute glare. Naime opened her mouth to speak, but he gathered her up in his arms, lifting her off the couch, the two books still in her lap.

"I'm working." She couldn't decide between amusement or annoyance. He set her on the bed and crawled in beside her.

"Do it here," he said in a sleep-rough voice, propping pillows behind her back. When he seemed satisfied with that he sprawled at an angle across the bed, his head in her lap and one arm over her thighs, curling toward her hip. Naime blinked down at him, but his face was pressed against her belly, his eyes closed.

At first she thought it would be impossible to do anything with him as he was. But she made a few adjustments, until she was comfortable, and set the books across her knees, opening Emer Saban's and turning the pages with one hand and carding the fingers of her other through his hair. What a much more pleasant way to study dry, mind-numbing material. Her hand wandered to his skin, tracing bone and muscle in absentminded strokes.

"Don't do that again," he mumbled against her stomach.

"Do what?" She brushed a few braids away from his cheek.

"Leave without telling me," he said. "I reached for you and you were gone."

"All right," she said. "Why were you half hanging off the bed this morning?"

He opened one eye, or both, she could only see the one. "This bed is enormous. I felt lost in it. Like I wouldn't be able to escape if I needed to."

"Did you think you would need to escape?"

He rolled onto his back with a sigh. "Not exactly." He closed his eyes. Naime traced a finger over his lips. He nipped her fingertip and adjusted his head against her legs.

"Habits?" she asked, wondering if he was simply too accustomed to the need to be able to be out of his bed and ready to fight at a moment's warning. He nodded once. Habits he might have picked up on the borders between Sarkum and the plains, where raids were frequent. And here she had spent every night of her life, save her trip to Sarkum, in a comfortable bed with sleep undisturbed by the chance of danger.

"What work is this?" He rolled his head away from her belly, taking stock of the books.

"I am due in the Council today. To defend myself as Regent. To explain the situation in Sarkum, to deal with my father's revelation about Ihsan. To explain that you wish to take the title of Mirza."

He lay still for a moment, staring at the books. His brow furrowed and he sat up. He reached for the books in her lap, closing them and moving them to the table beside the bed. Then he knelt near her feet and stroked his hands up her calves. With a little smile, he gripped her behind the knees and tugged, pulling her onto her back and guiding her legs around him as he pressed his hips to hers. She laughed, and thoughts of her books and ideas flitted away. She gripped his arms as he propped himself on his elbows and held his face over hers. He was so beautiful and strong and her heart so full of him she wanted only to reconnect, as they had the night before. But his expression was serious, and he brushed her hair away from her face.

"I do not wish to take the title of Mirza," he said.

Naime stroked her hands down his back, tracing his spine with her fingers, examining his face as she waited for the rest of his declaration.

He ducked his head, touching the tip of his nose to her chin and closing his eyes. "I have another in mind."

"Another title?" She kissed his brow.

"Mmm." The sound rumbled through his chest and so through hers. "Prince Consort."

The words lay between them for long moments before their meaning burrowed into her heart. Her hands stilled against his back, and she exhaled slowly. Not Sultan. Not ruler. Consort. To her. Her eyes burned suddenly, and her throat closed around any reply she might have given.

He lifted his head, his fingers tracing her jaw and throat.

"Why would you do that?"

When he smiled, lighting his face with gentle amusement, it broke something inside her and a tear slid free.

"I believe in you." He brushed the tear off her temple. "I believe you can change the world, and I want to be at your side to see it, to help you if I can. What is a title like Mirza when I could stand beside one of the greatest rulers in history?"

Naime closed her eyes against more tears, her body too full of emotion for her to speak without everything overflowing from her.

"Besides, the terms your Council sent to the Mirza did offer a marriage of alliance," he teased. "I have them with me, if you'd care to read over them."

"You are so certain you will defeat your brother?" She had to temper the inferno of emotion filling her chest with something practical.

He grinned. "If you say yes to me, there is nothing I cannot do, would not do, to stand beside you. You believe in me too, don't you?"

"Oh." She dug her fingers into his hair. "Yes."

"Yes you believe in me, or yes to marrying me?"

She smiled, a solution evolving in her mind at the same time that fondness and longing broke inside her. "To both," she said. "Yes, I believe in you. You who can destroy the old, broken ways and help me build them new. And yes"—she touched her mouth to his—"yes, I am yours."

His breath shuddered and his eyes locked on her mouth, sending a pulse of want through her body. "When do you have to go to the Council?"

"After breakfast," she said, shifting as he pushed his hips against hers, making his arousal known to her, "but we have to discuss my plans. We have to discuss the Circle, and—"

"Yes, yes to all of it," he mumbled before kissing her. A soft sound escaped her, and her body arched toward his.

"Makram," she sighed when he released the kiss, "you don't even know what I'm going to say."

"I trust you." He kissed her throat, brushing his lips across her skin. "And I want you. Right now. We can talk later." He reached a hand down and tugged her chemise up so he could stroke his hand over her hip and thigh. She closed her eyes and gave a playful, exasperated sigh and Makram responded by pinching her backside.

She squeaked in surprise and her eyes flew open.

"Beast," she giggled as he rose above her on all fours.

"Your beast." He grinned wickedly at her. "Yours."

Thirty-Five

A misty rain blotted the sun and sky when Naime met Bashir in the courtyard outside the Council Hall. He'd brought with him the six men he had chosen to be her escort when ceremony and exposure dictated she would need such. Lieutenant Terzi was one of them. They all bowed to her, Bashir's gaze touching on the belts she wore at her waist. One eyebrow cocked, and he adjusted his sword belt as he straightened, cutting his gaze to the Council Hall.

"They aren't going to like that," he said in a low rumble.

Naime ducked her head. Her father had not worn ceremonial House belts. It was a tradition from the Old Sultanate, and even if he had, she doubted he would have worn all six colors.

But today was the beginning of a new day, a new way of doing things. Or perhaps, more accurately, a return to the old way. Each belt was a thin silken rope tied over the silver embroidered cloth that wrapped her waist. Instead of tassels to decorate the ends, they hung heavy with stamped medallions bearing the sigil of each House, each cord dyed its respective House's color. White, blue, green, gold, red, and black.

Makram and Tareck joined them a few moments later. When they stopped, Makram's gaze slipped to her waist, to the six belts that swung heavily against her silver and white entari with each small movement she made. His expression mirrored Bashir's, but he said nothing.

"Did you not bring any other men? You're meant to look… commanding."

He lifted an eyebrow and spread his hands as he glanced down at himself. She pressed her lips together to stop her smile. He did look magnificent, to her eye, but this was neither the time, nor the place to say such a thing. Dressed from head to toe in unrelieved black, he appeared both regal and formidable, and every bit the dark and imposing death mage. Which was exactly how she needed him to look. For everyone else's benefit.

For hers, she preferred him as he had been that morning. There was something more than just sex in their nakedness, something vulnerable and sweet. Perhaps her gaze gave her away, because one corner of Makram's mouth perked up, his dark eyes holding hers.

"I can already tell this is going to be interesting," Ihsan said from behind Naime, as he strode up to join them. "Good morning," he said as he kissed her cheek. He ran his fingers across the colored belts and gave a heavy sigh as he met her gaze. "If we're lucky, the sight of these alone will give our Kadir a heart attack." His gaze flicked to Makram, down, up, and to his face. "Welcome back."

"Sehzade," Makram said. They didn't glare at each other, exactly, but the look they exchanged was tense, at best. They had only met in passing, after all. She'd have to give them a chance to get to know each other.

"It's Master, now," Ihsan corrected him.

Makram gripped his sword's hilt, making Naime realize the belt and sheath were not the usual, scarred and worn brown leather. They were black, marked with silver embellishments, the only adornment he wore besides the silver band that held his hair in its knot.

"Ah. So I've heard. I will probably keep the Sehzade, to antagonize your Grand Vizier."

Ihsan chuckled, and Naime thought perhaps their common ground would be in a common enemy.

"It's time," she said to Makram. "I'll send for you when I'm ready."

Makram rubbed a hand over his mouth and eyed the doors to the Council Hall, stepping back to make room.

Bashir nodded to his men and they surrounded Naime as Ihsan offered his arm. They walked into the Council Hall together, and the absence of her father felt more acute for Ihsan's company and the reminder of the same walk they had taken not so long ago. Her first time addressing the Council alone, when things had begun to go wrong.

Bashir shoved the doors to the hall open with such force they slammed against the walls, a sharp report in the cavernous space of the hall and foyer. The chatter of the Viziers ceased, and they all watched as Naime and Ihsan approached the dais. The guards and her six attendants, the number required of a ruler, formed the procession behind her.

Naime took note only of Kadir's face, which progressed through stages of surprise, confusion, and tension. When her guards took places to either side of the dais, and Ihsan sat, Kadir's attention fixed on the House belts she wore. His tension became a more palpable wariness, and she was pleased to have knocked him off-balance. Now, to keep him there.

The Sultans of Tamar had not worn House belts since the Sundering. Her choice to do so was silent declaration of her intentions, both to be Queen Sultana, and to stand the Circle, neither of which she had openly shared with her father's governors. Before the Sundering, the Sultan took council from the Circle of Chara'a, not his governors. The belts were threat to every man standing in the room before her.

She turned when she reached the bench, facing the room, and sat.

When the silence stretched on a beat too long, Naime gave Kadir a pointed look. He flinched as if surprised and tapped his staff to the floor. The Viziers sat. Esber Pasha elbowed the Vizier next to him, eyeing her and Kadir. The other nodded.

Kadir drew breath to speak, but Naime interrupted. "We are here to discuss the state of negotiations with Sarkum, my betrothal, and the Sehzade. Do you agree, Grand Vizier?" She kept her eyes on the room, not him.

He cleared his throat, bowed his head, and made a sound of agreement.

"Then let us begin. Sarkum is on the brink of civil war. I believe it is in our best interest to pick a side."

Yavuz Pasha's eyebrows rose. One of her guards shifted his feet, his head whipping around to look at her, but he corrected himself immediately, training his eyes forward.

"You told us you would not choose sides in a Sarkum war. To what end do you go against your word?" Kadir replied.

"I said I would not do so without good reason," she said, baiting her trap. Kadir sensed it, and held her gaze in silence until Yavuz Pasha finally spoke up.

"Please elaborate, Sultana."

She tugged her gaze from him to the doors and steadied her voice with a thread of magic. "I arrived in Sarkum to find that someone had sent a letter, and terms that were not my father's, to the Mirza in Sarkum."

Shock rippled through the room. Some weathered it in silence, but she heard a few exclamations of outrage. Yavuz Pasha's expression blackened, and the man to his right, Terim Pasha, gave a disbelieving laugh. That was one of the few times she'd seen the short, corpulent Vizier do anything more active than frown.

"Who?"

"I do not know, Yavuz Pasha. The documents were signed with my father's seal."

All eyes went to Kadir, whose face was the perfect picture of ire. Only the Sultan, his Grand Vizier, and the heir had access to the seal and the court calligrapher. Of course, Kadir had not used the calligrapher, who might have spoken against him.

"Are you accusing me of something, Sultana?"

"Of course not. I will accuse no one without proof. I am stating the facts of what I saw."

"Are they facts if there is no evidence? It could just be a story you've concocted," he said. The three Viziers who sat on the bench behind him, all of whom she knew to be firmly in his pocket, nodded sagely.

"That would only make sense if I intended to accuse someone, which I do not." She did not need to accuse him outright. The statement had sown suspicion, which would only grow stronger with each attempt he made to push the blame away. She could not topple him like a statue, with one great swing, but she could chip away at the base that supported him, the men who believed in him.

She said, "There remains a delicate situation though, which was created by Sarkum agreeing to false terms. I was offered in marriage to the Mirza."

Now the room broke out into full-volume protests. They wanted her married, a man on the Sultan's seat, but not an outsider. Not a Sarkum man. Naime held her face still, blank of emotion, though inside triumph flooded her. Only with monumental effort did she prevent herself a gloating look at Kadir. He had attempted to get her out of his way. Instead he had unintentionally handed her exactly what she needed to put herself in her father's place. An inescapable alternative they found even more abhorrent than the idea of a queen as ruler.

Naime waited for the noise to die down before she spoke again. "The Council is displeased?"

"Displeased? That is unacceptable! You do not intend to honor those terms, do you?" Yavuz Pasha asked and was echoed by many of the others.

"I may have no choice." Naime stood. When she gestured to Bashir, the Viziers looked as one toward the doors. Bashir's men pulled them open.

In the time since she had left him, Makram had been joined by eight of his men. He and Tareck entered the Council Hall surrounded by them, a miniature phalanx dressed in tones of grey and steel blue. All but Makram, whose onyx-colored clothes were the focus of every gaze in the room. Color was important in Tamar. It labeled a person indelibly with their House. Makram had never worn black, had been careful to keep to the greys his men wore.

He appeared at ease, confident and composed, as if he strode to a battle he was certain he would win, instead of through a gauntlet of political enemies. Naime's next breath came easier, unfurled in her belly and limbs more fully.

Their unexpected entrance shocked the Viziers enough to silence them for the moments it took Makram to approach the dais. When all his men, including Tareck, dropped to their knees before her, Makram did not. He bowed his head. That woke the Viziers from their silence, and though they broke into hushed chatters, Kadir stepped forward, surveying Makram, his black clothes, his sword, then the weapons carried by the others.

"Sultana," Kadir said without taking his gaze from Makram, "what is the meaning of this?"

"Gentlemen." Naime took her seat as Makram straightened and his men sat back on their heels. "This is about alliance. Kinus Rahal wishes to align with the Republic to end magic. The Republic's military is already a force we cannot hope to defeat. If Kinus gives them Sarkum and its military, which has far more knowledge of magic than the Republic does, they will be unstoppable. We would be better off surrendering."

The room echoed with disbelief, scoffing laughs and raised voices. Naime took note of those who did not speak up, who sat with their grave thoughts. Yavuz Pasha, Esber, Terim, and Yavuz' brother, who claimed the loyalty of the southern Viziers. They understood. So she spoke to them.

"There is an alternative." Naime waited for them to quiet. "The Agassi means to challenge his brother for the title of Mirza and the rulership of Sarkum. He is not interested in aligning with the Republic."

"He wants our help," Kadir announced in disdain. "And if we help, if we commit our magic and our sons to this foreign war, what do we gain?"

"Besides more power to hold off our inevitable destruction?" Yavuz Pasha asked. A few spoke in agreement with him, his younger brother and his comrades included.

"Have a care, my friend, that you do not sit for a half-told story," Kadir said. "We help put him on the throne of Sarkum, what guarantee do we have that he does not come for us next? A man who would usurp his own brother for power is not a man I trust in an alliance. What is the price?"

Naime nodded to Makram.

"The price is that which was offered to my brother by this Council. These terms, stamped with the Sultan's seal," he said, and held a hand down to Tareck, who unslung a carrying tube from his shoulders and handed it up.

Makram stepped closer to Kadir and handed him the tube. Kadir kept his gaze on Makram as he opened the case and withdrew the terms.

"Alliance by marriage," Kadir read, "the Sultana betrothed to the Mirza and resides in Al-Nimas. A regent rules in Tamar."

"Absolutely not!" Yavuz Pasha stood, his voice cracking through the room. Everyone agreed, loudly, and others stood as he did. Esber Pasha took a step away from his bench as if he meant to storm the dais.

Their agreement was an interesting and rare sight that made Naime smile. Many of them focused suspicious looks on Kadir. He had never meant for Naime to return from Al-Nimas. He had meant for her to go, to be forced into marriage or taken hostage, and to step in as Regent in her absence. Perhaps after murdering Ihsan. She shivered.

"The terms are otherwise the same that the Council legally signed before I departed for Sarkum. Mages dedicated to eradicating the crop Blight, the exchange of instructors and information by our Academy and your University. Our military to aid you."

"And those were barely acceptable. These are untenable," Yavuz Pasha said. "Grand Vizier, surely you agree?"

"We sit under rule of a regent now, Yavuz Pasha. How are these different?" Kadir rolled the terms and gave them a shake in the air.

"I have an alternative I would like to offer both the Agassi and the Council," Naime said. Kadir's mouth thinned, but he tipped his head to indicate she should continue.

"We will assist the Agassi in wresting control of Sarkum from the Mirza. Once he has taken the title of ruler from his brother, we will honor the alliance by marriage. When it is done, Sarkum will belong to Tamar."

"That is impossible, Sultana. The Sultan's seat has never been held by a foreigner." Kadir flicked his hand in dismissal.

"You do not understand, Grand Vizier," Makram replied. "I will cede rule of Sarkum to the Sultana and take the title of Prince Consort in Tamar."

Kadir turned his head slowly, his gaze fixing on Makram, his lips drawing back from his teeth. His hand tightened so hard on his staff that his knuckles washed of color. He would never have been able to foresee this. A chess piece that sacrificed itself.

Naime did not hide her smile this time.

"You are not a Tamar noble," Kadir enunciated carefully.

"He will be tomorrow, Grand Vizier," Naime said, using a gentle tone, not to calm him, but to mock him. "When I name him Sixth of the Circle."

Kadir whipped his head to look at her face, then the belts on her waist, then Makram once again. He recoiled, his expression twisting. Heat swelled around him, distorting the air. Other Viziers got to their feet, slowly, as if Makram were a lion whose notice they did not wish to draw.

Makram sighed, his gaze catching hers and a wry grin spreading over his mouth. They had not had much time to discuss this, the reaction of the Council to his magic. They'd been too busy with… other activities. She smiled back, using her magic to keep the heat from her skin.

"Sultana," Yavuz Pasha said, "please explain yourself. Is this man a destruction mage, a Charah?" Gold flashed along his cheeks, and the room rumbled with distant echoes as every earth mage readied himself.

Naime glanced at Bashir, who nodded. He was prepared to contain them.

"He is," Naime said. The room took a collective inhale, a pause, that feeling right before lightning arcs across the sky. Naime could not read their minds, but she could read their faces, their postures, their darting looks, the swirl of every power unleashed in the room.

"Have a care," Makram said, his voice deep with threat and magic, "that you do not attempt something you will regret." His men stood, turning as one to face the room, closing a circle around Makram.

"There will be no violence in this hall," Naime commanded. "I will remind the Council that this man has not once used his magic, not even when it would have saved him from injury and hardship. Do not show less restraint than he has and embarrass yourselves and my father."

"I will not hear another word of this. That man"—Esber Pasha pointed at Makram—"is a plague. If Sarkum is afflicted with a Blight, it was probably he who caused it!"

"Yes. I have decided to starve my own people while a conquering army gathers on my country's doorstep." Makram cast Esber Pasha a scathing look, and the rail-thin Vizier snapped his mouth closed.

"I will not allow a destruction mage anywhere near the throne of Tamar, consort or not," Kadir said. "And will absolutely not be party to giving him the autonomy of a place on a Circle. A Circle that does not even exist." Magic flared on his skin, flickering flames that seemed to originate in the red marrow of his bones. The other fire mages in the room took that as license to unleash their own powers. Ihsan stood, scarred face fixed in an expression of stone that barely hid the revulsion at the feel of the billowing heat.

When the tension in the room grew taut enough to snap, Makram questioned her with a look. She lifted her fingers in signal for him to wait. She had to be the one to quell them.

"You will not allow it?" Naime addressed the Grand Vizier. "Your job is to control this Council. To ensure their loyalty to the Sultan." She waited for a rise in the room's fluctuating strain. "You have failed."

The three men behind Kadir, minor governors of estates in the north, sat straighter in their seats, faces strained. Kadir's grip on the staff of his office tightened.

Naime narrowed her eyes. "Someone on this Council sent false terms to Sarkum. Because of that, I have been forced to negotiate to preserve the autonomy of Tamar. And because I can no longer trust my father's High Council, a Circle will stand." She kept her hands folded in front of her, instead of gripping handfuls of her clothes as reflex to hold her temper. "I am not standing the Circle to oppose the Council. They can and will work in tandem for the good of the people."

"You mean for what you decide is for the good of the people," one of the men behind Kadir accused.

"Yes," Naime said. "What I deem is right for the people, as advised by the Circle and the High Council."

"How do you intend to accomplish a full Circle?" Yavuz Pasha cut off what promised to be vile words from Kadir.

"There are no creation mages left, and no one has seen a Charah in generations," Esber Pasha added.

"There is a Charah before you now." She gestured to Makram. "And another resides in Narfour. That is two, I believe there must be others. A Circle will balance the Wheel, will give us power enough to stop the Republic taking everything from us."

"This man will bring plague and death and horror to Tamar!" Kadir barked.

Makram's hand twitched toward his sword. Tareck gripped his wrist, but all the Sarkum soldiers had already mirrored Makram's reflex. Hush and threat stretched, every man's eyes on Makram, magic crackling, half-leashed, through the room.

"This man"—Naime kept her voice calm, neutral of anger or of care—"saved my life, and the lives of every man and woman loyal to me, when we traveled to Sarkum. He has not harmed a soul in all the time he has spent with us, despite being threatened outright."

She cut her gaze to Kadir's then back to the room. "He has forsaken his home, and his brother, to stand in alliance with Tamar for the sake of the people of both our countries. And he is the only mage, at this moment, whose magic is not untethered. So tell me again, who in this room is a danger?"

Naime looked again at Kadir, whose fire licked and coiled around the staff he held, danced and flashed in his eyes.

The hush compressed, as Vizier turned to Vizier, as they considered Makram, considered her.

"Death comes to us all," Naime said crisply. "And can come to us all at the hands of any mage. Attaraya Agassi is a man and a mage as any other, as capable of greatness and folly as any of you. The Circle will bind him to the service of magic, of the people. Judge him by that service, not by accident of birth."

Makram bowed to her. Like a pin to a soap bubble, the action released the air and tension from the room.

At her nod, Makram stepped out of the circle of his guards and spoke. "I cannot agree to giving up all control of Sarkum. I have demanded the right to advise on its governance. The title of consort does not give me that power. The Circle of Chara'a does. It is as simple as that."

"It is not simple at all," Kadir said, words laced with fire.

"You do not like it, Grand Vizier, I understand. But that does not mean it isn't simple." Naime stood and stepped to the base of the dais. "A prince of Sarkum will sit on the throne, or I will."

"A son of Tamar must sit in the Sultan's seat." Kadir managed barely to rein in his fire. His restraint inspired the others in the room, and the crackle of magic receded.

"Whoever sent false terms to Sarkum has made that impossible," Naime countered. "I must honor my father's wish for an alliance with Sarkum, the Council's wish that I marry, and your demand that a foreigner not occupy the throne. Since Sarkum demands a bride, and the Council demands a Tamar noble, I will honor both by remaining on the throne."

She smiled, and Kadir tilted back a fraction, his eyes narrowing, lips pursed as he tried to follow her logic.

"The people will never accept a prince who has destruction magic, Efendim," Yavuz Pasha said, his words directed at her but his stare fixed on Makram as if he had just sprouted horns and a tail.

"I do not intend to marry him until after Sarkum has been secured. The people will have time to adjust," she said.

"A betrothal is all that is necessary to show good faith, for now," Makram added in a reasonable voice. "I have no wish to plunge Tamar into rebellion before I have even unseated my brother."

"This Council has say over what happens in Tamar, Sultana." Kadir's voice had steadied. "You cannot simply dismiss our concerns."

Naime interjected, before he could utter another word. "Give me the person or persons responsible for the terms that were sent to Sarkum, Grand Vizier, and perhaps I will reconsider this situation."

Kadir's eyes glittered with malice, though his mouth was set in a thin smile. Naime smiled back.

"I am afraid I cannot, Sultana," he said. If only Makram or his spy had been able to retrieve the letter with Kadir's handwriting, she could be rid of him for good. But he had not had time to comb his brother's palace for evidence against Kadir, and his spy had only been able to find the false terms before fleeing to safety.

"Then the decision is made, Grand Vizier. The Council will meet with me tomorrow to name the Agassi as Sixth of the Circle." She retook her seat.

The air rippled around her, Kadir's magic breaking free under the incendiary heat of his temper. Naime continued to smile, folding her hands in her lap, crossing one foot over the other, and leaning slightly toward him.

"I believe you wished to discuss the matter of my cousin." She indicated Ihsan, who was doing his best to remain quiet and uninteresting. Kadir's focus moved from her to Ihsan, and Naime could almost see the thoughts in his head, whirling, twisting, as he tried to think of something to turn in his favor.

"The Council believes he should be removed from the line of succession."

"He is the only son of the Elder Sehzade, and the last male heir who carries the Sabri name. I suggest"—Naime glanced at Ihsan then away when she saw only bitterness in his gaze—"he be allowed to remain in the name of the children he would father to carry on my father's line." She knew Ihsan was vehemently against the idea of marriage or children, for the same reason she had been. He was uninterested in being the ladder someone climbed to higher status.

"There is no guarantee he will father children," Kadir said, some private amusement turning his angry smile into a humored one. Ihsan was well known for his disinterest in women at court. He had attempted a few times, but wanted nothing to do with politics, and the few who shared his disinterest were unable to breach the walls of ice and bitterness around the warm heart he hid away.

"What if I gave you a guarantee he would marry by the end of this Great Turn, to a noblewoman?"

Sounds of interest came from the Council. Naime glanced at Ihsan, in time to see him grimace and hide it by ducking his head to stare at the floor. He pinched the bridge of his nose. She would have to apologize later, for inflicting on him something she had struggled so desperately to prevent for herself. But better this than him lose everything.

The Viziers were interested because many of them had eligible daughters, or at least considered them so. Many had already attempted to gain favor with Ihsan and failed. She was grateful, in some measure, for the distraction of Ihsan from the subject of Makram and his magic.

Kadir lifted a hand to his brow, pressing his fingers slowly toward his hairline as the others talked. Finally, he tapped his staff against the floor and waited for silence.

"We will give you until the end of water's turn. The Council will bring candidates to you."

That was only until the end of spring to find a way to prevent Ihsan from being stripped of his nobility and everything he owned or cared for, and her deprived of a powerful ally.

Naime did not allow her dismay to show on her face, only smiled and ducked her head in agreement. Ihsan sighed. There was no anger in his face, only resignation. Another blow dealt him by the Wheel.

"Very well." Naime stood. "I believe that concludes the Council's business for today. We will reconvene tomorrow, in the Hall of Chara'a, just before sunset." That was the Sixth House's time. Dusk. While the books she had on the subject had little in the way of ritual, she had gleaned bits as she read. And it simply felt right to bind a mage to the Circle when their House was at its strongest. Fortuitous that it was also the first half of winter, the season of the Sixth House as well. A powerful omen, if one believed in such things.

Makram strode forward as she descended the steps of the dais. But who needed omens and portents when they had reason, and logic? Or when one had the most powerful destruction mage in the world at her side…

Naime slipped her arm into his. Kadir appeared as if he were trying to swallow something bitter and failed.

"Tomorrow then, Grand Vizier?"

"As you wish, Efendim." He bowed to her.

Ihsan rose and fell in behind them, followed by her guards and attendants. The other Viziers bowed as she walked, though their gazes remained fixed on Makram.

Her hand squeezed his arm too tightly, and her jaw was stiff. Each step she took she waited for someone to shout out for her to stop, for chaos to unfold. But there was none. If she kept moving forward, one step at a time, perhaps she could drag them with her into a future that shined bright in her imaginings.

When they stepped into the foyer, where daylight streamed in through the doors ahead, she drew a deep breath. Her body felt lighter and her head clearer. She glanced up at Makram, who fought back a pleased smile.

Neither of them said anything but continued walking until they reached her rooms. Ihsan crossed the sitting area to flop onto a couch with a groan, tipping his head against the back and staring at the ceiling. Bashir dismissed his guards, and Tareck did the same for Makram's men.

Naime felt like bursting into laughter. Not because anything was funny, but to release the upwelling of energy and nervousness, turns' worth of tension. When she moved to slide her arm free of Makram's, he took her wrist and spun her against him, one hand circling the back of her neck as he bent to kiss her.

Samira gasped and hurriedly pushed the doors closed. Naime fisted handfuls of Makram's shirt to keep her balance at the ferocity of his kiss, and slapped his chest when he pulled back, glaring up at him. Her stare lacked heat, because it had all gone into her cheeks and neck.

"Your Grand Vizier once called you the best and the brightest," he said, apparently unconcerned with all the eyes watching them, "but I do not think he realized how right he was until today."

"Shall the rest of us leave?" Ihsan suggested dryly.

"No," Naime said, sliding a quick look at Makram. "I believe the Agassi was simply overtaken by emotion."

"Prince Consort," Makram corrected. She cast him an irritated simper, though in truth she warmed at the title. He knew. He winked at her, moving to take a seat on the couch across from Ihsan. The two men eyed each other in silence.

"You were amazing," Samira said in her ear, then held her arms open, shyly. Naime hugged her. "My queen," Samira said as they separated.

"This is only the beginning," Naime said to them, the people she trusted most in the world, "and perhaps the easiest battle of those to come." She nodded to Bashir. Warm golden magic flared in his eyes as he cast a dampening to protect their conversation from anyone who might try to listen. Tareck watched him with envy.

"Elder Attiyeh has begun gathering those who would support me in the Elder Council and the army," Makram said. "I will have to return when he sends word."

Naime clasped her hands and nodded, avoiding his gaze so she could maintain her unperturbed facade. It had been easy to pretend, when they had been lying together that morning, that everything was right with the world and war was not looming. It was easy to pretend she would not have to be parted from him, not have to worry she might never see him again.

"Word will spread about a destruction mage residing at the palace. I expect that to be met with resistance. Commander Ayan, I want you to work with Captain Akkas and the City Watch to maintain order," Naime said.

Bashir ducked his head in acknowledgment.

"Captain Habaal, I would like you and those men you have with you to assist Commander Ayan in determining a location for a refugee camp."

Tareck nodded.

"I want a contingent sent to the Engeli Gate and set measures in place for anyone fleeing Sarkum."

"Yes, Efendim." Bashir tapped an open hand over his heart.

"Samira, have the Hall of Chara'a prepared for the ceremony tomorrow."

"Yes, Sultana." Samira bowed.

"And me?" Ihsan asked. "Shall I hang a sign about my neck and take a stroll through the market?"

Makram snorted and tried to cover it by wiping a hand over his mouth.

"San," Naime said, sitting next to him. "I have a plan."

"I have no doubt," he replied and appraised her from the corners of his eyes. "Please tell me it does not include that damned woman."

"What other choice do we have? She is the best of them. If we allow Kadir and the Council to choose, you will be married off to one of their grasping daughters or a fire mage."

"Fire and water," Ihsan cursed, tipping his head back once again and covering his eyes with his hand.

"Who might that 'damned woman' be?" Makram asked. Naime censored him with a look and he huffed, leaning back and propping one foot against the opposite knee. He flicked his gaze to the window and the barren garden beyond.

"Amara Mutar," Naime answered, putting her hand on Ihsan's knee, "a merchant who has been interested in marrying Ihsan for Turns. She is the Charah of the Second House."

Makram took a breath as if he meant to speak, his brow notching. He had believed himself alone in the world. The only Charah. What an interesting pair they would be, a woman determined to rise and a prince who willingly fell. "Will I meet her?"

Naime did not have a chance to answer him because Ihsan spoke.

"You forgot the part about her not being noble born," he said, a little flare of hope in his hazel eyes.

"And you forgot she is completely self-made, uninterested in your money, and undeterred by your reclusiveness."

"It is impossible to forget those things," Ihsan grumbled.

"And, she will be a noble when I name her to the Circle."

"She has refused the Circle." But then his eyes widened and he dropped his head into his hand. "Spokes. You're going to use me to bribe her."

"She is the only one I would trust, San. She is a good person."

"Let's talk about this later." He stood abruptly. "I'm certain you and your intended have more important matters to attend to." Ihsan strode to the doors, lifting a hand in farewell as he left. Naime sighed when the doors slammed shut. Samira jumped in surprise, raising her eyebrows at Naime.

"Perhaps that is enough planning for today. The rest of you can go about your tasks," Naime said. Bashir released his spell, and Naime's ears popped as it fell away. Samira bowed, pulling the doors open again.

"Lets you and I have a chat, young pup," Tareck said to Bashir, who flashed his teeth in a grin as they left side by side. Samira followed, closing the doors behind them.

Makram said nothing as Naime stood and skirted the table to stand before him. Her heart hammered as if it were the first time she had ever been alone with him. Makram lowered his crossed leg to the floor and reached for her. She thought he meant to take her hand, but instead he pulled the belts loose from her waist and stretched all six between his hands, examining the sigils that hung at the ends.

He withdrew the black cord and tossed the others over the back of the couch.

Naime gave a cry of protest, but he leaned forward and held her wrists, tugging her forward. She collapsed beside him, one knee bent beneath her. He draped the black cord around her neck and tapped it with a finger.

"This is the only one of those colors you're allowed to like," he said.

Naime laughed. "Oh?" she teased. He nodded gravely, then stroked his fingers over her temple and hair.

"Tell me about this ceremony tomorrow."

"Unfortunately, I can tell you little, as it will be the first time I have performed it. Your magic should instinctually bind to the Circle. You will be asked in what manner you wish to serve. So, think about it." She straightened one of the braided buttons of his entari and lifted her eyes to his.

"Naime," he said, holding her chin and pressing his brow to hers. He took a deep breath and exhaled slowly. "I love you."

Her body constricted, as if squeezed, then relaxed, relief swelling inside her. All she could do was nod as words failed her. She could hardly breathe, let alone speak.

His eyes opened and he drew back, waiting. Tension drew lines on his face.

Naime forced herself to inhale a breath. "Yes," she said. "I love you. You cannot tell? I did name you my consort."

"I hoped, but"—he brushed his hand down her cheek—"even for me you are difficult to read. Remember you must tell me. Often." His beautiful, coffee eyes crinkled at the corners. "At least twice a day."

"Anything you want." She smiled, fighting back the bite of tears and the lump in her throat.

"Anything?" he asked, hopefully, a grin teasing the corners of his mouth.

Thirty-six

Makram walked beside Bashir toward the far north end of the palace. They were headed for the circular structure that dominated the palace's architecture. Its dome and six twisting spires were visible from the path down from the Kalspire and the depths of the city. The palace was always busy, but today there were more nobles and their families moving about the grounds. Curious stares followed him everywhere he went. Since they were curious and not frightened, he suspected the interest lay in news that he was to be Naime's betrothed, not that he was a destruction mage. Perhaps that detail had not yet spread.

He could not suppress a surge of joy and pride every time he thought the word betrothed, and this time it manifested as a grin, which he hid from Bashir by ducking his head. The commander had proven to be obedient and capable, and Makram could see from just their few interactions that his men respected and liked him, despite that he was a man of few words.

Naime did have a knack for surrounding herself with good people. Yet another trait his brother had not shared.

Regret pierced his chest. Kinus. War was not what Makram wanted. He wanted to reason with him. He wanted there to be another solution. But there could not be. To escape the men Kinus had sent after him when he left the prisons, Makram had been forced to collapse almost an entire wing of the palace in Al-Nimas. Thankfully the harem was empty when Makram reduced it to rubble. There was no reason left in his brother.

"May I ask you a question, Agassi?" Bashir said, his rumbling voice so reflective of his House it was almost comical.

"Always," Makram said.

Bashir paused in surprise. After a few more steps he said, "Your magic…it cannot accidentally harm her, can it?"

"Of course it can. Just like yours can accidentally collapse a house on innocents. Would you ever do that?"

"No."

"And you may rest assured I will stop my own heart before I ever allow my magic to hurt her. I own my magic, it does not own me."

Bashir gave a sound of acceptance. That would not be the last time he was questioned about his magic in Tamar, but it was likely to be the most easily accepted answer he would ever give. Bashir did not strike him as a man prone to paranoia. Makram lifted a hand and clasped the commander's shoulder. Bashir seemed surprised but said nothing.

They turned into a wide hall, with arched windows along both walls and carpets laid down the length. Crowds of palace dwellers had gathered to either side, and their conversations and musings filled the space with noise. Makram held his hands behind his back, checking behind for Tareck, who walked in loose formation with his men.

At the end of the hall two enormous doors stood open. They were wooden, lattice like honeycomb, so even when closed he would have been able to see the room beyond. Makram stopped to admire them, and to give himself time to consider the moment.

Tareck stopped at Makram's right side, looking up at the frescoed ceiling and the doors, which were the height of three men at least. He lifted a hand and stuffed something into his mouth.

"Are you eating?"

Tareck looked at him sidelong, chewing. He swallowed. "Do you know they've prepared a feast?"

"Checking on the quality, were you?" Makram could not decide if he was amused or appalled.

Tareck swiped his hands together to dislodge crumbs. “Samira obliged me in my inspection. They’ve made a tower of baklava into the shape of a swan,” he said. “Missing a beak though.”

“Was it always missing a beak?” Makram sighed.

“I wanted to make certain the food was up to the standards of a Sarkum prince. Now, are you ready?” He wiped a tenacious flake of pastry off on his caftan.

“For what?”

“Does it not feel like the last time you will be the man you are now?” Tareck rarely dabbled in philosophy. He preferred parables. Perhaps he had been inspired by the baklava.

Makram tugged at the top button of his entari. “You compared the man I am now to a beaten dog.”

Tareck scratched at his freshly shaven jaw. “I have no idea what you mean.”

“Of course you don’t,” Makram said. He adjusted his sword against his hip and strode forward.

The doors were dwarfed by the room beyond. Circular, it stretched on for hundreds of paces. Sandstone and marble tiles alternated on the floor to create the flowing pattern of the Wheel, each spoke ending in a wedge of colorful stone—white marble for air, turquoise for water, malachite for creation, yellow jasper for earth, red agate for fire, and obsidian for destruction. In the center of the Wheel lay more white marble, depicting a sun with curved rays that formed the boundaries between the Houses. Makram had never seen an illustration of the Wheel like this one.

The domed ceiling seemed to soar leagues above them, and windows circled the room, opening to views of the sea, the city, and the mountains. The moment Makram stepped across the threshold of the room, he had a sense of time. The ancient history of the room pressed inward, the echoes of the hands that had built it, of the magic that pulsed around him. Voices whispered, but not the gathered Viziers, who sat in risers circling the mosaic of the Wheel. They were silent, as weighed down by the gravity of the place as he felt.

Instead he heard magic, whispering as it did when he was in flux. Voices of the past, of mages who had walked before, magic linking them across time, through him.

Naime stood in the middle of the Wheel, in the center of the white marble sun depicted as the hub. Her father and Ihsan sat in the risers near their House spokes, and as Makram glanced around he noted the Viziers did as well. Bashir left his side, indicating to Tareck to follow him to the Fourth House spoke. Earth.

Those few of his men who possessed magic followed suit, moving to seats that rose away from each spoke. The five who did not have magic found places near the door.

The risers near the Sixth House spoke and its black glass wedge were empty. Makram walked toward it as if towed there. Loneliness filled him with its heavy despair. How could he live in a place where he was alone? How could he serve a people who wanted his magic gone from the world?

He stepped onto the obsidian, and was shocked to realize it was one piece, not tiles.

"Welcome to the Hall of Chara'a," Naime said, her voice pitched softly. It carried anyway, filling the vast space with its echo. "This hall," she said as he continued to the center of the spoke, "was built by the First Circle, and everything from the stones of the floor to the skeleton of the building are imbued with their magic. After it was created, enchantment of objects was outlawed in the Old Sultanate."

"Why?" Makram looked at his boots, or rather, the reflection of himself in the obsidian below them. It was like peering into infinity, into oblivion. He looked at Naime instead, his stomach twisting.

"Spells draw power from their caster," she said. "Items imbued with spells draw the lifeforce of those they come in contact with. They are dangerous and uncontrollable—as the Chara'a who built this hall learned. Many lives were lost in its construction."

She stepped aside, revealing something covered by a cloth with a much simpler depiction of the Wheel embroidered upon it. Horror became awe as Makram surveyed the building again, and the feeling like he was being watched, measured, weighed felt even more real to him.

"Today," Naime announced as she pulled the cloth free, "we are here to begin the Circle anew."

Samira hurried forward to take the cloth, exchanging it for an orb. At first Makram thought it was a mage orb, but those were ephemeral, made of nothing but light. This was heavy, judging from the way Samira and Naime handled it. Stone, perhaps. Not opaque like marble, but hinting at translucence. Moonstone maybe. He had not studied much about the use of artifacts in magic, nor had he seen any used. He did know that stones could hold magic, but it was attuned to its associated House. Obsidian could hold the spell to take a life, but it could not hold a spell to start a fire. Moonstone was not associated with any House, that he knew of.

The cloth Naime removed had covered a scepter set in a socket in the center of the hub. The scepter was empty—six twisted, reaching fingers of carved wood holding nothing. Naime set the milky, opalescent orb into the scepter's grasp.

"If no one objects, I will begin." Her sweeping gaze rested longest on her father before it cut to Kadir. Kadir wore a speculative expression, his gaze flicking from the Sultana to the stone cradled by the scepter, which sat at her waist level.

"Do you even know what will happen when you attempt this?" he asked, and Makram could have sworn concern passed over the man's face.

"Only what has been written. But the binding has been performed many times through history, and I believe it to be safe. Father, by your leave?" She deferred to her father, who nodded. Makram imagined he could see the man fighting back something, some other memory or person who wanted his mind. He gave a sharp, stiff nod when she faced him once more.

"Is this a danger to you?" he asked as he eyed the stone. It appeared innocuous enough.

"The First Circle bound the magic in this room. We are safe." She gave him a reassuring smile. "This requires you untether your magic," she said, releasing her hold on herself as she did.

Light spilled forth, from her eyes, her skin, shining through her pale clothes and filling the dusk-lit room with winter sun. The people in the chamber chattered excitedly, the same awe in their voices that squeezed his heart. He stared a beat too long it would seem, because even with the light of the sun obscuring her eyes he could see the irritation on her face.

Makram released his power. Wisps of inky smoke and tongues of black flame answered her outpouring of light, and the whispers of awe turned blacker, and louder, into fear. Makram heard it, and felt it, and the tension made his body a coiled spring, ready to run or attack the moment he had to.

"There will be silence, and peace in this room," Naime commanded. "This is a sacred place of balance and harmony." The words struck the walls and reverberated. The voices stopped, but for one.

"That's my girl," her father said, at full volume. Naime sighed softly, and Makram suppressed a smile.

"Makram Attaraya Al-Nimas, Agassi of the combined forces of Sarkum and Tamar, named Prince Consort, Charah of the Sixth House"—she pulled the scepter free of its socket and approached him—"to be bound to the Circle, you must choose the manner in which you will serve it."

"How do I do that?" He had tried to think of something, after she'd told him, but had no idea what she had meant. Naime fit the butt of the scepter into a small pocket in the stone, at the seam between the obsidian and the marble tiles.

"It is your choice, what is in your heart," she said. "Place your hands on the moonstone. It is conduit to the magic of this place."

As she said it she laid her hands over the top. Makram followed her lead, laying his hands on the stone, but curving his thumbs over her fingers. For a transient moment, his eyes met hers, void and sun colliding, before the tiny, twisting, searching pull in his gut, the one that had begun the first time he'd read the Book of Chara'a, engulfed him.

He was tugged from his body, or into his mind, he only knew a feeling like falling, momentum without sound or sight, tumbling through void. When it seemed to stop he was neither standing nor floating. He existed in this place not as a body, but as thought, or something else. He could not feel Naime's touch anymore, or sense her near him. He was alone. Again.

"Alone?"

The voice that whispered was his own, and thousands of others. Makram tried to look around, but he had no eyes, only awareness. And that awareness expanded, and before him lay a line of shadows, which rose and stood, one after the other, stretching back until they faded into the blacker shadow of the void.

They were shaped like people.

The first figure moved, shadowed arms breaking free of the greater darkness of its body, taking up a fighter's stance, and drawing a sword of void and night. The next did the same, and the next, and on down the line. Makram realized every figure was him, not his face, or his body, but his power. Understanding struck him, realization that would have stolen his breath if he needed to breathe in this place.

As he realized, a corona of light colored the edge of the void, and points of light winked into existence all around him. Mages. Destruction mages. Each one a beating heart, a thrum of magic. A brother, or a sister. And the shadows of himself were not reflections, but history.

He was not alone, could never be alone. His magic was not his tool, but an entity that had existed before man walked the world and would continue on long after he died. He was a link to all those born of the Sixth House, their tie to the Wheel, sustainer and sustained by them.

The shadow nearest him became his true reflection, its features blurred by shadow, its eyes black void. That void was a mirror the same as the obsidian glass he stood upon. Reflected back to him were all the Sixth House Chara'a who had come before. Their magic the sword that defined the end and carved the beginning, conflict that shaped peace, destruction that birthed creation, the dark before the dawn, the ruin of things broken, destroyer.

His reflection gave a sharp nod and was gone.

Makram blinked. He stood on the obsidian floor once more, his magic bleeding into the air around him. The black glass glowed with shadow, lines of it pulsing across the floor, outlining the entire spoke depicted beneath his feet, toward the heart of the marble sun in the center of the room.

"I serve by the sword," Makram said, because that is what he was. What his magic was. That little twist of longing, that searching feeling in his gut unwound, and reached.

Naime gave a sharp gasp and jerked as if struck, her eyes widening. Her light dimmed then brightened until Makram could not look at her, until the entire room was filled with the aura of her power and even the Viziers exclaimed in surprise.

When she spoke, her voice sounded hollow, like a chant, not like her voice at all. "So be it, Sword of the Circle. You are bound to its service, from this day, until your last."

The moonstone warmed beneath his hands, and the magic that had leached away through the floor rushed back to him. It sang with new awareness, those points of light that had been in his mind, other mages of the Sixth House, still there, in his periphery, giving and taking from the font of his power. Awake and alive.

"Welcome home, mage of the Sixth House." Naime had wound her magic into her mental grip and her brown eyes were warm and glittering with held tears.

He smiled, his own throat tightening, his chest constricting. He could feel it, a thread like spider silk, stretched between him and her. She was the center around which he spun, and would, for the rest of his life.

Makram lowered his hands to his sides. Bashir and his men, as well as Makram's, had dropped to their knees, hands spread before them in reverence. Some of the Viziers Makram recognized—Yavuz, Esber, Terim—seemed interested in what they had seen, unafraid. But they had shown themselves to be somewhat more reasonable than their comrades. In general, the Viziers who sat in the Fifth House spoke, with Kadir at their head, looked like a gallery of chastised urchins. Faces pinched, fists balled, glancing at each other in shared discontent.

"Did you see what I saw? Did you feel anything?" Makram asked Naime in a hushed tone.

"What did you see?" She appeared concerned. "I saw only that you touched the stone and claimed the sword."

When he hesitated, she lifted the scepter and carried it to the center of the hub. The stone glowed. Faintly, but there had been no glow before she'd named him to the Circle. Perhaps he should read more of what she had, so he might understand better what he had just blindly agreed to do.

Makram rubbed the back of his neck as she moved back to him.

"I saw…" He shook his head. "I think I saw the entire spoke. The Sixth House. I can…feel the others. All of them."

"Then it worked," Naime said, her mask-like facade cracking just enough for fervor to gleam in her eyes. "Chara'a are supposed to strengthen their House by their simple existence."

"You have strengthened the Sixth House before you even know if the others exist?" Kadir stood. "Who will stand against him if he decides to turn his power on us?"

"They exist," Naime said. "You yourself have met Mistress Mutar. And the others…I know they exist. I can feel it." She pressed a hand over her middle. Makram walked to stand just behind her shoulder, and the closer he got to the moonstone the more a sound like a song, like tinkling bells, filled his awareness.

"You can feel it?" Kadir scoffed. "Are we to trust a woman's intuition to guide us?"

"You are to trust…" the Sultan said, standing slowly. He wove in place but Ihsan rose beside him and steadied him with a hand on his shoulder. "You are to trust the edict of your queen."

Makram recognized the desperate, hurried way her father spoke, holding onto his moment of clarity with mental claws. He could feel the creeping destruction in the man's mind. Could he hold it? Even for a moment? Mathei Attiyeh had dabbled in such things, using destruction for healing, focusing his study on poisons.

"Sultan Efendim." Makram strode forward, dropping to his knees and bowing his head. "The magic of the Sixth House can do so much more than you believe. Will you allow me an opportunity to demonstrate?"

Viziers leapt to their feet.

"You will not unleash your magic on the Sultan of Tamar." Kadir started toward them, real fear evident in his face.

"Be still," the Sultan sighed, "be still, Behram." He lifted a hand, and Kadir stopped halfway between his seat and the Sultan's, his staff held before him like a weapon he meant to bludgeon Makram with.

Makram sat back on his heels.

"What are you going to do?" the Sultan asked him.

He pointed toward the Sultan's head. "I can feel what's happening in you, Sultan Efendim. I can hold it back, for a short time. Though I cannot cure it," he warned.

The Sultan sat and nodded.

Makram closed his eyes, dropping into the core of his power, the twisting void. The sounds of the room fell away, and he sought for and found the faint echo of destruction in the Sultan's mind. Makram followed it with tendrils of magic. Plaque like barnacles bloomed across the man's brain. And in the sight of his power, it shone deeper black, bruised shadow that prevented the uninterrupted flow of thought and self. Makram chipped away at it with destruction honed to a point. The damage could not be undone, but what he cleared would allow the Sultan command of his own mind, until the strange plaque reclaimed it.

Makram opened his eyes.

The Sultan stared back, clear-eyed and thoughtful. He took a deep breath, as though he had been unable to for a long time. Then he raised a single, salted brow. "I heard her call you Prince Consort. Was anyone going to ask me first?" he said, dry humor coloring his voice.

Makram suppressed a laugh, glad he was kneeling, because the working had left him dizzy. "You were indisposed, Efendim."

Naime uttered a warning, but the Sultan laughed, the sound booming through the chamber. His laughter riveted the Viziers, indicating this was a sound they had not heard in some time.

"Fair enough," the Sultan said. "Let me dispense with this before I am indisposed again." He clapped his hands to his knees and rose to his feet. Naime made a sound and moved as if to run to him. He waved her off. "I'm too old to care what these think, anymore." He waved at the Viziers arrayed around the room. Kadir bore the lone expression of fury. Everyone else seemed nonplussed by the declaration.

"Today, in this place, with my Council and generations of Chara'a as my witness, I command that when I am gone, my daughter will take my place. Queen Sultana."

Naime inhaled sharply, and her fingers curled together in front of her entari as she stared at her father. *Yes*. Thank the Wheel. The Sultan nodded to him, gratitude making his expression grave. Makram regretted he could not have known the man before his decline.

"Marry her, serve her. Protect her. She knows what is right, you keep everyone out of her way so she can accomplish it."

"Sultanim," Naime protested.

He held a hand up toward her. "Well?" he asked Makram.

"Ask, and I am commanded, Efendim." Makram ducked his head. He didn't need a Sultan to tell him that.

"And argue with her sometimes."

Naime sighed, and Makram repressed a laugh. "I will try," he said.

"Then so be it. Grand Vizier, you may mark down my blessing."

"As you wish, Efendim," Kadir said, bowing as he did. For once his face was as unreadable as Naime's normally was, but Makram could feel the heat of his discontent, the blistering inferno of his thoughts and schemes. He was not silenced, only stalled.

Makram stood and the Sultan offered his hand. He hesitated, then clasped the Sultan's forearm and was gripped in return. Makram faced Naime.

"In the future, Attaraya Charah, you will remember that Chara'a stand outside the hierarchy of the nobility. They belong to the people, and owe fealty to no one but those same," Naime announced.

The Viziers protested, those near Kadir were the loudest, but she ignored them.

"We bow to you," Naime said. She bowed. The room sat charged with surprise and silence. "All bow to you."

Everyone else followed her next bow with their own. Bowing to a mage of the Sixth House. The Tamar Sultans must be spinning in their tombs.

"It's Rahal," Makram said, taking the final step toward a destiny he could never have guessed at. "The crown prince of Sarkum has always borne the name Rahal."

"Rahal Charah." Naime's eyes reflected her understanding of the gravity of his decision, and that was all he needed. He flicked his gaze to Tareck, who gave a single, approving nod, though Makram had never seen his friend's face so alive with fervor.

"We are finished for today," Naime said.

The Viziers stood and made their way toward the doors. Some paused to chat with each other. Naime looked past Makram, shyly, toward her father. He spread his arms, and Makram imagined in his younger Turns he might have resembled a bear. Naime rushed to his embrace. Makram looked away from them, to afford them some modicum of privacy. He saw Tareck take Samira's arm, gesturing enthusiastically. There was a baklava swan that needed his attention.

Yavuz, Esber, and Terim approached Makram and bowed.

"Rahal Charah." Yavuz offered his hand. Makram shook it, watching for the man to flinch or recoil. If he wanted to, he curbed the urge, only continuing to smile what Makram loosely interpreted as a welcome.

"Terim Pasha." The short Vizier thrust out a pudgy hand. Makram gripped it.

"I am Esber Pasha," Esber said, offering the same bow and handshake. "You are not what I expected of a death mage. You seem human."

Makram's brows drew together. Yavuz Pasha set a heavy hand on his comrade's shoulder and steered him away with a click of his tongue.

Makram did not recognize Cemil Kadir until he was standing in front of him, his hand outstretched. The fire mage wore a smug half smile.

"I think I'd rather not." Makram nodded to Cemil's outstretched hand. Cemil lowered it.

"Perhaps we'll have a better-matched spar sometime. One where you aren't hobbled."

"I don't think you would like that, little Kadir," Makram warned. Cemil only continued to smile, lifting his fingers to touch his brow, then strode away.

"Don't taunt him," Naime warned as she moved to Makram's side. "He is every bit his father's son."

"I can handle myself. Are you ready to leave this place? It makes my skin crawl. Like the walls are watching me."

She gave a soft smile. "If you wish." Her gaze followed the Viziers as they made for the door, then went to the moonstone where it glowed gently in the grasp of the scepter.

"Something troubles you?" he asked. He wanted to pull her to him, to drape an arm over her shoulders or hug her, but this was not the place.

"No. Something finally makes sense." She pointed to the spoke of the First House on the floor. "I thought to stand the Circle I would need to start at the beginning. With the First House."

"But it's random?"

"Not in the least. I had to start at the end." Her point traveled to indicate the Sixth House spoke. "I had to start by destroying what came before, to make room for a new way. A new Circle."

She smiled, and his entire world contracted, to her. To his center. His new and only lodestone. "I could have started with no one but you."

"I see," he said, and lifted her hand to his lips. "So, my queen. Shall we begin?"

Thank you for reading!

If you enjoyed this book, you can continue on in the series, follow me on social media, and sign up for my newsletter (for fun FREEBIES!) here:

Acknowledgments

DESPITE THE GLORY HEAPED upon authors (queue internal laughter), a book is not a solitary endeavor. I did not sit down at my lovely desk overlooking a pond and trees in beautiful fall colors and knock this thing out over days filled with tea and silence, attended to by an unobtrusive maid. I desperately tapped it out in the pockets of time bought for me by my amazing husband, who whisked our child away for hours or days at a time in between his own work hours and never flinched, complained, or mentioned his lack of sleep or absentee wife. It was possible because of my parents, who also took the child, or sometimes washed our dishes, cooked our meals, did our laundry or otherwise cared for me as if I were unable to do these things (I was, because I was Consumed by Naime and Makram). It came about because my sister, also an author, believed in me when I could not believe in myself, who was cheerleader for each advancement I made, each time I suggested I might be ready to try and publish—who championed self-publishing and lit the way. She was alpha and beta, critique partner and friend, shoulder to cry on and the one to slap me around when I wallowed too long.

I brought this thing, this heap of words and ideas, to Michelle Morgan to edit into something resembling a cohesive story. Not only is she competent and amazing, she is also a lovely person who saw exactly what I wanted this to be and showed me how. She was patient with my ceaseless questions and concerns, and cared for this, my first ugly book baby, as her own. She did not just make this into a better book, she made me into a better writer—I hope. I will always be grateful to her and consider her just as much a friend as an editor.

Tatiana Anor is unbelievably talented, in both fine art and photography, and I was stupidly lucky to stumble upon her work and that she was willing to commit to six book covers for someone she had never heard of. She brought Naime and Makram to life so vividly that I am still reeling.

Eric C. Wilder took artwork and made it into the most beautiful (I am totally not biased) book cover I have ever seen, managed to take all my random, disparate ideas and turn them into something cohesive and stunning, and has the patience of a saint, I might add.

Terry Roy makes books beautiful. This could have been just a bunch of words piled on the page under Arial Font chapter headers. But it is not, thanks to her hard work and artistic knack.

Storm & Shield

SNEAK PEEK

NOW THEY WERE TRAPPED and miserable, someone wanted to kill them, and Aysel was stuck spending her time convincing that bonehead pack of useless ruffians that she should be allowed to do something about it. And their double-boneheaded, infuriating commander. Her mouth curved in a smile as she picked at the drying mud on the toe of her boot.

"Are you in there?" Bashir's gruff voice immediately set her on edge in the best and worst of ways. She got up and slapped one of the canvas pieces aside.

"I was just thinking about you," Aysel said. He raised an eyebrow and tossed a bundle of something at her. Aysel caught it, barely, and glared at him. It was her swords and harness.

"Should I be flattered?" he asked.

"Not at all. And I think you must have wanted to be an errand boy and fell into being a guard by accident," she said, shaking her swords at him. "This is the second delivery you've made for me, your most-wanted criminal."

"I'm the only person available to take this watch on you. Still sour?"

"I don't know why I would be." She arranged the harness and swords on another crate she'd set by the firepit. "The welcome here has been nothing but warm and lavish."

"Did you expect something different? Even if you weren't a criminal, you are a noble from Sarkum," he said.

Aysel crouched by the fire and began to poke at it with a stick that had been propped on the rocks that formed its edge.

"How am I a criminal? I took back my own belongings and rounded up a murderer for you. In Al-Nimas, my brother and I were the right and left hand of a prince," she said. "My father was an adviser to the Elder Sultan and then his sons, Commander of their armies. My mother was a respected and well-loved daughter of a family long known for their generosity and charity. I did not realize crossing an imaginary line in the rock would turn my entire family into dangerous villains."

Her vain hope that there might be a coal remaining to begin a new fire died a slow death as she poked and prodded through the ashes.

He watched her in expectant silence for so long she began to feel crushed by it.

"Do you know how to start a fire?" he finally asked.

Aysel pointed her stick at him. "Of course I do." She did not. Adem made all their fires, cooked their meals. It was a simple matter for a Fifth House Aval—he needed only to speak a word and fire obeyed his command.

"You can scale a cliff face to infiltrate a palace and fight off men three times your size—"

"Twice, maybe," Aysel corrected.

Bashir raised an eyebrow. "Three times your size, but you cannot start a cookfire." He felt about his belt as if searching for something, then tucked his hand into a small leather pouch tied to the thin leather sword belt that crossed over the fabric wound at his waist. "Only a noble," he sighed as he withdrew a stone of some kind, then drew a knife from a sheath at his hip.

Aysel silently mimicked his statement about nobles and stuck her tongue out at him. He nearly smiled as he rounded the firepit. "Hold these." He handed her the knife and stone as he crouched beside her.

Aysel watched as he dug about the pile of sticks and wood that Adem had scavenged for them. Bashir withdrew a handful of dead grass from the middle of the pile and set it in the center of the firepit, then fluffed it, reminding Aysel of watching her mother arrange flowers in a vase. She snorted, and he gave her a baleful, sideways look. "Do you want my help?"

"I'm not certain." She studied the knife he'd given her as he continued his work, building the grass into a little nest. "You're very brave, handing me a knife and then sitting right next to me." She danced the knife over the tops of her fingers and spun it into her grasp, leveling the point at his eye.

Bashir, without even flinching, reached up and took the knife from her hand, then the stone. "If you knife me in the eye, you can forget your fire." He held the stone over his pile of grass and began to strike the dull edge of his knife against it.

Aysel hugged her knees and set her chin against them, watching his short, quick strokes in fascination—she'd never seen someone start a fire without magic. A few times a spark landed and glowed, and Bashir blew carefully on them, but it took him four tries before the grass caught. He tended that for a few moments, as if it were the most fragile of infants, then began to feed it more grass and small bits of twigs, gradually building it up until it was steady and strong, and adding larger and larger pieces of wood until it was a proper fire.

He looked at her in irritation. "You probably can't cook, either. What are you doing out here? Go back to the palace and sleep in a dry bed and eat good food. Do you even have any food?"

"I'm not a child, Ox." She stood and ducked back into the shelter to sort through the rest of her things. She'd bought rice and lentils at the market, and two oranges. Only things she thought essential. Aysel fished the cookpot out from under the stack of pallets that was her bed and dumped some of the lentils into it, then placed an orange on top before carrying it back outside.

She handed it all to Bashir. "Do you know what one of your problems is?"

"You are my only problem." He settled the cookpot into a section of coals he'd pushed away from the main fire. He set the orange on the ground beside him, tugged her bucket of water over and dumped some into the pot, then put the lid on. Aysel touched her foot to his back and gave a little shove in reprimand for his sarcasm. He caught himself with one hand as he tipped forward and twisted to catch her ankle with the other.

Aysel grabbed his wrist in both of her hands and shoved her weight into her leg to break his hold, grazing his cheekbone with her knee as she threw her leg over his arm.

"No." She wrenched his arm up between her legs, putting her weight against the back of his elbow and torqueing his arm toward her chest. Bashir tried to yank out of her hold but only put more pressure against his arm and cursed. "The problem"—she gave his arm a little jerk that made him hiss—"is you keep underestimating me."

She released his arm with a shove and stepped over him like she might a little boulder in her path, swiping her orange as she moved to the other side of the fire. She sat in the dirt, folding her legs in front of her, and started peeling.

"I don't blame you really," she said, tossing a piece of orange peel into the fire as he glowered at her and worked his hand against his shoulder. "I've yet to meet a man who doesn't. And you think because I asked for your help once it means I need some kind of rescuer. But I don't. If you hadn't been around to use as a tool, I would have found another way."

Not entirely true, but mostly true. His comment about the cross-bows that morning still made her temper simmer.

"You say the most flattering things." Bashir dug his fingers against his arm. She doubted she had done any lasting damage, but it did ache for a bit after being extended backwards as she had.

"Oh, did you come up here for flattery? I thought it was to prevent me from looking for the men who want to kill my family." She pried loose a wedge of orange then freed the rest of the fruit from its peel.

"And I thought it was to cook your dinner," he said.

Aysel nibbled on a piece of the citrus, meeting his gaze across the fire. She held the other half out to him. "I didn't ask you to do that. You're just trying to rescue me again."

Bashir finally took the fruit and sat down, folding his legs up toward his chest and shoving a piece of it in his mouth. He'd looked strung out and spent when she had seen him that morning; now he appeared dead on his feet. There were dark circles beneath his eyes, and he moved with the same kind of slow determination as the exhausted refugees at the top of the pass.

The man was done-in. In fact she wouldn't be surprised if he fell asleep right in front of her.

"Where did you learn that?" he said after he had lifted the lid on the lentils to give them a stir.

"Well I'm not exactly going to win a fistfight, am I?" She ate her last piece of orange and brushed her fingers off on her salvar. She got to her feet and retrieved her harness and swords from where she'd set them. "My brother and I have been working through scenarios for Turns. We tried to find things I could use on someone if I were foolish enough to get caught." She sat down next to him and took another piece from the half she'd given.

"I doubt I underestimate you as often as you think," he said, quietly. "I've never met a woman like you."

Warm pleasure filled her belly at his praise, but she laughed softly. "I know you can't help it. You're so big, and you're the kind of man who can't help wanting to protect people, can you? And small animals too, probably, hmm?"

Red crept up his neck and she knew she was right.

"Well, rest easy, Ox. Cooking and fire-starting aside"—she drew one of her swords and looked at it—"I take care of myself very well."

She narrowed her eyes and brought the blade close to her face, then tapped her thumb against its edge. A thin line of blood bloomed across her skin. Aysel sighed, setting the blade in her lap and turning her gaze toward him. He busied himself with prying loose another wedge of orange.

"Who sharpened these?" She knew. She knew exactly who had sharpened them.

"I don't see a whetstone around this mudhole, do you?" he said around a mouthful of fruit. "You can't be running around with dull swords. And they were bouncing all over those cobbles last night. It'll chip your edge." Then he shoved the last piece in his mouth.

"What am I supposed to do with you? You insist I'm a criminal and I need to be guarded, but you came when that katil almost caught me. You should be sleeping, but you're here instead of sending your men. You don't want me hunting the katil, but you sharpened my blades…"

She motioned to the pot of lentils. "…you cooked my dinner!" Aysel held his gaze.

And waited.

Bashir rubbed his palms over his face. "I don't know." He shoved both hands into his hair. "I don't know what I'm doing."

"You know what I think?" She slid her blade back into its sheath. "I think you want to trust me, but you don't trust yourself or your judgment because the Sultana says something different."

"You can't possibly understand what I owe her."

"Don't be insulting. Even a simpleton can understand feeling indebted to someone." Aysel sighed, and reached up, tugging his hand away from his hair. "Come on."

"What?" He looked up at her as she stood. Aysel pulled again, and Bashir clambered to his feet, his fingers slipping between hers and tightening in a way that made her pulse flutter. She stepped toward her lean-to and he balked. Aysel jerked him harder, smiling a little.

"Don't be afraid, little Ox, I won't hurt you," she teased, stepping closer and sliding her fingers into the cloth at his waist, then walking backwards and towing him with her. He looked bewildered, and hopeful, and like he was trying not to feel either.

When he had ducked inside, she let go of him and turned to clear her purchases off the bed, right the crate she'd been kicking, and place them on it. Then she maneuvered him so his back was to the pallets.

"Aysel," he said, the censure in his voice broken with interest. "I thought we agreed…" He shook his head, but his hands found her waist.

"For right now"—she unbuckled his sword belt and tugged it free of his hips—"just this moment. Trust me." She set the sword on the edge of the pallets. "Lie down," she ordered.

Bashir frowned. Aysel put her hands on his shoulders and pressed until he sat, then positioned her knee next to his hip and pushed, following him as he fell back because his hands tightened against her waist. She swung her other leg over him so she straddled him on all fours. Wheel but she wanted to do so much more than she was about to, especially when desire unleashed in his gaze. Even if her intent was not what he thought, she liked that he was willing to give over his control to her.

Aysel bent her face over his. His body shifted as he tensed to lift his head to hers. "Go to sleep," she murmured.

"Wheel and spokes." He dropped his head against the folded blanket she used as a pillow and grit his teeth as he glared at her. "Is this funny to you?"

Aysel pushed up on her knees and put her fingers together in a circle, the symbol for the Wheel. "I swear on the Wheel that I will be right here"—she pointed toward the cookfire on the other side of the canvas—"when you wake up."

"Get up," he ordered, though he did not move his hands from her hips. Aysel dropped her hands back to his shoulders as he started to sit up.

"Go to sleep. You have taken care of me, and now you're going to let me repay the favor. I will stand watch outside until you wake up."

"You're going to stand watch on yourself? Why on the Wheel would I believe you?"

"Because your instincts are right. You can trust me." Aysel placed one hand by his head, lifting the other toward his hair and hesitating. "That's why you came to help me with the katil when I asked. And why you sharpened my swords, and why you haven't turned me into mincemeat for putting my grubby Sarkum hands all over you."

He frowned at her and shifted his head to butt it against her fingers. She smiled as she stroked them through his tawny hair.

"Bashir," she said, in the warm, unguarded way she would have always said his name if they could have started out under different circumstances. "You need sleep. How can you take care of your men if you won't take care of yourself?" She continued sliding her fingers through his hair, enjoying how it slipped through. It was softer than hers, softer than Mat's, lacking the coarseness that spoke of their mixed heritage.

He closed his eyes.

About the Author

J. D. EVANS WRITES fantasy and science fiction romance. After earning her degree in linguistics, J. D. served a decade as an army officer. She once spent her hours putting together briefings for helicopter pilots and generals. Now she writes stories, tends to two unreasonable tiny humans, knits, sews badly, gardens, and cultivates Pinterest Fails. After a stint in Beirut, J. D. fell in love with the Levant, which inspired the setting for her debut series, Mages of the Wheel.

Originally hailing from Montana, J. D. now resides in North Carolina with her husband, two attempts at mini-clones gone awry, and too many stories in her head.